For my baba, mama, and mei mei

Being deeply loved by someone gives you strength, while
loving someone deeply gives you courage.

— Lao Tzu

"I loved the insight we got into the Chinese culture and tradition through Wei and the curiosity that Glory expressed in her Chinese heritage." -Juliana, *Goodreads*

"Grace Callaway is such a treasure. Her books are sooo sexy, and the historical details are just right. Some HR authors seem to leave out so much of the little day-to-day details of the time period, but not Callaway. I love all of the history she sprinkles throughout the book." -Leelee, *Goodreads*

"Love Wei and Glory's relationship. I love how they fit so well together. Wonderful characters! The mystery is fun and the plot is fast moving. An enjoyable read." -May, *Netgalley*

"Glory Cavendish was just as bright and spunky as she'd been before, and it's always refreshing to see a female character embrace her attraction, and in this case, even seek out counsel from her friends. In fact, their antics in trying to make Glory more appealing to Wei was rather hilarious. Glory is stubborn, but that is part of her charm, and that is what keeps Wei coming to her aid. She's self-aware in a way that doesn't necessarily make her self-deprecating (or an NLOG), she's just who she is and doesn't mind that she's different." -Madame Amy, *Goodreads*

"Wonderful elements of steadfast loyal friends, familial affection and unique cultural and social details combine for an interesting and memorable story. The romance between two sensitive yet upstanding individuals is a great balance of passionately sensual and sweetly delightful connections." -Allison, *Bookbub*

"There are honestly no words to express how much I adored this book. It was so captivating that my mind was blown, and I could not put it down once I started." -Di, *Netgalley*

Her Husband's Harlot

Her Wanton Wager

Her Protector's Pleasure

Her Prodigal Passion

Glory
AND
THE
MASTER of SHADOWS

Lady Charlotte's
SOCIETY of
ANGELS

GRACE
CALLAWAY
USA TODAY BESTSELLING AUTHOR

Cover Art: EDH Graphics

Cover Image: Jenn Le Blanc

Typography Design: KM Designs

Formatting: Colchester & Page

PROLOGUE

1836, Coastal village near Canton (Modern-day Guangzhou)

"Heavens, Wei, that feels good." On her hands and knees, Chun arched her neck, her hair a river of onyx rippling down her back. "Do it harder."

Gripping her slender hips, eighteen-year-old Wei Chen obliged his lover. He pushed inside her, groaning at her slick warmth. She pushed back at him and moaned loudly...too loudly.

Wei curved over her and whispered, "Have a care, my love. We cannot risk discovery."

"This cottage has been abandoned for years. No one is going to find us here." Chun twisted her head to look at him, her doe-brown eyes gleaming with defiance. "And I do not care if my husband finds us. He's a useless old fool. He blames me for not giving him an heir, but it is not my fault that his prick is as wilted as a dying chrysanthemum. He cannot even find it beneath the folds of his belly."

Now five-and-twenty, Chun had been married to Fulin Li, the village governor, for a decade. The union had not produced children, and Governor Li publicly blamed Chun for this. Wei understood her bitterness, yet her husband was a rich and powerful merchant who ruled over their village on the coast of the Pearl River Delta. If he discovered that his wife was committing adultery, it would be within his rights to have her and her lover killed.

Trepidation knotted Wei's chest. Nearly a year ago, he and Chun had had a chance encounter in the village market. Chun had spilled a basket of apples, and as he'd helped her to retrieve the shiny red fruit, he'd fallen under her spell. She was as beautiful and unattainable as Chang'e, the Goddess of the Moon, and he still couldn't believe that she had chosen him, the undistinguished son of a soldier, to be her lover.

At the same time, Wei knew the risk he was taking. He didn't care about himself—he had made his bed and would sleep in it—but his family would also bear the brunt of his dishonor. Shame flooded Wei as he thought of how his father, the righteous Captain Qiang Chen, would react to his illicit affair.

The Qing Emperor had sent Captain Chen to this coastal village to wage war against opium. While the dangerous substance had long been illegal in China, foreigners—especially the British—were smuggling in the drug by the boatloads.

"The barbarians do not care about the devastation they are causing to our people, son," Wei's *baba* would say grimly. *"They are governed only by greed. By their insatiable desire for silver to trade for our tea and silk. Yet equally treacherous are the traitors within our borders. Our fellow countrymen who would betray their own people and aid the injection of poison into the veins of their own society..."*

The captain's mission to stamp out opium required continual travel. Wei had resented the upheaval, the constant cycle of having to leave old friends behind and earn the respect of new ones. He'd been an outsider his entire life, and his ten-year-old sister Meiling, known as Ling Ling, was suffering the same fate.

Whenever he complained, his *mama* would chide, *"Your baba follows the orders of the Emperor. It is your duty and privilege to support him in this."*

Wei had heard enough lectures about filial piety to last a lifetime. Yet his resentment was tempered by guilt. He *did* respect his father; who wouldn't revere such a dedicated and stalwart soldier? A man who, for meager army pay, fulfilled his duty with unfailing diligence. Who stood strong in the face of bribes and threats, all in the name of justice and loyalty to his country.

Yet the captain was also taciturn and critical. He had one ambition for his only son: he wanted Wei to become a scholar-official. He was determined that Wei would bring honor to the Chen name by studying hard, passing a series of rigorous imperial examinations, and attaining an elite position in civil service.

Easier said than done. Scholarship did not come naturally to Wei, a fact that not even his tutor's bamboo cane could rectify. Nonetheless, he'd done his best and taken the first round of local examinations this year.

His failure had humiliated himself and his family.

"Wei, darling, let us stop talking." Chun's husky words jarred him from his thoughts. "We have far better things to do, don't we?"

She squeezed her inner muscles, the decadent massage making him grunt.

"You're so big," she purred. "Do it to me, Wei. Satisfy me the way only you can."

While studying had never been Wei's forte, he'd always been good at physical activities, and lovemaking was no different. By now, he knew what pleased Chun—knew she liked it when he was rough. When he took her hard and used filthy words, she turned wetter than a rice field.

"Want my big prick, do you?" He shunted his cock forcefully into her passage. "Want it hard and deep?"

"Yes, yes, *yes.*"

Egged on by her mewls of delight, he took her, harder and

harder still, his queue whipping against his back with the power of his thrusts. She came with a carelessly loud shriek that echoed through the empty cottage. As his own finish boiled over, he had just enough sense to yank himself free of her spasming sheath. He bit his lip against a shout, tasting blood as he shot his seed onto the grimy floor.

Panting, he gazed at Chun. She'd collapsed onto her forearms, her cheeks flushed, a smile on her lips. Pride puffed his chest that he'd satisfied this beautiful lady, made her happy, and while he knew it was foolish, he wanted to protect her—even from her husband.

"I love you," he blurted.

She met his gaze, and her lips formed a beckoning curve.

"Then show me again," she said.

After two more rounds of lovemaking, Wei escorted Chun as far as he dared back to the extravagant governor's compound. Then he continued his way to his family's small house. The path took him along the cliffs overlooking the Pearl River Delta. The sky flowed seamlessly into the water, forming an ink-black canvas, but he didn't risk using a lantern. Instead, he relied upon the crescent moon to light his way.

As he trudged toward home, the pleasure was already fading, replaced by gnawing shame. He knew what he was doing was wrong. While he loved Chun, he knew that their affair could come to no good end. Once, he'd tried to end things with her; she had cried, and he'd tried to comfort her...and the next thing he knew, she was beneath him, her legs circling his hips as he pounded into her.

"*You're an animal. A filthy beast,*" she'd moaned. "*You make me wild.*"

She was not wrong, Wei thought starkly. He was no better than a beast. Perhaps that was why he'd never be the good son his *baba* deserved. Why he'd failed the examinations and dishonored his family. Why he was addicted to the taste of Chun, the feel of her, and all the dirty things they did under the cover of darkness.

He reached his home, a single-story building with a walled courtyard perched at the highest point of the cliffs. *Baba* had chosen it so that he could scout for clandestine opium vessels docking in the coves below. Ironically, the only smuggling going on tonight was the captain's son trying to get back into the house unnoticed.

Moving stealthily along the perimeter of the wall, Wei found the lowest point. The top stones had crumbled, leaving the partition about three times his height.

If I had proper training in kung fu, *this wall would be no barrier,* Wei thought bitterly.

While academics had a sedative effect upon Wei, martial arts awakened his appetite for learning. His family had never stayed in one place long enough for him to train with a *shifu*, but he'd picked up techniques here and there. He wanted to be a fighter... maybe a soldier like his father. When he'd told his *baba* of his desire, the captain had given him a stern lecture.

"You will obey me and become a scholar. You must show filial respect, set a good example for your younger sister. Bring the family honor, and do not fail again."

It was how every conversation with *Baba* went.

No negotiation. No room for personal desires. Nothing but duty, duty, duty.

Clenching his jaw, Wei gazed up at the wall. *I can handle this.*

In the village his family had lived in prior to this one, there'd been a *shifu* who taught a technique known as *"qing gong"* or "lightness *kung fu*." The method emphasized agility and speed, resulting in a seeming ability to defy gravity itself. The *shifu* had given Wei a few tips, and Wei had practiced ever since.

Ling Ling had begged him to teach her as well.

"When you're older," he'd told his *mei mei*, tugging on one of her pigtails.

His irrepressible little sister had stuck her tongue out at him. Yet that hadn't stopped her from keeping him company as he trained, whooping and cheering as he'd learned to scale trees and walls of increasing height.

The memory made Wei grin. Backing up, he took a running start, pairing his muscles and breath to maximize the lightness of movement. The soles of his shoes whispered against stone as he swiftly ascended the vertical surface. He'd almost reached the top when he made the mistake of looking down—and the distraction cost him.

He slipped backward, flailing, one hand managing to grab the top of the wall. Gritting his teeth, he pulled himself up and swung over the edge. At least his landing in the courtyard was soft, his queue swishing behind him.

Wei straightened, his senses on sudden alert. The windchimes his mother hung to ward away hostile spirits tinkled eerily. Shadows shrouded the courtyard, broken here and there by shards of moonlight. As he wondered why the lanterns were out, a figure exploded from the darkness and barreled into him. He sprawled onto his back, the newcomer leaping atop. In the next heartbeat, a blade arced toward his face. He reached out, grabbing the assailant's wrist as the glinting tip hovered above his throat.

The attacker pushed downward; Wei resisted with equal force.

While the other was heavier and had the upper position, Wei was stronger. He glimpsed pale eyes in the holes of the attacker's mask as he shoved the knife away from his throat. He gave his foe's wrist a sharp twist that made the bastard mutter, "Bloody hell!" and drop the blade, which skittered across the stones.

Wei threw off his foe, handspringing to his feet. The enemy recovered with equal speed and charged again. Wei dodged the blow, delivering a palm strike to the man's solar plexus. The barbarian stumbled back, and Wei attacked, going in with a barrage of punches and kicks. He grabbed the man's arm; the man wrenched away, leaving Wei with a handful of fabric and a glimpse of inked vines crawling up the other's forearm.

The man suddenly dove to the ground—*the knife*. Wei ran over, and the bastard jumped up, throwing gravel into Wei's eyes. Momentarily blinded, Wei leapt back instinctively, heard the whoosh of steel cutting through the air. Hot pain sliced across his shoulder, but he reacted with a high kick. The man cursed as the knife went flying, clattering in the distance.

His vision blurry and eyes burning, Wei held his fists up, ready for more...but his foe's footsteps pounded away in the opposite direction. The coward was retreating like a cur with its tail between its legs. Wei considered following, but a new fear drummed in his chest.

Ling Ling, Mama—I must make sure they are all right.

He raced out of the courtyard into the central hall. The air was heavy with incense from the ancestral altar, the darkness too thick for him to see. As Wei headed to the altar to find matches, he tripped, barely catching himself. Grabbing the matches, he lit one to see what had caused him to fall...and his heart slammed into his ribs.

Old Wong, the servant who'd been with his family since he was a boy. Who'd tended to Wei's scrapes and secretly given him salty dried plums after each beating and lecture he'd received from *Baba*. Old Wong, who was as wrinkled as a *shar-pei* dog...and who now stared blankly up at Wei, his throat sliced from ear to ear.

Wei covered the old retainer's eyes with a shaking hand.

Then he raced to his family's chambers, shouting their names.

ONE

LONDON, 1851

"I can handle this evening on my own," Lady Glory Cavendish declared.

She took a seat in the well-appointed drawing room of her bosom friend Lady Olivia Wodehouse, the Duchess of Hadleigh. Her faithful companion, Ferdinand the Ferret the Second, nicknamed FF II, leapt onto the cushion beside her. Curling into a furry white crescent, he settled in for an afternoon nap.

From adjacent chairs, Olivia, Mrs. Pippa Cullen, and Lady Fiona Morgan, the Countess of Hawksmoor, were exchanging looks. These days, Glory's closest friends did that *a lot*...as if they knew something that she did not. Those knowing glances made her feel a bit left out. Truth be told, she'd felt that way since the other ladies had been felled by love, toppling like dominoes one by one. With her twenty-first birthday approaching, Glory was the only member of the group left standing.

She didn't mind, for she had better things to do than fall in love. For the past three years, she and her friends had been part of a covert investigative agency founded by their indomitable leader, Lady Charlotte "Charlie" Fayne. On the surface, the Society of Angels was a genteel female charity. The polite world believed that Glory and her fellow "Angels" were volunteering their efforts in the usual fashion: writing pamphlets, raising funds, and bringing baskets to the poor. The Angels were indeed helping others...just not in the way people assumed they were.

Charlie conducted discreet investigations on behalf of women in dire straits. The clients believed that Charlie had a network of "contacts" who helped with their cases. The subterfuge was necessary to protect the Angels' reputations, and ironically, society's beliefs about female limitations worked to their advantage. Thus far, no one had suspected that young ladies were capable of conducting investigations and solving crimes.

Charlie had trained her charges thoroughly in the art of detection. Glory and her friends had practiced their skills, from clandestine surveillance to combat. They had worked on cases involving everything from blackmail to murder. And just as they were coming into the prime of their abilities, three-quarters of the group had decided to become wives.

And *mamas*, to further complicate matters.

"Gloriana Cavendish, you are not going to a club in Covent Garden by yourself. And one crawling with the criminal element, for heaven's sake." Olivia, a petite brunette who wore her hair in fashionable looped braids over her ears, rolled her green eyes. "It wouldn't be safe for any of us to go alone. Unfortunately, no one is free to accompany you tonight. Or rather, I *am* free, but I would not be of much use hobbling around on a sprained ankle."

She gestured at her foot, which was propped up on a velvet stool.

"Does it hurt, Livy?" Pippa, a sunny blonde, asked with sympathy.

"My pride is injured more than my ankle," Livy said ruefully.

"I have bested villains in combat, yet here I am, felled by a toy my two-year-old left on the nursery floor."

Pippa placed a hand on her midsection, where the pleats of her butter-yellow carriage dress had been let out to accommodate her pregnancy. Her blue eyes turned dreamy.

"I hope Cull and I have a girl," she said. "Then our daughters could be playmates."

"Perhaps they could wear each other out?" Livy looked hopeful.

"Better yet, they could have adventures together." Glory made her selection from the refreshment tray on the coffee table, adding pointedly, "The way we used to when we were girls."

The way we did until recently. Now everything is changing. And I am not certain I like it.

Feeling peevish and guilty because of it, Glory munched on some biscuits and cheese. She loved her friends unconditionally and wanted them to be happy. But she also wished that things weren't changing so rapidly.

An unconventional girl, she had never fit in with her peers. She'd grown up in a small village in Dorset, where her curiosity and love of adventure had made her stick out like a loose nail. The schoolmaster and village children had tried to hammer her into place; when they failed, they labeled her a peculiar hoyden and washed their hands of her. Pride had kept Glory from showing how much the rejection had hurt. She'd kept her chin up as her mama and Aunt Hypatia had taught her to do and carried on.

Then, when she was just shy of nine, Papa had entered her life. After a whirlwind romance, he'd married Mama and taken the family to London. As the newly minted daughter of a duke, one would think Glory would fare better socially, but she proved even *more* awkward with her new peers. It didn't take long for the well-bred misses to begin whispering about her.

"Why does she keep a ferret, of all things? Why not a normal pet like a cat or bird?"

"Goodness, what a muddled excuse for hair she has, neither a proper shade of red nor brown. And did you see her freckles? Hasn't she heard of a fading lotion?"

"There is no lotion that can fade her un-English looks, alas." A sly pause. *"I suppose she gets it from His Grace."*

The latter was a reference to the fact that Papa had Chinese heritage from his mama's side, and the resemblance between him and Glory was too obvious to be ignored. Before their wedding, Glory's parents had told her the truth: they'd met years earlier and had a brief affair that had resulted in Glory's conception. Papa had left without knowing that he'd fathered a child, and Mama had married Paul Foley, Aunt Hypatia's brother.

Glory had grown up believing that Paul was her father, and she'd mourned the gentle, middle-aged scholar deeply when he died. Yet from the instant she'd met Rhys Cavendish, the roguish Duke of Ranelagh and Somerville, she'd felt an inexplicable sense of kinship. In truth, she hadn't been all that surprised to learn that she was his daughter in blood. Her parents, however, had wanted to protect her from the scandal of illegitimacy, and officially, she remained the duke's daughter whom he'd adopted after marriage.

Even so, rumors about Glory swirled as fiercely as the surf along the Dorset coast. She had resigned herself to being an outcast...until she met Livy and Fiona at age nine. The girls turned out to be her sisters in spirit. Livy and Fi didn't care about Glory's unusual interests, origins, or looks; they liked her for who she was. Dubbed "the Willflowers" for their spirited ways, the girls had bonded over countless adventures, and for the first time, Glory had experienced the bliss of belonging.

Now, however, it was as if her bosom friends had joined some secret club to which she did not belong. They were all swooning over their husbands while she hadn't the slightest clue what romantic love felt like. Certainly, no fellow had held her interest more than a case. To be fair, she wasn't precisely an object of desire to the opposite sex either. Not with her freckles, reed-like figure, and peculiarities.

"Ugh."

The faint gargle stirred Glory from her thoughts. It came from Fiona, a redhead known for her beauty and charm. Currently, however, her face was an alarming shade of green.

Worried, Glory asked, "Is something the matter, Fi?"

"No. Well, yes," Fi choked out. "What kind of cheese is that?"

Glory looked at the blue-veined crumbles on her plate. "Roquefort, I think?"

"The *smell*—excuse me..."

Fi shot up, her peach satin skirts billowing as she dashed from the room.

"Poor Fi," Livy murmured. "My morning sickness wasn't as bad as hers."

"Hers isn't just in the morning; it's morning, noon, and night." Pippa pushed herself to her feet. "I'll go check on the poor thing."

After Pippa toddled off, Glory said, "Do you think Fi will be all right?"

"She ought to be fine in a few weeks. And she has Hawksmoor looking out for her. She told me that the earl is taking impending fatherhood quite seriously. He takes notes at every physician's visit and has apparently read multiple manuals on childbirth. Fi says that he is so involved that he has even begun experiencing some of her *symptoms*."

Glory had to grin at the thought of the stoic Earl of Hawksmoor getting queasy. His attunement to Fi didn't surprise her, however. Like all the Angels' husbands, the fellow adored his wife and was inordinately protective of her. Glory was glad that her friends had chosen their mates well.

I, however, have made a different choice. While I might be a dismal failure as a debutante, I am a jolly good investigator. And I am not letting my skills go to waste.

"About tonight." Glory straightened her shoulders. "I will be in disguise. You know my Cockney is first-rate. I'll pop in, do a bit of reconnaissance, and be out before—"

"We never embark on missions alone. It's too dangerous," Livy said firmly. "If Charlie were here, she would say the same."

Botheration. As usual, Livy was right. The motto for their society was "Sisters first," which meant the Angels always looked after one another. The strength of their bond made them a formidable team. But what if Glory's friends got too distracted by their new lives to focus on investigating? With Livy injured, Fi casting up her accounts, and Pippa about to pop like a champagne cork, the Angels were presently a shipwreck. And not just the Angels...the entire organization had hit the rocks.

The Angels' instructors, Hawker and Mrs. Peabody, who'd also served as Charlie's de facto butler and housekeeper, had married a few months ago. To everyone's surprise, Hawker had inherited a duchy; now the Duke of Ryedale, he and his new duchess were managing their estate in Yorkshire. Although the pair promised to return when things were settled, Glory missed her teachers dreadfully.

Then Charlie had begun to take frequent trips as well. When she left town yesterday, she claimed it was to visit an ailing friend, but Glory's intuition told her something else was afoot. Some secret mission, mayhap, that their mentor could not speak about.

Someone has to woman the fort, Glory thought resolutely. *That woman might as well be me.*

"We have an urgent case," she reminded Livy. "We promised Mrs. Mumford-Mills that we would recover Sir Barkley, and there is no time to lose."

As Glory stroked her snoring ferret, her heart ached for their newest client. A wealthy widow who lived alone, Mrs. Mumford-Mills doted upon her bull terrier, Sir Barkley. She'd been out shopping when dognappers snatched her beloved companion from her carriage. That night, a shady fellow had paid a visit to her home.

He claimed he was a "middleman" who didn't know Sir Barkley's location but was working on behalf of the dognappers to negotiate a ransom.

Not knowing what else to do, Mrs. Mumford-Mills had paid the twenty pounds he demanded. The next week, the same fellow reappeared, without Sir Barkley and demanding fifty pounds to ensure the dog's continued well-being. He had warned Mrs. Mumford-Mills against contacting the police, saying that the dognappers would kill Sir Barkley on the spot if she did so.

Distraught, the poor widow had confided in a friend, who'd told her about Charlie's secret organization. Mrs. Mumford-Mills had begged Charlie to help, even providing a miniature portrait to aid the search. The painting showed a sprightly white-and-brindle bull terrier with pricked ears. Upon his collar was a charm Mrs. Mumford-Mills had commissioned for him, the letter "B" topped with a small garnet-studded crown.

Disguised as sweeps, Glory and Livy had lain in wait outside Mrs. Mumford-Mills's home three nights ago. Sure enough, the middleman had shown up to collect his payment, and they'd tracked him to an establishment in Covent Garden with the dubious name of Fanny Bottom's. The club was open to members only, and the Angels, unable to gain entrée, had lost their target.

Since then, Charlie had managed to obtain a pair of membership cards. In a stroke of luck, Glory's parents were away on a trip to promote her papa's political campaign against the opium trade, leaving her under the charge of her aunt. A proud bluestocking, Aunt Hypatia was delightfully supportive of female autonomy. Thus, it would be easy for Glory to come up with an excuse to leave the house tonight and, hopefully, rescue Sir Barkley.

All she needed was a partner for the mission.

"I understand the urgency," Livy said. "And I have a solution."

Glory sat up straighter. "You do?"

"Initially, I thought Hadleigh could escort you. But he insists on being here to carry me up and down the stairs." Although Livy cast her gaze ceilingward, her blush betrayed that she didn't mind her husband's attention. "In his place, he has asked Master Chen to accompany you."

At the mention of Hadleigh's friend, Glory felt a strange quiver of excitement. Wei Chen was an austere gentleman who operated a clinic that treated opium addicts in the East End. Although a social connection between a Chinese commoner and an English duke was unusual, to say the least, Livy had confided in the Angels about the men's history.

Before marrying Livy, Hadleigh had struggled with opium use. The drug had wreaked havoc upon his life, taking him on a downward spiral that had led him to an alley in Whitechapel, where he'd been attacked by cutthroats. He might have died had Master Chen not intervened. A master of both healing and fighting arts, Chen had saved the duke from the murderous thugs and helped him to stop his opium habit.

Glory was fascinated by the noble master. He was around Hadleigh's age, yet his broad cheekbones, straight nose, and chiseled jaw had an ageless quality. His hair was the black of midnight, and the short, thick layers had a slight wave. Beneath his straight eyebrows, his eyes were an intense, clear brown—like tea brewed strong. To Glory, those eyes revealed everything and nothing.

Truth be told, she had never met anyone with Mr. Chen's degree of self-possession. It was as if he observed the world from some high and motionless perch, unaffected by the vagaries of human emotion. For a girl who preferred action, his quality of stillness was as puzzling as it was intriguing.

Yet he was fully capable of acting when warranted. He'd assisted the Angels on several missions, and his *kung fu* had filled Glory with awe and, truth be told, a bit of envy. While she wasn't pretty or popular, she did pride herself on her athleticism. Growing up in Dorset, there hadn't been a tree or cliff she couldn't climb or a boy she couldn't outrace. She loved physical activity and sports...although her competitive nature sometimes got the best of her. At a recent party, she had decimated the other debutantes at archery. The gentlemen, too. When it came to dancing, she was often quicker and nimbler than her partners, which resulted in her unfortunate habit of taking the lead.

As sporty as Glory was, however, Master Chen's physical abilities cast hers in the shade. With his muscular frame and absolute control, he seemed capable of conquering gravity and air. She'd never seen anyone move like him, fight like him. He combined the power of lightning with the stealth of shadows.

What she wouldn't give to learn some of his techniques.

She was also intrigued by another commonality they shared. From her papa's side, she was a quarter Chinese, but Papa's mother had died when he was young, and he knew little about that part of his legacy. Glory had pestered him into finding her a tutor; she'd learned to speak rudimentary Chinese, but there was so much more she wanted to learn about the culture.

Nothing excited Glory more than discovering new things.

She tried to sound casual. "Did Master Chen agree to accompany me?"

"He said, and I quote, *'This is a bad idea'.*"

Drat.

Livy smiled, reaching for her teacup. "Hadleigh, however, talked him into it."

Hooray!

"Where shall I meet him?" Glory asked eagerly. "What is our cover story?"

"Don't worry, dearest." Livy sipped her tea, her eyes twinkling over the rim of her cup. "I have a plan."

Two

"Shall we go in now? Or should we wait?" Lady Glory Cavendish peeped through the drawn curtains of the carriage window. "What do you think, Mr. Chen?"

"I think that this is a bad idea," Wei said.

Actually, he *knew* it was. Yet he'd agreed to this escapade anyway, which puzzled him. He was not a man who acted against his better judgment. Once upon a time, he'd allowed selfish desire to be his compass, and his family had paid the price. He felt the familiar sear in his chest, the agony of a scar too deep to be healed. His mistake was a part of him, woven into the essence of who he was, the unrelenting force behind his every action.

In the next breath, he let go of the feeling. Unhooked himself from it like a rowboat from a rotting dock. As Master Lam had taught him, he let himself float on the waves of anger and despair, riding the tide until it once again calmed. It had taken him years to develop this ability; now detachment was a reflex. He was able to channel his inner turmoil so that it flowed through him without disturbing his outer calmness.

He taught this practice to the students who flocked to his East End clinic looking for a cure to their opium habit. Many were quick to declare his methods "un-English," and they were not wrong. He had no snake oil or miracles to sell. The secret was that there was no secret: everyone had to work at their own healing. Benedict Wodehouse, the Duke of Hadleigh, had been one of Wei's successful pupils and was now a friend. Thus, when the duke had asked him, as a personal favor, to accompany his wife's friend to a disreputable club, Wei had agreed.

Wei reasoned that friendship and loyalty were acceptable explanations for his presence tonight. Yet he couldn't deny that there was another reason too. That reason being the lady disguised as a foppish, curly-haired gent sitting across from him. At present, Lady Glory had her small nose pressed against the carriage window like a child peering into a toy shop. And it was precisely her innocence that drew Wei to keep an eye out for this wayward duke's daughter.

He had become acquainted with Lady Gloriana Cavendish over the course of three years. He'd only been in her company a handful of times: when he'd assisted with the Angels' cases and during social occasions hosted by the Duke and Duchess of Hadleigh. The time spent in her company had solidified his perception that she was a rare and untamed spirit.

As outrageous as Lady Glory's covert activities were, they were driven by her crusader's heart. She had a genuine desire to do good and help others. These qualities, coupled with unquenchable idealism, were admirable...and more than a little worrisome.

Wei flashed back to memories of his sister, Ling Ling. She, too, had been a fearless campaigner for good, even at ten years old. No matter where their *baba*'s orders took the family, Ling Ling had been sure to stand up for those who needed help. In the last village where they'd lived, she had organized the other girls to travel in groups and look out for one another to avoid being harassed by some of the older boys.

"When everyone adds fuel, the flames rise high," she'd declared.

Her apple-cheeked face had glowed with pride as she'd

informed Wei of her plan's success. He'd gravely offered her his congratulations while keeping his bruised knuckles hidden. Although he knew the true reason for the bullies' retreat, he'd wanted to protect his sister's optimism.

Ling Ling had also been a lifelong lover of animals, which resulted in rescued chickens, pigs, and assorted creatures running amok in the Chen household. One day, she'd proclaimed that she would no longer eat meat. When she tried to convert the entire family to vegetarianism, *Baba* had put his foot down.

"I am a soldier, daughter, not a monk or rabbit," he had said with exasperation. *"I cannot survive on grass and hay."*

Yet even the taciturn captain had been fighting a smile. That had been Ling Ling's effect on people. Her goodness had lit up everything around her...until it had been snuffed out. The image of his baby sister lying in a pool of blood, her eyes unblinking and pigtails shorn and missing, caused Wei's insides to churn with rage.

When I let go of who I am, I become what I might be.

He took in a breath and released it. Emotions were mere leaves floating on the surface of his larger purpose. He would not allow them—or anything—to distract him from his goal.

Vengeance required a cool head and calm heart.

"You are not going to be a wet blanket, are you?" Turning away from the window, Lady Glory shot him a disgruntled glance. "The last thing I need is a killjoy for a partner."

"I have no intention of being a killer of joy. Merely the guardian of good sense."

Lady Glory directed her gaze upward toward her curly brown wig. While her disguise was first-rate, Wei thought that her eyes gave her away. They were the color of jade illuminated by sunlight; if one looked closely enough, one could see specks of bronze embedded in the irises. Wide, tip-tilted in shape, and fringed by lush sable lashes, her eyes brimmed with a mix of intelligence and innocence. Her gaze was that of a female who saw what was wrong with the world and believed she could single-handedly fix it.

Her naïveté underscored her youthfulness. The dozen or so years that separated her and Wei in age might have been a hundred when it came to life experience. He couldn't recall ever being that idealistic, that unspoiled by the darkness of life. Perhaps that was why she pulled at his protective instincts.

"I do not require a guardian of any sort," she retorted. "As this is a Society of Angels mission and I am the sole Angel present, I shall be in charge. You, sir, are second-in-command."

She was naïve *and* a little tigress. A dangerous combination. Not for the first time, Wei wondered about her parents. English aristocrats usually prized modesty, sophistication, and propriety in their female offspring...traits that were conspicuously absent in Lady Glory. Not that he was complaining. He much preferred her honesty, loyalty, and caring heart.

He inclined his head. "I am happy to serve, my lady."

"Jolly good." Even the fake mustache could not hide her jubilant smile. "Now that we have an understanding, Master Chen, I think we shall rub along well. Indeed, I have long admired your *kung fu* and would love to learn some techniques."

During a supper party at the Hadleighs', Lady Glory had asked him countless questions about his martial arts training, her expression as inquisitive as that of the ferret who'd been perched upon her shoulder. At present, the animal was in a small cage on the seat beside her, his back turned to them. Glory had claimed that FF II was giving her the "cold shoulder" because she wasn't taking him into Bottom's.

"Proper training takes time," Wei replied. "Years of cultivation."

"I haven't got years. Just tonight." She furrowed her brow. "Won't you give me a tip or two?"

He kept his expression bland. "Patience is power. With time and patience, the mulberry leaf becomes a silk gown."

She wrinkled her nose. Although she'd covered her features with a layer of face paint, he knew that her pert little appendage was sprinkled with golden freckles. He liked her freckles and her unaffected nature in general. In the stifling, smoke-choked world of London, Lady Glory was a blast of fresh air.

"But I don't want a silk gown," she protested. "I wish to have lessons in martial arts."

He gave into the rare urge to tease. "Lessons come from unexpected places."

"*Ugh*. All right, you win. No pointers this eve." She gave a huff that was, for lack of a better word, cute. "Then we'd best focus on our strategy."

Rummaging through a satchel, she pulled out a pair of tickets, handing him one. The voucher was made of silver-plated tin and engraved with a symbol that resembled a curvy "W." Below the symbol was the phrase, "Bottom's Up."

"This is our way in. If anyone asks, I am Adam Smith, newly minted baronet." She gave him an expectant look. "And you will be..."

"John Wong," he decided. "Former sailor. Currently in the import-export business."

"An excellent cover." Her nod was approving. "Now the suspect we are looking for is a burly, brown-haired fellow. He has the mien of a prizefighter with a nose that looks like it has been broken, barrel chest, and limp favoring the right side. When Livy and I followed him here previously, the guards at the door greeted him by name as Farwell so we believe that he is a regular patron at Bottom's."

"What is the plan if we see this Farwell fellow?"

She beamed, clearly delighted to be asked. "We will monitor him and try to get information on the whereabouts of Sir Barkley. As Farwell is merely the go-between for the dognappers, his knowledge of their operation may be limited. We cannot afford to tip him off to our investigation, or Sir Barkley's life will be at risk."

"Then the goal is surveillance." Wei preferred a hands-off

approach, as it provided less opportunity for Lady Glory to get into trouble. "Observation only."

"Generally speaking, yes."

He didn't trust the zealous gleam in her eyes.

"But if the opportunity arises for us to get close to Farwell, we should take it," she said decisively. "Get into his good graces and loosen his tongue with flattery and drink. You know how males like to talk about themselves."

He lifted his brows. "Do I?"

"I am not referring to you specifically." She gave an airy wave. "You happen to be the exception to the rule. Trust me, after three Seasons, I've become an expert on male behavior."

That she believed her words was a testament to her innocence.

"Surveillance is a sound strategy," he said. "Being unfamiliar with Bottom's, we are at a disadvantage. When thrown into a lion's den, it is wise not to draw attention to oneself."

"Adaptability is the key to survival." With a jaunty grin, the indomitable miss jammed a hat onto her curly wig and reached for the door handle. "Let us play it by ear, shall we?"

Before Wei could respond, she opened the door and hopped down. She made a beeline for the den of iniquity, every movement of her slender frame imbued with boundless energy. Amused and resigned, he alighted and went after her.

THREE

"That was easy," Glory said under her breath. "The guards didn't blink an eye."

She and Mr. Chen had passed the first gate of entry and were now in a corridor leading to the inner sanctum of Fanny Bottom's. Her partner greeted her comment the way he did most things: with an impassivity that might be mistaken for indifference. Yet she could tell that he was far from unconcerned. Although his noble features gave little away, she noted the subtle tension in his broad shoulders and the alertness of his gaze.

A gentleman who is ready for anything. How refreshing is that?

"The evening's journey has only begun," he said.

"Every journey begins with a single step," she said cheerfully. "Wasn't that one of Lao Tzu's famous sayings?"

"You know of Lao Tzu?"

Mr. Chen's brows shot upward. For him, that was the equivalent of a shout of surprise.

Glory shrugged, admitting, "I know a lot of things."

Her curiosity was rarely viewed as a desirable quality and, indeed, had oft landed her in the suds. From schoolteachers to peers, most people found her inquisitive mind disconcerting (if not downright annoying). Only her family and closest friends understood and accepted her. It was one of the reasons why she adored Aunt Hypatia, who had not only tolerated her precociousness as a girl but encouraged it.

"Reserve your right to think." Aunt Patty had been fond of quoting her namesake, Hypatia of Alexandria. *"For even to think wrongly is better than not to think at all."*

Mr. Chen's forehead furrowed. "I was not aware that there were English translations of Lao Tzu's writings."

"There aren't. I read a translation by the French sinologist Monsieur Julien," Glory explained. "After that, I attempted to read it in Chinese, but I stumbled my way through. My oral ability is far superior to my reading and writing skills, unfortunately."

Mr. Chen gave her an unfathomable look and said nothing.

Glory stifled a sigh, realizing that she was being a bit boastful. For some reason, she wanted to impress this taciturn master...probably because she wanted him to agree to teach her *kung fu* and other aspects of Chinese culture. She'd always been curious about that part of her heritage, and now she finally knew someone who had knowledge to share.

Remembering how he'd smiled when she had spoken in Mandarin at the Hadleighs' supper party, she asked in that language, "Perhaps *you* could teach me how to read Lao Tzu in his original language?"

"Perhaps." A smile flitted through his eyes. "For now...focus."

They arrived at a second set of doors flanked by guards. The robust fellows checked their membership cards again, the taller one eyeing Mr. Chen with obvious suspicion.

"Don't get many o' your sort 'ere," the guard sneered.

"And what sort is that?" Mr. Chen asked.

The shorter guard cut in. "Just let the bloke in, Barnes. We don't need no trouble."

Barnes yanked open the door, releasing a raucous swell of noise that didn't muffle his parting shot. "All I'm saying is that we don't need the stench o' opium dens stinking up the club."

At the injustice of the accusation, Glory felt her blood boil. Mr. Chen *helped* people recover from their opium use. If anyone pushed opium, it was the British traders who grew, distributed, and profited from the drug. As she opened her mouth to relieve the guard of his ignorance, Mr. Chen slung an arm around her shoulders, his touch causing her to start. She caught a whiff of his scent—clean male musk combined with something herbal—and her tummy gave an odd flip.

"Let us not ruin the evening's purpose, Smith," he said casually.

Beneath his companionable tone was a warning.

Right. The mission.

Getting her impulses in check, Glory bestowed a look of loathing upon the guard before continuing into the club. Mr. Chen dropped his arm as soon as the door closed behind them.

"How can you abide such ignorance?" she said in a furious whisper.

"Practice." As self-contained as ever, he circled his gaze around the large hall. "I suggest we start canvassing for Farwell before we encounter more of the guard's ilk."

Glory forced herself to focus on the task at hand. Paneled in dark wood, the main hall was spacious with a vaulted ceiling and hanging candelabra. Patrons from all strata of society, from local riffraff to louche bluebloods, mingled in their shared search for depravity. Serving maids sashayed about with trays of drink and food, and Glory's eyes widened at their obvious commonality: all were generously endowed in the derriere. The snug fit of the barmaids' skirts showcased their curvy bottoms, much to the leering appreciation of the customers.

Slanting a look at Mr. Chen, Glory felt a spark of approval. He was surveilling the room and took no notice of the barmaids' charms. It was, she decided, quite professional of him.

He cut a swath through the throng, and she hurried to catch up. They circulated around the hall before entering another chamber, this one dedicated to gambling. Crowds surrounded the tables where players wagered on cards and dice. As Glory scouted for Farwell through the haze of cigar smoke, she noted the way Mr. Chen navigated his way around inebriated louts. He moved like water, finding the path of least resistance. When men found themselves stumbling out of his path, they did not even register that he'd displaced them.

I wish I knew how to do that, she thought wistfully.

They continued into another section of the club, and Glory was so caught up in admiring the master's technique that she failed to see him halt. She collided into him, stumbling back a few steps.

Heavens, it is like running into a brick wall.

Pivoting, Mr. Chen steadied her. "Any sign of Farwell?"

Balance regained, she surveyed the patrons drinking at long tables facing a curtained stage. As she scanned the faces, a voice boomed. A portly man had come through the velvet curtains, dressed in a garish red jacket with epaulettes and braided gold trim.

"Gents, I've a real treat for ye all this evening," he announced. "The show you've all been waiting for, the jewel o' Fanny Bottom's crown. The amazing spectacle that cannot be seen anywhere but within these walls. Put your 'ands together for the one, the only... Fantastical Female Fighters!"

The crowd whistled and stomped as the curtains swept apart.

At first glance, the revealed sparring ring was not unlike the one in the Angels' training chamber. Then a pair of footmen appeared, efficiently rolling off the cloth that had covered the floor of the ring to reveal a sunken pit filled with a dark, oozing substance...mud? Moments later, a brunette and a redhead strutted onto the stage, and catcalls erupted from the audience.

Heat bloomed in Glory's cheeks as she took in the women's voluptuous forms. Their ensembles were skimpy: strips of cloth bound their rounded breasts, and tiny loincloths barely hid their lower parts. The brunette's costume was embellished with green baize cutouts in the shape of leaves while the redhead's bore sequined orange flames.

"Sit your arses down! You ain't made o' glass, you know," a voice shouted behind Glory. "Paid good money to see me some tits this eve."

Glory turned to look at the florid-faced fellow sitting behind her. He made a rude hand gesture.

"Pardon," Mr. Chen said calmly. "We did not mean to block the view."

He nudged her toward the nearest bench.

When they were seated, he said in an undertone, "Do not get distracted. Stay focused on finding the suspect."

Once again, Glory was impressed by the master's indifference to the debauchery. Unlike the other males who were howling like rabid hyenas, he ignored the half-naked women now wrestling in the mud.

"Sitting near the exit, to the right of the stage," he said in a low voice. "Is that Farwell?"

Glory's nape tingled at the sight of the large, pugnacious-looking fellow.

With a quiver of excitement, she said, "That's him."

She started to rise. Mr. Chen closed a hand around her arm, keeping her in her seat.

"If we get up now, we'll block the view and cause a ruckus. We don't want to scare Farwell off. Wait until after the show."

He had a point, of course. Patience truly wasn't one of her virtues.

Tapping her foot, she glanced back at the stage, where the brunette and redhead were still tussling. To the delight of the roaring crowd, the women were now topless.

Glory slanted him a glance. "You just don't want to miss the show."

Amusement flashed in the master's eyes.

"I prefer less obvious displays," he murmured.

For some reason, her cheeks burned at his comment. Thank goodness she'd worn sideburns and a mustache; otherwise, her blushing might give away her disguise.

The fight finally came to an end, with the brunette emerging victorious. She performed a victory lap around the stage, her bare, mud-smeared breasts jiggling. She brought the crowd to their feet as she blew kisses and bent to collect the coins they tossed in tribute.

Glory craned her head in Farwell's direction. "He's on the move."

Mr. Chen was already standing. "Let us go."

They headed toward Farwell, their progress slowed by the jostling throng. Farwell disappeared down a corridor next to the stage. Glory led the charge after him, passing through a curtain to another hallway. Mounted sconces cast flickering shadows over the row of closed doors.

"Do you think Farwell is in one of those rooms?" Glory chewed on her lip. "We should check."

"Our plan was to observe only," Mr. Chen said. "This is a recipe for getting caught."

She came to a quick decision. "If someone catches us snooping, we'll pretend we got lost."

"I shall, of course, bow to your greater experience."

She couldn't tell if he was teasing her. He did, however, accompany her to the nearest door. She tried the knob...locked. Removing her trusty lockpicks from her pocket, she made sure the coast was clear before gaining entry. Inside, she surveyed what appeared to be a bathing room. Pipes ran up one of the marble-tiled walls, connecting to an overhead brass spout.

"There's no one here," Mr. Chen said. "Let's go."

But Glory was distracted by the large wardrobe in the corner.

Open me, its double doors seemed to whisper.

Curious, she headed over. "Let's see what is in the wardrobe."

"There will be nothing of import..."

Ignoring Mr. Chen's exasperated sigh, she reached for the wardrobe doors. With tingling anticipation, she opened them... and saw a lone sateen robe hanging in the cavernous interior.

Mr. Chen stood with his arms over his chest. His version of an *I-told-you-so* sort of look.

Feeling slightly foolish, she said, "Onto the next room then—"

Approaching voices cut her off. As the door to the bathing chamber opened, she acted on instinct and jumped into the wardrobe. Mr. Chen followed her, swiftly closing the doors behind them.

Four

Every journey began with one step. As did every disaster.

The enormity of his mistake struck Wei. Lady Glory had a way of affecting his better judgment. Despite her noble intentions, she was a virginal miss and a duke's daughter. She might be out to save the world, but the world would not reciprocate the favor. If she were discovered in this nefarious club, her life would be ruined beyond repair.

I will not let that happen. I will protect her. From herself, if necessary.

He glanced at his charge. As the wardrobe barely fit them both, they were crammed together, mere inches apart. A narrow gap between the doors provided a direct view of the bathing area and let in enough light for him to see Lady Glory's face. She did not look concerned; in fact, her eyes sparkled with unholy excitement.

Turning to him, she mouthed, *It's Farwell.*

She pointed gleefully at the gap, through which the pair of newcomers was visible.

Stifling a sigh, Wei peered over her head to observe. Farwell was with the brunette who'd won the fight. She'd thrown on a short green robe but no shoes, leaving muddy footprints over the pristine tile.

"I'm glad you won the bathing rights tonight, Farwell," she cooed.

"I've 'ad my eye on you for a while, Christabel." Farwell stalked her into the showering area. Hulking and square-jawed, he had the look of a man who made his living with his fists. "Just 'ad to wait for my ship to come in so I could bid for you."

"I like a winner." Christabel let her robe slip, baring a shoulder as she turned to him. "Was it a very big ship that came in?"

"Very big." Farwell trailed a finger along her shoulder. "Can you keep a secret, dove?"

"As well as I can wrestle."

In a flash, Christabel grabbed Farwell by the arms, pressing him against the bathing room wall. She rubbed against him like a cat, slowly and sinuously. She turned, gyrating her bottom against him while he panted. When she stepped back, he had a noticeable bulge in his trousers.

Sweat trickled beneath Wei's cravat. The air in the wardrobe had grown warm, and Lady Glory's scent tickled his nose. It wasn't perfume—she was too clever to compromise her disguise—but her own subtle essence, sweet and elusive. It reminded him of something that he couldn't quite put his finger on. As she took in the debauched scene, her eyes were the size of supper plates, and he had the distinct urge to cover her all-too-curious gaze.

"My lips are sealed." Christabel's vow was sultry. "You can tell me anything."

His eyes glazed with lust, Farwell said, "I've landed meself a plum job with one o' the premier East End outfits. The Fancy... you've 'eard o' them, eh?"

Bloody hell. The situation is worse than I thought.

When Wei had opened his clinic five years ago, he'd been shocked by the lawlessness in the East End. Police had seldom patrolled his Whitechapel neighborhood; he didn't know whether the cause was fear or bribes. What he did know was that when he'd asked for help, they'd turned him away. No stranger to corruption —he'd dealt with his share of it in his homeland—Wei had not been deterred.

He had organized a night watch made up of his students and neighbors. The concerted efforts of the community made life harder for the thieves, pickpockets, and cutthroats who preyed on the vulnerable. This did not endear him to the underworld element; some of the gangs had even issued threats, leaving pigeons with broken necks on his doorstep as warnings.

On a few occasions, they'd done more than threaten. This had required Wei to demonstrate, through force, his commitment to keeping his neighborhood safe. Most of the gangs had learned to steer clear of him, but the Fancy was the most brutal of the lot. They ran everything from protection rackets to burglary rings, terrorizing local denizens into submission. The few who resisted suffered injuries or ended up floating in the Thames.

Now it sounded like the Fancy was behind the dognapping scheme. Wei's gut knotted. He did not want Lady Glory anywhere near the bloodthirsty gang.

"If you're a member o' the Fancy," Christabel said, "then you must be a very powerful fellow."

"Ain't a member exactly," Farwell admitted. "I'm more o' what you'd call a consultant."

Christabel walked her fingers up his chest. "Important *and* powerful. An irresistible combination."

"Went to 'em, I did, wif an idea," Farwell said proudly. "I discovered a product that folks'll pay anyfin' for. Even be'er, these goods are simple to obtain...why, you can practically scoop 'em right off the street. The Fancy stashes the goods while I collect the blunt from interested parties. Everybody wins."

Feeling Lady Glory bristling beside him, Wei put a staying

hand on her shoulder. She turned to him; even in the dimness, he could see the fire in her eyes.

Observe only, he mouthed.

But the blighter is operating a dognapping ring!

He had to bite back a smile at her response, which she'd managed to make emphatic despite only mouthing the words. His attention was diverted by the sound of running water and Christabel's suggestive words.

"Time to get me wet, sir."

Lady Glory swung her gaze back to the viewing hole. Wei saw that Christabel had shed her robe, revealing her generous mud-caked breasts and hips, with only a strip of cloth covering her sex. Water rained from the overhead nozzle, and she stepped beneath the spray, rivulets of dirty water streaming over her full, glistening curves.

"Use the soap," Christabel said huskily. "I'm a *very* dirty hussy this eve."

Farwell shed his clothes as if they were on fire. When he reached for his waistband, Wei couldn't stand it any longer. He clapped his hands over Lady Glory's eyes and pulled her away from the viewing hole.

Feeling her struggle against him, he whispered in her ear, "This is not fit for a lady's eyes."

Unfortunately, it wasn't fit for a lady's ears either.

"Bleeding 'ell, you've fine tits." Farwell's voice was thick with lust. "Big and plump, wif nipples like cherries."

"Keep soaping me," Christabel purred. "You're getting me into a real lather."

Wei wished he could plug Lady Glory's ears. At least she had stopped squirming. Perhaps she'd finally realized the dire risk of the situation. He had to protect her modesty as best he could... which wasn't easy, given the increasingly degenerate talk.

"You don't need my 'elp to get soaked down 'ere." Farwell's

words seemed to reverberate within the wooden closet. "What I wouldn't give to dip my wick in that hot, wet pussy o' yours."

Wei felt Lady Glory grow very still, her cheeks warm beneath his palms. Warm and...soft. In the steamy air, her mustache had come unglued, dangling from one end and exposing her mouth. It was a good thing that she'd thought to hide her lips, for they were feminine, full and soft-looking. Her tongue flicked out, wetting the rosy rim, and sudden heat flooded his groin.

Shock washed over him, followed by an undertow of self-disgust.

What the bloody hell is wrong with me? This is Lady Glory, and I am responsible for her.

Wei's churning thoughts were cut short by Christabel's firm voice.

"Now, you know the rules." She tut-tutted. "Bathing rights include *hands* only. You may touch but nothing else, naughty boy."

"But I'm 'ard as a bloody rock," Farwell grumbled. "'Ow am I supposed to walk out with my prick in this state, eh?"

"You can't finish in me, but that doesn't mean you can't finish, eh?" Christabel's tone turned suggestive. "Frig yourself, big fellow, and show me what I'm missing."

As the lewd exchange continued, Wei anchored himself in reason. What he'd felt had been a mere physical reaction. What any man might feel when observing depravity in close confines with an attractive young female. Especially when said man had practiced celibacy for the last thirteen years.

Thus, he would ignore what amounted to naught more than a meaningless bodily reflex and concentrate on extricating Lady Glory from this mess. Beneath his palms, her cheeks were more than warm now—they were blazing hot. With maidenly mortification, undoubtedly.

Protectiveness surged over Wei. While his charge had a brazen streak, she was pure of heart. The poor girl's sensibilities must be offended beyond repair. He had to get her out of here as soon as possible and salvage what he could of her innocence.

Glory was having rather strange feelings.

During her adventures as an Angel, she'd been exposed to a variety of improper situations, although never as up close and personal as the present one. She had an intellectual understanding of what was going on between Christabel and Farwell. Yet nothing in her experience prepared her for the way she was feeling right now. Breathless and hot...which made sense since she was trapped in a stifling wardrobe. The thing was, she wasn't hot from the outside. The heat felt like it was coming from *within*. A fever seemed to have started in her belly, spreading outward in sweltering waves.

She burned hottest where Mr. Chen was touching her. Even though the contact was light, the rasp of his callused palms made blood pulse in her cheeks and...well, elsewhere. The tips of her breasts had stiffened, tingling against their cloth binding. That feeling of heightened sensitivity swirled over her skin. She was twitchy and uncomfortable, overwhelmed by an urge to move.

"Stop wriggling."

The master's quiet command warmed her ear and somehow made matters worse. She became acutely aware of him behind her, the coiled tension in his powerful frame. Without the usual obstacle of fluffy skirts, she was standing closer to him than she had any man, her trouser-clad posterior mere inches away from his front.

Heat licked her insides at the scandalous thought. She clenched her thighs together, shocked to feel an odd smear of dampness there.

Dash it, what is happening to me?

"Christ's blood, I'm about to unload my cannon," Farwell panted.

With her sight blocked, Glory could only hear the suspect grunting and the slippery sounds he was making. Her heart thumped with wanton curiosity. What *was* Farwell doing, exactly?

As if reading her thoughts, Mr. Chen kept his hands over her eyes, drawing her against him. Her entire being shivered when their bodies made contact. She felt the unyielding edges of his strength. He was like a brick wall...but one that was warm and alive.

"You've a cock like a stallion," Christabel breathed. "Rut that fist o' yours."

Zounds. Images bounced through Glory's head.

"It will be over soon," Mr. Chen murmured. "Try not to listen."

Certainly. While I'm at it, I could also try not to breathe.

"I'm going to spend, dove," Farwell said hoarsely. "Want to do it on your tits."

"That'll be five pounds extra, love."

As guttural sounds emerged from Farwell, Glory gave in to the urge to squirm. She felt something hard and large wedged against her buttocks. *Did Mr. Chen bring a weapon with him?* An instant later, the master released her. When she twisted her head to look at him, he was adjusting his frock coat, his expression stern.

His lips formed a single word. *Quiet.*

She rolled her eyes in reply. As if she would be otherwise. The conversation beyond the wardrobe drew her back to the viewing slit.

"Farwell, you wicked fellow." Christabel pouted as she held up her green sateen robe. "This were my favorite, and you got it dirty."

"Just giving you somefin' to remember me by." Farwell smirked. "Don't worry, I'll pay for another."

"A true gent you are, to be sure." Christabel blew him a kiss. "Luckily, I 'ave a spare robe..."

Glory's heart hammered as the brunette headed for the wardrobe.

A strong hand gripped hers; she shot a look at Mr. Chen as the door opened.

His eyes steady, he said, *"Run."*

FIVE

The door to Wei's study flung open, and Yao stomped in. While such behavior was uncommon among butlers and majordomos, Yao was also Wei's *shidai*, or junior disciple of the same *shifu*. Wei had known Yao since the latter was a sixteen-year-old fisherman's son who'd become ensnared in opium's net. Disowned by his family and disgraced, Yao had tried to drown himself. Shifu Lam and Wei had found him barely breathing on the shore, and they'd brought him home and helped him to recover.

Since then, Yao had been a boisterous and sometimes annoying part of Wei's life. He was like a little brother...although at six foot five and weighing seventeen stone, Yao could hardly be called "little." While Yao tended to be unruly and idle, he was also loyal, with a heart to match his physical size. When Wei had set off on his quest to avenge his family, Shifu Lam had suggested Wei take Yao with him.

Wei rose from his desk. "What is it, *shidai*?"

"*Shihing.*" Yao remembered to bow and use the respectful form of address for a senior disciple...which was surprising, given his general disregard for things such as protocol. "We've got a bolter. Guess who?"

Wei didn't have to guess. "The American."

"And that is why you're the *shifu* around here." Yao lifted the jade seal from Wei's desk—a gift from their master—tossing it from hand to hand...and promptly fumbling it.

Wei moved, catching the carved stone before it smashed on the ground. He set it back down on the desk.

Stifling a sigh, he said, "Let's see to the American."

They exited the main building, which contained Wei's study and the main hall, and headed to the patient wing.

The property had once been used as a warehouse by a varnish maker, who'd happily sold it to Wei for a song. Wei had seen the potential of the three tumble-down buildings connected by two courtyards. With Yao's help, he'd rebuilt the place, modeling it after their *shifu*'s Spartan compound, adding a latticed railing to the walkways and tiled roof to give it the feeling of home.

They arrived at the patient wing, a stark and orderly chamber with a dozen cots arranged behind dressing screens. At present, the sole occupant was Joseph Williams, an American sailor. He was in his twenties, but his gaunt features made him look at least a decade older. He sat on his cot, his head in his hands, a battered valise packed beside him.

"How are you feeling, Williams?" Wei asked.

"Like hell." Looking up, Williams ran a hand through his ragged blond hair. "Since you gave me that vile potion this morning, I cannot keep anything down."

"That is the point." Wei sat beside Williams and took the other's pulse; it was chaotic but improved since the start of the treatment. "The tonic contained opium ash paired with purgative herbs. Soon the mere thought of opium will remind your body of this unpleasant reaction, which is an effective antidote to craving."

"You've explained this before, Doc." Williams scrubbed his hands over his face before turning desperate eyes to Wei. "But I don't think I can take any more. I'm not strong enough. I...I want to go."

"There is nothing keeping you here," Wei said. "Nothing but your determination to get better."

"What if I can't get better?" Williams's face was etched with despair. "I've tried everything—even had a friend lock me in a room for a week so I couldn't get my hands on opium. But the craving...it's too overpowering. I reckon I'm too weak to resist it."

"Accepting that one's willpower alone is not enough is half the battle. Here at the clinic, you have met men, many sailors like yourself, who share the same struggle. Do you think them all weak?"

Williams shook his head. "No, Doc, I surely do not."

Wei nodded to his *shidai*, who stood on the other side of the cot. "What about Yao? Do you think he's weak?"

"I'd be shaking in my boots if I met Mr. Yao in an alley." Williams's eyes had a glimmer of humor as he tilted his head back to look at the larger man. "You look like you could best Hercules, sir."

"It's true that I was known as the 'Strongest Man in Shandong.' But opium was stronger," Yao said frankly. "I couldn't wrestle free of its grasp...until I tried the tonic you just took. Tastes and feels like shite, doesn't it?"

"Worse," Williams said, grimacing.

"But it worked," Yao replied. "After a month, the smell of opium smoke made me queasier than a sailor on his first voyage. After two months, even the thought of opium made me want to puke my guts out."

"I've been at it for a month already. The tonic makes me sick, all right. But I...I..." Williams forced the words out. "I still have cravings. What kind of pathetic bastard does that make me?"

And there it was: shame. A feeling as detrimental to progress as any craving.

A feeling that Wei knew well.

"It does not matter how slowly you go as long as you do not stop," he said quietly.

A spark came into the American's eyes. Hope...a refusal to give up the fight.

Wei knew Williams would be all right.

A deep, cultured voice came from the doorway. "Still beating your pupils over the head with Confucius, Master Chen?"

"Your Grace." Wei rose as the Duke of Hadleigh strode into the room. "I am gratified that you recognized the wisdom of the world's greatest philosopher."

"Heard it often enough, old boy," Hadleigh said wryly.

In the eyes of English society, Benedict Wodehouse, the Duke of Hadleigh, was a gentleman who had everything: status, wealth, and a lovely young wife and daughter. To look at the robust dark-haired duke, immaculately garbed in the latest fashion, one would not guess the destructive path he'd once traveled.

"Doc's philosophy ain't half bad," Williams said shyly. "And it's a hell of an improvement over the thoughts running through my head."

The wry humor dropped from Hadleigh's countenance. His blue gaze sharpened.

"Williams, is it?" he said in imperious tones.

"Y-yes, sir." Looking awed that a duke was addressing him by name, the American stammered, "I m-mean, er, Your Majesty."

"Take it from me, the treatment works. Don't give up on it...or yourself."

Williams gave a reverent nod.

Amused, Wei asked, "Do you have time for tea, Your Grace?"

"If your fine lapsang souchong is on offer, I shan't refuse."

As Wei and the duke headed back to the study, they passed students practicing *kung fu* in the courtyard. The men bowed, chorusing, "Good morning, Shifu Chen." Wei acknowledged their greetings with a nod and waved them on to continue their drills.

"I could use a training session myself," Hadleigh remarked. "My skills are getting rusty."

"You are always welcome to practice here."

"I know. I've had my hands full of late."

Wei cocked his head. "How is Her Grace's injury?"

"Her ankle is coming along, and she wishes to convey her thanks for the poultice you prescribed." Hadleigh's eyes crinkled at the corners. "If you have a similar poultice to cure her impulse to get up and about before she is ready, I would forever be in your debt."

Wei felt his lips twitch. "I am a healer, Your Grace. Not a miracle worker."

It would take a miracle to cure the duchess of her headstrong nature; fortunately, Hadleigh cherished his wife's spirit. Indeed, willfulness seemed to be a quality shared by Her Grace's friends. On cue, Lady Glory burst into Wei's head. Since their adventure last night, she'd intruded constantly upon his thoughts, and even years of contemplation practice could not rid him of the memories.

Of being trapped in that wardrobe with her. Of her scent. Of her innocent-yet-wanton curiosity, that instant when arousal had broken through the barrier of his self-control, his cock rising hungrily against her sleek curves...

Thoughts are like rambunctious children. It will not do to indulge them.

Pushing the wayward duke's daughter firmly out of his head, Wei led the duke into his study. Like the rest of the clinic, his sanctuary was stark and uncluttered, furnished with simple rosewood furnishings. A pair of his *shifu*'s calligraphy scrolls graced the wall behind his desk, and his meditation cushion sat on the floor next to the ancestral altar.

With a bittersweet pang, Wei ran his gaze over the three spirit tablets on the altar: one for his *mama*, *baba*, and *mei mei*. The narrow wooden plaques were carved with their names, and the incense he'd burned for them earlier lingered in the air. Next to the tablets, the offering of oranges gleamed in their bowl...Ling Ling's favorite.

I hope the oranges are sweet, little sister. As sweet as the vengeance I vow to one day offer you.

The thought focused him, reminded him of everything at stake. For fifteen years, he had been hunting down the villains who'd murdered his family. He'd delivered justice to one, but a job half-done was a job not done at all. He had another killer to find, and he would not let anything—least of all a fleeting and irrational physical reaction—distract him.

The maid arrived with tea. Wei and his guest sat at the round table, the smoky aroma of the lapsang souchong rising from their porcelain cups.

"I came to thank you," Hadleigh said. "For escorting Her Grace's friend last night."

"It was my pleasure."

Do not associate Glory Cavendish with pleasure. Do. Not.

"Was it?"

The note of knowing humor in Hadleigh's tone made Wei wary.

"From what I hear, there was rather a lot of mayhem, which is to be expected where the Angels are concerned," the duke went on. "But you apparently took everything in stride. Lady Glory was singing your praises to Livy this morning."

Wei ignored the kick of warmth in his chest. "I was glad to lend a hand."

"According to Lady Glory, you rose to the occasion."

Bloody hell, she didn't notice my arousal, did she?

Wei's heart thumped. "Pardon?"

"The way the chit told it, you had wings on your feet. She claims that after the two of you were discovered, you engineered an ingenious escape that involved evading an army of guards and scaling a towering gate."

The speed and agility of Wei's lightness *kung fu* had proved useful as he'd navigated Lady Glory to safety. Yet she had also played her part. He had never met a female with her energy and stamina. Moreover, she was fearless...

Dangerously so.

"I take it Lady Glory mentioned our discovery of the Fancy's involvement," he said grimly.

"She did, yes."

Hadleigh's reply was somber. He had participated in Wei's neighborhood watch and witnessed firsthand what happened to those who stood up to the Fancy. When Mr. Calder, a grocer who owned a shop close to the clinic, had refused to pay protection money, the gang had set fire to his property. Wei and his team had arrived in time to put out the flames, but Mr. Calder had suffered burns that required treatment to this day.

The idea of Lady Glory attracting the Fancy's notice chilled Wei.

"You know, as I do, that the Fancy is not to be trifled with," he said. "This case is not suitable for your duchess and her friends."

"Be that as it may, the Angels tend to decide for themselves what is suitable." Hadleigh took a drink of tea, replacing the cup in its saucer. "In this instance, they remain committed to helping their client recover her pet."

"It is far too dangerous. Surely you can dissuade your wife—"

"You have met my Livy?" Hadleigh quirked a brow.

Wei clenched his jaw. "Don't you English have a saying about a man being the master of his own house?"

"I am undoubtedly Livy's lord and master. When it suits us both."

Seeing the male gleam in the duke's eyes, Wei felt the bite of frustration. While Hadleigh deserved the hard-won happiness he'd found in his marriage, there were more pressing concerns to contend with, Lady Glory's welfare being at the top of the list.

"Perhaps if we inform Lady Fayne of the dangers associated

with the Fancy, she will listen to reason," Wei said tightly. "When does she return?"

Hadleigh tilted his head. "Why do you care?"

"I beg your pardon?"

"About the Angels."

As a *shifu*, Wei was used to providing advice and guidance to others. Now he found himself in the unaccustomed, and not entirely comfortable, position of explaining himself.

"As a gentleman, I extend my assistance to those who require it," he said stiffly.

"The Angels are hardly damsels in distress. You've seen them in action."

Wei gave his friend a pointed look. "You are saying you are comfortable with Her Grace traipsing into the Fancy's territory?"

"Hell, no. Livy is my wife, and I will see that she is protected by any means necessary." Hadleigh lifted his brows. "Who are you protecting, old chap?"

Heat crept up Wei's jaw. "I don't know what you mean."

"Don't you?" Hadleigh rotated his cup a half-turn. "Lady Glory is an unusual chit. Quite refreshing, in her own way, don't you think?"

"I have not pondered the matter." *Not intentionally.*

"It would not be wrong if you had." Hadleigh cleared his throat. "Next to my wife, you are the one who knows me best, Chen. You know the darkness of my past and, indeed, helped me to slay some of those demons. I am in your debt. And yet it occurs to me that I know very little about you."

Because I cannot compromise my goal. Vengeance requires secrecy. I cannot entrust my family's honor to any Englishman...even you, my friend.

"There is no debt," Wei said. "You have more than repaid my services with your generous donations to the clinic."

"My skills may be rusty, but I still recognize an evasive maneuver." Although Hadleigh smiled, his eyes were serious. "I know you are a private fellow, and my intention is not to pry. Only to reciprocate what you have given me in the past: a willingness to listen and understand."

"Your offer is appreciated."

"But you are not going to take it." The duke relented with a nod. "The offer stands, nonetheless. I know you value self-discipline, old boy, but no man is an island."

Wei flashed back to the early years after his family had been slaughtered. He hadn't been disciplined then; he'd been hotheaded and reckless, his actions fueled by rage and grief. Then, when he'd failed to avenge his family, he'd numbed himself with violence, drink, and women. In truth, his journey had not been so different from Hadleigh's. At his lowest point, beaten to a pulp and robbed by dockside ruffians, he'd been rescued by a former monk named Lam.

Master Lam had become Wei's *shifu*, reshaping his character and imparting the skills he needed to restore his family's honor. Patience, restraint, humility—these had become Wei's guiding principles. One of Shifu Lam's teachings surfaced in Wei's head, and he voiced it now.

"Ordinary men hate solitude," he said quietly. "But the master embraces his aloneness."

If solitude was the price Wei had to pay to hunt down the man who'd murdered his kin, then he would be an island. He would cut himself off from temptation. From anything—or anyone—that threatened to distract him from his purpose. Perhaps then he could finally let go of the pain festering inside him. Perhaps then he could be at peace.

"I suppose one cannot argue with Confucius," Hadleigh said with a sigh.

Before Wei could correct the duke on the source, he heard Yao's heavy steps, followed by lighter ones...and the rustling of expensive skirts? He rose, his pulse giving an odd stutter as Yao led Lady Glory into his study. She was accompanied by an older female who wore a lace cap over her silver curls, her narrow figure encased in a no-nonsense gown. The chaperone's bespectacled gaze simmered with intelligence.

"The ladies wished to see you, Master Chen," Yao announced.

Wei's *shidai* was doing a piss-poor job of hiding his curiosity about the women, especially Glory. The big bastard couldn't take his eyes off her.

Hadleigh bowed. "Mrs. Newton, Lady Glory. What a pleasant surprise."

Wei narrowed his eyes. Despite the duke's words, he did not seem surprised in the slightest.

"Good afternoon, sirs," Lady Glory said cheerfully.

Today she looked like what she was: the daughter of a wealthy duke. Her rosewood hair was styled in a topknot, with curls framing her heart-shaped face. Her striped bamboo-green gown showcased her lissome figure and brought out the verdant sparkle in her eyes. Her freckles had reemerged, specks of gold leaf upon her dainty nose. The only exception to her fashion plate perfection was the ferret perched on her shoulder.

Wei's confidence returned. While she was fresh and appealing, he knew that he could resist temptations of the flesh. He had done so for years.

"However, Your Grace, I think you are mistaken," she went on.

Hadleigh cocked his head. "About what?"

"The source of the adage is not Confucius."

Lady Glory turned to Wei, and her smile affected his cool self-discipline like a blast of sunshine. Her playful dimple turned his blood molten, sending a hot rush straight to his groin.

"That saying is attributed to Lao Tzu, I believe," she said.

Six

Although Glory had heard about Mr. Chen's clinic from Livy, this was her first visit. She was bubbling over with curiosity about the operation and the man behind it. As Mr. Chen and Hadleigh guided her and Aunt Hypatia on a tour, she took in the tiled roof, rock gardens, and latticed wood walkways with a thrill of excitement. Since she was a girl, she'd been fascinated by her Chinese ancestry, reading as many books as she could find on the subject. She had the strange sensation that she was simultaneously visiting a foreign place and coming home.

She adored the spare elegance of the setting, which suited its owner. Today the master was dressed in his native style, wearing a long blue-grey tunic over matching trousers. The drape of the linen emphasized his broad shoulders and narrow hips. He moved with the grace of a predatory beast, the fabric flowing along with him as if it didn't dare get in the way. Recalling his callused touch against her skin, how close she'd been to him in the wardrobe, she felt an odd flutter in her belly. An awareness that hadn't been there before last night and that made her feel like a gawky schoolmiss.

Stop acting like a ninny, or Master Chen will never grant your request.

Glory's instincts told her that the master would not welcome silliness. He was the epitome of dignity and reserve. She wondered what sort of female might appeal to a man like him...if, indeed, he had any interest in romantic pursuits. Livy had mentioned rumors that the master had trained as a monk.

Despite Mr. Chen's asceticism, Glory suspected that he was a man of strong passions. His commitment to helping others and mastery of martial arts conveyed the power of his convictions. His intense gaze also had a worldly quality...as if he'd seen too much of life to be surprised by it. And despite his stoicism, she suspected that he enjoyed teasing her.

No, she could not imagine Wei Chen as a monk. Yet it was equally difficult to imagine the type of female he might be interested in. Since like drew like, he might choose someone whose temperament and habits matched his own. A lady who never took a misstep, never had a hair out of place. A paragon of refinement and propriety.

As the thought was oddly depressing, Glory pushed it aside. Her purpose today was professional, not personal. The flit from Fanny Bottom's had made her more determined than ever to learn from the master. She had never seen anyone with his physical prowess. If he would teach her even an iota of his martial arts, she would be *unstoppable* as an investigator.

Hence, she had arranged the visit today. It hadn't been difficult to get Aunt Hypatia on board. Glory had mentioned that the Hadleighs knew a respected teacher in the art of self-defense, and wouldn't it be wonderful if he might agree to teach her a few skills? She'd added that Mr. Chen was also a famed healer who specialized in Chinese remedies. Aunt Patty, whose love of knowledge was equal to Glory's, had taken the bait and agreed to chaperone her.

It was a stroke of luck that Livy's husband happened to be here. The duke's patronage lent credibility to the establishment, although even that was unnecessary: Aunt Patty appeared as intrigued by the clinic as Glory was. At present, they were in a chamber that resembled an apothecary shop, the air scented with herbs and other earthy smells Glory couldn't quite place. A large cabinet with dozens of small drawers took up an entire wall while a neatly organized worktable stood at the center of the room.

"What a remarkable operation you run, sir." Aunt Patty glanced around the room, her bespectacled gaze glimmering with interest. "How did you become a healer?"

"I was taught by my *shifu*, Master Lam," Mr. Chen replied. "For decades, he belonged to an order of monks whose practices included healing, contemplation, and martial arts."

"Were you, um, a monk as well?" Glory blurted.

He raised his brows, and her cheeks flamed at her own impertinence.

"Not in a technical sense," he said after a pause. "Master Lam had left his order long before he took on pupils. While he advocated austerity as a life principle, he ran a school, not a monastery."

Glory was relieved that he didn't seem offended by her curiosity. And by his answer...not that his non-monastic status had anything to do with her. She also thanked her lucky stars that he was keeping mum about her extracurriculars. While Aunt Patty supported female independence, she had limits and would never approve of Glory's covert life as an investigator. Fortunately, Master Chen was proving the soul of discretion.

Glory's heart did a giddy somersault. *Could any gentleman be more perfect?*

Their eyes met; at the unfathomable flash in his intense brown gaze, she was suddenly afraid that he could read her thoughts. Nervously, she looked away, and while Mr. Chen responded to her aunt's next query, she wandered to the worktable where three lidded ceramic jars stood in a neat line.

She traded looks with FF II, who was curled around her shoulders.

"I wonder what is inside these?" she murmured.

She interpreted his reply of *tuk-tuk* to mean, "Let's find out."

Bending over, she reached for one of the lids.

"Don't touch that..."

Mr. Chen issued the warning just as the lid came loose in her hand. Air exploded from the jar with a loud *poof*. She and FF II both squeaked as a dark, sticky substance flew out and splattered them.

"...it is in the middle of fermenting," Mr. Chen finished saying.

He strode over as Glory stood frozen in shock. Holding her chin between his finger and thumb, he took out his handkerchief and began to wipe the sticky mess off her face.

She blinked at him. "What...what is this stuff?"

His features remained impassive. "A ginseng compound I am experimenting with. There is no cause for concern." He turned her head this way and that, examining his handiwork. "It is good for the skin."

When he proceeded to clean off FF II, the latter chirping happily at his gentle strokes, gratitude filled her.

"Is it good for fur as well?" she quipped.

Mr. Chen's mouth gave a betraying twitch. "Ferdinand's coat will have extra shine, no doubt."

"Thank you, sir." Glory smiled at him. "You are ever so kind."

The master stared at her as if she were a creature he'd never seen before.

The clearing of a throat made them both start, and he took a hasty step back.

"My niece informs me that you teach martial arts, sir," Aunt Hypatia said.

Mr. Chen turned to her. "I have a few students, ma'am."

"Chen is being modest," Hadleigh said. "Word of his prowess has spread, and now pupils from all corners of society are knocking on his door. His school is poised to become the biggest craze since Apollo Fines's boxing saloon."

Aunt Patty looked impressed. "In your culture, Mr. Chen, do women also train in martial arts?"

Wariness flickered in the master's gaze.

"Women do learn *kung fu*, yes. I, however, have not taken on female pupils," he said. "Given the rules of English society, I do not think it prudent."

"We English do have a Draconian view of female propriety," Aunt Patty muttered.

Sensing that the pendulum was swinging in the wrong direction, Glory cut in.

"I saw some of your students training earlier. Could we take a closer look?" she cajoled. "My aunt and I would find a display of *kung fu* most elucidating."

Seeing that she had witnessed him in action on multiple occasions and participated in a mission with him last night, her naïf act was doing it a bit brown. But she needed an opportunity to talk to him.

"For a well-educated young lady such as yourself," he said, "I doubt a demonstration will offer much in the way of novelty."

Luckily, Glory's chaperone did not seem to register his irony.

"We shall be the judge of that," Aunt Patty said crisply. "I believe that a lady's thirst for knowledge ought to be encouraged and would be obliged if you would show us some *kung fu*."

Did Glory detect a slight sigh from Mr. Chen?

"Right this way," he said.

He led the group outside to the courtyard where his pupils were training. They all paused to bow respectfully; Mr. Chen instructed them to carry on. The students resumed their drills, standing in a wide stance, their feet pointed forward and knees deeply bent, their thighs parallel to the ground. They held the position motionlessly, as if they were sitting but without the support of a chair.

Glory canted her head. "What is the purpose of this exercise?"

"It is called horse stance," Mr. Chen replied. "The position builds core stability and strength and is the foundation for other skills."

"Horse stance is harder than it looks," Hadleigh said. "I still cannot hold the position beyond a few minutes."

Intrigued, Glory studied the stance so that she could practice it at home.

"How long can you maintain horse stance, Master Chen?" she asked.

"As long as is required."

His reply was matter-of-fact, with no hint of boasting, and Glory believed him. She found his blend of humility and quiet confidence so very appealing.

As Aunt Hypatia and Hadleigh discussed the intricacies of horse stance and some of the other exercises, Glory took the opportunity to draw Mr. Chen aside. They remained in view of her chaperone but were out of earshot. Just in case, she spoke in Chinese.

"I must apologize for showing up with my aunt," she said.

"You should be chaperoned," he replied in the same language. "A young woman ought not to run about on her own."

His rebuke made her stiffen. As did his stern expression. In his native tongue, he sounded even more authoritarian—like a *shifu* who expected obedience.

"What is your problem?" She kicked at a pebble, her green skirts swishing. "You seemed more reasonable last night."

"About that." His jaw tautened. "The mission last eve was far too perilous. If we had been caught, the consequences to your well-being and reputation would be too dire to contemplate."

"But we didn't get caught, did we?" Because Chinese wasn't her first language, she had to work harder to summon the words, which made her impatient. "There was no harm done. In fact, there was a lot of good accomplished, for we now know who is behind the theft of Sir Barkley. And not only him...it sounds like Farwell is operating a much larger dog-stealing ring. We will start investigating the Fancy forthwith—"

"Out of the question."

"I beg your pardon?" she asked incredulously.

"Getting embroiled with the Fancy is a hazardous proposition for anyone, let alone a lady of your station."

Annoyed that she couldn't argue as well in Chinese, she switched back to English. "I am not some milk-fed miss—"

"I am aware of that." While he reverted to English as well, his dictatorial manner did not change. "Nonetheless, you are a duke's daughter, and the Fancy is a ruthless, bloodthirsty gang. I am certain that when Lady Fayne returns, she will agree with my assessment that this case is not suitable for the Angels."

Glory felt her temper rising. "And I am certain that Charlie will agree with *my* plan to proceed with assisting our client."

"There are other ways of retrieving the dog. You could hire an investigator—"

"I *am* an investigator."

The retort burst from her, and she glanced around hastily to make sure that no one had heard. Luckily, the duke was keeping Aunt Patty engrossed in conversation.

"You have seen the Angels at work," Glory said in a furious whisper. "You know how capable we are."

"It is not your ability that I question, but your impulse to court danger," he said with irritating calm. "The Fancy is unlike other foes you have faced in the past. They are a well-connected organization, with police and politicians in their pocket. They rule with fear, and anyone who crosses them suffers the consequences. I currently treat a shopkeeper who was nearly burned to death because he refused to pay them protection money."

Her heart squeezed with compassion and outrage. "How *dastardly* of the Fancy."

"They have done worse." Mr. Chen's gaze was relentless. "Trawling the Thames would harvest ample evidence of the gang's brutality. Which is why you must delegate this case to those who can handle it."

Of all the arrogant and idiotic presumptions.

"Mrs. Mumford-Mills came to the Angels for help," Glory said through her teeth. "And we have made progress toward finding Sir Barkley. Now that we know who stole him—and, likely, other dogs—we are responsible for returning him and the other pets to their owners. Case closed."

"Be reasonable," he insisted. "Think of the consequences. If not for yourself, then for your family."

Guilt pierced her armor of resolve. He'd found her Achilles' heel: she loved her family dearly, and the possibility of hurting them was her greatest fear when it came to her investigative work. If word of her covert activities got out, the scandal would undoubtedly ruin Papa's political career and undo all his efforts toward stopping the opium trade. Her disgrace would affect the reputations of her mama and younger brothers, Horatio and Theodore, as well.

While Glory's family had never blamed her for being different, in her darker moments she secretly wished that she could be popular for their sake. If only she could be more like Lady Aileen, the Earl of Darlingford's daughter, whose charm, refinement, and beauty were said to have helped her father secure a seat in Russell's cabinet. Glory, however, only knew how to be herself: outspoken, curious, and plain.

When she'd tried to support her father by speaking up at balls about the evils of opium smuggling, she'd done more harm than good. People had either made a rapid exit...or they'd started to snore. A dowager had famously described Glory's conversation as "soporific."

It shamed Glory to admit that when it came to social matters, she was a liability to her family.

The least I can do is make sure I don't get exposed for being an Angel. For my family's sake, I must never get caught.

Glory took a breath. "If you want to protect me from harm, then help me help myself."

"I beg your pardon?"

"That is why I am here, Master Chen," she said. "To ask you to become my *shifu*."

He drew his brows together, then shook his head.

"That is not possible," he said curtly. "I do not take on female pupils."

"I could be your first," she wheedled. "You said so yourself that females learn martial arts in China."

"This is London, not China. And you are not just any female; you are a duke's daughter." He frowned at her. "You must know that what you're proposing is beyond the pale. I cannot train you. In fact, your very presence at my clinic stretches the bounds of propriety—"

"As her chaperone, I disagree." Aunt Patty came toward them, Hadleigh behind her. "There is nothing improper about my niece's desire to acquire new skills. As a former governess, I speak with authority when I say that Glory is one of the brightest pupils I've had the pleasure of teaching. From languages to sports, there has yet to be a subject she has not mastered. Why should she not have the opportunity to learn martial arts as well? A healthful practice, evidently, that will also provide her the tools for taking care of herself should, heaven forbid, the situation arise."

Glory had never loved her aunt more.

"The attainment of knowledge must not come at the cost of Lady Glory's reputation," Mr. Chen said tersely. "Society will not tolerate the presence of a popular debutante at an East End clinic for opium users."

"I can hardly be described as popular," Glory countered. "I am neither pretty nor socially accomplished. I am prone to social blunders...and my dance card is never full. Most of the time, my partners are fortune hunters or the husbands of my friends." She jerked a thumb at the duke. "Hadleigh, for instance, only stands up with me because Livy makes him."

The duke cleared his throat. "It has been my honor to dance with you, Lady Glory."

Glory snorted. "My point is that my reputation is not going to suffer unduly if I come here chaperoned by my Aunt Hypatia."

Aunt Patty nodded. "I would be delighted."

Mr. Chen remained silent. Thinking...but Glory had no idea what.

"If you will not have a care for your reputation," he said at length, "then have a care for mine."

Glory knitted her brows. "Why would *your* reputation be affected?"

"In my experience, the English do not harbor a particular fondness for foreigners. The escalating tension between China and Britain over opium smuggling does not help matters. While I am fortunate to have supporters such as His Grace, many of your countrymen would like to see my clinic closed and need only the slightest excuse to act upon their desire. Some have even conjured up falsehoods to shut me down, accusing my establishment of being its very opposite: an opium den."

Indignation flared beneath her breastbone. "How dashed unfair—"

"If it were to be known that I entertained a well-bred young lady here, rumors would fly. And the truth would not matter to the mob," Mr. Chen said flatly. "They would tear down every brick of this place."

She stared at him. "That cannot be true."

"I'm afraid Chen is right about some of the local folk," Hadleigh said with disgust. "Despite all the good that he's done, they still view him with suspicion. Moreover, he has made enemies: by protecting the neighborhood, he's made life harder for criminals who would jump at the chance to get rid of him."

Stricken, Glory said, "I...I didn't know. I would never wish to put you at risk, sir."

"Now that you do know," the master said, "I hope you understand why I cannot grant your request."

"Yes. Of course." Ashamed of her selfishness, she blurted, "I fear my presence may be compromising your establishment at this very moment. Aunt Hypatia, we must go."

Looking concerned, Aunt Patty said, "It is probably for the best, my dear."

"Allow me to see you to your carriage." Hadleigh gallantly offered Aunt Patty his arm.

Glory followed with Mr. Chen.

Biting her lip, she peered up at him. "I *am* sorry if I inconvenienced you in any way."

"There is no harm done, my lady," he said quietly. "I am relieved, however, that you have been swayed by reason and have given up your initial plans."

"Do not worry about a thing." Seeing that Aunt Patty was engaged in conversation with the duke, she lowered her voice. "I shan't involve you any further in my mission."

Mr. Chen's brows snapped together. "You cannot mean to continue your quest. Not after what I told you about the Fancy. You cannot handle the situation on your own—"

"I won't be on my own," she assured him. "Charlie is returning tomorrow, and we will come up with a new plan."

"You must listen to me, Glory."

Her breath lodged as he closed a hand around her upper arm, pulling her toward him. His touch sent ripples of heat over her skin. Her stomach did that funny flip again, her knees as wobbly as an aspic. She couldn't look away from the blazing intensity of his gaze.

"Steer clear of the Fancy, do you understand?"

It wasn't really a question. Even in her flustered state, her initial reaction was to resist his edict; she'd never taken orders well. Yet his command pumped her heart, warmth rushing beneath her skin, the tips of her breasts prickling against her corset. Uncertain how to answer, she wetted her lips and saw his gaze track the path of her tongue.

"Are you all right, Glory?"

Aunt Hypatia had turned around, regarding her with a frown.

Mr. Chen released her instantly and took a step back.

"I just, um, tripped, and Master Chen caught me," Glory extemporized.

"Thank you for looking after my niece, sir," Aunt Patty said. "And for the edifying visit."

"It was my honor, ma'am." Mr. Chen bowed, his reserve back in place. "And Lady Glory, I hope you also learned something of value today."

Glory heard his unspoken message. *Heed me and stop your investigation.*

Now that she'd regained her equilibrium, her reply came naturally.

"According to Confucius, the essence of having knowledge is to apply it." She performed a smart curtsy. "Good day, Master Chen. Your Grace."

She followed Aunt Patty to their waiting carriage; at the last moment, she couldn't resist glancing back. Master Chen was watching her, a banked fire in his eyes. With a shiver, she wondered what lay behind his wall of control.

SEVEN

As he stumbled through the smoky corridor of the flower boat, one of Canton's infamous floating brothels, Wei's gut churned. Not because of the boat's bobbing—working as a pirate had earned him his sea legs—but because of self-disgust. Because he couldn't escape the dirty and immoral part of his nature. Memories clawed at him; at least the potent rice wine he'd downed dulled the pain.

The shame and self-loathing, however, remained.

Drinking, fighting, fucking, his inner voice sneered. *That is all you're good for, you worthless scoundrel. Two years since your family was murdered, and what do you have to show for it?*

Nothing but failure.

Feeling the familiar surge of frustration and rage, he shut out his thoughts. The corridor was lined with curtained doorways, and he chose one at random. So long as the room offered oblivion, he didn't care what was inside. He staggered through the red silk panels into the dim chamber.

A naked prostitute sat playing a lute. Her gaze beckoned him as her rouged lips moved in a mournful song. A barbed wire tightened around Wei's heart, for in the muted glow of the silk lanterns, the whore could be Chun's twin. She appeared young and fresh, her scant tits topped by coy buds and her skin smooth as porcelain. Catching Wei's gaze, she widened her narrow thighs, displaying her dark thatch. The feigned desire in her doe-like eyes made his insides roil.

I am sorry about your family, Wei, but I cannot run away with you. Chun's reproachful voice played in his head. *How would we live...how could you support me? You ask too much.*

Wei clenched his hands, trying to shut out the past.

The madam glided into the room, her smile as painted on as her eyebrows.

"More *baijiu*, sir?" she offered.

Grabbing a cup from her tray, he tossed back a shot of the strong alcohol, followed by another. He swiped his sleeve over his mouth and caught the disdain in the bawd's gaze. He felt grim satisfaction in knowing that his vulgarity offended her. He was no longer recognizable as Captain Chen's clean-cut son. Two years of making his living as a ruffian had hardened him. If the job paid well and in silver, he'd taken it. He needed money to fund his vengeance...although he had little to show for his efforts.

"Perhaps, sir, you would care to partake of my flower boat's other diversions?"

The madam's question came at the right time, stalling his emotional spiral.

"What do you have to offer? I want something"—he flicked a glance at the lute-playing whore, whose pout was so like Chun's that he felt a surge of nausea—"less contrived."

"Of course. Please follow me."

The madam led the way back into the passageway, taking him to an entrance at the far end. This one was barricaded by a door.

"Welcome to the Chamber of a Thousand Delights, sir. A place we reserve for our most exclusive and *generous* clientele. Here, you are guaranteed to find whatever your heart desires."

My heart has nothing to do with this.

He withdrew a coin bag, dropping it into the bawd's waiting palm. "This should cover it."

She grasped the sack, her pointed fingernails reminding him of claws. She unlocked the door and pushed it open, guttural sounds spilling out.

"Indulge in whatever you fancy, sir." She smirked. "Everything, and I do mean *everything*, is included in the fee."

Smoke from incense and opium swirled through the air, offerings to appease the gods and the devils. Through the haze, Wei saw that eight canopied beds lined the perimeter of the room, the wooden frames shaking due to the vigorous activities taking place upon them. A dozen men and women were fucking at the center of the chamber, their bodies a writhing train of flesh on the silk carpet.

An unsteady feeling crept over Wei.

You're an animal. You belong here. Slake your lust.

He stumbled forward. A man sat on the nearest mattress, his hands clenching the heads of the two whores performing fellatio upon him. The women's mouths sandwiched the man's prick, gliding in unison along his glistening shaft before they took turns licking his stones. One of the whores caught Wei's gaze; as she sealed her lips around the other man's crown, she crooked a finger at him.

Wei shook his head and walked on.

The bawd hadn't lied; every kind of depravity was on offer. Even Wei, who thought he'd seen every carnal variation, lifted his eyebrows at some of the acrobatic positions. Yet nothing stirred his lust to a sufficient degree. Nothing promised the forgetfulness he sought.

Then he saw her.

Lithe and slender, she had her back to him, the red glow of the lanterns making her hair gleam like rosewood. Her long, luxuriant tresses reached her buttocks, swaying as she moved and giving him glimpses of a sleek and delectable ass. He found himself following her, pushing past others to keep her in his line of vision.

She pivoted slightly; a white veil hid her face, exposing only her eyes. From this distance, he couldn't discern their color, but they were wide and fringed with thick lashes. As she gazed at him, her head tilted inquisitively. Heat flooded his groin, his cock instantly hard.

This was what he'd come for: mind-robbing lust.

She gave him another look over her shoulder before moving on. Giving chase...a game he enjoyed. He stalked her through the chamber, and he could almost hear her giggle as she hastened her pace like a playful little tigress. She exited through a curtain, and he followed her.

The new chamber was scarcely larger than a wardrobe. Wei's quarry stood against the wall, studying him with huge eyes, her veil adding to her captivating aura of mystery. Her breasts were small and delicately rounded, topped with berry-like nipples that he knew would be sweet. Between her sleek thighs, her shy little pussy beckoned.

He closed the short distance between them and reached for her. She melted into his arms, gasping when he spun her around.

"Put your hands on the wall," he said. "Keep them there."

At her ready obedience, his prick strained against his trousers.

He swept her hair over one shoulder, baring her neck. He kissed her down-soft nape, inhaling her alluring fragrance...not perfume, but a subtle, natural scent that reminded him of his mother's prized orchids. Hungrily, he hunted for more of the elusive aroma as he fondled her tits.

The slender curves nestled perfectly against his callused palms. He tweaked her nipples, and she moaned, arching against him, caressing his erection with her taut ass. Over and again, she rubbed against him, teasing him with sinuous movements that seemed charmingly unpracticed. With desire that seemed real.

"Naughty little tigress," he growled. "Let's see if you're ready to play. Put your hands on your bottom and spread those pretty cheeks for me."

With a bashful whimper, she did as she was told. Her long, slender fingers cupped the firm mounds of her bottom and held them apart. He got down on one knee to inspect her offering. In the dim light, her slit had the dewy sheen of petals after a rain, and his cock throbbed as he imagined burying himself in that lush hole.

"Your cunny looks wet. Did you oil yourself?" he asked sternly.

"N-no, sir."

Her reply sounded breathy and puzzled, as if she were an innocent who didn't know the tricks of the trade. What a delightful actress she was.

Yet the scent of her feminine arousal did not lie. Lust darkened his vision, and he rose, tearing off his trousers, his gaze fixed on the target she kept exposed for him. Fisting his erection, he rubbed the engorged head along her rosy gash, grunting at her wetness. Her dew coated his cockhead, dribbling down his shaft and over his knuckles.

She was more than ready; she was hungry for it. Needing to be fucked.

By the gods, he was going to oblige her.

"Hands back on the wall," he said hoarsely.

She rested the side of her face against the wall, placing her palms on either side. Gripping her hip, he brought his cock to her pussy. He thrust inside, panting at the exquisite constriction. She was tighter than he expected; he could feel her stretching to take him. Luckily, she was also dripping wet, and he pushed in deeper.

"Damn, you feel good," he gritted out.

Her needy moan spurred him on. Bracing her slim hips with both hands, he held her steady for his pounding. With greedy eyes, he watched the thick meat of his shaft tunneling inside her. Her passage milked him like a fist. His vision darkening, he let himself go, rutting her like the animal he was. His stones smacked her pussy, the wet, squelching sounds adding to his frenzy. He slapped her bouncing ass and groaned when he felt her start to spend.

The rippling of her sheath brought him to the edge as well, and he had the sudden urge to see who he was fucking. He jerked out, spinning her around and slamming her onto his prick once more. Then he ripped off her veil.

His eyes widened at the sight of her freckled nose and dimpled smile. She wetted her pretty lips, taking him over the edge. His balls swelled, heat blasting up his shaft...

Wei jerked awake. His heart was galloping, and it took him a moment to register that he was in his own bed. He was perspiring, the sheets clammy against his skin. Sitting up, he pushed aside the blankets and discovered with shock that sweat wasn't the only wetness on his person. His erection was a throbbing bar against his stomach, the tip glossy with seed.

I nearly came in my sleep like a bloody green lad.

Need buzzed in his veins. Stunned, he dragged both hands through his hair, trying to think through the haze of desire. Through the hunger clawing at his insides. Inhaling, he assumed the cross-legged position he used for contemplation...and grimaced when he had to adjust his rigid cock.

He took several deeper breaths, willing his body and mind to calm. Yet all he could think about was Glory—some confounding mix of fantasy and reality that made him even harder. He let out a huff of impatience. The harder he tried to block her out, the stronger she pulled at him.

What did the dream mean? Why was he having debased thoughts about her? A lady who was too innocent, too young, and too far above him. Who would be a reprise of the worst mistake he'd made in his life. For years now, he'd kept his urges at bay; why were they emerging now, filthier and stronger than ever?

He gritted his teeth. *What the bloody hell is wrong with me?*

"The stronger the will, the weaker the result." Shifu Lam's voice

surfaced like a leaf floating on dark water. *"In meditation and in life, Wei, the doing is in the not doing."*

Wei focused on his breathing. On letting go—which had never come easily to him.

He remembered the day he had left his *shifu*'s compound in the mountains. The old master's eyes, milky with cataracts, had nonetheless seen straight into the heart of Wei's fears.

"You will not find what you seek, Wei," Shifu Lam had said. *"You are not ready."*

"But I have trained diligently for the past seven years, Shifu. Practiced everything you have taught me. I have even studied with that Jesuit priest, learning the language of my enemy so that I may hunt him down in London." Frustration had raked Wei's insides. *"If I am not ready by now, when will I ever be?"*

"When you can relinquish that which drives you, then you will find your way. Do not do, Wei. That is the answer."

As much as Wei revered his *shifu*, the old man's obfuscated wisdom could drive him mad.

Just a sign that Master Lam is right. I am not ready. Not worthy.

Sighing, Wei got out of bed. His mind was too unruly, tugging him this way and that, jumping between past mistakes and future fears. He needed to stay anchored in the present. If he could not achieve that through meditation, then he would employ other means.

He dressed for *kung fu* practice. Then he paused, removing three items from his dresser. The piece of fabric, dagger, and sketch of the ink drawing were a reminder of his purpose: clues to the murderer he was hunting.

The stamp on the dagger indicated that it had been made in London. Taken with the knowledge that the British traders in Canton had sailed from England's largest city, Wei had decided to start his search here. Five years later, however, he'd made little progress, running into countless dead ends. For instance, after months of canvassing, he'd located the bladesmith, but the fellow had produced so many of the daggers that he had no idea who'd purchased the one Wei had shown him. Due to the shady occupations of his patrons, the bladesmith did not keep any receipts.

The scrap from the killer's jacket proved even less identifiable.

Thus, Wei's only hope was the inked design he'd seen on his enemy's arm. He'd made a sketch of the tangle of vines, leaves, and bell-shaped flowers that had branded itself upon his brain. Consulting with several experts, he'd discovered that the plant depicted was the *Atropa belladonna*...more commonly known as deadly nightshade. While it was fitting that the assassin would carry the mark of a poison, Wei's inquiries about the deadly nightshade tattoo did not yield further information.

He did discover that tattoos were considered barbarous in England, associated with seamen and criminals, and he could find no establishment that openly practiced the art. He'd resorted to frequenting the places where he was most likely to see inked skin. He'd visited dockside taverns, underground prizefights, and bathing houses, looking for the symbol of his family's killer. Thus far, his forays had yielded nothing but invitations to fight...and to engage in other activities. Apparently, patronizing places where men were in a state of undress and surveilling them for signs of a tattoo could lead to misunderstandings.

Wei continued his weekly incursions into the darkest parts of London, searching aimlessly for clues. Last week, he'd infiltrated a gaming hell in the Seven Dials and ended up fighting a band of ruffians who'd tried to rob him. Bruised knuckles were all he had to show for his trouble. He knew he was flailing—struggling to stay afloat in a swamp of failure. He left his bedchamber and went to his study, where he lit incense at his ancestral altar and faced the wooden plaques carved with his family's names. The silence felt as heavy as an accusation.

"I am sorry, *Baba*, *Mama*, Ling Ling." His eyes burned. "I have yet to fulfill my duty to you. All these years, and I have only served justice to one of the men responsible for your deaths. But I vow to work harder, be better, and not let anything distract me from my purpose."

Of course, Glory flashed in his mind's eye. Her words about "applying knowledge" tightened his gut. Clearly, she did not intend to heed his warning to stay away from the gang, and why would she? He had no hold over her. Yet he knew someone that Glory *would* answer to, someone he hoped would listen to reason when he paid her a visit this afternoon.

After that, he would let go of Glory Cavendish...dimples, freckles, and all.

Resolved, he exited to one of the courtyards. The sun had not yet risen, and the air was thick with fog. He filled his lungs with coldness, breathing out warmth. He stretched, readying his body for practice. Bending his knees, he adopted a horse stance, grounding himself in the power of the pose.

As minutes passed, his thigh muscles bulged and strained. The burn shot from his buttocks into his calves. His heart thumped pleasantly as sweat misted on his skin. Finally, he began to move. He started with a punch, then another, his accompanying steps gaining momentum. He spun in a crouching kick, plumes of gravel rising around him. Springing into the air, he used his fists and feet to take on an invisible enemy.

And for these few moments, his mind was clear.

EIGHT

"Do you have an appointment to see Lady Fayne?" From beneath bushy grey brows, the butler named Sutton peered at Wei with suspicion.

As a foreigner, Wei was used to such looks, yet something about the manservant rubbed him the wrong way. Perhaps it was the crusty old fellow's posture: he blocked the doorway as if he feared Wei might charge into the Mayfair residence and run off with the silver.

Wei kept his manner polite. "My name is Wei Chen. I sent a note earlier, and Lady Fayne replied that she would receive me at two o'clock."

"Wait here while I verify your request."

Sutton slammed the door. Left waiting on the doorstep, Wei bridled his impatience. Finally, the butler returned, skewering him with a bright-blue gaze.

"Lady Fayne will see you," Sutton announced as if the Queen had granted Wei an audience.

As the butler led the way, Wei noted that the servant walked with a slight limp, favoring his left foot. Gout, probably. Age weighed on his broad shoulders, giving them a slight hunch.

When Sutton reached to open the door, Wei observed the butler's hands were curiously smooth and at odds with the wrinkles on his face.

Sutton said in a surly voice, "Mr. Chen to see you, my lady."

"Very good, Sutton." The lady rose from behind an elegant rosewood desk carved with flora and fauna. "Mr. Chen, a pleasure to see you."

Lady Charlotte Fayne was an attractive widow in her thirties. Her plum-colored dress complemented her upswept blonde hair and grey eyes. During their past interactions, Wei had found her manner cool and cordial. She surveyed the world with a detachment that he admired. When one's work involved dealing with the darker side of human nature, it was necessary to keep one's sentiments in check.

He wondered if Lady Glory would ever learn to curb her emotions. Probably not, he concluded. Her passion for life was a flame that no amount of cynicism or despair could dim. Her naïveté came not from a lack of experience, but an inexhaustible well of idealism. As she was too reckless to protect herself, someone had to step in.

Wei bowed. "Thank you for seeing me on short notice, my lady."

"Your note said the matter was of some urgency." Lady Fayne gestured to one of the chairs facing her desk. "Please have a seat."

Wei folded himself into the chair, noting that tea was waiting for him on a small side table. The cup was fashioned in the Chinese style, with no handles and a lid. Lifting the lid, he took a polite sip, unsurprised to find that he was drinking his favorite blend.

Despite her gentility, Lady Fayne had a mind like a steel trap. Her powers of observation were first-rate, and she'd developed ways of collecting information that cast police work in the shade. Because of her gender, she was undoubtedly underestimated, a fact that she used to her advantage with her secret society. She was a strong, independent female, and Wei guessed that she would not welcome his interference.

Nonetheless, he had to try.

"It is about Lady Glory," he began.

"I heard that you escorted her to Fanny Bottom's whilst I was out of town." While amicable, Lady Fayne's smile did not reach her eyes. "That was kind of you, sir, but in the future, pray do not inconvenience yourself on behalf of my group. I've had a talk with my Angels, reminding them that our organization does not rely on the kindness of strangers."

"I am hardly a stranger," Wei said stiffly. "Having assisted before."

"Things have gotten a bit out of hand when it comes to accepting help from outsiders. I expect it began with the ladies' husbands wanting to be involved." Lady Fayne tapped a silver pen against the blotter in an annoyed ditty. "Not my preference, of course, but I believe in giving my Angels full autonomy and have left it up to them to manage the degree of spousal participation. I must, however, draw the line at the *friends* of husbands insinuating themselves into my society's affairs."

"I have no desire to insinuate myself. I wish merely to speak to you, as one teacher to another."

Lady Fayne tossed the pen onto a tray, folding her hands on the desk. "Go on."

"I gather Lady Glory told you what we discovered at Bottom's. About the Fancy's involvement in the dognapping scheme?"

The lady's response was a cool nod.

"Are you familiar with the Fancy, my lady?" he pressed. "They are a brutal and ruthless gang. You cannot allow Lady Glory to—"

"I am aware of the dangers, Mr. Chen. As the Angels' mentor, protecting their welfare is my job," Lady Fayne said pointedly. "But I must also empower them to be the best versions of themselves. And nothing damages a lady's independence like being underestimated and needlessly shielded from life's realities."

Wei drew his brows together. "It is one thing to be independent, another to be foolhardy. You cannot allow Lady Glory to put herself in danger—"

"I do not impose restrictions upon my Angels. I provide them with information, and they make their own decisions." Lady Fayne's gaze was flinty. "As a woman who does not like being governed by others, I treat my charges the way I expect to be treated. Now, if there is nothing else..."

"I can provide you with a list of people who have crossed the Fancy, never to be seen again," Wei said tightly.

"And I could have that list before you even dip your pen in an inkwell."

"I am not questioning your capability, madam, but your understanding of Lady Glory. She is too idealistic and brash, and her desire to help others blinds her to her own vulnerability—"

"I do not care to repeat myself. Glory is *my* charge, and I will see to it that she has the proper knowledge to make her own choices."

Wei's frustration mounted. "She cannot be trusted to put her own welfare before the needs of the case. To help Mrs. Mumford-Mills, Glory would venture alone into the Fancy's territory—"

"She will never go alone on any mission. Angels work together and look after one another," Lady Fayne stated. "That is the policy of my society."

"The Duchess of Hadleigh, Mrs. Cullen, and the Countess of Hawksmoor are out of commission, at least temporarily. The Angels' instructors, Hawker and Mrs. Peabody, have recently wed and left your service. Who is left to escort Lady Glory?"

Lady Fayne arched her brows. "Rather familiar with my affairs, aren't you?"

"My intent is not to interfere, my lady." Wei strove to keep his tone collegial. "Only to ensure the safety of your young pupil. I am speaking as one *shifu* to another and hope you understand my concern."

"Hmm. Your interest is purely professional, then?"

Subjected to the lady's keen perusal, he felt his neck prickle. Guiltily, he recalled his dream, which had been the furthest thing from professional. While he could not control the workings of his sleeping mind, however, he could control his waking actions.

"That is why I am here," he affirmed.

"Then your concern is without merit. I will see to it that Glory has the proper reinforcement on her missions. Although we are regrettably short of hand, I intend to bring in new recruits soon. Until then, I have hired an experienced agent to assist the Angels on their missions."

Wei frowned. "Who is this agent? How do you know that he or she can be trusted?"

"He came recommended by Fiona's husband, the Earl of Hawksmoor." Lady Fayne's clipped tone conveyed her displeasure at being questioned. "In point of fact, I'm meeting with him after this, and he ought to have arrived." She reached for the bell pull. "I'll have him brought in."

Moments later, someone rapped on the door. When Lady Fayne gave permission to enter, a gentleman strolled in.

"Hope you don't mind, Charlie." The fellow's cultured accents matched his urbane exterior. "Since I'm to be part of the inner circle, I told Sutton I would let myself...oh, pardon. Didn't see you there, old chap. Francis Devlin, at your service."

"Wei Chen." Wei's reply was curt.

Lady Fayne's new hire was the epitome of the man about town. Wearing clothes that had undoubtedly come from Bond Street, the Adonis had gleaming copper curls and blue eyes. The casually complicated cravat beneath his square chin had likely taken his valet hours to perfect. He had the look and manner of a rake, oozing a trail of confidence in his wake.

"In the past, Mr. Chen has been a friend to our society," Lady Fayne said by way of introduction. "He accompanied Glory on her most recent assignment. Given his knowledge of the

Fancy, he came to express his concerns about her continued involvement."

"I see." Devlin sauntered over, offering Wei his hand. "Thanks for your efforts on the Angels' behalf, old boy. But you needn't worry. I am here to take over the reins."

"I do not believe the Angels require anyone to 'take over'." Wei's gaze narrowed as he took the other's hand. "Do you prefer to be called Devlin...or Sutton?"

For a moment, Devlin looked nonplussed. "What gave me away?"

"Your hands."

"One of which you're, ahem, crushing."

Wei loosened his hold. Devlin yanked his hand away, rubbing it.

"That's quite a grip you've got there," he said with a grimace.

"Master Chen is a practitioner of Chinese fighting arts," Lady Fayne said.

"I've heard of that but never seen it for myself." Devlin straightened his lapels and smirked. "Involves kicking, does it not? Unsporting, if you ask me."

"I did not ask." Wei felt a muscle twitch in his jaw. "What did you say your background was to qualify you for this present position?"

"If I told you, I would have to kill you."

Devlin's light words did not sound entirely in jest.

Wei's gaze did not waver. "You are welcome to try."

"Enough, gentlemen." Irritation sharpened Lady Fayne's tone. "There will be no cockfighting in my study. Devlin, I will remind you that you are currently on a probationary trial. You will act upon my orders and my orders alone. Any missteps, any attempts to 'take over', and this trial will be over before it began."

Devlin looked at Lady Fayne, and admiration—the first genuine emotion Wei had seen from the cove—flickered in his gaze.

"Understood," he murmured.

"As for you." The lady transferred her steely regard to Wei. "Do not mistake my patience for compliance. I do not countenance others telling me what to do, especially when it pertains to my Angels. As one *shifu* to another," she said smartly, "I am sure you understand."

Leave it be. You cannot change the direction of the tides.

"Don't worry your head over it, old sport," Devlin drawled. "Lady Glory will be in excellent hands Friday night."

The thought of the bastard's hands anywhere near Glory ignited a fire in Wei's belly. Nearly as much as the idea of her going on another mission this Friday—one that would, undoubtedly, take her into the Fancy's territory. Lady Fayne's shuttered expression told him that trying to find out the details would be futile.

She leaves me with no choice. If she will not protect Glory, then I will...be it from a gang or a bloody rake.

"Then I will take my leave." Wei issued a curt bow. "Good afternoon to you both."

He left the study, a plan taking shape in his head.

NINE

"First time, dearie?" the buxom brunette serving maid asked. Seeing the kindness in the other's gaze, Glory gave a rueful nod. "Is it that obvious?"

"You do look a bit nervy. Probably on account o' the rumors you've 'eard about the Fancy's parties, eh?" The maid gave Glory a sisterly pat. "This'll be my sixth or seventh go-around, and I lived to tell the tale. Name's Pru, by the by."

"I'm Nellie," Glory said.

Through her contacts, Charlie had learned of the Fancy's monthly ball. Held at the gang's flash house in Whitechapel, the event was a show of the Fancy's power, with other gangs invited to join the festivities. Charlie had secured employment for Glory as a serving maid.

"I know you do not need to be told to be careful." Charlie had pursed her lips. *"Nonetheless, the Fancy's masquerades are notorious for violence and vice. Blood can flow as freely as ale, and from what I gather, their newest leader, Wulfric Scott, is as ruthless as they come. Your job is to observe only; at the first sign of trouble, you and Devlin will leave immediately."*

Glory currently sported a wig of straw-blonde curls and a thick layer of face paint. Her serving maid uniform consisted of a stained white blouse and black skirt layered with tattered petticoats, discreet padding giving her the appearance of curves.

At present, she was in the cavernous kitchens. The cook barked orders, the makeshift staff swarming like a disorganized hive. Thumping footsteps and boisterous voices from above signaled that the party had officially begun.

"There ain't nofing to worry about if you keep your wits about you." Loading a tray with pork pies, Pru dispensed wisdom in a manner that befitted her name. "The fellas can get rowdy once the drink starts flowing, so stay in the public rooms and stick close to the other serving maids. Avoid the top floor—those chambers are reserved for the ranking members o' the Fancy, and from what I've 'eard, anyfing goes up there. Unless you're looking to earn a bit o' extra on the side—"

"I ain't serving nofing but refreshments," Glory said quickly.

"Wouldn't judge you any which way." Pru shrugged. "Meself, I don't mind giving 'em a feel or two. It lets off some o' that manly steam and keeps the tips coming."

"Thanks, um, for the advice."

"My pleasure, dearie. We serving wenches 'ave to stick together—"

"What are you 'ens clucking about?" The cook marched up to them. "Ain't paying you to wag your tongues. Get the food up to the buffet table and be quick about it!"

Winking, Pru shoved the loaded tray at Glory. "Good luck, Nellie."

With a nod of thanks, Glory scurried up the creaking steps. The sprawling main floor had been split into several areas to accommodate eating, dancing, and gambling. Alcoves along the room's perimeter were shaded by dressing screens, providing some convenient "privacy." A stone fireplace pumped out a smoky haze that gathered in the vaulted ceiling.

Guests were entering in droves, wearing elaborate masks and

garish costumes. They greeted one another with a mix of excitement and suspicion; the sparkle of jewels was accompanied by the glint of ill-concealed weapons. As the attendees flocked to the bar for libations, Glory noted the adjacent staircase leading to the upper floor.

The private chambers Pru mentioned must be up there. Might Sir Barkley be hidden in one of them? How can I get up there without being noticed?

"Good evening, dove. What do you 'ave on offer tonight?"

Pivoting, Glory saw that a dark-haired fellow wearing a half-mask and maroon velvet jacket was smirking at her.

"Pork pies, sir," she said crisply.

His blue eyes glinted in the holes of his mask as he drew close. He had overdone the cologne, the pungent spice tickling her nose. As a matter of fact, he was doing everything a bit brown.

"I'm more in the mood for a buttered bun." Leering at her, he trailed a finger along her shoulder. "Where can I find one, I wonder?"

Glory's cheeks warmed. Although she wasn't completely certain what Mr. Devlin was referring to, his tone was enough to make the sexual innuendo clear. When Charlie had introduced him as Hawker's temporary replacement and Glory's partner for this eve, Glory had been surprised. The younger son of an earl, Mr. Devlin moved in the same circles as she did. Debutantes, however, were warned to avoid him due to his reputation as a rake.

Glory, herself, didn't mind rakes so much. Prior to marriage, her papa had been a rather infamous one, yet his devotion to Mama had turned him into what he called "a walking cliché" about reformed rakes. While Mr. Devlin's reputation did not concern Glory, the business between him and the Earl of Hawksmoor did.

Fi had told Glory that Mr. Devlin had once deliberately put Hawksmoor in harm's way. True, Mr. Devlin had made amends—and Hawksmoor had recommended his former spy colleague to

Charlie—but as a woman who placed great value in loyalty and friendship, Glory couldn't fathom how he could betray a member of his team in the first place.

She would have preferred having a partner she trusted implicitly. Someone whose integrity was unquestionable, who was wise and protective and kind. Someone like...

Don't think about him, she told herself firmly. *That is water under the bridge.*

She hadn't heard from Mr. Chen since her visit to his clinic. Not that it was surprising; he had made it clear that he would not teach her martial arts. What *did* astonish and annoy her was that he had gone over her head and talked to Charlie. Charlie had told her about his visit and inquired why he was taking such an interest.

Glory could provide no explanation. She was befuddled by Mr. Chen's behavior. On the one hand, he wanted her to stay away from him; on the other, he kept interfering in her business. It was enough to drive a lady mad.

Stop fixating upon it. Concentrate on the mission.

She returned her focus to the setting. Guests were getting into their cups, and prostitutes had arrived, parading their wares to whistles of approval. As couples twirled on the dance floor, they rubbed against each other, their movements growing more salacious by the minute. It wouldn't be long before the place descended into a depraved free-for-all.

Once that happens, I can slip upstairs. And maybe Mr. Devlin can prove of use after all.

Directing her gaze to the upper floor, Glory said in suggestive tones, "I 'ave me break coming."

Devlin's gaze glinted with instant understanding. At least he wasn't slow-witted.

"Upstairs, one hour," he said softly. "Don't be late, dove."

Kissing her hand with roguish flourish, he melted into the crowd.

Glory spent the next hour serving food and eavesdropping.

While she caught some griping over rival gangs and territorial disputes, nothing was said about a dognapping scheme. What she did learn was that the job of the serving maid was as difficult as a balancing act at Astley's Amphitheatre. Not only did she have to balance a heavy tray and distribute refreshments, but she also had to dodge groping hands whilst keeping a smile on her face.

As she was wiping down a table, a sudden hush came over the room. She looked up to see two men entering the party. From the information Charlie had provided, she could guess who they were. The taller, leaner one was the Fancy's leader, Wulfric Scott. Even though he looked to be in his twenties, his thick, brown mane had swaths of silver, and he exuded a leader-of-the-pack confidence. The blond and bearded fellow next to him was likely Jimmy Bryant, his second-in-command.

Scott circled his narrow blue gaze slowly around the room, his manner predatory and intimidating. Glory could see the nervousness of the guests, some of whom might be his rivals. A few men placed their hands on their weapons. His lips faintly curled, Scott stalked to the bar, where he picked up a foaming tankard, holding it high.

"Tonight, we celebrate friendship," he declared. "Enjoy yourselves, compliments of the Fancy!"

The cheers were accompanied by a few sighs of relief.

Pru sidled up to Glory. "The Wolf's a splendid beast, ain't 'e? 'Is manner's fine as any toff's, and females fight o'er who gets to kick up their 'eels for 'im. But 'e's also dangerous, that one. After the old leader was found shot through the 'eart, men vied for the top position, and the transition weren't a peaceful one. When the dust settled, the Wolf was the only one left standing, and some of 'is opponents vanished, never to be seen again."

Glory shivered. "'E sounds like a man not to cross."

"You've got that right, dearie," Pru agreed. "If you're wise, you'll stay out o' 'is path."

The place soon descended into an orgy.

Guests were staggering around, three sheets to the wind. The whores had abandoned most of their clothing, strutting through the crowd, showing their wares. Once prices were negotiated, they retreated behind the screens with their patrons, the primal sounds of coupling swelling with the music of the quartet. The dance floor became a mass of grinding, heaving bodies, partners traded as easily as kisses.

The air was sweltering, the lights had dimmed.

Time for me to make my move.

Glory made her way up the staircase as quickly as she could. Reaching the top, she found a hallway lined with doors. She was early for her rendezvous with Mr. Devlin, but she could do some preliminary sleuthing until he arrived.

By the sounds of the muffled groans, most of the rooms appeared to be occupied. Glory made her way along the corridor and turned the corner, not sure where to start her search. Her ears perked at a sudden sound. Pausing, she listened...yes, there it was again.

What sounded like a *bark.*

Is that Sir Barkley?

With thudding excitement, she followed the barking. But then it stopped. At that moment, a ghostly hand brushed her nape; she pivoted...and saw nothing but shadows.

Aarf. Aarf aarf.

She tracked the barking to the room at the end of the hall. She glanced this way and that before pressing her ear to the wood. No voices...but there was a scratching on the other side of the barrier, followed by faint whines. She tried the knob—locked. The whining turned into plaintive whimpers.

"There's a good boy," she murmured. "I'll have you free in a moment."

Plucking a set of hairpins from her wig, she made short work of the lock. She slipped inside and was instantly attacked by a ball of white fluff. The dog bounced on its short hind legs, black eyes bright with joy and tail sweeping like a feather duster.

The pup was adorable but not Sir Barkley. Fighting disappointment, she bent to give him a scratch behind the ears...and her eyes widened at the sight of the golden charm attached to his leather collar. It was shaped like the letter "B," with a tiny garnet-studded crown on top. She removed the charm from the collar and examined it.

"This looks like Sir Barkley's charm," she said with hushed elation. "The one he is wearing in his portrait—that Mrs. Mumford-Mills said she had specially made."

The dog tilted his head and thumped his tail against the carpet. With a worried pang, Glory wondered if he was a victim of dognapping as well. At least he looked happy and well cared for. His coat was brushed into a cloud, his nose moist and twitchy. Looking around the chamber, she spotted a dog-sized bed that was a charming miniature of the massive tester bed beside it.

She pocketed the charm and gave the pup a pat before starting her search for clues. She began at the desk; the surface was meticulous, writing implements ordered in silver trays. Finding the drawers locked, Glory again made use of her makeshift picks. She pulled a leather-bound appointment book from the top drawer. She turned to the first page and hesitated at the boldly inked warning.

Property of Wulfric R. Scott.

Straightening her shoulders, she flipped through the pages, stopping at an entry made a month ago. *"F, Jacob's Island"* was scheduled for nine o'clock on a Friday evening. Could "F" stand for "Farwell"? Had the meeting been about the dognapping scheme? She found an identical entry scheduled for the following Friday.

Replacing the appointment book, she rummaged through the other drawers. In the bottom one, she found a folded map of the East End. A dozen or so properties had been circled, their addresses noted in the margin...

Sudden awareness ghosted over her nape. She spun around, and her heart stuttered at the sight of the figure standing inside the room.

He'd entered as noiselessly as a shadow. His all-black attire accentuated his lean and powerful physique and gave him a dangerous air. He was masked, the brewing intensity of his gaze sending a quiver up her spine.

"Mr. Chen," she breathed. "What are you doing here?"

"Keeping an eye on you," Wei said sternly.

He advanced toward her, stopping when his knees were attacked by a bundle of snowy fur.

"Sit," he commanded.

The dog obeyed, beating its tail against the carpet.

Wei continued to his target.

"How...how did you find me?" Lady Glory asked.

"Without much difficulty," he said shortly.

As usual, her disguise was compromised by her eyes. He wondered if the shining idealism in those wide orbs could ever be dimmed. He'd been surveilling her all evening from the rooftop, watching her pull off a convincing performance as a serving maid.

From a distance, however, he hadn't noted how scandalously she was dressed. The scooped neck of her blouse revealed far too much of her smooth, flawless bosom while the high hem of her skirts flaunted her trim ankles. No wonder she'd been swarmed all evening; he'd wanted to tear those groping bastards limb from limb.

He tamped down his protectiveness. He wanted to get her out of here as quickly as possible. Knowing her, she wouldn't leave until the job was done...which meant the best strategy was to help her.

He exhaled through his nose. "Have you found what you were looking for?"

She beamed at him. The disarming flash of her dimples propelled him back into his dream. Of her smiling just this way as he pounded into her hot little quim from behind. Heat flooded his groin, his cock hardening.

Stop this madness. Concentrate.

"I have, actually."

Elation brought out the golden sparkle in her eyes as she told him about the dog charm she'd found and the entries in Scott's appointment book regarding "F," whom she suspected was Farwell. Then she showed him a map.

She tapped on the circled locations. "What do you make of these properties?"

Wei looked them over. "They all fall within the Fancy's territory."

"That was my first thought as well," she said eagerly. "Perhaps the dogs are kept at one of these addresses—"

The little white dog barked. It ran to the door, bouncing eagerly on its stubby back legs and running in a happy circle.

"Someone's coming," Glory whispered.

She folded the map, shoved it into her skirts. Not a moment too soon, for footsteps and voices stopped outside the door. With cool efficiency, Wei ran through his options. Escaping through the window was too risky; he'd used lightness *kung fu* to scale the building, but Glory did not know that technique. He couldn't risk her falling from this perilous height. He scanned the chamber for a place to hide, jerking in surprise when Glory flung her arms around his neck.

"Hurry," she said with quiet urgency. "Kiss me."

Keys jangled. Someone fumbled with the lock.

Looking down into Glory's wide gaze, Wei made his decision. He swung her up in his arms and carried her to the bed. Tumbling her onto the mattress, he crushed his mouth to hers.

TEN

Lying beneath Mr. Chen's muscular length, Glory thought dreamily, *So this is kissing.*

Her stratagem had been to create a plausible reason for their presence in the room. All they had to do was put on a convincing show as lovers. Of course, she had very little experience with this sort of thing—none, to be precise—but she'd hoped Mr. Chen would take the lead.

And did he *ever*. He was as expert at kissing as he was at everything else.

The rumors that he'd been a monk could not possibly be true...

Her thoughts turned hazy as Mr. Chen consumed her senses. He tasted of smoky tea and himself, a strangely addictive flavor. His lips were firm, warm, and exploring. She tried to pull him closer, but he cupped her face and controlled the kiss.

The rasp of his calluses against her cheeks sent a wave of heat over her skin. Held steady by him, she felt both overwhelmed and safe. There wasn't anything to do but to surrender to him, to the need bubbling inside her. She melted into the mattress, and he made a low sound, licking the seam of her mouth. Shivering, she opened for him, the demanding plunge of his tongue dissolving her bones.

His sensual mastery awakened her dormant desires. She was struck by a fusillade of sensations. The drugging pressure of his lips. The hard friction of his chest against her throbbing nipples. The sensual weight of his hips pinning her down.

Through her flimsy skirts, she felt a heavy iron bar prodding her thigh; with a jolt, she realized what it was. Goodness, Mr. Chen's manhood was substantial. Just then, he shifted over her, rocking his hips and driving his hard length against an exquisite peak.

She gasped as bliss sparked between her legs. Desperate for more, she tugged on his hair, pressing against him. His thrusts were firm, disciplined, and she could feel herself dampening her drawers. When he tongued the rim of her ear, she quivered. He sucked the lobe into his mouth, and the warm tug seemed to pull at her very core, releasing a damp gush.

"Good boy."

The deep, drawling voice punctured Glory's erotic reverie. Simultaneously, she felt Mr. Chen still above her, his breath a harsh pant against her ear. She twisted her head toward the door... and found herself staring into narrow blue eyes.

Wulfric Scott.

His collar hung open, cherry-colored lip stain smudged along his slashing cheekbones. In the crook of his arm was the dog, who was ecstatically licking him. Brunette twins flanked him, one in pink, the other green, their gaping bodices revealing identically plump breasts with rouged nipples.

Glory's world spun as Mr. Chen came to his feet, pulling her with him. He placed himself between her and the newcomers.

The twin in pink said with a giggle, "From the way the serving maid was carrying on, the cove must be a *very* good boy indeed."

"Who doesn't like a gent who knows what 'e's about, eh?" the other twin purred.

When she gave Mr. Chen a sly wink, Glory clenched her jaw.

"The 'good boy' I was referring to is my dog, Beauregard." Whilst clad in irony, Scott's tone had a core of menace. "Not the uninvited cove in my chamber."

"Apologies, sir." Mr. Chen was calm and in command. "Me and the miss 'ere were wanting a bit o' privacy and stumbled upon this empty room."

"The room was locked," Scott said coldly.

"Begging your pardon, sir." Gathering her wits, Glory resumed her role, coming forward with a contrite smile. "This is all me fault. I'm new 'ere, and downstairs, they said I could make a bit o' the ready, so long as it were on me break. The gent 'ere made me an offer I couldn't refuse, so I brought 'im upstairs. The door weren't locked when we came in...maybe one o' the maids didn't close it properly? I'm ever so sorry, sir." Nerves injected an authentic quaver into her voice. "Please don't dismiss me. I promise it won't 'appen again."

She held her breath as Scott perused her with predatory eyes.

"What's your name?" he asked curtly.

"Nellie, sir. Nellie Eccles."

He directed his gaze to Mr. Chen. "And you?"

"The name's Wong. I'm wif the Limehouse Lads."

As Scott lifted his brows, Glory felt a rush of admiration for Mr. Chen's bold and quick-witted move. The Limehouse Lads were one of London's notorious dockside gangs, tales of their violent misdeeds regularly splashed over the front pages of newspapers. Their name invoked fear...even in their rivals, it seemed.

Scott's eyes slitted; Mr. Chen returned the stare with a level one of his own. Neither man backed down. As the staring contest went on, shouting erupted outside the door.

"Smoke! Fire! Everyone run!"

Sure enough, grey wisps began seeping in from beneath the door. Glory sent up a prayer of thanks to Mr. Devlin. He must have set off smoking devices to extricate her from the situation.

The twins began to shriek, Beauregard barking in unison.

Scott swore under his breath. "Bloody night. All right, everybody out."

They all exited the room. In the hallway, the billowing smoke created mayhem. People rushed for the stairs in a panicked wave, their momentum carrying Glory along.

An arm circled her waist from behind, anchoring her against a familiar hard form.

"I'm sorry." Mr. Chen's hoarse words heated her ear. "It won't happen again."

Before she could reply, he let her go, and the crowd swept her toward the stairs. Heart thumping, she twisted around, trying to look for him. But all she saw was smoke and shadows.

Eleven

"Glory, dear, we've a letter from your mama." Aunt Hypatia waved a letter during luncheon the next day. "I'll read it aloud, shall I?"

As Glory dissected a slice of ham, she tried to listen to her aunt, but she kept getting distracted by thoughts of Mr. Chen. The memories were like a lodestone, drawing her back to their kiss: the warm command of his lips, the thrilling weight of his chest pressing her into the bed. She'd awakened several times, panting and perspiring, tingling in unmentionable places. Even now, she was aware of a gnawing sensation in her belly. A hunger that had nothing to do with food.

This must be desire.

Glory finally understood what the fuss was about, and it made her feel giddy, nervous, and a teeny bit afraid. Like an explorer venturing into uncharted territory, she was excited yet tentative. She wasn't certain how to proceed.

Was Mr. Chen only playing his role when he kissed me? Did he feel anything? Did he apologize because he is a gentleman...or because he regretted kissing me?

"Glory, are you listening?"

She yanked her gaze up to her aunt's frowning countenance.

"Beg pardon," she said hastily. "You were saying something about, um, my family's trip?"

Aunt Patty resumed her summary. "Your mama writes that the tour to support your papa's campaign has gone smoothly. They've arrived at their last stop, Mr. Emmett Rothwell's estate in Hampstead, where they will be staying the week. She says that your brothers are enjoying themselves thoroughly. Horatio jots in the margin that 'the refreshments are tip-top, especially the pheasant pie,' and Theo has sketched a hunting hound he saw in the kennels."

When Aunt Patty displayed her brothers' handiwork, Glory smiled affectionately. As much as she was enjoying her freedom, she missed her family. She felt a prickle of guilt that she'd asked to stay behind...but they were probably better off without her. Her social gaffes would not contribute to her papa's cause.

"His Grace has given several well-received speeches," her aunt read on. "In fact, Mr. Rothwell has apparently pledged his full financial support."

"That is a coup for Papa," Glory said with pride.

With a fortune amassed through investments, Mr. Emmett Rothwell had turned to philanthropy in recent years. Reformers vied for his support as he had both deep pockets and social influence due to his recent marriage to a widowed countess. Rumor had it that Sarah Rothwell, formerly Lady Gowerville, had helped her husband build his humanitarian reputation to such an extent that he was being considered for a knighthood.

"With the Rothwells as allies, His Grace will have the backing he needs to fight the good fight in the House of Lords," Aunt Patty agreed.

Glory was struck by the similarities between Papa and Mr. Chen. On the surface, the two could not be less alike, yet they were both men of purpose and conviction. While Papa took on opium in the glittering arena of politics, Mr. Chen fought his battles in the shadowy streets of London. They were both tenacious, determined to stand up for what was right, and she admired them for it.

She contemplated what her parents would think of Mr. Chen...and then chided herself for putting the cart before the horse. She didn't even know if Mr. Chen was interested in her. His apology and vow to never kiss her again indicated otherwise. Her hopes deflated like a rapidly descending hot air balloon.

Was I bad at kissing? Does he find me unappealing?

"What *is* the matter, Glory?"

"Nothing," she mumbled. "I was just, um, woolgathering."

"At this rate, you'll have gathered enough to knit scarves for all of London." Aunt Patty's gaze gleamed keenly behind her spectacles. "It isn't like your mind to wander. Is there something going on?"

I had my first kiss, and it was wonderful. But the gentleman didn't seem to feel the same way, and I need to figure out what to do next. Meanwhile, I have a dognapping case to solve...

"I, um, didn't sleep well last night."

"Then be sure to have a lie-down, my dear. The Castlebury ball is this eve."

Botheration. She'd forgotten about the ball. With her bosom friends out of commission, she would have to blunder through the evening alone, a prospect she dreaded. She would much rather be investigating Scott's map. Under the pretense of a charity emergency, she'd secured Aunt Patty's permission to visit Charlie this morning. Her aunt had allowed her to go accompanied by Elsie, her lady's maid, whom she'd hired on Charlie's recommendation.

A discreet sort, Elsie had enjoyed a cup of tea in the kitchen whilst Glory met with her mentor. She'd filled Charlie in on her adventures last eve...most of them, anyway. She'd glossed over the intimate details of Mr. Chen's involvement.

Charlie, however, hadn't been fooled.

"What does the master want from you, Glory?" Her steel-grey gaze slitted, Charlie had drummed her fingers on her desk. *"First,*

he had the temerity to tell me how to run the Angels, now he has interfered with one of our missions. I am of a mind to pay him a visit—"

Glory had begged Charlie to let her take care of the matter, and luckily her mentor had relented. Yet Glory knew that the reprieve was temporary; if she didn't sort things out with Mr. Chen, Charlie would not hesitate to step in.

The rest of the visit had gone better. Glory had produced the charm taken from Beauregard's collar, and it was a precise match with the letter "B" Sir Barkley sported in his portrait. Charlie would verify their finding with Mrs. Mumford-Mills. In the meantime, Mr. Devlin would begin surveilling the locations on the map. On a positive note, Livy and Fi appeared to be on the mend and would be ready to check out the remaining properties this week.

Glory was looking forward to being with her friends again. She badly needed their advice when it came to Mr. Chen, even though the thought of disclosing her first kiss made her squirm with embarrassment. It wasn't easy for her to discuss matters of the heart. As a lady of action, she was more comfortable scaling cliffs and chasing after villains than disclosing her feelings. Yet these were desperate times, and her friends could be counted upon for excellent advice.

Greaves entered the room.

"I beg your pardon," the butler said in his sonorous voice. "A gentleman has arrived."

Aunt Patty frowned. "We are not expecting visitors."

"He says his name is Mr. Wei Chen. Shall I send him away?"

"*No.*" Glory bolted to her feet, rattling the china. "Master Chen is my...a friend."

"Direct him to the drawing room, Greaves." Aunt Patty rose as well, her brows arching over her spectacles. "I wonder what Mr. Chen wants?"

Excitement fluttered in Glory's chest.

With any luck...me.

As Wei followed the butler through the stately Mayfair mansion, he noted all the luxuries. The grand double staircase, gleaming marble floors, and gilt-framed portraits created an ambiance of old and established wealth. He passed spacious rooms with high ceilings and decadent furnishings, the fragrance of lemon polish and fresh flowers blocking out the odors of the streets. This was undoubtedly a house fit for a duke.

Wei had a sudden memory of being in Governor Li's compound. In the early days of his affair with Chun, he'd taken a job delivering furniture in hopes of seeing her. He recalled the awe and despair he'd felt seeing his lover's home for the first time. He'd realized then that he could never offer her such comforts. That love might not be able to bridge the gap in station between them. That what he was doing was wrong on so many levels.

If only he'd acted on those realizations. If only he'd ended the affair.

If only.

But he was no longer the gawky lad he'd once been. He was older, hopefully wiser now. After the events at the flash house, he'd gone home and engaged in contemplation. He had spent hours meditating upon Lady Glory Cavendish...specifically, how he ought to handle his disgraceful behavior toward her.

He had not lost control like that in *years*. It was as if all his training, all his hard work to become a *shifu*, had gone up in smoke, and he had regressed to the uncouth ruffian he'd once been. He thought he had mastered his wicked urges and put them behind him, but one taste of Glory's sweet innocence had proved him wrong.

The touch of her lips, the feel of her nubile form beneath him, had unraveled his self-control. He'd wanted to teach the bold miss not about martial arts but about pleasure. Wanted to master every inch of her lithe body while she moaned his name. To bury himself inside her untried passage, feel her blossom around his cock, and hear her scream his name when she came.

Desire had bombarded him while he'd meditated. His prick had swelled, becoming so stiff and hard that he could no longer sit comfortably cross-legged. Letting out a string of oaths—another bad habit he'd previously conquered—he had paced his chamber, willing his lust to subside. He'd battled the urge to take himself in hand and find some bloody relief. Instead, he'd stripped down to his trousers and stalked into the dark courtyard. He'd practiced *kung fu* for hours until he regained control over his body and mind.

His muscles quivering and dripping sweat, he'd come to a conclusion. He could no longer deny his attraction to Lady Glory, which wasn't just physical. He...he liked her. Her spirit, optimism, and intelligence. He even liked her curiosity, which often landed her in trouble but was so endearingly authentic. Endearingly *her*. Combine all that with her rare beauty, and she was the most potent of drugs.

His gut roiling, he'd thought of Chun. Of their toxic, addictive passion. Of how he'd sacrificed everything, even his family, to plow her eager cunt.

He would never do that again. Never again abandon his principles for desire.

He was in London for one reason alone: to hunt down his family's killer. He couldn't afford distractions. Couldn't let himself get entangled with a reckless maiden, knowing that no good—and likely all bad—would come of it. His honor had demanded that he come here today to offer her an apology and make amends however possible. Lady Glory deserved that courtesy before he extricated himself from her life.

Greaves led him into the drawing room, and his resolution suffered a blow. Not just because Lady Glory shone like a pearl in her native setting, but also because of her greeting. Unlike most ladies of her class, she did not remain reposed upon the settee with her skirts artfully arranged. She didn't flutter her eyelashes or wait for him to do the pretty.

Instead, this duke's daughter leapt up and rushed over to him, her ferret bounding behind her. She stopped just short of him, her lavender skirts swishing to a halt, her eyes shining with unaffected welcome. At her smile, which came complete with dimples, his heart hammered until his chest ached with pleasure.

Glory Cavendish was always lovely, but when she smiled, she was beyond compare.

"Master Chen, I am so happy you came," she said breathlessly.

He remembered to bow. It wasn't easy because he didn't want to look away from her glowing face. Even her freckles seemed to sparkle.

Mrs. Newton came forward. "We are surprised but pleased by your visit, sir."

As a fighter, Wei was trained to assess his surroundings, yet he hadn't registered the presence of the chaperone until this moment. That was how fully Glory absorbed his attention—how completely he fell under her spell.

This is why she is dangerous. A threat to your purpose. Do what you came to do, then go.

He inclined his head. "I beg your pardon for arriving unannounced—"

"I know why you've come, Mr. Chen," Mrs. Newton said.

Does she?

Wei shot a glance at Lady Glory. Her subtle shake of the head told him she hadn't disclosed their encounter.

"You do, madam?" he said politely.

"Indeed." Mrs. Newton's reply was crisp. "You have come to regret the rashness of your decision, haven't you?"

You have no idea.

But he caught himself in the lie. As appalled and ashamed as he was by his ungentlemanly conduct, he couldn't bring himself to regret it. His experience with Glory had been like stumbling upon a cozy cottage on a long winter's journey; the memory of her passion would warm him in the cold and lonely days ahead.

He cleared his throat. "Rash decision, ma'am?"

"Your refusal to teach my niece martial arts. That is why you are here," the lady concluded triumphantly. "You have come to your senses and realize that Glory would make the perfect pupil."

Wei furrowed his brow. As he tried to formulate a reply, Glory cut in.

"May I discuss the matter with Master Chen in the garden, Aunt Patty?" she asked. "It is too lovely a day to be cooped up inside. And I would like to show him Mama's peonies."

"Very well," her aunt said. "I will chaperone here from the window, so mind you don't wander out of sight."

"Master Chen and I will observe all proprieties," Lady Glory promised. "Won't we, sir?"

There is a first time for everything.

"Of course, my lady," he said.

When he offered his arm, the chit took it with a bright smile. The mere brush of her fingers against his forearm sent an alarming rush of heat to his groin. For once he was glad to be dressed in the English fashion, his arousal obscured by the folds of his frock coat.

There is no room in your life for selfish desire. You must focus on vengeance. You cannot fail again.

Resolved, Wei squared his shoulders and committed to doing what was right.

No matter how he longed to do the opposite.

Twelve

The garden was alive with spring, brimming with blooms and birdsong. Glory led Mr. Chen to the rectangular walk. Lined with manicured hedges, the path had several points of interest, including her mama's prized flowers, statuary, and a stone fountain. Glancing back, Glory glimpsed Aunt Patty standing at the drawing room windows.

If you want to know if Mr. Chen has any romantic inclination toward you, then you must act now. Don't be a wilting violet.

Glory slid a look at her guest. He was as austerely handsome as ever, the stark tailoring of his smoke-grey frock coat and dark trousers emphasizing the honed muscularity of his frame. Beneath his chin, his neckcloth was tied in an unfussy yet elegant knot. The thick waves of his hair gleamed like a raven's wing, his gaze clear and fathomless.

She tried to summon the courage to ask him what his purpose was, but the words got stuck in her throat. Blocked by the fear that the reason might be the opposite of what she wished.

"I am glad you came today," she said inanely.

"Needs must, my lady. We have unfinished business to discuss."

At Mr. Chen's blunt statement, her excitement fizzled. Even though she was a novice at courting, she wasn't an idiot. He did not resemble a lover about to declare his undying devotion. In fact, he looked more like a fellow being marched to the gallows.

"Why don't you call me Glory as my friends do?" She nervously laced her fingers as they strolled. "After everything we've been through, formality seems unnecessary."

"Decorum exists for a reason, my lady," he said severely. "And that is why I have come. To beg your forgiveness for my unpardonable behavior last evening."

Of course that is why he's here. To apologize. Because he regrets kissing me.

The realization should have come as no surprise, yet she felt her bottom lip wobble. Luckily, pride saved her from acting like an utter ninny.

"Think nothing of it, sir." She managed what she hoped was a professional smile. The kind she'd seen Charlie use when dealing with bureaucrats and men who talked too much. "Ruses are part of the job. As an experienced agent, I assure you that I have participated in my fair share of them."

"Have you?"

Mr. Chen's gaze was so dashed intense that she couldn't lie.

"Well, not that particular kind of ploy." Her cheeks heating, she blundered on. "But only because I haven't worked with a male partner before. Well, there was Hawker of course, but he was more of a driver, and he would never have taken liberties—not that you did, of course," she said in a rush. "I was an equal participant in the stratagem. In fact, it was *my* idea. If anyone is to blame, it's me—"

"You are faultless." Mr. Chen's tone was grim. "You are an innocent young lady, and I bear full responsibility for what happened."

"I am not *that* innocent," she protested.

"Aren't you?"

At the glint of amusement in his eyes, she felt her face grow hotter.

Was my inexperience that obvious? Was I that dreadful at kissing? Dash it, does he find me that unattractive?

Her insides sank like a soufflé past its prime. Not that she'd ever risen to any great heights when it came to attracting the opposite sex. But it had never mattered to her...until now.

"It's true that I was a bit of a novice when it comes to, um, what we did." She kept her gaze trained on her shoes as she forged onward. "I pray you will forgive my inexperience. Kissing is like any other skill, I suppose, and as you've surmised, I haven't had much practice at it. Or any practice...I don't count the time a fortune hunter tried to compromise me. But next time I shall —*what on earth?*"

Startled, she looked at the long fingers circling her upper arm. Then higher, into Master Chen's face. At the blazing intensity of his gaze, her heart pounded as if she'd gulped down an entire pot of strong tea.

"Who touched you?" he gritted out.

She blinked. "I b-beg your pardon?"

"Who was the bastard who laid hands on you? What is his name?"

As she registered what he was asking—and why he might be asking it—she felt a giddy flutter.

"It doesn't matter. It was ages ago," she said breathlessly. "Anyway, I handled the situation with a well-placed knee to his, um, unmentionable parts. He doubled over, then fell to the ground, and I *may* have accidentally kicked him on my way out of the orangery."

A muscle twitching in his jaw, Mr. Chen continued staring at her.

She babbled on. "I could have inflicted more damage, but I didn't want to risk exposing my skills as an Angel. Anyway, no harm was done, and he never came near me again. I suppose my dowry wasn't worth the bother. Or," she added impishly, "the pain."

"The bastard wasn't after your dowry. Not only that, anyway."

She furrowed her brow. "What else would he be after?"

Mr. Chen drew her closer, and her pulse raced at the fire in his eyes. His touch burned through her sleeve. His hold was firm, its purpose to anchor her attention rather than to detain her. She knew she could free herself at any time...but she didn't want to.

Unfortunately, he released her and took a step back.

"You are a lovely young lady," he stated.

She waved a hand. "Pishposh. I know I'm plain."

"The fact that you are oblivious to your own charms makes you all the more vulnerable to scoundrels," he said sternly.

Even though he was clearly lecturing her, thrills zinged down her spine.

"You think I have charms?" she blurted. "Even though I wasn't good at kissing?"

He frowned. "What makes you think you weren't good at kissing?"

"I don't know." She kicked a pebble the way she wanted to kick herself for bringing up the subject. "You're the first gentleman I've kissed. And since you have no desire to repeat the experience, I assumed..."

"There is nothing wrong with the way you kiss."

"Be still my beating heart," she muttered.

"What I meant to say was that you are a natural at it." He cleared his throat. "A perfectly fine kisser. In no need of practice at all."

Her heart careened like a runaway carriage. "Truly?"

"Truly."

She blew out a breath. "Well, that's a relief."

His mouth quirked, but his expression remained solemn as he held out an arm. He nodded subtly toward the window where her aunt was keeping watch. Hurriedly, she took his arm, and they continued their promenade.

"The point is that I acted disgracefully. I know you say it was a ruse"—he cut off her protest with a severe glance—"but it went too far. You are a virginal duke's daughter, and I am not from your world. Not fit for you. In any way."

She furrowed her brow. "I don't care about things like money and station—"

"Which proves how naïve you are. From experience, I know those differences are irreconcilable," he said ominously. "Moreover, I had no business kissing you that way when I have no intentions in that regard."

His last comment was a pinprick to her ballooning hopes.

He's just making excuses. The truth is he has no interest in an awkward hoyden like me. It was absurd of me to entertain the possibility.

As if reading her mind, he said, "My lack of interest in courtship has nothing to do with you."

"Right."

"It is the truth." He hesitated. "May I tell you something in the strictest confidence?"

She tilted her head, then held out her finger. "Shall we pinky swear on it?"

His eyes crinkled at the corners. "Your word of honor will do."

"You have it," she vowed.

"I came to London with a purpose."

"To help those suffering from opium dependence, you mean?"

"While my work is meaningful, I have another goal that is more personal in nature. There is no room in my life for anything else."

Despite her disappointment, she was also intrigued. "What is your goal?"

"To regain something," he said quietly. "Something that was taken from me years ago."

"What was taken from you?"

"Something dear and irreplaceable. That is all I will say on the matter."

Her instinct was to push, to find out more about Mr. Chen's quest. Yet she saw pain slice through his gaze, the welling of emotion so deep that her heart squeezed. While she might be a greenhorn when it came to romance, she was an expert at knowing when people needed her help. She'd never been one to stand by if she could lend a hand. That very propensity had driven her to become an investigator.

"Let me help you," she said.

He shook his head. "That is kind of you to offer, but you cannot."

"How do you know? As an Angel, I've had oodles of practice at finding things."

His smile did not reach his eyes. "This is a private matter."

"Only because you won't confide in me," she pointed out.

"I have confided in you more than I have anyone since arriving in London."

He sounded earnest and a bit puzzled, and she felt a tingle of pleasure.

"I am disclosing all this not to involve you in my affairs but to explain why an intimate relationship is impossible between us," he went on. "Why we would be better off as friends."

"Friends," she echoed.

"And as *shifu* and student, if that is your wish."

Not so long ago, she had wanted him to be her teacher more than anything. Now her desires had taken a decidedly different turn. Yet he had made it clear that he had no interest in her romantically...wasn't it better to have a relationship based on friendship and a mutual interest in martial arts than none at all?

"I do wish it," she said with a bittersweet pang.

I want you to be my shifu. *And so much more.*

"Then I shall instruct you. On one condition."

At that, she paused. In her experience, conditions were a euphemism for rules, and she wasn't overly fond of either.

She narrowed her gaze. "That being?"

"You will keep me apprised of any missions you plan on undertaking."

"So that you can stop me? Thank you, but—"

"So that I can assist you," he corrected.

"After all the times you've warned me away from the Fancy?"

"Things are different now."

"What has changed?" she asked bluntly.

"I have learned my lesson, namely that it is pointless to try to stop the tides." He shrugged. "You will do what you do, regardless of my opinion. The only way I am going to protect you is by teaching you the skills to protect yourself."

I always knew he was an intelligent fellow.

"As your *shifu*, I will be in a position to do just that," he went on. "It will be my responsibility to help you achieve your goals, safely and sensibly. I could, for instance, teach you how to use lightness *kung fu* to escape dangerous situations."

As Glory wasn't stupid, she knew a carrot when it was being dangled. Yet she couldn't resist the opportunity. To learn some of Mr. Chen's techniques...

Don't pretend it's only about the kung fu. *You want to spend time with him.*

She bit her lip. "But Charlie might not welcome your involvement—"

"You can discuss my offer with Lady Fayne before you make any decisions." He guided her around a corner, where the patch of peonies awaited ahead. "Or, if you prefer, I will speak to her."

"If you do, bloody murder is likely to happen, and I don't want that on my conscience." Glory inhaled and came to a decision. "I'll talk to Charlie. But I do have a question."

He lifted his brows.

"When I asked you to teach me before, you said that my presence at your clinic could lead to problems. Is that still the case?"

He halted in front of the flowers, and knowing that her aunt was observing, she made a show of describing the varietals as best she could.

"These are the, um, pink ones. And those are white and yellow," she said.

His lips twitched. "Thank you for the edification."

"Flowers are my mama's hobby, not mine. She is accounted an expert...in fact, people come from all over to see the roses she cultivates at our seat in Dorset," Glory said proudly. "Don't ask me about them, however. I cannot tell a flower from a weed."

"Duly noted."

Flustered by the teasing glint in his eyes, she said, "You, um, haven't answered my question."

"In short, I've changed my mind. I now realize that it is better for all parties concerned to keep you close rather than at arm's length."

"I don't understand. What about the reputation of your clinic? You said that I might compromise your work."

"First of all, it is your reputation that I am concerned about, not my own. I can handle whatever comes my way. Secondly, a young lady should not be traipsing around the East End. I will give you lessons here at your home and not at the clinic."

"Why didn't you offer that option before?" She gazed at him with dawning suspicion. "Was your prior argument a mere ploy to dissuade me from pestering you for lessons?"

His expression remained bland. "The supreme art of war is to subdue the opponent without fighting."

"Is that Lao Tzu?" She canted her head. "I don't recall coming across that quotation."

"The philosophy comes from another source." His mouth quivered, as if at some private jest.

Wrinkling her nose, she said, "You know, for a noble *shifu*, you have a sneaky streak."

"For an eager pupil, you have a cheeky one."

At the warm humor in his eyes, her heart somersaulted.

"Do we have an understanding then?" he asked.

I understand that we'll be spending time together. That despite my better judgment, my heart wants what it wants. That this could be the most brilliant—or devastating—adventure I've ever embarked upon.

"Yes," she said breathlessly.

"Splendid. Then let us secure your aunt's permission." As they circled back toward the house, he said, "What is your next move regarding the case?"

She slid him a glance. True to his word, he seemed encouraging rather than disapproving. The fact emboldened her to tell the truth.

"Charlie and I reviewed Scott's map," she said. "We plan to surveil the marked locations for signs of Sir Barkley and any other stolen dogs."

"When will you be going on a scouting expedition?"

"Not soon enough." Glory blew a curl out of her eye. "The soonest I'll be able to go is tomorrow since I have a ball tonight."

He cocked his head. "You do not sound happy about it."

"Balls are the bane of my existence," she confessed. "Especially when my friends won't be present. I will have no one to talk to, and the only ones who'll ask me to dance are fortune hunters and aging roués."

"Surely you underestimate your own charms," he said gravely.

"Surely I do not. I told you before that I am the opposite of popular."

"I find that difficult to believe."

"You wouldn't if you saw me at one of these affairs," she said candidly. "I am not like the other debutantes. I don't fit in and never will."

"To my mind, there is no finer trait than authenticity."

His gentleness and wisdom made her long for things she couldn't have.

Shrugging, she trudged on. "I don't wish to complain. Grin and bear it, as my papa would say."

"How pragmatic." Mr. Chen sounded amused. "At any rate, I hope you do not stay out too late."

"Why?"

"Because I plan to be here tomorrow morning for your first lesson."

"Oh." For a giddy heartbeat, she stared into his deep-brown eyes. "I would, um, like that."

More than I probably should.

Blushing and tongue-tied, she looked away.

Thirteen

"You know, the English have a saying. About needles and haystacks," Yao grumbled from across the booth.

Wei nodded but kept his attention trained on the surroundings. He was on his weekly excursion into London's seediest neighborhoods, looking for clues to his family's killer. Yao had wanted to come along, and they were staking out the White Hart, a dockside tavern in Blue Gate Fields. The place reeked of smoky grease, stale ale, and sewage from the Thames…which wasn't a bad thing as it masked the pungency of its unwashed clientele.

Wei had undertaken tonight's surveillance out of habit rather than hope. It was also a form of penance. For failing to let go of Glory Cavendish.

He told himself his solution was just as good, if not better than his original plan of exiting her life completely. The *shifu* and pupil relationship set strict boundaries between them, making romantic entanglements forbidden. His honor would not allow him to dally with her. Instead, he would focus on protecting her and teaching her skills to keep her safe. It was the best outcome for all involved.

"You're deceiving yourself, *shihing*," Yao said.

Wei stilled. "Pardon?"

Yao took a slurp from his foaming tankard. "You're not going to find what you're looking for tonight."

Right. He's talking about my family's murderer.

Wei loosened his grip on his own untouched drink. "If you're worried about wasting time, you could have stayed at the clinic."

Yao aimed his gaze at the sagging ceiling. "And let you court danger alone? What kind of a *shidai* do you take me for?"

"One who could use a napkin." Wei gestured to his upper lip.

Yao swiped a sleeve across his mouth to rid himself of the foam mustache.

"Anyway, you need me here. There's a reason I earned the moniker 'Sharpest Eyes in Shandong.' That's why *Shifu* sent me to look after you."

"And here I thought it was because he wanted you out of his hair," Wei said wryly.

A spiritual man, Shifu Lam embraced an ascetic lifestyle. He spoke only when necessary, valuing silence and peace...neither of which were likely to be found in Yao's presence. Since the arrival of his youngest disciple, he'd escaped to the forest behind his cottage to do his meditation, and he hadn't disclosed the location.

Yao grinned. "I'm our master's favorite pupil."

"If by favorite, you mean 'loudest,' then you're probably right."

While Yao finished his drink and started on Wei's, Wei surveyed the usual assortment of dockhands and sailors packed into the dingy establishment. Some looked deep into their cups and into other substances as well. He recognized the glaze of opium over the dilated stares of more than a few men slumped in the scarred wooden booths. At the center of the room, two burly coves were arm wrestling to the cheers of a betting crowd.

Their rolled-up shirtsleeves revealed hairy forearms...but no tattoos.

"I reckon you are as likely to find that tattoo tonight as you are to hire some companionship for the eve." Yao waggled his thick brows. "I plan to make a stop at a nunnery after this. I don't suppose you want to join me?"

Their *shifu* had recommended but not required celibacy of his pupils, and Yao took full advantage of this liberal policy. The "nunnery" he referenced was a well-known bawdy house in Covent Garden.

Wei shook his head.

"Be honest. Don't you miss the feeling of..." Making a circle with his thumb and forefinger, Yao poked a finger of his other hand through, his huge shoulders shaking with laughter.

Wei's *shidai* had the strength of five men and the sense of humor of a small child.

"There is this thing called self-discipline," Wei said mildly. "You might try it sometime."

"Having seen your version of self-discipline, I will decline. Any routine that involves practicing *kung fu* half-naked in the court-yard before dawn and taking ice-cold baths is not for me."

"To each his own."

"I suppose every fellow has his own way of dealing with his, uh, needs." Yao's expression grew crafty. "I've noticed, for instance, that your, er, self-discipline habits have grown in frequency ever since a certain miss paid us a visit."

Bloody hell.

Years of training allowed Wei to prevent heat from rising in his face.

"I don't know what you mean," he said.

"Ha, I knew it." Yao slapped the table. "That still-as-a-wind-less-pond expression might work with other people but not with me. It's a dead giveaway, *shihing*: you're hiding something."

"There is nothing to hide."

"You like the little lady."

Wei...did. As wrong as it was, he couldn't bring himself to deny it. Lady Glory had countless charms, the most endearing one being her obliviousness to her own appeal. *I am the opposite of popular,* she'd said. *Plain*, she'd called herself. The men of her acquaintance must be stupid indeed not to recognize what a rare jewel she was. Her curiosity, intelligence, and desire to help others made her even more special. As the English would put it, she was the genuine article, inside and out.

The knowledge that he'd been the first man to kiss her filled Wei with dark and unspeakable pride. A word had flashed in his head, one he knew to be dangerous and impossible. One that he'd never before applied to any woman. But, hell, he'd wanted to kiss Glory in that sun-drenched garden and give the little tigress another lesson in the ways of desire.

He cleared his throat. "The lady in question has many fine qualities. But that does not mean I have designs upon her."

"She is pretty, spirited, and rich." Yao counted on his fingers. "And, for some reason, she seems to like you. You could do worse, you know."

"She is the daughter of a duke. She belongs to a different world."

Wei's experience with Chun had taught him that love did not conquer all. On the contrary, love had rules like everything else. Breaking those rules—violating the laws of the universe—was an invitation for trouble.

"Don't be so old-fashioned. These are modern times." Modernity was one of Yao's favorite topics, one he could wax poetic about for hours. "Here in England, working-class folk are demanding reform. Women are too. People are questioning the so-called natural order of things. You don't have to settle for your lot in life; you can take on the establishment, make a change."

Instead of arguing, Wei said, "As it happens, I am taking on the lady in question. As my pupil."

Yao's jaw slackened. "You *idiot*. Why would you do such a bloody stupid thing?"

"Because it sets the proper boundaries," Wei replied.

"It erects a bleeding steel wall is what it does." Yao shook his head. "Now that she is your pupil, you cannot court her."

"Precisely. In the end, she will thank me for doing the right thing."

"Well, your cock certainly won't," Yao said with a snort. "A lifetime of *kung fu* at dawn and cold plunges is a lonely way to live, *shihing*."

Wei ignored the clenching in his gut.

Whatever it takes. I will sacrifice anything for my family's honor...and that includes letting go of my selfish desires.

"I have my purpose," he said. "Everything else is irrelevant."

"An unyielding army will not win," Yao said loftily.

At the familiar precept, Wei raised his brows. "You read the *Tao Te Ching*? All the way to chapter seventy-six?"

"Of course not. But Shifu Lam told me that if you ever start acting like a rigid oak...or was that oaf—"

"Get on with it," Wei said curtly.

"No need to shoot the messenger." Yao held up his hands. "Those are *Shifu*'s words, not mine. He said that if you ever got too, ahem, inflexible, I should say that bit about the army. Which I just did." He scratched his head. "Can't believe I remembered it, actually."

Frustration knotted Wei's insides. The cryptic message was typical of Master Lam.

The stronger the will, the weaker the result. The doing is in the not doing.

Wei curled his hands on the table. "How in blazes am I supposed to avenge my family without hunting down the murderer?"

"Don't ask me. I didn't understand half of *Shifu*'s teachings." Yao mimicked their master's unflappable tones. "*Do not do. To go up, first look down. The perfect square has no corners.* What does all of it mean, anyway?"

"That we haven't achieved the Way." The sense of failure

smothered Wei like a familiar old blanket. "That we've wasted our master's time and dishonored his teaching."

"Nonsense." Yao waved away the conclusion with an ease that Wei could only envy. "You take everything too seriously, which has always been your problem."

"This is who I am. I don't know how else to be."

"If you want to be something different, do something different."

Wei frowned. "I don't recall that maxim from *Shifu*'s teachings."

"That's because he didn't come up with it." Yao slapped his chest. "*I* did."

Wei's reply was cut off by a roar rising from the crowd. One of the arm wrestlers had defeated the other, and people were cheering or groaning, depending on how they'd placed their wagers. The winner strutted around the table, flexing his brawny biceps as he took his lap of victory to the chants of, "Ha-rold! Ha-rold! Ha-rold!"

"Who's next?" A slim ginger-haired man threw the challenge out to the crowd. He gestured to the pile of money on the table. "For a mere crown, you can wrestle Harold the Hammer for a chance to win this purse!"

"You should do it," Yao said in an undertone. "The winnings could pay for equipment at the clinic, and you could beat that fellow without blinking an eye."

Wei ignored his *shidai*. He had no interest in participating in tavern games.

Others didn't hesitate, however. A cove stepped up, big as a mountain, with a ragged scar running down the side of his neck and into the collar of his shirt. Beneath his bushy salt-and-pepper hair, he had a craggy face and deep-set eyes.

He slapped the required coin on the table.

"Name's Jacob," he said in a deep, rumbling voice. "I'll wrestle with you."

He and Harold the Hammer took their places at the table. As Harold made a show of stretching his arms, Jacob rolled up his sleeves...and Wei's heart pitched into his ribs. For an instant, he didn't trust himself, wondered if it was an illusion. Like a mirage a lost traveler in the desert conjures out of desperation.

"Blimey," Yao whispered. "Do you see what I see?"

The tattoo twisted like a vine up Jacob's forearm. It wasn't an exact replica of the one Wei had glimpsed on his enemy, but the pattern was undeniably similar. Similar enough to be inked by the same hand.

This Jacob could be a link to my foe.

Wei was on his feet, Yao at his back as he strode to the table. He shoved past several men who grumbled, but whatever they saw in his face made them back down. He got next to Jacob, his blood rushing as the similarity between this tattoo and the one he sought was even more pronounced up close. The creeping vines and leaves were nearly identical; in place of the deadly nightshade flowers, however, this man had crosses on his arm.

Wei reached to grab the other man and found himself held back.

"Patience, *shihing*," Yao said softly. "If you start a brawl, we'll have to take on the entire tavern. You don't want to risk losing the cove in the melee."

Wei realized that Yao was right. He nodded, forcing himself to breathe, to think.

"Take your positions, fellows," the ginger-haired man said.

Harold and Jacob planted their elbows on the table and clasped hands.

"On your marks. Ready, set...wrestle!"

The shouts of the audience were deafening as each man struggled to gain the upper hand. Yet for Wei, the sounds faded to nothing. His mind grew quiet, his focus sharp. He saw only the man named Jacob whose forearm bore the key to finding his family's killer. Jacob's face was ruddy with exertion, sweat trickling down the deep grooves of his forehead. His tattoo slithered and quivered like a live thing as he fought to bring down his opponent.

The men's hands moved a fraction in one direction, then in the opposite way. Their muscles straining, they glared at each other, jaws clenched. On the outside, they appeared equally matched, but Wei knew who would win. He saw it in Jacob's gaze: the glinting assurance of a cat playing with a mouse. It allowed him to plan his own trap.

Seconds later, Jacob slammed his opponent's hand down on the wood.

In the ensuing explosion of groans and cheers, Jacob took his lap around the table. When he returned, Wei was waiting for him. He eyed Wei up and down, and a slow sneer spread across his features.

"Want to play, Chinaman?" he taunted. "For you, it'll be a pound for a chance to win this 'ere pile o' blunt."

At the inflated price, murmurs shot through the crowd.

Wei withdrew a coin purse, letting the contents jingle. "There are five pounds in here. If I win, I don't want your money."

Jacob's gaze was focused on the purse. "What do you want, eh?"

"Answers."

"Is that some kind o' foreign trick?" Jacob asked suspiciously.

"No trick," Wei said calmly. "If you win, I give you five pounds. If I win, you answer my questions."

Jacob narrowed his eyes. "Easy as that, eh?"

"Take the Chinaman's money!" someone called out.

Amidst howls of laughter, Jacob dropped into his chair, holding up an arm.

"Ain't got all night, Chinaman," he said.

Wei took the opposite chair, posture relaxed, feet braced apart. Leaning slightly, he gripped his opponent's hand, which was larger and had fingers like sausages.

He met Jacob's gaze levelly. "Whenever you are ready."

The ginger-haired announcer took up his place again. "Ready, set...wrestle!"

Immediately, Jacob applied brute strength, trying to push Wei's hand toward the table. Wei resisted, grounding himself in his posture. Years of *kung fu* training had honed his muscles, and they worked together against his adversary's strength. The bands of his abdomen turned to steel, his thigh and leg muscles anchoring him like iron. His hand did not budge from its initial position.

Jacob's eyes widened, then he clenched his jaw and pushed harder. Wei withstood the onslaught, watching as sweat dripped down the other's face. Only when he felt the tell-tale quiver of Jacob's arm, the sign of tiring muscles, did he attack.

Bending his wrist slightly to improve his leverage, he pulled his opponent's arm toward him. Jacob struggled to resist, but he'd drained too much of his energy in the initial moments. Drawing power from his stance, Wei pressed downward. Gravity always loved a winner, and the farther he bent the other's arm, the less effort it took.

An instant later, he pinned Jacob's hand to the table.

"The winner is...the Chinaman." The announcer sounded as astounded as Jacob looked.

As the grumbling crowd dispersed, Wei released his foe's hand. He met Yao's gaze. His *shidai* nodded and posted himself close to the table, shooing away patrons to afford Wei privacy.

"Now to my question," Wei said.

Scowling, Jacob rubbed his hand. "Get on wif it then."

"I wish to know about your tattoo."

"Why the devil do you care about that?"

"I am doing the asking," Wei said evenly. "Who gave you that tattoo and where?"

His gaze shifting around the room, Jacob pulled his chair closer.

"Newgate," he said in a low voice. "When I was there five years ago, one o' my fellow prisoners gave it to me, all right?"

It made perfect sense that the bastard who'd killed Wei's family had spent time in prison. Unfortunately, if Jacob had been there only five years ago, he would not have met the killer…but he could tell Wei more about a person who had.

"Tell me about this tattooist," Wei said.

"Ain't much to tell. He was known as the Don o' Newgate on account o' his fine manners and 'ow 'is fingers were always stained with ink. Like a don's, you see." Jacob scratched his head. "'E'd been in the clink for decades when I arrived and was still there after I left."

If this Don fellow was in Newgate for decades, then he could have inked my enemy. He could be the clue I've been searching for. The missing link to my family's killer.

Despite his excitement, Wei managed to keep his tone neutral. "Did the Don give similar tattoos to any other inmates?"

"I can think o' a few blokes 'e inked, but no design like mine. Most coves only wanted a small symbol, and most couldn't stand the pain. Me, I liked the feeling, so I kept going back for more." Jacob pursed his lips. "Come to think o' it, the Don did mention that there was one other fellow like me. One who'd liked the prick o' the needle so much that he asked the Don to tattoo 'is entire forearm with flowers and vines."

Wei's chest thudded. "What was this fellow's name?"

"Damned if I know. The Don just mentioned it once in passing." Jacob rose, sweeping his winnings into a sack. "That's all I know."

Sensing that he'd extracted as much information as he was likely to get, Wei did not try to stop the other man from striding off. Yao took the vacated chair.

"Learn anything important, *shihing*?" he asked.

"As a matter of fact," Wei said with surging anticipation, "I think I've picked up the trail to my family's killer."

Fourteen

"Thank you for the dance, my lord," Glory said. "And for the escort back to my chaperone."

"The...the pleasure..." Beneath the blazing light of the ballroom chandeliers, Viscount Lyttle's face was florid, and he was gasping like a landed fish. "Was all...all mine."

"Are you unwell, my lord?" Aunt Hypatia turned from her intellectual debate with a fellow duenna to peer at him. "The polka was rather strenuous. Perhaps you ought to sit down?"

"I am fine," he wheezed.

Shrugging, Aunt Patty returned to her discussion.

Seizing the opportunity, the viscount edged closer to Glory.

"I'm fit...fit as a fiddle," he said with a wink. "A red-blooded male in the prime of life, don't you know."

Privately, Glory thought that the thrice-widowed viscount might be a bit past his prime. He was shaped like a teapot and possessed a waddling gait. A conspicuous raven shade, his hair was combed in thin strands over his balding pate. He was still huffing from their polka.

"Perhaps I could claim the honor of another dance later this eve, my lady." Viscount Lyttle discreetly mopped his forehead. "If you happen to be free, that is."

At his smirk, her cheeks warmed. Having signed the dance card attached to her wrist, he could not have missed its barren state. Eccentric hoydens weren't in fashion this or any Season, and as her friends were not in attendance this eve, she didn't have their husbands to fill in the blank spaces. She had no excuse to avoid another dance.

And even if she did, what else would she do? She'd tried chatting with other debutantes but had nothing to contribute when it came to fashion and gossip. When she'd tried to shift the conversation to politics, the ladies had made excuses one by one until she was left standing alone. As always.

"Your card, Lady Glory?"

She looked at Lord Lyttle, who was leering at her, ready to pencil in his claim. That was when she noticed the dark streaks starting to run from his sideburns. It took her a second to grasp the cause: he'd dyed his hair, and his perspiration was leaching the color. Rivulets of inky sweat wended their way toward his snow-white collar.

Zounds, he looks a frightful mess! And it is my fault for over-taxing him.

Twisting her fan in her gloved hands, she tried to think of a discreet way to warn him.

"Perhaps you would, um, care to refresh yourself, sir?" she suggested.

"I'm perfectly well."

Botheration. A black bead traversed his large jowl and reached his jaw.

"A visit to the necessary is never a bad idea," she said desperately.

"Delicacy, my dear gel." Lord Lyttle gave her a reproving look. "*Delicacy.*"

The droplet clung to his jaw, trembling as it resisted gravity's force.

Glory could stand it no longer. Opening her fan, she ducked behind it. "Your sweat has washed off your hair dye, my lord," she whispered. "It is about to stain your shirt."

Lord Lyttle's eyes bulged. He reddened several shades until he appeared apoplectic.

"Well, I never," he sputtered. "The impertinence, sirrah!"

He stomped off, inky droplets splattering his collar. Titillated eyes turned to Glory. Her face flamed as fans waved madly, tongues wagging behind them. She could imagine what they were saying:

"Did you see Lord Lyttle give Lady Glory the cut direct?"

"I wonder what the peculiar gel said this time…"

"Maybe he reprimanded her for leading their dance…"

Why am I such a social disaster? she wondered miserably. *Why do I only attract men like Lord Lyttle? And why does the only gentleman I* am *interested in have no interest in me…*

"Mind if we join you?" a melodic voice chimed in.

"Fiona!"

With a squeal of surprised joy, Glory spun around to face her smiling friend. Fiona looked ravishing in a cerulean gown with frothy skirts, her red curls artfully arranged over one shoulder. Her eyes were bright and her cheeks a healthy pink. Her husband, the Earl of Hawksmoor, stood by her side. He was a brown-haired fellow with serious grey eyes, and his stark handsomeness was the perfect foil to Fi's dazzling charms.

After greetings were exchanged, the Hawksmoors offered to relieve Aunt Hypatia of her chaperonage duties. Glory's aunt went off to inspect the buffet table with her friend.

"I am so glad you are here," Glory said happily. "I didn't know you were coming tonight."

"I wasn't planning on it, but my symptoms are vastly improved." Fi glanced mischievously at her husband. "Hawksmoor's symptoms are as well."

"Minx." The earl shot his giggling countess a look before saying with great dignity, "I was merely under the weather."

"Whatever the case may be, it is splendid to have company," Glory said with feeling. "I was having a rather dismal time of it before you arrived."

"Was that Lord Lyttle I saw stomping off?" Fi asked.

Sighing, Glory told her friends about the incident involving the hair dye.

"The *nerve* of him, calling you impertinent when you were trying to help," Fi said indignantly.

Gratitude warmed Glory like a cup of chocolate. It was so nice to have friends in one's corner.

Fi wrinkled her nose. "What I don't understand is why you danced with that old roué in the first place."

"Beggars can't be choosers," Glory said philosophically.

"Gloriana Cavendish, that is utter claptrap." Fi gave her a stern look. "You could have your pick of suitors if you wanted. Isn't that right, Hawksmoor?"

"Quite right," Hawksmoor said gallantly.

I don't want my pick of suitors. Just one.

"That is, um, nice of you to say."

Chewing her lip, Glory debated whether she should share what had happened with Mr. Chen. Yet her feelings were raw and confusing. She wasn't ready to expose herself to scrutiny, even from friends.

Fi and Hawksmoor exchanged a look. It was one of *those* looks —the kind that couples shared when they'd developed the ability to read each other's minds. Glory had seen it often enough between the Angels and their husbands and between her parents.

Hawksmoor cleared his throat. "Ladies, may I fetch you some lemonade?"

"Thank you, darling," Fi said. "That would be lovely."

Brushing a kiss against Fi's temple, the earl departed. Fi took Glory by the arm, tugging her to a divan set in an alcove by the dance floor. It was the ideal place for a tête-à-tête. A wall of potted palms provided some privacy, and the orchestra muffled their conversation to passers-by.

"Out with it," Fi said.

Glory fiddled with her yellow satin skirts. "It's nothing…"

"Please." Fi aimed her gaze toward the plaster-decorated ceiling. "Not only am I a trained professional, but I also happen to be your bosom friend. I can tell something is afoot. Does it have to do with last night? I stopped by Charlie's earlier, and she filled me in on your adventures."

Not all of them.

Glory hesitated. While she didn't know quite how to bring up Mr. Chen, she did want her friend's advice. Charming and popular, Fiona understood males better than anyone.

"Fi…do you think there's something, um, wrong with me? As a lady, I mean."

Her friend's gaze thinned. "Why would you ask such a thing? If that horrid Lord Lyttle said something—"

"He didn't," she said in a rush. "I was just, um, wondering. Since all I seem to attract are gentlemen of his ilk."

Fi canted her head. "Do you want the truth, Glory?"

She nodded.

"The main problem is that you don't flirt," Fi said. "You don't act in ways that would invite male attention. And, frankly, you have never seemed interested in putting forth the effort."

Glory couldn't argue with that.

"Furthermore, when it comes to your charms, you sell yourself short. I've always said that beauty is ninety-nine percent presentation. Take me, for instance: I make use of every asset." With a charming lack of false modesty, Fi flicked a hand at herself. "This doesn't happen on its own, you know. It takes cultivation."

"If I were to put in more of an effort at flirting and presenting myself," Glory ventured, "do you think gentlemen would find me attractive?"

"Without a doubt," Fi said promptly. "You are a lovely young lady and delightful company. Any gentleman worth your time would see it." Her expression turned shrewd. "Do you have a particular fellow in mind?"

"Um, maybe?"

"It's Master Chen, isn't it?"

As Glory's cheeks burned and she tried not to squirm, Fi squealed.

"I *knew* it," she crowed. "Livy and Pippa each owe me an ice from Gunter's!"

"Hold up." Glory drew her brows together. "The three of you were wagering on whether or not I liked Mr. Chen?"

"Oh no, dear." Eyes twinkling, Fi clarified, "We were wagering on *how long* it would take for you to recognize the fact. I said you would come to your senses before your fast-approaching birthday. Livy predicted by summer, and Pippa went for autumn."

Glory blinked. "My feelings were that obvious?"

"Only to your bosom friends, who have been through the mill themselves." Fi's smile was understanding. "You all figured out that I was in love with Hawk before I did, remember?"

"I suppose that is true." The fact that even Fi, who understood the male psyche better than most, had had her blind spots made Glory feel better. "But I am not certain that I am in love with Master Chen. That is, I like spending time with him, and being around him feels, well, different than being around other fellows."

"Different in what way?"

In every way.

When he was near, she felt a breathless, quivering tension. Her blood seemed to quicken, her heart raced, and she ached in unmentionable places. And those were just the physical sensations. She experienced other novel desires as well. She wanted to dig beneath Mr. Chen's calm austerity and discover what lay beneath. She wanted to learn from him and teach him how to play. To have adventures with him and feel the warmth of his approval. In sum, she wanted to discover who he was not just as a *shifu*...but as a man.

"We kissed," she blurted. "To avoid getting caught during the mission, we had to pretend. That we were lovers."

"I am familiar with that ploy," Fi said demurely. "How was it?"

"The kissing, you mean?"

Fi rolled her eyes. "What else would I mean?"

"It was, um, nice." Glory blushed so hard she feared her skin might melt from her bones.

"Just *nice*?" A divot appeared between Fi's curving brows. "In that case, perhaps you ought to look elsewhere—"

"The kiss was perfect," Glory admitted. "Indescribable, in a thrilling and tingly sort of way. Until Mr. Chen, kissing didn't seem that interesting. Now I think about it all the time, and I cannot imagine kissing anyone else."

Fi smiled. "In that case, I think you've found your match."

"But I haven't really."

"Why not?"

Glory's shoulders slumped. "Because Mr. Chen isn't interested in me."

"That is not possible."

"It is entirely possible," Glory countered. "He is a man of great character and purpose, you see. He has important responsibilities and doesn't have time for a relationship."

Recalling that she'd given Mr. Chen her word, she didn't want to say more...although, truth be told, he hadn't revealed all that much about his secret quest. What had been taken from him, and why did he want it back so badly? She would give her eyeteeth to know. Not to assuage her curiosity, but so that she could help him.

Even if there was to be no romantic involvement between them, friends stuck together. He, for instance, seemed intent upon teaching her skills to protect herself. Why couldn't she return the favor and aid him in his pursuit?

"Did he say that he doesn't have time for you?"

"More or less," Glory said. "He apologized for kissing me. He said it was wrong of him to do so, even as part of a ploy, when he has no intentions in that regard. He claims it's not because I'm undesirable, but because he has other commitments."

"The old *it's not you, it's me* bit?" Fi asked with sympathy.

Glory gave a glum nod. "He did offer to be my *shifu* so that he could teach me to better protect myself. I said yes..." She trailed off when Fi clasped her hands in delight. "Did I do something wrong?"

"No, dearest. You did everything *right*," Fi exclaimed. "You'll have Mr. Chen proposing in no time, if that is what you want."

Confused, Glory said, "Perhaps you misunderstood what I said—"

"Oh, I understand *perfectly*. The gentleman in question kissed you. Then he apologized, vowing it will never happen again. Am I correct so far?"

"Yes."

"Then he offered to be your *shifu*, which means he will be spending time with you. Lots of time and in close proximity, facts that he is surely aware of. And the reason he wants to teach you is because he wants to keep you safe. Ergo, he is being protective... which means he has formed an attachment to you!"

Glory's jaw dropped at her friend's gleeful logic.

"But...but he kept apologizing for kissing me," she stammered. "He said he would never do it again."

"My dear girl, gentlemen say things they don't mean *all the time*. Do you recall what Hawksmoor said about me before we got together?"

Glory recalled how indignant Fi had been after she'd eavesdropped on the earl's private conversation.

"He said you were the last lady he would be interested in." Glory chuckled. "Poor fellow. He didn't know what hit him."

"Cupid's arrow is capable of felling the mightiest of men," Fi agreed with a twinkle. "And your Master Chen is no exception."

Hope rattled against Glory's ribs. "You truly think there is a chance that he might like me?"

"No man gives a woman an indescribably thrilling and tingly kiss unless he is attracted to her. And he certainly does not keep showing up and protecting her because he *lacks* interest."

Hmm. Fi does have a point.

"Like asses, men can be stubborn creatures and sometimes need to be led. If you wish to encourage Mr. Chen's attentions—"

"I do," Glory said earnestly. "Ever so much."

"You may have to work at it," Fi warned.

"I'll do it. Whatever it takes."

"Then you've come to the right lady." Fi gave Glory's hand a confident squeeze. "I'll show you what worked with my husband. If you follow my guidance, I guarantee that you will have Mr. Chen at your feet in no time."

Fifteen

Awaiting Mr. Chen's arrival the next day, Glory paced the music room, FF II hopping at her heels. She thought the space with its soaring ceiling, wood floors, and mirrored walls would be an ideal setting for her first lesson. She paused in front of one of the mirrored panels to check her appearance. Seeing the wide-eyed and uncertain lady who looked back, she felt a nervous flutter.

She consulted FF II. "Do you think Fi knows what she's doing?"

The ferret twitched his nose and cocked his head.

Glory sighed. "I am not certain her plan is going to work either."

A true sister in spirit, a yawning Fi had arrived early this morning to help Glory prepare for her lesson with Mr. Chen. Fi had rummaged through Glory's entire wardrobe before choosing the present coral-colored walking dress with an elongated bodice and fluffy skirts.

"But this dress is too restrictive for practicing *kung fu*," Glory had protested as Elsie laced her up. "How am I supposed to run, punch, and kick?"

"Needs must. I am certain you'll find a way." Fi's reply had been a bit tart for she wasn't an early riser. "It is not as if we have time to order a new frock from Mrs. Quinton."

A famed modiste, Mrs. Q was a close friend of Charlie's who did special work for the Angels. The gowns she'd designed for Glory were beautiful and allowed for freedom of movement, but Glory had always chosen more modest styles, which Fi had ruled out for the occasion of seducing Master Chen.

"The color of this dress is perfect for you," Fi declared. "The coral shade brings out the red in your hair and the blush in your cheeks. All we need to do is alter the neckline a little."

By "alter," Fi had meant "lower" and by "little," she had meant "a lot."

Glory blushed at the amount of skin exposed by the newly sloping vee of her neckline. The center dip showed a hint of the shallow crevice between her bosoms. When she had protested that the dress was too revealing, Fi had pinned a rose at the lowest point.

"There," Fi had said. "That covers everything."

Looking at her reflection, Glory feared the rose might do the opposite and bring attention to how uncovered her breasts presently were. It didn't help that Fi had instructed Elsie to style her hair in a more sophisticated fashion than usual. Dispensing with Glory's sensible topknot, Elsie had created a looser style. The front of Glory's hair was tied back with black velvet ribbon whilst the rest hung in loose, flowing curls.

Feeling the silky, unaccustomed brush of hair against her bare shoulders, Glory shivered. She didn't look or feel like herself. But if she wanted Mr. Chen to see her as a woman, then perhaps this was a good thing?

Fi's parting instructions rang in her head.

"While looks are important, you must also act like a lady who is confident in her charms," her friend had instructed. "Try the suggestions I gave you, and remember that flirtation is an art form.

When done properly, the object of your interest doesn't even know it is happening, only that he is falling irrevocably under your spell."

If only it were that easy.

As Glory mentally reviewed Fi's tips—which could have filled an encyclopedia—the knock on the door made her jump. She glanced at the clock. Dash it all, where had the time gone? She'd spent all morning getting ready only to be caught unprepared when her guest arrived.

She dashed to the settee. Fi had advised her on the specific pose to adopt, but in her panicked state, she couldn't replicate it. There had been a lot of talk about achieving the perfect angle between sitting and reclining...some posture Fi called "languid repose." Throwing herself upon the cushions, Glory did her best.

Aunt Patty entered, followed by Mr. Chen. Glory's belly flipped at his undeniable virility. His somber clothes hugged his lean form, his thick hair gleaming. He moved with that innate self-assurance that she could only admire.

"Since I was headed this way, I told Greaves I would take Mr. Chen in..." Her aunt trailed off, peering at her with a frown. "Are you unwell, my dear?"

"No," Glory said. "Why would you ask?"

"Because you are lying down in the middle of the day."

Drat. So much for the languid repose.

Glory pushed herself ungraciously to a sitting position. "I was, um, just trying out the cushions."

"How odd." Aunt Hypatia frowned. "Are you certain you're well? Your cheeks are rather flushed."

"I'm fine," Glory bit out. "And ready to start my lesson with Mr. Chen."

"Carry on, then," Aunt Patty said. "I daresay my presence isn't required. We'll leave the door open, and I shall be across the hall in the library if you need me."

Hallelujah.

Although Fi had said to let a gentleman come to her, Glory

couldn't wait. The moment her aunt departed, she jumped to her feet and met Mr. Chen halfway.

Seeing the smile in his eyes, she was suddenly tongue-tied.

"Good morning, *Shifu*," she said shyly.

"Good morning, my lady." His gaze dropped lower, below her face, and he cleared his throat. "Are you, er, ready for a lesson?"

The promise of learning martial arts took some of the edge off her nerves.

"I jolly well am," she said eagerly. "What are we starting with? Lightness *kung fu*?"

"Actually, I thought we would start with this."

Mr. Chen removed a cloth-bound book from the satchel he carried.

She knitted her brows. "We're...reading?"

"Before one can run, one must walk. I have taken the liberty of translating my *shifu*'s fundamental precepts for us to review. He compiled them based on the works of great philosophers. They are the basis of his training and what I plan to teach you."

Striding to the writing table, he held out the chair. Sighing, she went over and sat. He placed the book in front of her, and she immediately leafed through to the end.

"It must have taken you a while." She peered at him, wide-eyed. "To translate *one hundred* precepts."

"It was a worthwhile exercise," he said blandly. "One can never review the fundamentals too often. Let us begin with the first precept: *Patience is the key to knowledge. Without patience, there is no learning...*"

Around precept number twenty-eight, Glory started squirming in her seat.

It wasn't that the lesson was boring...all right, it was a *bit* boring, especially when she'd been expecting to learn how to scale walls and outrun pursuers. But reviewing the text didn't bother her as much as Mr. Chen's presence did. And by bother, she meant that she had difficulty keeping her mind on the lesson and off *him*.

He paced in front of the desk as he lectured. She loved how knowledgeable and intelligent he was; was there anything the man did not do well? He, himself, must have been a first-rate pupil. He did not need to consult the book, seeming to know everything by heart, and when she had a question, he answered thoughtfully, a crease of concentration between his brows. He looked serious, stern, and cerebral...

And so dashingly attractive. Her heart sighed.

"Humility is the basis of learning. Now, what do you suppose Shifu Lam means by that?"

She forced herself to focus. "Um, knowing what one knows and admitting what one doesn't know is how one learns?"

"An excellent answer."

His approval made her toes curl in her shoes.

"My *shifu* likes to say that the most profound knowledge is self-knowledge." Master Chen rapped his knuckles against the desk to emphasize the importance of this point.

As he continued to pontificate on the inherent virtue of seeking knowledge, he trailed his long fingers idly along the table. Back and forth, back and forth. Glory found herself mesmerized by his hand. The back was tanned and veined, rippling with tendons. She saw calluses on his fingertips and palms, badges of an active man. A warrior and a healer.

Strong and capable, his hands told the story of the man himself. Recalling the feel of them cupping her face, the way he'd held her steady for his kiss, she became aware of a needy throb between her legs. Flushing, she realized how damp she'd become there. She squeezed her thighs together, trying to quell the ache. She reminded herself that her aunt was just across the hall—could come in at any moment.

It didn't help that Mr. Chen continued to trail his fingers along the table. Caressing the wood the way he might a...a lover. She imagined him touching *her*, and the tips of her breasts pulsed beneath her bodice. What would his hands feel like there, cupping her bosoms, touching the straining peaks? Would he touch her like a healer, soothing the ache of her nipples with gentle strokes? Or like a warrior, capturing those needy points between his fingers and demanding her surrender...

"What do you make of that precept?"

Jolted out of her sensual daze, she stammered, "Um, I...I beg your pardon?"

"Am I interrupting your daydreaming?"

Mr. Chen's sternness did something funny to her insides. Between her legs, she grew even wetter.

"No. Um, not really."

"Not really?" He leveled a look at her. "Your attention is required during lessons, Glory."

Hearing him address her informally, even if it was a reprimand, sent a pleasant quiver through her.

"Yes, *Shifu*," she said contritely. "I'll do better."

"See that you do." His expression softening a fraction, he said, "You have had enough for today. We will resume the lesson at another—"

"Oh no, please. I would love to spend more...to learn more," she said quickly. "Perhaps you could show me something different. Something other than the precepts?"

After a moment, he relented. "I suppose an application of the concepts is in order. Why don't we go over to the sitting area?"

"That sounds capital!" Glory exclaimed.

Before Wei could assist her, she bounded from her chair. He

smothered a smile as she made a beeline for the sitting area. Some men might find her feminine energy wearying, but Wei was captivated by her vitality. If she moved that way in bed...

Do not go there. You are her shifu *now. She is your student... which means she is forbidden.*

The fact that he'd had good reason to establish these new boundaries did nothing to change his visceral reaction to her. Always a pretty minx, she was especially toothsome today. He blamed the dress she was wearing. As he followed her to the seating area, he noted how the color brought out the rich fire of her hair. Her curls swayed like a sensual curtain against her back, and his fingers itched to touch those shiny tresses. To tangle themselves in that silk, tug her head back, and—

"Will we be standing or sitting for this exercise?"

Glory stood at the edge of the Aubusson, peering at him. It required all his willpower to keep his gaze from dipping to her breasts. The dress was cut too damned low, and the rose pinned to her bodice didn't help matters, luring his attention to her dainty tits. Earlier, as he'd lectured on the virtue of abstemiousness, an image had floated into his head: of plucking that flower from its place and burying his nose against her orchid-scented skin.

"Shifu?"

"Sitting," he said hastily. "We will be practicing breathing."

"Breathing?" Her brow pleating, she plopped onto a settee. "I know how to do *that*."

"The lesson is not just about how to breathe—although I think you will learn something about that as well. Mainly, the lesson is about paying attention to your breath." He gave her a pointed look. "And paying attention in general."

"I *do* pay attention."

When he lifted his brows, she amended, "Most of the time."

"Then you will have no trouble with this lesson. To begin, keep your posture upright and place your hands palms up in your lap. Feel the ground beneath your feet." He paused, giving her time to follow his directions. "Once you are comfortable, you may close your eyes."

It took her a few moments to get settled, her long lashes brushing her cheek.

"I want you to start by paying attention to the sensation of breathing," he said. "The feeling of the air as it enters your nose and leaves your lips."

Glory obeyed, albeit in her own adorable way. She wrinkled her nose, her golden freckles dancing as she inhaled. When she parted her lips and blew out an exaggerated breath, he had to fight a smile.

"Just breathe naturally," he advised. "You don't have to try; your body knows what to do. As my *shifu* would say, *Do not do*."

Even with her eyes closed, she managed to look exasperated. And cute...much too cute.

"What in heavens does that mean?" she grumbled.

"It means trust in your instincts and don't overthink it."

She seemed to take in his advice. Gradually, her breathing changed, deepening. Her lashes fluttered like butterfly wings as she relaxed. Her lips parted, and he envied the air that passed between that plump, rosy portal. Her tongue darted out, moistening the rim of her mouth and yanking back the curtain of his self-control.

In a flash, he was engulfed by his erotic dream. He saw her kneeling before him on the flower boat, peering at him with jade-and-sunshine eyes as he fisted his cock. Threading his fingers through her satiny curls, he brought her mouth toward the dripping tip.

"Lick me," he said huskily.

Her gaze shining with ardent curiosity, she ran her tongue over his engorged dome, swirling fire over his senses. With a hum of approval, she parted her lips, and he thrust his cock into her welcoming kiss—

"Doing it this way feels different."

Wei jerked, returning to the present. His blood was rushing

through his veins...and one large vein in particular. He was shocked to discover that he was hard, his cock a visible ridge at the front of his trousers. Luckily, his pupil's eyes were still closed. Wei's fingers were unusually fumbling as he buttoned up his coat to hide his arousal.

"Pardon?" he managed.

"Breathing this way. I never realized how involved breathing is. How it affects different parts of one's body."

Tell me about it.

With each breath, Wei felt his erection throbbing, straining against his smalls. His lack of self-discipline bewildered him. While he could blame the element of surprise for his response to her at the flash house, now he had no excuse. He'd told her that he had no romantic interest in her, that they could only be friends. Hell, he'd come up with the plan to be her *shifu* to guard himself from temptation. Yet being in her presence tossed his honorable intentions out of the window like a bucket of dirty water.

Get control of yourself, man.

He inhaled and exhaled before speaking. "How does it affect your, er, various parts?"

His stones pulled up taut; talking about her parts was not helping his lust.

Tilting her head, she replied, "I hadn't really thought of how deep a breath went."

Do not go there. Do not think of how deep you could go.

He cleared his throat. "Go on."

"Well, usually I'm aware of my breath here." She placed a hand on her chest, on the bare skin below her collarbones. "But it goes farther than that. All the way down here to my belly"—she placed her other hand at the lowest point of her elongated bodice—"when I breathe fully."

"You have made an important discovery."

Pride joined desire, a jarring combination. She was as bright as she was beautiful, and he'd always enjoyed her intelligence. Respected the original workings of her mind.

"I have?" Her eyes flew open.

At the eager wonder in her gaze, his chest seized with a feeling that only she elicited in him. One that was foolhardy. That made him long for things that he could not have.

"Breathing is energy," he replied. "When you can experience the fullness of your breath, you can learn to harness its power. To direct that energy to different parts of your body, to help you move in ways you have not before. Allow me to demonstrate."

He scouted a route around the room that had multiple obstacles and took off in a light sprint. Engaging his breath and his muscles, he first leapt over the back of the sofa, then a wingchair. Next was a rosewood console holding a vase and other delicate objects. He soared over the table without disturbing a single object and landed noiselessly on the Aubusson.

Using the impact of landing to propel himself forward, he dashed toward the side of the pianoforte. He gauged the height of the propped lid, and at the precise distance, he powered himself off the ground. He flipped easily in the air above the gleaming wood panel. The somersault was a bit of showing off, but he couldn't resist it.

"*Zounds,* that was incredible, *Shifu*!"

She raced toward him, clapping. She flashed her dimples at him, and his sudden breathlessness had nothing to do with his demonstration.

"I would like to learn how to do that straightaway," she announced.

He laughed—couldn't help it. He didn't know why he found her impatience so damned endearing. Perhaps because it was part of her irrepressible zeal for life.

"One must walk before one runs," he reminded her.

"Can't I learn both at once?" she wheedled. "Please?"

"Practice feeling your breath first." He gave in to the impulse to chuck her under the chin. Told himself it was a friendly gesture even as his insides tightened at the downy softness of her skin.

"And if I master it?" It was her turn to sound breathless.

"Then I will teach you a lightness *kung fu* technique at our next lesson."

Sixteen

The following afternoon, Glory received her aunt's permission to go to Charlie's.

Thus far, Mr. Devlin had turned up nothing related to the stolen dogs, and Glory and the other Angels set off to scout one of the final locations on Scott's map. Disguised as a grumpy and foul-mouthed hackney driver, Mr. Devlin was taking them to a locale on Jacob's Island, a notorious slum south of the Thames in Bermondsey. They were on their way to the London Bridge but were mired in traffic.

Mr. Devlin was cursing loudly at a costermonger whose over-filled cart had gone over a bump, scattering apples and halting the flow of transport.

"If you don't gather 'em apples quick, I'll come down and stuff 'em up your arse!" Mr. Devlin yelled from the driver's perch.

Inside the hackney, Glory sensed the former spy was rather enjoying himself. She didn't mind the delay, for it gave her time with her friends. Livy, Fi, and Pippa were all feeling more the thing, and it was a treat to be together again. For the mission, the Angels had transformed themselves into middle-aged morts in mob caps and stained aprons. Wigs concealed their hair, and they'd aged themselves with artfully applied face paint.

Anyone eavesdropping upon their conversation, however, would have been confounded to hear four older women chatting and laughing like young ladies. Fi had already informed Livy and Pippa about Glory's situation with Mr. Chen, and Glory finished filling everyone in on her first lesson.

"Mr. Chen chucked you under the chin?" Fi said from beside her. "That is all he did?"

When Glory nodded, Fi pitted her brows.

"I was certain that dress would do the trick," she muttered. "After the alteration Elsie did to your neckline, you were nearly falling out of it. One would think he would get the hint."

"*Fiona*," Glory said, aghast. "You said the neckline was fashionable, not fast."

"Fashionable, fast." Fi's shoulders rose and fell. "What's the difference?"

Glory bit her lip. "What if he thought I was too forward—"

"Obviously, you weren't forward enough if all you got was a little tap under the chin. I was expecting a kiss at the very least."

"In my experience, getting chucked under one's chin can be a positive sign," Livy said from the opposite bench. "Hadleigh did that to me while we were courting. As a matter of fact, he still does it."

"Yes, but he does *other* things as well," Fi said.

Livy turned pink. "Really, Fi."

Undeterred, Fi said, "My point is that Master Chen has only kissed Glory once, and she was aiming for a repeat performance. Or at least a sign of his romantic interest."

"I think Mr. Chen has given several signs," Pippa said.

"You think so?" Glory asked keenly. "What signs?"

Pippa smiled. "More than once, the master has come to your aid, and now he has taken on the role of your *shifu*. Clearly, he wants to spend time with you."

"I already noted that Mr. Chen is inordinately protective of Glory," Fi chimed in.

Glory chewed on her lip. "But an older brother or friend can also be protective, and I don't want him to think of me that way."

"How well I understand that dilemma," Livy said with feeling.

"How did you convince His Grace to see you as a woman and not a sister or friend?" Glory wanted to know.

"We have circled back to the 'other things' category," Fi said, giggling.

"You are familiar with those things as well, Fi," Livy retorted.

"I'm not denying it," Fi said blithely. "Just pointing out that seductive tactics can be an invaluable tool when one's goal is gaining a gentleman's attention."

"And therein lies the problem." Slumping against the seat, Glory blew out a breath. "I have no talent when it comes to seduction."

"Surely you are underestimating yourself—" Livy began.

"I wish I were. I found Fi's tips dreadfully confusing," Glory admitted. "When I tried them, I felt silly and awkward and not like myself at all. I don't know how to repose languidly. Or how to flirt and get a gentleman under my spell. Mr. Chen didn't even seem to notice how I was dressed. Maybe he's not attracted to me. Maybe he was using his commitments as an excuse. To let me down gently."

"Or maybe you are going about this the wrong way," Pippa said.

"How do you mean?"

"Forget about Fi's tactics for the moment." Pippa pursed her lips. "How do you *feel* in Mr. Chen's presence?"

Giddy and hot. Damp in unmentionable places.

"Bothered." Cheeks flushing, Glory amended, "In a good way, though. I cannot stop thinking about how much I admire him. Not just because he is handsome. I respect *everything* about him: his physical prowess, nobility, and integrity. He has such conviction and purpose." Squirming a bit in her seat, she forced out the next words. "When I'm around him, I feel breathless and...um, tingly. All over. At the same time, I feel oddly *tense*, and I'm dying to know if he feels the same way about me. Am I...am I making any sense?"

"*Yes*," her three friends said in unison.

"You are falling in love with Master Chen," Pippa confirmed. "When Cull first came back into my life, I felt tense and tingly too." Her blue eyes dreamy, she rubbed her rounded midsection. "I still do."

Am I falling in love?

The answer prickled through Glory, the sensation like that of a foot that had fallen asleep but was now stirring. She knew she was attracted to him, but the truth was that her feelings ran deeper. Until now, she'd been an eccentric hoyden who hadn't cared what gentlemen thought of her. Yet when it came to Mr. Chen, not only did she care...she cared *deeply*.

She wanted him to teach her about lovemaking, *kung fu*, and their shared heritage. She wanted to get through his reserve and earn his smiles and admiration. She wanted to know his innermost thoughts and help him in his quest, to be his companion through thick and thin...

"Zounds." Dumbfounded, she looked at her friends. "I *am* falling in love with Mr. Chen. But what if...what if he has no interest in me?"

"There is only one way to find out," Pippa said. "You must ask him."

With a shiver, Glory said, "I cannot just *ask* him if he likes me."

"Why not?" Livy tipped her head to one side. "You're outspoken by nature. You always say what you mean, even when your view is unpopular. Your habit of being direct is part of your charm."

"You told Lord Lyttle that his hair dye was leaking," Fi added.

"Not many people would have the courage *or* care enough to do that."

"But this is different." Glory knotted her fingers together, feeling how clammy her hands had gotten. "This would involve talking about my private feelings, and I am not good at that."

What if I say what is in my heart, and Mr. Chen rejects me? What if my growing attachment scares him away? Wouldn't it be better to have him as a friend and shifu *than nothing at all?*

"Being vulnerable is hard for all of us." Pippa's tone was gentle. "Which is why falling in love rarely goes smoothly. But sometimes *not* knowing is worse than the truth itself."

"You're right." Glory took a breath. "I shall lay my cards on the table and ask him if he has any interest in me at all."

"Hooray," Fi and Livy cheered.

"Now that I've decided to have this conversation with him," Glory said ruefully, "waiting until my lesson next week seems intolerable."

"Then don't wait," Livy said. "Hadleigh is planning to visit the clinic tomorrow, and we shall pick you up on our way. We'll be your chaperones whilst you and Mr. Chen have your tête-à-tête."

With a heady mix of dread and anticipation, Glory nodded.

Mr. Devlin deposited the Angels in an alleyway close to their destination. The area was one of the worst rookeries in London. The dilapidated patch sat next to St. Saviour's Dock, and as Glory hopped down from the carriage, she wrinkled her nose at the foul smells. Surrounded by tidal ditches, the area had been dubbed "the Venice of Drains," with many buildings backing up against stagnant canals teeming with waste. Even though it hadn't rained, the ground was soggy. Mud and heaven knew what else squished beneath Glory's worn shoes.

"Ugh, it smells like a rubbish heap." Fi grimaced. "I just got over my nausea."

"Are you certain you don't want to stay in the hackney with Pippa?" Glory asked.

Due to her advanced pregnancy, Pippa was on surveillance duty with Mr. Devlin. The pair would discreetly circle the environs while the other Angels searched the property. At any sign of trouble, Pippa would alert her fellow agents with a whistle that emitted a shrill and distinctive sound that resembled a bird's call.

"I am not missing out," Fi said firmly. "I want to have as much adventure as possible before I get as big as a house. No offense to Pippa."

Pippa's dry reply came from the carriage. "Why would I be offended to be likened to an edifice?"

"We'll reconvene here in an hour," Livy said to Mr. Devlin.

"If you're late, I'll be chargin' you for me time," he grumbled.

Glory admired the way he stayed in character; it reminded her to readjust her tatty apron and make sure her wig was in place. After he and Pippa drove off, the remaining trio headed to their destination. Dusk was falling, bringing along drifting fog as they crossed a rickety bridge. Crammed jowl to jowl, the buildings they passed had sagging roofs and peeling paint, drying linens hanging limply from poles extended out the second-floor windows. There were occasional storefronts, light flickering through the dirty glass. Everywhere, babes were squalling, adults shouting, and even animals joined in on the ruckus.

Glory's ears pricked at the sound of barking in the distance.

"Do you hear that?" she said. "It could be Sir Barkley."

"It sounds like more than one dog," Livy replied. "Perhaps we've found the dognappers' stash."

Excitement shot through Glory as they approached the two-story building at the end of the street. It sat on a larger lot than the others and was enclosed by a rusty iron gate. There was just enough light to make out the faded sign: "Seyfried & Sons Leather

Dressers." The boarded-up windows and ramshackle state suggested that the place had long been abandoned.

"This is the final place on the map," Livy confirmed.

After a quick glance around, Glory discreetly checked the gate. Locked.

"Let's go around back," she said in an undertone. "We don't want to invite attention."

The Angels continued along the side of the building. The fence ended where the place butted up against a ditch, a wooden gallery extending over the rivulet of sludge. Here, there was no one to witness them making their entry. Glory sent FF II to do some initial scouting. He easily scaled the fence, his long, furry body arcing as he leapt onto the gallery. He bounded along the perimeter of the wooden deck, then stood on his hind legs and made a *dook-dook* sound.

The ferret equivalent of a thumb's up.

"Good boy," Glory whispered. "Looks like the coast is clear."

She went first, the other Angels following her onto the deck. With expert speed, she picked the lock on the back door, and the trio crept into the shadowed interior. The former tannery had a rotting odor distinctive from that of the sewage outside, no doubt from the years of animal carcasses being treated and stored within its walls. Grabbing a lantern from a hook, she lit it.

Glory's breath caught as the light gleamed off metal bars.

"Heavens," Fiona breathed. "This has to be where they are keeping the dogs."

The massive cage took center stage in the cavernous room. The cell went halfway up to the high rafters and was wide enough to keep dozens of animals. As Glory walked around the cage, she saw dark stains soaked into the floorboards, and her throat clenched.

Behind her, FF II let out a low hiss and scampered off.

"Where are the dogs now?" Glory's voice trembled. "Do you think they are all right?"

"Who knows?" Livy said darkly. "Whoever took those dogs is a monster, and this place is a veritable dungeon of horror."

Shuddering, Glory thought the description was apt. Like the floor, the thick posts that supported the rafters were also splattered with unidentifiable gore. The tanner's old tools still hung on the walls, and the double-handled fleshing knives, hooks, and skivers added to the unnerving ambiance.

"We should check the other rooms—"

She was cut off by a warning shrill.

Pippa's whistle.

"We have to go," Livy whispered.

Livy and Fi ran for the back door, but Glory couldn't find FF II.

"Come here, boy," she said urgently.

When he didn't respond, she dashed to the other rooms, looking for him. No luck. She sprinted back into the main room as voices and heavy footsteps approached the front door. Simultaneously, she heard a soft squeak from overhead; FF II was perched on one of the beams. Snuffing the lantern, she left it on the ground and ran to one of the posts, climbing it quickly. She reached the safety of the shadowed rafters just as the door opened.

Looking at FF II, she placed a finger to her lips. He seemed to understand and scurried to the safety of her shoulders. She pressed into the nook where the wall met the ceiling, her heart pounding as two men entered the room. The blond one with the beard was holding a lamp, and she recognized him from the flash house: Jimmy Bryant, Scott's right-hand man.

"The room needs to be bigger." Bryant's tone was brusque. "Last month, coves were nearly trampled trying to watch the fights, and this time we're expecting an even larger crowd."

"But you said the event is this Friday." The other man scratched his head. "That's three days from now, guv. Not sure I can—"

"The Wolf's orders. Do you want to be the bloke who upsets 'im?"

"N-no, sir." Even in the dimness, the man's fear was visible. "I'll, er, take down a wall, expand this room into the others—"

"Mary's tits, I don't care 'ow you do it. Just get it done." Bryant sounded annoyed. "While you're at it, put in some extra seats. Scott upped the admission ticket to twenty pounds and says the swells expect somefing soft beneath their arses."

The door squealed open again, and another man appeared. With a rush, Glory recognized the pugnacious face and stocky figure of Farwell.

Bryant looked none too pleased to see the newcomer.

"What the devil are you doing 'ere?" he hissed.

"M-my apologies," Farwell stammered. "But I 'ave an urgent matter to discuss, and I didn't know what else—"

"Shut yer bleeding gob. We'll talk in my carriage." Turning to the other man, Bryant said tersely, "This place be'er be fixed up by Friday, or 'eads will roll. Understand?"

"Y-yes, sir."

Bryant stalked out, Farwell trailing at his heels.

As the remaining man went to investigate the other rooms, Glory took the opening to clamber down and exit out the back door. Fi and Livy were waiting for her on the gallery.

"Thank heavens you're all right," Livy whispered. "We couldn't see what was going on."

"That bastard Scott is holding illegal dogfights," Glory said grimly. "The next event is Friday—the perfect opportunity for us to rescue Sir Barkley and the other dogs."

Seventeen

Shirtless and seething, Wei took out his frustration on the wooden dummy. Sweat dripped down his face as he punched the inanimate figure. His knuckles were raw and burning, but he didn't care. The sensation was nothing compared to the pain of letting his family down again.

I thought I picked up a trail. But it led to another dead end. He clenched his jaw. *Yet another failure...on today of all days.*

Before his lesson with Glory yesterday, he'd gone to Newgate to find the tattooist known as the Don. A guard had stopped him at the gate, stating that an appointment was required for all visits. When he asked to schedule one to see the Don, the guard eyed him suspiciously and questioned his relationship with the prisoner. Wei could only say that he was an acquaintance, and the guard had refused his entry pending an interview with the warden, which could not be scheduled until this morning.

Chomping at the bit, Wei had complied with the bureaucracy. He'd contemplated breaking into Newgate but discarded the plan for being too high risk. Besides, a part of him had believed that *yuan fen*, or destiny, was at work: today was his sister's birthday. It would be fitting that on the day Ling Ling had taken her first breath, Wei would finally discover who had made her take her last.

Simmering with anticipation, he'd shown up to meet with the warden...who'd informed him that the Don was dead. Apparently, the cove had passed away in his sleep a few weeks ago. As no kin had come forward to claim his body, he'd been buried in a pauper's grave.

Progress is an illusion. I think I am getting closer to my vengeance, but it slips like water through my fingers. All this time and I have accomplished nothing.

Wei punched harder, trying to block out his spiraling thoughts. He couldn't give up—*wouldn't* give up. But he didn't know what to do, how to give his family the peace they deserved. Years of rage welled inside him, and with a roar, he jumped into the air, issuing a spin kick. His foot connected with the dummy's head, sending it flying across the courtyard.

He landed on his feet, panting, hands fisted at his sides.

"Are we, er, interrupting anything?"

He twisted around to see Hadleigh at the entrance of the courtyard. The duke wasn't alone. His wife was there...and Glory. She was staring at him with wide eyes, looking so pretty and concerned that desire joined Wei's swirling emotions.

He struggled to compose himself.

"Pardon," he muttered. "I was not expecting company."

Wei reached for a towel, slinging it around his neck. As he hadn't brought a shirt with him, it was as decent as he could make himself. At the moment, he wasn't sure he cared. He didn't feel civilized or calm or any of the things he'd trained himself to feel.

"We saw Yao, and he said to come in." Hadleigh's voice held a note of apology.

Yao would say that. Since the disaster this morning, Wei's *shidai* had been overly solicitous, hovering and asking if Wei needed anything. He probably thought Wei could use the company.

Wei gripped the ends of the towel. "Was there something you wanted?"

He was curt, bordering on rude. But he wanted to be left alone. Wanted to rage at the universe and lick his wounds in private.

"Actually, there was something," Her Grace said.

Hadleigh gave his wife an oddly warning look, which she ignored.

"Glory wished to speak with you," she said, nudging her friend forward.

Seeing Glory's face turn rosy, Wei frowned. "What about?"

The duchess answered. "As it is a private matter, Hadleigh and I will make ourselves scarce. We'll be in the other courtyard if you need us."

Like a determined tugboat, she linked her arm through that of her much larger husband and pulled him toward the exit. Hadleigh went with her, shooting one last concerned glance at Wei over his broad shoulder.

Alone with Glory, his emotions surging, Wei had a bitter moment of clarity.

He wanted her.

A lady who was too well-born and innocent for the likes of him. A lady whom he'd taken on as his student because he was afraid of what he might do otherwise. A lady who trusted him when she ought to have left him to his misery.

His throat clenched with anger at the world—but mostly at himself.

I haven't changed at all, always doing the wrong thing. Making the wrong choices.

As furious as he was, he knew he was in no state to be around Glory. He had to get rid of her.

"What do you want?" he asked brusquely.

Glory's mouth was completely dry. In all the time she'd known Master Chen, she'd never seen him in such a state. So raw and exposed...and she wasn't just referring to his lack of a shirt. Although, heavens, she didn't know men had that *many* muscles on their torsos. She blinked, momentarily mesmerized by the sweat-sheened blocks of his chest and the defined bands on his abdomen. Even his hips were lean and cut, girded by an intriguing slant of sinew. As he clenched the ends of the towel looped around his neck, his biceps and forearms bulged, popping with veins.

"Well?" he asked shortly. "What was so important that you came all this way?"

Another lady might have been offended by his harsh tone. Yet Glory knew intuitively that she was not the cause of his mood. She sensed that something had happened. Something bad. He seemed, for lack of a better word, *shaken*.

His mask of calmness was askew, raw emotion seeping through. His pupils were dilated, his eyes brewing with emotions he was barely keeping in check. Even his hair had given into an unruly wave.

He is hurting. The realization constricted her heart. *And he needs a friend.*

"Has something happened?" she asked.

"I should be the one asking you that question. After all, you show up without notice—"

"We'll get to that later." She wanted to help and wasn't going to get distracted. "Right now, I want to know what has left you so shaken."

"Shaken?" He made a scoffing sound. "I do not get shaken."

"Well, you're not precisely calm, are you?" she pointed out. "You are not yourself, and I wish to know why."

"It's nothing."

"Something is going on," she insisted. "And you know how curious I am. If you do not tell me, I will pester you until I find out."

He shot her a fulminating glance. "It is disrespectful for a pupil to pester her *shifu*."

"Right now, we are just Glory and Wei." In her concern for him, she did not even blush at using his name. "You said you wanted to be friends, and this is what friends do. They talk to each other."

"There is nothing to talk about—"

"Does it have to do with your purpose? The thing you're trying to find?"

She knew she'd guessed correctly, for his shoulders grew rigid, his chest rippling with tension. And his eyes...she swallowed at the anguish flaring in his pupils. At the pain he must work so hard to keep hidden.

He averted his gaze.

"You can talk to me, Wei."

She came closer, and with great daring, touched his jaw. His gaze swung back to meet hers. Yet he did not pull away, his tight muscle quivering beneath her fingertips before she let her hand fall.

"Talk to me," she urged. "You can trust me."

She saw the moment pain broke free from the bonds of his self-discipline.

"It...it is my sister's birthday today."

Hearing his simmering emotion, Glory had a terrible premonition.

Carefully, she said, "I didn't know you have a sister."

"I had a sister." His hoarse words confirmed her fear. "Her name was Ling Ling. Today she would have turned five-and-twenty."

"I'm sorry," Glory said gently. "When did she pass?"

"Fifteen years ago." Grief saturated his voice. "She was...she was only ten."

He turned his back to her, his shoulders hunching, and Glory let him be. Knowing how private he was, she didn't want to push too hard and have him regret taking her into his confidence.

Seeing the taut grooves of his back, she ached for him. Wei was so strong and self-possessed; how difficult it must be for a man like him to accept the things he could not control. She did not know how one would cope with the loss of a younger sibling. She couldn't imagine life without her brothers...couldn't bear it if anything happened to Theo or Horatio.

"Were you and Ling Ling very close?" she asked tentatively.

"Yes." Wei's voice was gruff. "Even though I was older than her by eight years, Ling Ling liked to follow me around. I used to tease her for being a pest. But she was spirited and headstrong; once she set her mind to something, nothing could stop her from accomplishing it. She loved animals, hated bullies, and always stood up for what was right." He turned his head, sliding a glance at Glory. "You remind me of her, actually."

Drat. Now I have my answer: he does think of me like a younger sister.

Glory hid her deflated feeling behind a smile. "Are you implying that I am a pest?"

"Sometimes."

He faced her fully, and despite her disappointment, she was glad to see that his anguish had subsided. The intense brown of his irises was back, breaking through the shadows.

"But mostly you are like Ling Ling in your spirit and sweetness. In your optimistic campaigner's heart." The line of his mouth softened. "She, like you, had causes and people she fought for. While she did not always fit in, she knew who she was. She knew what mattered, and she never gave up."

"I would have liked your sister very much," Glory said sincerely.

"And she you."

Hesitating, she asked, "What happened to her?"

"I am not going to talk about that. Not today." His voice was quiet and firm. "You have reminded me about who Ling Ling was, and today I want to just remember her. To honor her memory. I will burn some incense and wish her a happy birthday."

"If you want company, I'll do it with you," she offered.

"I would like that," he said solemnly. "And thank you, Glory. For being here and being"—his eyes crinkled slightly—"a disrespectful pest."

It wasn't exactly a lover-like statement, but she was glad he could tease again.

She rolled her eyes. "You're welcome, O Great *Shifu*."

He smiled then, so warmly that her heart flip-flopped as helplessly as a fish caught on a line. She thought she could drown in his gaze...which was why she wasn't prepared for his question.

"Now, what did you wish to speak with me about?"

Botheration. Panic set in. *How can I tell him I'm falling in love with him when he just told me I remind him of his sister?*

"Nothing," she said quickly.

He tilted his head. "You came all the way to the clinic to speak to me about nothing?"

"I mean, it is nothing important. Nothing to concern yourself over. Not today when you have other matters—"

"Glory." He cut her off with a stern look. "Tell me."

"I...I..." Inspiration struck. "I wanted to tell you that the Angels have made progress on the case. Yesterday, we learned that Scott plans to stage dogfights at an old tannery on Jacob's Island this Friday. While the dogs weren't there, we found a large cage, and there were what appeared to be bloodstains on the floor."

"The bastard," Wei said, his jaw clenching.

Relieved that her distraction had worked, Glory nodded.

"We have a plan to rescue Sir Barkley and as many of the dogs as possible," she went on. "At the tannery, Farwell showed up, wanting to speak to Bryant, Scott's right-hand man. Farwell might not know where the dogs are being kept, but Bryant surely does. Mr. Devlin has started shadowing Bryant, and hopefully, the latter will lead him to the dogs soon. If Bryant doesn't do so by Friday, however, the Angels will infiltrate the dogfight and rescue all the animals."

"This plan is dangerous." Wei drew his brows together. "If you must go Friday, I will accompany you."

She thought about arguing. Yet they were short-handed, and given that their adversary was the Fancy, any missteps could lead to dire consequences. Hadleigh and Hawksmoor had already insisted on escorting their wives, and Charlie couldn't object to one more male coming along. Especially one with Wei's particular abilities.

"If you insist," Glory said.

"I do. And after we make an offering to Ling Ling, you and I are getting to work."

She canted her head. "What are we working on?"

"The basics of lightness *kung fu*."

Her eyes widened, delight zinging through her.

"Hooray!" She clapped her hands. "You're going to teach me here? Now?"

"Here and now." He was once again her calm master, though his eyes held a trace of amusement. "Let me get dressed, and then we shall start by having my cheeky pupil demonstrate her progress with the breathing exercises."

Eighteen

Over the next two days, Mr. Devlin's surveillance of Bryant did not uncover the location of the stolen dogs. Thus, the Angels proceeded with their plan to infiltrate the dogfight. On Friday, Glory obtained Aunt Hypatia's permission to stay the night with Livy, and she and Livy headed over to Charlie's to get ready.

In the courtyard behind Charlie's mansion was a carriage house that she had turned into a training facility. Inside was a sparring chamber and a newer room that the Angels had dubbed "Backstage" due to its resemblance to that area of a theatre.

Standing amidst the dressing tables and wardrobes was Vera Engle, the woman responsible for Backstage. The Angels had met the former actress during an investigation; impressed by her skills and character, they'd introduced her to Charlie, who'd brought her on board as mistress of disguises for the Angels. Vera had jumped at the opportunity to leave the shady theatre where she'd worked and proved both talented and exacting in her new role.

"You're late, doves." Curvy and raven-haired, Vera stuck her hands on her generous hips. "Disguises don't put themselves on, do they?"

"It is my fault," Glory said contritely. "My aunt had to stop at Hatchard's before she dropped me off at Livy's, which is why we're late."

"You ain't the only tardy ones," Vera grumbled. "Fiona's note says that she's running behind too. 'Ow am I supposed to transform you into toffs in less than an hour's time?"

"If anyone can, it's you," Livy said.

"Then let's not waste time tipping over the butter boat." Vera waved them to the dressing screens where she'd already hung their costumes. "I'll give you a hand getting changed."

After Glory and Livy donned their male attire, Vera sat them in front of adjacent dressing tables and set to work.

"So, luv," she said as she brushed cosmetic onto Glory's face. "I 'ear you've a follower."

Beneath the sweeping bristles, Glory's cheeks burned. "Um, where did you hear that?"

Vera snorted. "Where do you think?"

Glory and Livy looked at each other.

"Fiona," they said in unison.

"Well, is it true?" Vera said. "'Ave you found yourself a fellow?"

As Glory chewed on her lip, debating what to say, Livy spoke for her.

"She has, but the fellow in question doesn't know it yet." Livy looked at Glory. "I still say you should have told him."

"How could I?" Glory said miserably. "Mr. Chen had just finished telling me how much I reminded him of his sister."

"One o' those situations, is it?" Vera's face was sympathetic as she thickened Glory's eyebrows. "The bloke you care for don't return your affections?"

"He called me a 'disrespectful pest'." Glory heaved a sigh. "Even though he was teasing me, I wager he wouldn't say that to a lady he was attracted to."

"The attraction *is* two-sided," Livy insisted. "Hadleigh and I both think that there is a special connection between you and Mr.

Chen. You just need to work up the nerve to clarify the situation."

"It's not that simple." Frustrated, Glory tried to explain. "Mr. Chen is my teacher and my friend. And even though I might want more, I don't want to risk losing what I have. I am afraid that if I tell him my feelings, he'll stop giving me lessons. That he might disappear from my life for good."

To prepare her for tonight's assignment, Wei (having called him by his given name, she now couldn't stop thinking of him that way) had given her lessons each of the past three days. Their time together had brought home how much she enjoyed his company. It didn't matter what they were doing. He could be teaching her martial arts, or they could simply be bantering. Since he'd told her about his sister, she felt a deeper connection to him, and she thought he might feel the same way. In his presence, she felt happy and accepted for who she was.

Paradoxically, Wei also set off a trembling tension inside her. Images of him, his gaze smoldering and bulging muscles sheened with sweat, intruded constantly upon her thoughts. At night in her bed, she dreamily reimagined their kiss in the flash house. This time he wasn't wearing his shirt, and she'd felt every hard, rippling ridge of his chest. Beneath her nightgown, her nipples had started throbbing, and she'd touched them, imagining it was Wei's fingers rubbing and pinching. That it was his hand that had traveled lower, between her ribs and down her belly...

"Sorry I'm late!" Fiona tripped in, her cheeks pink and eyes bright.

Flushing, Glory asked, "Is everything all right, Fi? Was it nausea that kept you?"

"Quite the opposite." Fi pranced behind a dressing screen, her voice muffled as she undressed. "I haven't felt this full of energy in ages."

"Then why were you late?" Livy called out.

Fi peered coyly around the edge. "As it happens, Hawksmoor was also feeling rather frisky."

"Fiona Garrity Morgan, you are shameless." Livy's smile was knowing.

"I know. Isn't it wonderful?" With a giggle, Fi ducked back behind the screen.

Witnessing the exchange, Glory felt a wistful pang. She'd always valued her independence; as a young girl, her mama and aunt's self-sufficiency had made an indelible impression. Even after Papa and Mama had reunited, Glory had retained the notion that she would not rely on anyone for her own happiness.

Since meeting Wei, her dreams had undergone a shift. She saw with new clarity what her friends had. A partner who adored them and whom they adored in return. A connection that was passionate and playful, that allowed both partners to grow. She wanted all of that too...if only the object of her affections could feel the same way.

With Vera's help, Fi was soon dressed like a fashionable swell. She took the dressing table next to Glory's.

"Did I miss anything?" she asked.

"Before you arrived, Glory was telling us about 'er fellow." Vera pinned a curly brown wig over Glory's netted hair. "Giving excuses for why she hasn't asked if 'e likes 'er."

"I wasn't making excuses," Glory protested. "Mr. Chen might end our friendship if I tell him I want something more."

"*Or* he might give you something more." Fiona's smile turned sly. "From Livy's description of him when you caught him training, he has rather *a lot* to give."

Glory shot Livy a look.

"What? While I have eyes only for Hadleigh, I am not blind." Livy ruined her attempt at virtuousness by giggling. "I didn't know a man could have that many muscles."

"Mr. Chen's muscles are beside the point," Glory said primly.

"Silly girl, that *is* the point," Fi said. "Physical attraction is part and parcel of falling in love. There is naught to be embarrassed about."

"All right, I do find Mr. Chen excessively attractive," Glory said with a sigh. "But how do I get him to see *me* that way?"

"That's easy, dear." Reaching over, Livy patted her arm. "Just be yourself."

At the tannery, Glory observed the crowd milling around the cage. She recognized some of the gentlemen...which was no surprise. Upper-class men were known to seek thrills in rookeries and slums, trying to cure their ennui with doses of sordidness and danger. Scott was providing his audience with exactly what they wanted.

Scantily clad light-skirts were serving "punch" that was stronger than anything Glory had ever tasted. The mere fumes from her cup made her woozy. Most of the guests looked soused, and some tittered at the sight of Scott's armed cutthroats planted throughout the room. The guards were likely more for theatrics than to prevent any real danger—the louche blue-blooded audience hardly posed a threat—but they did make the Angels' plan a bit trickier to carry out.

Where there's a will, there's a way, Glory thought with determination.

She passed a pair of gentlemen toasting each other.

"Been looking forward to this fight all week, sirrah," one said in a slurred voice. "Nothing like a fight without rules to stir the blood, eh?"

"Watching beasts battle in a cage for their survival is delightfully primitive," his companion drawled, grabbing the derriere of a passing whore. "Well worth the cost of admission, I daresay."

The despicable blackguards. Anger smoldered beneath Glory's breastbone. *Imagine finding such a cruel sport entertaining. Well, no dogs will suffer tonight...not if I can help it.*

In the pockets of her frock coat were a pair of silver flasks. The flasks were in fact devices that emitted a dense and powerful grey smoke when lit. Livy and Fi carried the smoking devices as well. The plan was simple. When the dogs were released into the cage, the Angels would set off the devices. As the crowd panicked and ran for the doors, they would rescue Sir Barkley and as many of the other dogs as possible. Mr. Devlin had a wagon waiting nearby, ready to make a quick escape.

Livy and Fi's husbands were here to assist. As was Wei.

Glory discreetly scanned the audience. Three rows of benches had been arranged on each side of the cage, and Wei had secured a seat in one of the front rows. Sporting fake sideburns and a mustache, he was dressed like a prosperous merchant, his striped waistcoat complete with shiny fobs. Through the metal bars, his gaze met hers, and his poise bolstered her confidence.

The ringing of a bell signaled that the fight was about to begin. As planned, each Angel positioned herself on a different side of the cage, and Glory chose a seat in the section adjacent to Wei's. With simmering anticipation, she watched Bryant climb onto the small platform next to the cage. Tonight, Scott's lieutenant cut a flashy figure in a scarlet jacket with brass buttons.

"Welcome, gents," he announced. "Are ye ready to see some fighting?"

The throng stomped their feet and whistled their approval.

"We ain't talking about polite sparring," Bryant went on. "What you'll be witnessing 'ere tonight will be bare-knuckled and no-holds-barred, a true test of the will to survive!"

The cheering became deafening even as Glory furrowed her brow.

Bare-knuckled? That's an odd way of describing dogfighting.

"The fight will be to the finish. Only one man will be leaving the cage tonight on 'is own two feet."

Man? What man? What is going on—

"Without further ado, 'elp me to welcome the prevailing champion...the one, the only, *the Wolf!*"

The audience surged to their feet, and Glory followed suit. Sure enough, it was Wulfric Scott who came charging into the cage. His silver-brown mane loose and flowing, the leader of the Fancy strutted around the perimeter of the bars, flexing his arms to thunderous cheers. He wore a loose white shirt that was unbuttoned to show the heavy muscles of his chest.

"And his opponent for the eve: the Bulgarian Bear...Ivan Petrov!"

This underground fight is between men...*not dogs.*

As Glory came to that realization, she made eye contact with her team. Fi, who was closest, widened her blue eyes and gave a tiny shrug, as if to say, *"We'll have to wait it out and see what happens..."*

Leaving now would arouse suspicion. They were stuck watching the fight between Scott and the lumbering, shirtless Petrov, who was as bulky and hirsute as his moniker implied.

"The Wolf or the Bear...which shall prevail?" Bryant asked.

"Wolf, Wolf!" the crowd cried.

"In your corners, gents," Bryant said to the fighters. "And remember this: the only rule o' the fight is that..."

He held a hand to his ear, gesturing at the audience to reply.

"*There are no rules,*" the crowd shouted.

Scott shook his head in anticipation. Petrov cracked his beefy knuckles, his smile a checkerboard of stained and missing teeth.

"On your marks...get ready...fight!"

Despite Glory's frustration that Sir Barkley's rescue would not occur this eve, she found herself absorbed by the action in the cage. Petrov swung first, Scott ducking the blow easily. Petrov looked to be the stronger of the two, but he was slower...in all respects. Glory could tell Scott was toying with the Bulgarian, luring him to expend energy. Petrov swung and swung. Finally, he landed a punch, but the blow glanced off Scott's shoulder, the latter looking unfazed. The Bulgarian, however, was breathing heavily, his furry chest heaving and dripping with sweat.

Bouncing on his feet, Scott taunted, "Ain't tired, are you?"

Petrov growled and swung again. The force of his movement took him off-balance, and he staggered forward. Scott pounced.

Glory thought the Wolf was effective, albeit flashy, in his movements. He issued a series of punches to Petrov's gut, causing the other to grunt in pain. Next, he aimed for Petrov's face; his knuckles met the other man's nose in a sickening crack. Petrov doubled over, his blood spurting and splattering the floorboards, and the crowd went wild, stomping their approval.

Grimacing, Glory checked Wei's reaction. He looked unimpressed.

Feeding off the frenzy, Scott pranced around the cage, punching his fists in the air. He was celebrating too soon, however, for Petrov rushed him, pinning him to the bars. Using his weight to trap Scott, the Bear proceeded to pummel his opponent with his outsized fists. Glory winced and the audience grew quiet as the bashing continued.

Suddenly, Scott roared, and with some hidden well of strength, shoved off Petrov. Petrov stumbled, and Scott ran full tilt into him. Tackling the Bulgarian to the ground, Scott leapt astride and hammered his foe in the face. Again and again, he planted his fists, turning Petrov's face into a pulpy mess. The Bulgarian's efforts to stop the onslaught grew weaker and weaker until he stopped moving altogether, his head turning limply to one side.

Finally, Scott rose. Blood dripping from his fists, he turned a ferocious gaze upon the crowd like a predator eyeing his next prey.

"Who's next?" he growled. "Who wants to challenge the Wolf?"

The audience went *mad*.

"*Wolf! Wolf!*" They chanted his name, showering the cage with coins and banknotes.

Scott ripped off his shirt, tipped back his head, and howled. As he stalked around the cage, whipping up the adulation of specta-tors, Glory noticed a jagged scar next to his left shoulder blade... and a distinctive marking on his arm. As he raised his fists, vines of black ink seemed to twist along his right forearm. She couldn't make out the tattoo clearly, but it looked like blooms adorned the creeping lines.

The crowd grew wilder—a cue that the Angels could make their exit. No one would take notice while Scott was giving a show. She looked over at Wei to give him a signal...and drew her brows together at the empty seat.

Where has he gone?

She looked over at Fi, who'd risen but stood frozen, her gaze transfixed on the cage. Glory yanked her own eyes in that direction as Bryant announced, "Gents, we 'ave a challenger!"

Zounds. Her heart toppled into her ribs. *What is Wei doing?*

For her *shifu* was standing in the cage, facing Scott.

"You want to take me on?" Scott taunted.

"Yes."

Skin prickling, Glory had never heard Wei's voice sound so cold. To a stranger, he might seem calm and collected, but she knew him and knew that he was anything but. His hands were clenched at his sides, his broad shoulders taut. His total focus on Scott was nothing short of menacing.

Does Wei have a personal problem with Scott? Why hasn't he mentioned it before? What in heaven's name is going on?

Scott was either unaware or uncaring of the danger he was in.

"Sure are you, that you want to risk your life for money?" Scooping some banknotes, Scott threw them in Wei's face.

Glory's breath caught at the insult, but Wei's grim expression did not alter.

"I don't want money. Only a boon," he stated.

"What kind of boon?" Scott sneered.

"One within your power to give. Assuming you are not afraid to fight me." Wei paused. "If you win—"

"*When* I win, I'll have the satisfaction of knocking that smug expression from your goddamned face," Scott snarled.

"*Wolf! Wolf!*"

The crowd's chanting grew deafening, drowning out the rest of the exchange.

But Scott made his intentions clear by putting up his fists. "Get ready to be pounded into a fare-thee-well."

Removing his coat, Wei tossed it aside and shifted into horse stance. To the uninformed eye, the posture might not look like much, but Glory knew her *shifu*'s power. He was grounded and strong, his thighs rooted like tree trunks. Years of practice, of relentless self-discipline had every one of his honed muscles at his command.

Scott charged, and Wei blocked his swing easily. Scott came again, and this time Wei not only parried but redirected the momentum of the attack to send Scott sprawling. His movement was so smooth, so lightning quick that Scott looked stunned as he picked himself up. Then the Wolf's face contorted with rage, and in that moment, Glory knew her *shifu* had already won.

Scott charged at Wei, who this time stopped the other's fist with his palm. Scott tried to pull free from Wei's grip, and with a look of shock, discovered he could not. With a bellow, he threw a punch with his other hand, only to find that fist trapped by Wei as well. With breath-stopping power, Wei spun and flipped Scott over his head, the movement as fluid as water.

The audience let out a collective gasp as the gang leader landed on his back with a thud.

Nervously, Glory noted that Scott's guards were closing in on the cage. A half-dozen men, their hands on their weapons, prepared to intervene. She looked at Fi and Livy. She drew out one of her flasks; they nodded, doing the same. With that wordless communication, she knew they were ready to act on her signal.

Scott staggered to his feet, sputtering, "You're going to pay for that, you bugger."

Wei said nothing as he sank into a crouch, the weight balanced on his back leg while his front leg pointed straight out. He held out a hand, bending his fingers in a beckoning gesture.

With a snarl, Scott charged at him. Wei sprang into the air with an athleticism that made Glory's heart thump with wonder. His kick caught Scott in the jaw, the power of it sending the latter flying backward into the side of the cage. A second later, Wei was there, his hand around Scott's throat, pinning the gang leader to the bars.

She swallowed at the bloody murder in Wei's eyes.

NINETEEN

The roaring crowd faded to nothing. Wei's focus was only on his purpose.

He tightened his grip on Scott's throat.

"Give me my boon," he said.

"Wh-what the bloody hell do you want?" Scott snarled between gasps.

"Answers." Wei was cold inside—as cold as the vengeance that his instincts told him was finally within reach. "Another man bears the same tattoo as you. He would be in his forties or thereabouts. Pale eyes. Do you know him?"

As the question left Wei, he already knew the answer. Felt it in Scott's compulsive swallow, the widening of the other's gaze.

He knows. Wei felt an icy blast of triumph. *He knows the man who killed my family.*

"Go bugger yourself," Scott gritted out. "I don't have to tell you anything."

Scott struck out. Parrying the flailing fists was child's play.

Wei dug his fingers into the other's throat. "Tell me his name."

"F-fuck you."

Wei squeezed until Scott's face turned red. If he wanted, he could crush the other's windpipe, crumple it like a piece of paper in his fist. But Scott wasn't the one whose blood he wanted on his hands.

"Tell me your friend's name," he said steadily.

Scott made a gargling noise.

"Let 'im go, you bastard, or I'll shoot!"

A quick glance revealed that three guards had entered the cage, surrounding Wei. They were large and obviously slow-footed since it had taken them this long to intervene.

Wei moved, yanking Scott from the bars and switching their positions. Scott now faced his men, Wei behind him. Wei twisted Scott's arm behind his back whilst continuing to grip the man's throat.

"Shoot, and your leader dies first," Wei said.

The brutes looked indecisively at one another, their weapons wavering. Stupid as well as slow, which worked to Wei's advantage. He was going to get his answers from Scott, and he wouldn't let anyone stand in his way.

"Wei, look out!"

Glory's voice punctured Wei's concentration. He turned his head, seeing a guard outside the cage a few feet away, his pistol aimed in Wei's direction. Before the man could shoot, Glory dove into him, tackling him to the ground. But the brute was huge, outweighing her by at least five stone. He rolled atop her, getting the upper hand.

Wei's vision flashed scarlet.

No one hurts Glory. She's mine.

In a raging heartbeat, he made his decision. With a frustrated growl, he struck his palm into Scott's back, the force of his hit sending the other flying into two of the guards. The brutes toppled under the weight of their leader while the remaining man tried to get off a shot. Wei leapt into the air, a bullet whizzing past him an instant before he planted his foot into the guard's chest. The man sailed backward, smacking his head against the bars and slumping to the ground.

With a last fierce look at Scott, who was struggling to get up, Wei exited the cage. He shoved past the fleeing crowd, getting to Glory. He yanked the attacker off her and knocked the bastard unconscious with a strike to the head.

He pulled Glory to her feet just as Scott and his men staggered from the cage. Shielding her body with his, Wei readied to do battle.

"Don't worry," she whispered. "I've got this."

He saw that she'd lit a match and was holding it to the bottom of a flask. He spotted the other Angels doing the same. Glory lit the fuse, tossing the device to the ground, and thick grey smoke billowed into the air. He had an instant to meet Scott's slitted stare, and his shoulders bunched with fury—with the need to seize what had so long eluded him.

I'm so damned close—

Glory slipped her hand into his, tugging urgently.

"Let's go."

Glory, Wei, and the rest of the team made a quick escape to the alley where three carriages were waiting. Fi and Hawksmoor went off with Mr. Devlin while Livy and Hadleigh boarded their own vehicle.

When Glory didn't follow, Livy poked her head out the window. "Aren't you coming?"

Glory looked at Wei, who returned her gaze stonily.

"I'm going with Mr. Chen," she said.

Livy narrowed her eyes. "Are you certain that's a good idea? After he—"

She was cut off by Hadleigh, who murmured something in her ear.

After a moment, Livy turned back to Glory with a sigh. "All right, but do be careful—"

"I'll be back at your house soon," Glory promised.

Then she quickly followed Wei to his conveyance. On the driver's perch, Mr. Yao winked at her, tipping his cap, and she smiled back. Yet her smile faded as she found herself alone in the carriage with Wei. Removing their wigs and mustaches, they sat facing each other in silence. Seeing the stark set of his features, his twitching jaw, she waited for him to speak first. But after they crossed the Thames, she couldn't wait any longer.

"What happened back there?" she asked.

"You should not have interfered," he said curtly.

"*I* interfered?" She gawked at him. "We were in the middle of a mission, and out of nowhere, you attacked our main suspect. What was going on?"

He clenched his jaw. "I had my reasons."

"And I would like to know what they are."

"A student does not question her *shifu*."

"This particular one does." Taking a breath, she went to sit beside him. "What made you go after Scott like that? I have never seen you so...so out of control."

"I had everything in hand." Emotion flashed in his eyes. "If you hadn't risked your bloody neck—"

"That guard was going to shoot you! I couldn't stand by and let that happen. Not when you mean..." She cut herself off, shaking her head fiercely. "When you're my teacher and my friend. But you're avoiding my question. Do you know Scott...have some sort of quarrel with him? If so, why didn't you say anything—"

"Because I didn't know until tonight." Wei's eyes smoldered, his hands curling.

"Didn't know what?"

"I don't wish to talk about it."

"But you will," she insisted.

"Why? Because you are a duke's daughter who is used to getting her way?"

She flinched. He'd never spoken so coldly to her before. Yet the soft snarl in his voice was like that of a wounded animal; she knew he was hurt and trying to push her away.

"Because I am your friend," she said steadily. "Whatever is going on, I want to help."

"You cannot help."

"How do you know unless you let me try?"

"I don't want you involved." His expression was harder than granite. "That is final."

Final? He might as well wave a red flag in front of a bull.

"This has to do with your quest, doesn't it?" She plowed on, trying to put together the pieces of what she knew. "You said you're trying to retrieve something irreplaceable. Does Scott have it?"

"Leave it be, Glory," he ordered.

Anguish smoldered in his gaze, held back by rigid self-control. Like the time at his clinic.

Her intuition flashed. "Does this have to do with Ling Ling?"

The answer carved itself onto his face. Lines of pain bracketed his eyes, his mouth. His chest surged, and her own tightened with horrible empathy. With the knowledge that she'd unintentionally twisted a knife.

"I'm sorry," she whispered. "I didn't mean to cause you pain—"

"You didn't. You weren't the one who murdered my sister," he said flatly.

Murdered...Ling Ling was murdered?

Stunned, Glory stammered, "But who...who could be so cruel? To a little girl..."

For long moments, only the clopping of hooves filled the carriage. Time seemed to still, and Glory sensed a parallel between that swaying darkness and Wei's mood. He was fighting something, going back and forth trying to decide if he could release the shadows he kept locked inside.

"You can trust me," she said.

Wei expelled a breath. "I know."

"Then talk to me."

A pause.

"Fifteen years ago, while I was away, an intruder broke into my family's home. He was looking for something...and killed my parents and sister. Our old servant, too. I have been hunting him down since, and that is why I am in London."

Although Wei's tone was matter-of-fact, the horror of what he shared swept through Glory like a winter storm. She felt chilled, inside and out.

"Wei, I...I'm so sorry."

The words were stupid, wholly inadequate. Yet what would be a comforting response to such a random act of violence?

Her eyes damp, she tried again. "I cannot imagine the pain of... of losing your family. And in such a fashion."

Wei gave a nod, that small, controlled movement conveying a world of grief.

"When I arrived home that night, I fought the murderer, but he got away." Wei's knuckles gleamed bone-white in the darkness. "He was masked, so I saw only his eyes, which were pale...the exact color, I could not say. He spoke with an Englishman's accent. During our battle, his shirt ripped, and I saw a tattoo on his arm— the same tattoo that I saw on Scott's arm tonight."

Glory drew her brows together. "But if this happened fifteen years ago, Scott would be too young to be the killer, wouldn't he?"

"Yes. But he knows the man with whom he shares that tattoo. I saw it in his eyes tonight," Wei said grimly. "He chose to protect that bastard, but I vow on my family's honor that I *will* get my answers from him. I will find the murderer and avenge my family."

"I will help you," Glory said immediately.

Now that she understood what was at stake, she would do everything in her power to assist Wei. To help him find the justice he and his family deserved.

"You will stay out of it," he said sharply. "This has nothing to do with you."

"If the situation were reversed and I was on a quest to right a horrendous injustice, would you stand by and do nothing? Would you abandon me in my time of need?"

Her questions were rhetorical. From the time they'd met, Wei had always been there when she needed him. Had offered her his protection and friendship and care.

"That is different," he bit out.

She narrowed her eyes. "I sincerely hope that statement does not conclude with 'because I am a man and you are a woman'."

"This is different," he said through gritted teeth, "because if anything happened to you because of me, I...I could not stand it. Do you understand?"

"I think I do," she said tremulously.

Because, she thought, she finally did. Everything she'd wanted she saw now in his glittering gaze, the sentiments he was rigidly holding in check. And it gave her hope...hope and courage.

"Good," he said stiffly. "As your *shifu*, it is my responsibility to keep you safe—"

"I want more," she said.

"I beg your pardon?"

"I want to be more than your pupil." She reached out and took his hand before she lost the nerve. "Wei, I...I have feelings for you."

His strong, callused fingers closed over hers. An instant later, he released her as if she were a burning-hot coal.

"You are mistaken," he said gruffly. "You are a young and innocent lady—"

"Who knows what she wants," she reminded him. "You know that about me. Well, I know I want *you*...as more than a *shifu*. More than a friend."

As his silence stretched, some of her courage deserted her, and she dropped her eyes to her lap, to her nervously clasped hands.

"I've known since we kissed, even though I was too afraid to admit it. Too afraid that you didn't feel the same way about me." She drew a shuddering breath but couldn't force herself to look up and find rejection staring back at her. "I know I'm not pretty or popular or what most gentlemen would consider attractive. But I *am* a lady who is true to her heart. I suppose what I'm trying to ask is...do you think you could want me? Want to be more than my friend?"

TWENTY

She was killing him. Laying waste to his defenses and self-control. In his thirty-three years, Wei had never felt such a potent mix of admiration, tenderness, and desire.

He tipped her chin up, stared into her embarrassed eyes. The most beautiful eyes he'd ever seen. Eyes that stripped away thoughts of honor and revenge, right and wrong. The shining light of her honesty illuminated the truth he'd tried to hide—from her and himself. The longing that he'd tried to stave off with *kung fu*, denial, and whatever he'd had at his disposal now washed over him in an overwhelming tide.

"Glory," he said hoarsely. "I want you so damned badly."

Her smile, one of surprise and relief, made his heart contract. He didn't know how this enchanting young woman could doubt herself. All he knew was that her vulnerability laid him bare. Years of frustration, anger, and despair suddenly morphed into a yearning that was beyond lust. Beyond anything he'd ever felt for a woman. He held her face in his hands, sweeping his thumbs over her silky cheeks.

Then he kissed her.

Her lips were as warm and soft as he remembered, her taste

even more intoxicating. He'd intended to kiss her with more finesse this time, but she slid her hands into his hair, pulling him closer, and her eagerness unleashed an ungovernable hunger. He began devouring her mouth, and she kissed him back with equal ardor. Dragging his lips over hers, he ran his tongue over her plump, rosy seam.

With a breathless sigh, she let him in, and he shook with lust at her sweet surrender. He plunged his tongue into her warmth, and she licked him back, shyly at first, then with growing boldness. A quick study at this like everything else. Recalling her abashed confession that he'd been the first man to kiss her, he felt a surge of pride and primal satisfaction. Her tongue moved with his, a wet, delicious dance that made his pulse race as if he'd been training for hours. She moaned, pressing herself against him, impatient as always.

He lowered her onto the cushions, taking his time with their kiss. Exploring her slick, sweet heat until she was wiggling beneath him. Her male garb made her femininity even more pronounced. He could feel the softness of her slender form, her delicate curves designed to fit against his hard edges.

He nuzzled her ear. "Patience, sweeting. We're in no hurry."

"Speak for yourself."

He had to smile at her breathless words and wondrous eyes. Then he drew her earlobe into his mouth. Sucking and licking until she was clutching his shoulders, her sweet desperation causing his blood to rush. He tugged off her neckcloth and unbuttoned her waistcoat. He kissed the downy line of her throat, his mouth pooling at the scent of her orchid-fresh skin.

"What is the rush?" he murmured.

"You...you might change your mind. About wanting this. Wanting me."

He jerked his head up and saw that she was in earnest.

"A lack of wanting has never been the problem, Glory." Despite his pounding lust, he matched her serious tone because he didn't want to leave her with any doubts. "I've always wanted you, but I tried to deny it. Because you belong to a different world. Because you deserve someone better than me. Because I should be focused on my—"

"You're the only one I want," she said adamantly. "And I won't get in the way of your quest, I promise. We can work together."

His throat tightened. For fifteen years, he'd walked a lonely path. To be offered such sweet and unconditional companionship now unraveled the vestiges of his self-control.

"I am done fighting my desire for you," he said hoarsely.

Because he was. Done wasting his energy. Done trying to deny the word that had flashed in his head from their very first kiss: *mine*. It was something he'd never had, a woman who was truly and exclusively his. Yet from the start, Glory had pulled at his protective instincts, as if some part of him had known she belonged to him. Even if she was forbidden.

Right now, all that matters is that she's mine.

Her lashes quivered. "I am so glad—"

Whatever else she meant to say was lost as he lay claim to her mouth.

If their first kiss had ignited the spark of passion in Glory, then their second one threw tinder on the flames. She'd never felt this desperate before. Like she was burning up with a fever yet needed more heat. And she knew the only cure for this condition was Wei.

Wei, the only man who'd ever made her feel this way.

Who, miracle of miracles, felt the same way about her.

Trembling with joy and desire, she gave herself over to his plundering kiss. She needed more, all, everything she could have of him. His touch sent need pulsing through her veins, making her skin itchy and hot. His lips skimmed over her nose, her jaw, into the open collar of her shirt. He kissed her throat, and she squirmed.

"Are you this sensitive everywhere, my sweet?" he murmured.

"I don't know," she said breathlessly. "No one has ever kissed me there before."

"Good."

His proprietary tone sent tingles flowing up her spine, as did the dark flare of promise in his eyes.

She trembled as he undid her waistcoat, then moved on to the buttons of her shirt. His fingertips rasped against her skin as he parted the linen panels with care, as if unwrapping a present. Her heart bumped against her ribs as he exposed her breasts, which weren't exactly a gift of bounty. Her curves were so scant that she hadn't bothered to bind them. Would he find her lacking?

His nostrils flared. "You're delicate. So pretty."

She felt herself flushing. "They're not much—*ooh*."

She moaned again as he thumbed the stiff buds, teasing them with his callused pads. When he pinched one throbbing tip, she jerked and felt a rush of wetness at her core.

"Sensitive, as I thought." Satisfaction deepened his voice. "Let's see what else you like."

She gasped as he closed his lips around her nipple. At the hot, wet swirl of his tongue, her spine arched off the cushions. He went back and forth, licking a trail between her pulsating peaks until she thought she might go mad with bliss.

"Heavens," she panted. "What are you doing to me?"

"I'm kissing your delectable breasts. They are sweet and perfect"—he did something with his tongue that forced the air from her lungs—"just like you."

"I don't know if I can take anymore. I feel so strange, so awash..."

She couldn't describe what she was feeling...the twisting desperation, the ever-tightening coil in her lower belly.

"Are you wet, sweeting?"

Heat flooded her cheeks. His gaze was knowing and male; it made her aware of the gap in experience between them. In this and martial arts, she was clearly the novice. Even though she was an eager student, modesty made it impossible to answer him.

When she wriggled in embarrassment, a wicked glint came into his eyes.

"Can it be that my bold little tigress is bashful?" he asked softly.

She bit her lip. "I...I just can't..."

"Let me help you then."

He shifted, and suddenly she felt his hard thigh wedging between her legs, against the place where she'd grown shockingly damp. He pressed that sinewy ledge deeper, rubbing against her neediest place, setting off sparks of delight that pushed a whimper from her lips.

"There," he rasped. "Does that feel good?"

"Y-yes."

"Move your hips, sweeting. Rub your pussy against me."

Mesmerized by his sensual command, uttered in a tone like the one he used during their lessons, she couldn't help but obey. The friction of his muscular thigh against her sensitive cleft created waves of pleasure. The coil of need tightened and tightened, and she gave in to the impulse to move her hips faster, blushing as he stared down at her with unyielding intensity, gauging her every response.

"You are so lovely." He cupped her cheek, his gaze like glittering onyx. "I can feel how wet and hot you are. Ride my leg harder, sweeting, and make yourself come."

His naughty instructions blazed fire through her veins. She rocked her hips, chasing the relief that seemed just out of reach. Whimpering, she felt need winding tighter and tighter as she rubbed herself against his rock-hard thigh...

Suddenly, he bent his head, capturing her nipple between his lips. The hot suction seemed to pull at her very core. He drew on her nipple as he thrust his leg against the sensitive peak of her pussy, and she felt something spring free.

Pleasure flooded her, and she chanted his name. He kissed her, pressing and circling his thigh against her fluttering cove, prolonging the waves of her release. Afterward, as she floated in a blissful cloud, he set her to rights, the brush of his calluses against her skin making her satiated nerves quiver anew.

He sat her up, cuddling her against him. The carriage was still moving, the horses clip-clopping along. Yet everything felt different...changed.

She gazed at him in wonder. "I never knew."

"Knew what, sweeting?"

She tried to explain. "What all the...the fuss was about."

His lips curved. "And now you do?"

At her tremulous nod, his smile reached his eyes.

"I am glad." He tucked a stray strand behind her ear. "Was it worth the wait?"

"*You* were worth it," she said with feeling.

His gaze smoldered, and he leaned toward her. When she placed a hand on his chest, he stopped, tilting his head in question. She slid a glance at his lap, where the thick, unabated ridge of his arousal was clearly visible.

"What...um, what about you?" She chewed on her lip. "Should I do anything?"

"You've had enough adventures tonight, love. And I am a patient man."

When she furrowed her brow, not sure that she wanted him to exercise his much-vaunted powers of restraint, he kissed her. His hot, commanding claim vaporized her arguments, turning her into boneless mush. He framed her face with his hands, rubbed his thumb over her swollen lips, and what he said next made her melt even more.

"After all, little tigress, you were worth waiting for, too."

TWENTY-ONE

The following afternoon, Wei descended the carriage in front of Glory's home. The sun filtered through the leafy bowers, gilding the spotless brick-fronted mansions. The pavement looked freshly swept, and birdsong and blooms were in abundance. When Wei had left the clinic, fog and smoke had choked the sky, a brisk wind skirling leaves and litter over the muddy roads. Mayfair seemed not just like a different neighborhood, but a different world.

Standing amid that bastion of privilege, Wei felt his misgivings rise like specters.

She is too far above you. You are not worthy of her. The last time you crossed this line, it led to disaster.

But this was Glory, not Chun. Glory was different—unlike any lady he'd known. He thought of her vulnerability, her sweet avowal that all she wanted was him. The way she'd lit incense for his sister and offered to help him in his quest. The way she'd rubbed her wet little pussy against his thigh and cried his name when she came.

"Don't lose your nerve now, brother." From the driver's perch, Yao spoke in their native tongue.

Wei shot his *shidai* an annoyed look, answering, "When have I ever done that?"

"There's always a first time. And in all the years we've known each other, you have never gone courting." Yao smirked. "An activity that is known to incite fear in the bravest of men."

Wei felt his neck heat. Denial was pointless since Yao had been the one who'd driven him and Glory last night. As Yao had taken an extended detour around Regent's Park, he'd undoubtedly known what was happening inside the carriage. He had also spotted Wei practicing *kung fu* at dawn. With his arousal unabating, Wei had been trying to work off some of his humming energy because he didn't want to find pleasure by his own hand.

He hadn't lied when he told Glory he was a patient man. Some things in life were worth the wait, and she was one of them. When he ended his self-imposed celibacy, he wanted it to be with her. Wanted to plant himself deep inside her snug pussy, to hear her breathless whimpers, and to feel her come and come around his cock.

He made a clearing sound in his throat and rapped on the side of the carriage. "Don't bother waiting. I'll take a hackney back."

"Good luck." Yao took up the reins. "It's good to see you focused on happiness for a change."

As Wei watched his *shidai* drive away, he was troubled by Yao's words. He understood that Yao had intended them to be supportive, but his *shidai*'s observation had an opposite effect, stirring up his guilt. How could Wei think about his own desires when he had yet to avenge his family?

You promised Glory that you would call today. That you would discuss the Scott situation with her before taking further action. Maybe she can help with your revenge after all.

It had been the one thing Glory had asked of him before he'd dropped her off at the Hadleighs'. She'd begged him not to go after Scott until they'd had a chance to strategize. Since the gang leader was now of interest to both him and the Angels, she'd argued that they should coordinate their efforts, especially since Scott would be on guard now and even more difficult to corner. She'd reasoned that the key to success for both their missions was to work as a team.

He also knew that his little tigress would have more questions about his past. Last night, he'd provided a bare-bones version of his history; if they were to be a team, he would have to tell her the truth...all of it. The shameful secrets he hadn't shared with anyone except his *shifu* and *shidai*. What would Glory think of him if he told her why his family had been killed? Would she despise him— want nothing more to do with a man whose despicable behavior had destroyed the people closest to him?

His chest knotted. She was such an honorable little thing, fiercely loyal to those lucky enough to be in her circle. How could she accept the scoundrel he'd once been? Hell, there were times when he could barely stomach himself...and he'd spent years meditating, trying to come to peace with what he'd done. Yet acceptance still eluded him.

Still, he owed it to her to tell her everything. Not because of their mutual purpose but because he had made love to her. Last night, he had crossed a line—several lines, actually. While he could not bring himself to regret their encounter, he knew things were far from settled. She deserved to know the man she had become involved with. To have full knowledge of the facts so that she could decide whether she found him a worthy suitor.

For his part, he needed to figure out how to negotiate his honor with his desires.

Can I avenge my family and find joy for myself? Is it right for me to court a lady so far above me...and who is my pupil to boot? Now that I've tasted her sweetness, can I bring myself to let her go?

Thus, Wei had many things to discuss with Glory today. His past, their present, and perhaps even...even their future. While the agenda was not a little daunting, he felt a churning anticipation. He'd never known a woman whom he trusted enough to share his innermost thoughts and secrets. Never known that a female could incite such a heady mix of lust, liking, and longing. Never thought he'd find her in London of all places, when he'd all but abandoned that old dream of happiness.

Eager to see his little tigress, he strode to the door and rang the bell.

The butler greeted him, ushering him into the antechamber. "Wait here, sir."

But he didn't have to wait because Glory came rushing in, pretty as a picture in her butter-yellow dress. Then he noticed her wide eyes; she looked...oddly panicked? Before he could ask what was amiss, a tall, well-dressed gentleman emerged from the hallway behind her. With mahogany hair threaded with silver and a neatly groomed mustache and beard, the fellow had the kind of dashing good looks and lazy confidence that undoubtedly made him popular with the ladies.

His golden gaze, however, was sharp as a blade as he looked Wei up and down.

His eyebrow winged. "You must be the chap I've been hearing about."

"Papa, may I present my *shifu*, Master Chen." Glory wetted her lips nervously. "Master Chen, this is my father, the Duke of Ranelagh and Somerville."

Waking up this morning at Livy's house, Glory had felt groggy. Her body had been warm and relaxed as if she'd engaged in vigorous exercise...and then reality had hit her. Wei had said that he was attracted to her—and proved it in the carriage last night! Hugging a pillow to her chest, she'd dreamily relived those steamy moments.

Wei had been as masterful at lovemaking as he was everything else. His kiss, his touch...he'd gifted her with pleasure and made her feel beautiful. Her pussy fluttered, as did her heart. For Wei had also shown his trust in her by confiding about his past. About his unimaginable loss. And she was determined to help him find his family's killer.

With that thought in mind, she'd rung for the maid, dressed, and went to find Livy. Fiona and Pippa had already arrived, cake box in hand, all agog to hear about Glory's adventures last eve. Over a breakfast of Gunter's delectable treats, Glory had blushingly acknowledged that Wei was indeed attracted to her, and the Angels had cheered and shared a happy dance around the drawing room. They'd created such a ruckus that Hadleigh had looked in. Used to his wife's foibles by now, he'd shaken his head, lips twitching, and continued on his way.

After the celebrating, Glory had had to answer her friends' questions about Wei's behavior at the tannery. Since she could not betray Wei's confidence, she'd merely affirmed that he'd had valid reasons for confronting the gang leader.

"Scott is proving a popular fellow." Livy had tapped her chin. "Yet it was clear last night that the cages serve a human, rather than canine, purpose. And we saw no signs of Sir Barkley or any other dog. We have no actual proof of Scott's involvement in the dognapping scheme...except for the charm worn by his dog Beauregard."

"But Farwell showed up at the tannery," Glory said. "That cannot be a coincidence."

"You have a point," Fi replied. "But the one he was talking to was Bryant, not Scott."

"We should tail both Scott and Bryant." Livy's nod had been decisive. "Round the clock, and we shall see where that leads us."

The Angels had divvied up shifts for the week. Then Glory had hurried to get ready, for her aunt was due to pick her up, and Wei had promised to come by her home this afternoon under the guise of giving her another lesson. She couldn't wait to see him.

She'd lapsed into a romantic daydream when her ride arrived. To her surprise, it wasn't Aunt Hypatia who'd come to fetch her but her parents. They had returned early from the house party. Glory had been excited to see them, but during the reunion back at home, Aunt Patty had mentioned Glory's lessons with Wei. This had led to a barrage of parental questions; Papa, in particular, had seemed concerned about Glory's unconventional new interest. While Glory adored her father, he tended to be overprotective. The only thing that had stalled his interrogation had been the arrival of Wei himself.

Which brought her to the present moment.

Papa and Mama were seated at the ends of the table, Glory and Wei across from each other in the middle. Glory's aunt sat beside her whilst her brothers, twelve-year-old Horatio and ten-year-old Theodore, flanked Wei. Having seen a recent show at Astley's Amphitheatre that had included Chinese acrobats and a demonstration of martial arts, the dark-haired boys were bombarding Wei with questions.

Can you break a stack of boards in half with your bare hand, Mr. Chen? How high can you leap into the air? Can you swallow a knife and jump through a ring of fire?

An amused glint in his eyes, Wei responded to her brothers with admirable patience. Yet they were not the only ones expressing curiosity. The reason her father had insisted that Wei join them for the meal soon became clear. In addition to lunch, Papa was apparently serving the Spanish Inquisition.

"Hypatia tells us that you are an accounted expert in pugilism and healing." While Papa helped himself to pressed tongue and potted asparagus offered by one of the footmen, his gaze was narrowed upon Wei. "Odd combination, that."

"I teach *kung fu* at my clinic, Your Grace," Wei replied. "It is a healthful discipline that trains both the body and the mind. My teacher, Shifu Lam, belonged to an order of monks famed for their fighting and healing skills, and he passed on his knowledge to me."

Glory was relieved at his courteousness. He'd been the perfect gentleman, handling her father's grilling with remarkable equanimity for the last half hour. Since he'd dropped her off early this morning, he must have gone to bed later than she had, yet he radiated virility, the black waves of his hair gleaming, his somber clothing hugging his sculpted form.

"A monk, eh?" Cutting his meat into precise pieces, Papa smiled sardonically. "I don't suppose you adhere to that tradition as well."

Glory didn't know what horrified her more: the personal nature of Papa's inquiry or the possibility that he'd somehow guessed what was going on between her and Wei. With the exception of her investigative work, she tried not to keep things from her parents. But she wasn't ready to expose her fledgling relationship to them. She and Wei had acted upon their attraction mere hours ago; they hadn't addressed the topic of the future...which would, most likely, prove to be a complicated topic. She did not want to add outside interference to the mix until they'd had a chance to talk.

"No, Your Grace." Wei met her father's gaze squarely. "I have not taken any monastic vows."

Glory's heart pitter-pattered at his direct response. While many men kowtowed to her father's ducal status, Wei did not. She adored his confidence and how comfortable he was in his own skin.

"What a surprise," Papa said under his breath.

"I, for one, would like to hear more about your clinic, Master Chen." Mama cut in smoothly, her emerald gaze warm and her smile genuine. "Hypatia has shared her admiration for your pedagogy, and I must say I am impressed that you've established such a unique clinic in London."

Glory sent her mother a grateful look. Although Mama appeared every inch a duchess with her cinnamon hair arranged in ringlets, her voluptuous figure draped in a fringed cassis-colored walking dress, she retained the friendly and down-to-earth manner that had once made her an excellent businesswoman. Born into a working-class family, Mama had not forgotten her roots nor made any attempt to hide her origins since marrying Papa. Her lack of pretension had, ironically, garnered the respect of high society.

That and the fact that she, a fossils shop owner and former barmaid, had managed to land Papa, who'd once been dubbed the Duke of "Ransom"—a witty amalgamation of his titles and reference to his ability to steal female hearts.

"Like many things in life, my work at the clinic started by chance, Your Grace," Wei said politely. "During my sea voyage to London, many of the sailors had problems performing their duties due to their opium use. The captain even threatened to abandon them at the next port. Since I had assisted my *shifu* in treating this problem, I convinced the captain to let me have a go at helping these men. I encountered success, and when I arrived in London, the captain continued to send me clients. Word spread, and over time I was able to help people from all walks of life stop their use of opium and instead engage in more healthful practices, such as *kung fu*."

"What a novel approach," Mama said.

"I suppose your countrymen have advanced methods for treating the opium habit," Papa said with grudging interest. "Given the prevalence of the problem in China."

"Due to the smuggling of opium into China by foreign interests," Wei said flatly.

"You will find no argument from this quarter." Creases deepening around his mouth, Papa rotated his teacup a quarter-turn in its saucer. "The opium trade is a disgrace and stain on our national honor."

"Papa is one of the foremost advocates in the House of Lords against the opium trade," Glory said proudly. "In fact, he has a plan to educate the public about the atrocities and to introduce a bill to ban the unlawful commerce."

"The plan will soon become a reality." Papa's eyes had a zealous gleam. "At the house party, Emmett Rothwell agreed to back my campaign and roped in several of his well-connected cronies as well. We are gaining momentum, and if all goes smoothly, I hope to introduce that bill next month."

"Jolly well done, Papa," Glory said happily.

"Papa deserves credit for his commitment to the cause. While Mr. Rothwell has clout, it was your father who convinced the guests with his eloquent arguments. He worked day and night at the house party," Mama said proudly.

"Not every night, Maggie mine."

Papa smiled lazily at Mama, and she blushed.

"And the effort was not mine alone," he went on. "Rothwell's nephew and private secretary, Matthew Winslow, took up the banner as well. He orchestrated several key meetings with new donors to the campaign."

"You are far too modest, darling." Beaming at Papa, Mama raised her teacup. "We are so proud of you."

"It was nothing really," Papa said.

But he looked rather pleased as they toasted him.

Glory thought that Wei was looking at her father with new respect.

Soon thereafter, her brothers began pestering Wei again.

"Will you teach me some *kung fu* after lunch, Mr. Chen?" Horatio wheedled.

"Me too!" Not to be left out, Theo exclaimed, "I wish to have lessons too."

"That will be up to your parents, Masters Horatio and Theodore," Wei said gravely.

Papa shook his head. "Lads, I am not certain—"

"Please, Papa," Theo cajoled. "We want to learn how to smash boards and swallow swords!"

Glory stifled a smile as her parents exchanged dubious looks.

Theo's arguments weren't exactly helping his cause. When it came to negotiation, the ten-year-old still had a lot to learn.

"If Glory gets to learn *kung fu*, then so should we," Horatio stated. "It would not be fair otherwise."

Her other brother, on the other hand, was a more seasoned negotiator. He was at an age where fairness was the principle by which everything was measured. He kept track of the privileges accorded to each sibling and at what age each was allowed to do what. As Papa had dryly remarked, Horatio would someday make an excellent man of business.

"Whether Glory continues her lessons is a matter still up for consideration," Papa said. "I would not tie my argument to that particular ship as yet, lad."

All amusement fled Glory as she realized that her own position was in jeopardy.

"What is there to consider, Papa?" she said swiftly. "You know the incidence of crime has soared. As a young woman, I need to have the skills to protect myself—"

"As your papa, it is my privilege to safeguard you and your reputation," Papa countered. "You are a well-bred young lady. No offense to Chen, but his student population consists mainly of opium users. He is hardly the best choice of teacher for you, poppet."

She flushed at his endearment, which made her sound all of eight years old.

"I am not a little girl." She angled her chin up. "I can make my own decisions."

"Be that as it may, you are my daughter and will do as I say." Papa stirred his tea with undue care. "Until further notice, your lessons will be put on hold."

"That is dashed unfair!" Glory turned pleading eyes to her mother. "Do something, Mama. *Please.*"

"Rhys, darling, why don't we discuss this in private after

lunch?" Mama said pleasantly. "Cook has prepared a soufflé for dessert, and we should enjoy it at its prime."

With a sigh, Papa relented. "As you wish, Maggie mine."

"I cannot believe my papa," Glory fumed as she accompanied Wei to the antechamber. "He has no right to stop my lessons."

"Actually, His Grace has every right," Wei said somberly. "He is your father, after all."

She cast a quick glance around. They only had a few moments of privacy before Greaves returned with Wei's outerwear.

"Well, he is not going to stop me from seeing you," she said fiercely.

Wei's frown sent a sudden chill through her.

"Unless...unless you don't want to see me?" she asked.

"I do want to see you, little tigress."

The firmness of his reply and the endearment eased her fear.

"There are things we need to discuss," he said quietly, "but I do not wish to create problems with your father—"

"We'll talk when I come to the clinic tonight," she whispered.

"What? No." He lowered his brows. "I forbid it. It is not safe—"

The crisp resonance of leather soles against marble made them both spring back.

"Your hat and coat, sir," Greaves said.

As Wei donned the items, he leveled a stern look at Glory.

"As I was saying, my lady," he said. "I advise patience when practicing your lessons. No hasty moves."

"Of course, *Shifu*." Glory's reply was airy. "I would not dream of doing anything rash."

Twenty-Two

"Maybe this was a *teensy* bit rash," Glory said breathlessly.

Winding himself tightly around her neck, FF II hissed his agreement into her ear.

At present, she was clinging to a drainpipe, hovering some thirty feet off the ground. Her plan had seemed simple: exit her bedchamber via the rear balcony, climb down the metal pipe, and hail a hackney to Wei's clinic. Afterward, she would return the way she left, with no one the wiser.

Unfortunately, the pipe chose not to cooperate.

It had held when she'd tested it. But a few feet into her journey, the metal brackets securing the top section to the wall had snapped off, and Glory found herself holding on for dear life as the pipe swayed and bent over the courtyard below. As she chanced a glance down, her cap fell off, falling a dizzying distance. She debated resuming her downward climb, but the slightest movement caused the metal to curve further. The pipe gave an ominous groan that suggested it might snap and send her crashing onto the stones below.

She was too far to get back to her own balcony. Nor could she reach the balcony on the other side. In essence, she was trapped, and the only way to go was down. The pipe groaned again, and she knew there was no time to waste. She could cry for help, but by the time anyone reached her, it would be too late.

I'll have to make a go for the balcony. Swing as hard as I can and try to grab the railing. I'll use lightness kung fu, *and hopefully it will carry me the distance.*

"FF II, it's safer for you to climb down. The pipe will hold you," she whispered. "You have to go."

The ferret made a *tuk-tuk* of refusal and wound himself tighter around her.

"Go, boy. Please, we haven't much time—"

"Don't move." Wei's urgent command came from the darkness below. "I'll be right there."

Relief flowed through her even as the pipe bent further. Turning her head as much as she dared, she saw Wei in the courtyard. He took a running start and jumped onto the side of the house. Her panicked heart thumped even faster at his power and agility. Even though she knew he was using lightness *kung fu* to find the footholds and position his body for maximum momentum, he seemed to be doing the impossible and running up the side of the wall. Reaching a balcony, he sprinted along the balustrade, his movement so light and quick it was nearly invisible to the eye.

With a mighty spring, he soared from one balcony onto the next. He repeated this, going from balcony to balcony, each jump taking him higher and exposing him to greater risk. As he reached the balcony closest to Glory, the pipe squealed, and she felt the metal slipping beneath her palms as she bent backward into nothingness—

Wei's arm circled her waist like a steel band, his momentum carrying them through the air and to the nearest balcony. They landed in a tangle, Wei twisting to break her fall. She ended up atop him, breathless.

"Are you all right—" They spoke at the same time.

The absurdity of the situation and her near escape were too much for her overwrought nerves. A relieved giggle escaped her.

Wei narrowed his eyes while FF II chittered around her neck.

"What the bloody hell were you thinking?" Wei said in a low voice.

"It seemed like a good plan. At the time." She tried to clear her throat, but another anxious chuckle escaped. "Now I realize that I ought to have thought it through better. Thank heavens you were there."

He opened his mouth, then closed it.

Instead, he jerked his chin toward the balcony door. "Is the chamber occupied?"

She shook her head. "This is the guest wing."

Rising, she gave him a hand up and tried the door. It was locked but with the use of hairpins, she swiftly gained entry. She led the way into the shadowy chamber, Wei closing the balcony door behind them.

"My family's bedchambers are on the opposite side of the house," she whispered. "We'll still need to be quiet, however—"

She gasped as Wei grabbed her by the waist, hauling her against a wall.

"Don't *ever* do anything that foolish again," he growled.

She would have replied, but he slammed his mouth onto hers.

Fear and anger and panic morphed into raging lust. Wei was powerless against his surging emotions, powerless to stop his true nature from smashing the chains of his self-discipline. Glory resurrected his most primal self, the shadowy beast that he'd locked away for years. Intuition had told him that she would not stay put at home tonight. Luckily, he'd arrived in time to witness her perilous exit from the house. Seeing her dangling above death's gaping jaws, feeling her fragility as he'd snatched her onto the balcony had shattered his control.

I cannot lose her too. Yuan fen *cannot be that cruel.*

The possibility drove him into a frenzy. He clasped her throat between his palms, feeling her fluttering pulse as he consumed her mouth. Reassuring himself with each lick, each taste, each bite that she was alive. She moaned, winding her arms around his neck as if she would never let go. And, bloody hell, he needed that from her...needed *her* like he'd never needed anything or anyone else.

He tore his mouth from hers.

"You're mine." The words he'd buried clawed themselves free. "I want to hear you say it, little tigress."

Her pulse quickened against his palm, moonlight illuminating the wonder in her gaze.

"I'm yours, Wei."

She whispered it like a vow, and it was all he needed to hear. Gripping her loose tresses in his fist, he exposed her neck, burying his nose against her fragrant skin. He nipped his way down a delicate tendon as she squirmed. She was dressed in male attire for her little flit tonight, and his lingering buzz of fear turned into dark, pounding lust as he gained easy access. At least her outfit was good for something.

He stripped off her jacket and waistcoat, then ripped open her shirt, buttons skittering across the floor. She trembled as he covered her breasts with his palms. He adored her delicate shape, the contrast between her subtle curves and impudent nipples. He thumbed her stiff peaks, tweaking one between finger and thumb, and relished her gasp against his lips.

"I can't wait to taste you again," he murmured. "To feel these pretty buds against my tongue."

She panted his name as he dragged his mouth along her collarbones. He licked between her breasts and inhaled her natural orchid scent. When he captured a saucy nipple in his mouth, she clutched his head. He swirled his tongue then suckled, and her hips bucked with wanton need.

As he lavished the same attention on her other sweet tit, he unfastened her trousers, sliding his hand between her legs. She gasped as he fingered her warm, wet slit.

"Shh, sweeting," he said, his voice low and husky. "You don't want anyone to hear us, do you?"

Eyes wide, she shook her head.

He brought his mouth to her ear. "You shall have to be very quiet while I pet your little pussy and make it feel good. Can you do that for me?"

She nodded, trembling.

His blood thrummed as he delved deeper into her quim. Her virginal dew coated his fingertips as he stroked her plump seam. He found her pearl, circling it with his thumb, and she shook like a leaf. She was so sweet and responsive, already close to coming, and he wanted to watch her face as she climaxed in his arms. He frigged her harder, his erection straining at the slick sounds.

"Do you like me touching your pussy?" he murmured. "Playing with this naughty pearl?"

His carnal words had their intended effect. As Glory spent with a breathless cry, she did something no other woman had done before. Instead of closing her eyes, she gazed into his. She shared her pleasure with him without shame or pretense. As if she wanted to share everything with him. As if they could do anything together—even explore the darkest depths of desire—and remain anchored by the purity of their bond.

Her honesty stole his breath and ignited his blood. He craved more of her. Needed to feast on the wanton sweetness he'd always longed for.

He went down on one knee. Her belly slipped like silk beneath his lips, and he felt her quivering aftershocks. Grasping the waistband of her trousers, he tugged them down in a smooth motion, lifting her slender feet from the garment one by one.

In the moonlight, her beauty shone like the rarest pearl. Wearing only an open shirt, her nipples playing peekaboo through the linen folds, she was both wholesome and wild...his fantasy come true. He ran a proprietary touch up her long, supple legs, savoring her tremors. He followed the path of his hands with his lips, and when he reached her thigh, she gave an adorable—but too loud—squeak.

He gave her a warning look.

"Wh-what are you doing?" she said in a hushed voice.

"I am going to kiss you," he murmured. "Wherever you are sweet."

"Not *there*, surely."

He nipped the crease of her leg. "Especially there."

Then he put his mouth on her pussy. Swiping his tongue along her lush cleft, he had to hold back a groan of pleasure. She was even sweeter, juicier than he'd imagined. He lapped hungrily, and her legs began to shake. Parting her folds, he exposed her bold little pearl, tickling it with his tongue. She bit her lip to stifle a moan even as she rewarded him with a gush of honey.

Greedy for more, he slung one of her legs over his shoulder, propping her against the wall and his mouth. She slid her fingers into his hair, holding on to him as he feasted. Devil and damn, she was delicious. The best bloody thing he'd ever eaten, and he wanted to sample all of her. Opening her with his thumbs, he probed deeper with his tongue and shuddered when he felt the squeeze of her untried cunny.

Unable to resist, he brought his middle finger to her lush hole, easing it into her. His prick throbbed as her muscles pulled him deeper. By the deities, she was tight but ripe for plowing. Looking up at her, seeing nothing but dazed pleasure on her face, he thrust all the way to the knuckle. His balls swelled as her juices drenched his palm, and when her passage softened around him, he added another finger. Simultaneously, he put his mouth back on her pussy, sucking on her pearl.

As she neared another climax, he suddenly froze. Were those footsteps outside the room? He surged to his feet, pressing his hand over Glory's mouth just as she came. With her moan trapped against his palm, her quim contracting around his fingers, he waited in suspended agony.

The footsteps faded. He kept listening, his heart thudding, but heard nothing beyond the sounds of his own breathing and Glory's.

He removed his hand from her mouth, easing his fingers from her pussy. Seeing the glistening proof of her pleasure, his blood quickened...with desire and frustration.

"That was close," he said quietly.

She nodded shakily. "I don't think anyone heard us."

"Even so, we shouldn't tempt fate. I must go."

"But we didn't get a chance to talk." She chewed on her lip. "About Scott or about...us."

"I know."

He raked a hand through his hair, resenting the barriers between them. Resenting the fact that he and she came from such different worlds that they couldn't have a conversation without sneaking around. His gut seized as he recognized the parallels between the present situation and the one with Chun.

The same mistake, his inner voice sneered. *When will you learn that you are not good enough? How many people have to get hurt?*

"Tomorrow," Glory said softly. "Could you meet me at Livy's? Around one o'clock?"

Shutting out the voice, he forced himself to nod.

"You...you're not angry, are you?"

The uncertainty in her eyes cut through his brooding. With her hair tumbling over her shoulders and dressed in a man's shirt, she looked achingly young and beautiful. Despite everything, temptation gripped him.

"Never at you, little tigress." He brushed a finger beneath her chin. "I will see you tomorrow."

He left...while he could still make himself do so.

TWENTY-THREE

The next morning, Glory sat curled up on a chaise in her bedchamber. Shifu Lam's book of precepts lay open on her lap, but she couldn't concentrate. She was on pins and needles, waiting for the time when she could leave to meet Wei. Despite the incandescent pleasure they'd shared—or, more accurately, that he'd given her—their parting had left her feeling unsure about where things stood between them.

It wasn't just that they hadn't had time to discuss the future. Before Wei left, his mood had turned brooding...and she didn't know why.

Did he regret making love to me again? Was I too wanton to let him kiss me on my...my pussy? But it was his idea, and he seemed to enjoy it. Or maybe I wasn't brazen enough. Maybe I ought to have done something for him...

Her cheeks flamed as she realized how inexperienced she must seem to a worldly man like Wei. What if she didn't measure up to the lovers he'd had in the past? What if she wasn't good at lovemaking and had disappointed him in some way?

A knock interrupted her spiraling thoughts.

"Come in," she said hastily.

Mama entered, her rose satin skirts rustling. "Hello, dearest. I wanted to catch you before you left for Lady Olivia's."

Glory set aside her book. "Was there something in particular you wanted, Mama?"

"Nothing in particular. I just wished to chat."

Obligingly, Glory made room on the chaise, and her mother sat beside her, their voluminous skirts brushing.

"What do you want to chat about?" she asked.

Mama's emerald gaze was disturbingly keen.

"You know I have always respected your independence, dearest. Especially now that you are almost one-and-twenty and capable of making your own decisions. But no matter what, I am your mama, and I hope you feel that you can confide in me about anything."

Glory felt a pang of guilt because she *couldn't* discuss the two most pressing concerns in her life. Her work with the Angels had to be concealed for obvious reasons, and her relationship with Wei was too tenuous and complicated to address. While Mama was no snob, she would likely have concerns about the differences in Glory and Wei's backgrounds, and she *definitely* would not approve of the intimacies they'd shared.

Glory settled for, "I know, Mama."

"I am glad. You and I...we've been through so much together, haven't we?" Mama took Glory's hand and gave it a squeeze. "From the fossils shop in Dorset to this."

She waved at the chamber, referring, Glory understood, to their life of luxury.

"Through it all, you have been true to yourself, and I have always admired that," Mama said.

"I learned it from you," Glory said sincerely. "You and Aunt Hypatia taught me to be independent and free-thinking."

"I suppose we did, didn't we?" Mama's reminiscent smile faded. "I know life as a debutante hasn't been easy, especially with Papa's political work bringing attention to our family."

Glory's guilt deepened. Instead of blaming her for being a social failure, her parents were worried about her happiness.

Swallowing, she said, "I wish I could..."

Contribute to Papa's important work. Be more of an asset to this family. Like the Earl of Darlingford's daughter, who helped her father achieve his political ambitions.

"Yes, dear?"

"I wish I could do more," she mumbled. "For Papa's cause."

"Why, you have been one of his staunchest supporters," Mama said brightly. "He is proud of your knowledge of the opium trade and your willingness to speak up about the injustice."

But is he proud of the way I bore people at balls? My empty dance card? The way I cannot seem to do anything right in society?

"As a matter of fact, I will be planning a luncheon for Papa's supporters. Perhaps you would care to help?"

I'll try my best.

"Of course, Mama."

"I appreciate it, dearest. Until Papa introduces the bill, he will be under a lot of scrutiny and pressure. We must do our best to support him."

Unease slithered through Glory as she thought of Wei. If word got out that she was romantically involved with a man who treated opium users in the East End, the scandal would be colossal. Enough to compromise her father's aspirations. While she wasn't ashamed that she was falling in love with Wei, she couldn't allow her desires to damage the progress Papa had made toward stopping the despicable commerce.

I have nothing to worry about yet. Beyond the Angels, no one knows about Wei and me. Uncertainty gripped her heart. *Truthfully, I don't even know what his intentions are...whether he would want to marry me.*

"Papa is worried about you, you know."

Glory forced herself to focus. "About me? Why?"

"You know Papa: he cares so much about your happiness. He

wants to give you the best of everything and make up for the years when he wasn't in your life."

"It wasn't his fault," she protested. "He did not even know of my existence."

"I've told him that so many times." Mama's gaze clouded over. "If anyone was to blame, it was me."

"You are not to blame either," Glory said firmly. "Anyway, this is all water under the bridge. Why concern yourself over it now?"

Mama took a breath. "Papa and I were talking last night."

Uh oh. Parental talks seldom led to favorable outcomes.

"What about?" Glory asked warily.

"Your future." Mama hesitated. "Papa and I have noticed that you haven't taken a particular interest in any suitors."

"That is because I haven't had any. The fortune hunters don't count."

"You are a lovely girl, and I think it is fair to say that if you had encouraged the attentions of any eligible gentlemen, you would have your pick."

"Because you are not at all biased." Glory snorted.

"I am serious," Mama insisted. "Since your debut, Papa and I have never seen you have that, for lack of a better word, *spark* with any gentleman. We didn't worry because you are young, and we don't wish to rush you into anything, let alone something as important as marriage. Going into your third Season, however, we began to worry that perhaps you were avoiding forming attachments because...because of us."

Glory stared at her mother in confusion. "Because of you and Papa?"

Mama nodded. "Our relationship was not conventional, and you suffered for it. We did not set the finest example of how a relationship should be—"

"Mama." Glory took her mother's hand and looked into the other's fretful eyes. "I would consider myself the luckiest woman on earth to one day have a marriage like the one you and Papa have."

Mama's eyes sheened. "Do you mean that? Even after the mistakes we've made?"

"Whatever mistakes happened, love brought you back together. Love gave me a father who spoils me rotten. Love gave me brothers whom I adore and can always out-argue."

Mama gave a watery laugh.

"You and Papa showed me that love leads to happily ever after," Glory said sincerely. "How could I ask for a better role model than that?"

"Dearest, I cannot tell you how much that relieves me."

As Mama discreetly dabbed her eyes with a handkerchief, Glory glanced at the clock. It was nearing noon, and she didn't want to be late for Wei.

"If you wish, we can talk again later," she said. "But for now, if there is nothing else—"

"Actually, there is. Papa and I have decided that you may continue your lessons with Mr. Chen if you wish to do so."

Relief rushed through Glory. "I do, Mama. *Thank you.*"

"What do you think of the master, my dear?"

At the unexpected question, she faltered. "Um, I am not certain what you mean."

"I think he is an intriguing fellow. Aunt Hypatia does too, and you know her opinion of most men." Mama arched her brows. "The Duke of Hadleigh also apparently counts Mr. Chen amongst his trusted cronies. Given all that, I was curious what *you* thought of him."

"Master Chen is a man of integrity and honor," Glory said. "I admire his sense of purpose—he is much like Papa in that way."

"A commendable trait, I am sure." A small smile played on Mama's lips. "Is that all?"

"Well, he is a wonderful *shifu*. He has taught me how to defend myself."

"Very useful," Mama acknowledged.

Glory warmed to the subject. "And we discuss philosophy and all sorts of teachings that Master Chen's own *shifu* passed down to him. I am even beginning to see the value in patience."

"Goodness, Master Chen is not merely a teacher. He is a magician."

"*Mama.*"

Her mother laughed. "I am merely admiring the fact that your *shifu* has made progress where Papa and I have failed to. I do believe I would like to get better acquainted with Master Chen. What do you think of inviting him to your birthday ball next week?"

Glory's pulse raced with excitement. Here was an opportunity for her family to get to know Wei. If they spent time with him, they would surely come to admire him as she did...but would he want to attend her party?

"I would like that," she said. "I shall ask him at my next lesson."

"While we are on the topic of your birthday, do not forget to schedule a final fitting with Mrs. Quinton. We want your birthday gown to be just right."

"Yes, Mama."

"Then I shan't keep you any longer. Have fun with Lady Olivia, dear." Rising, Mama headed to the doorway, where she abruptly turned. "By the by, did you hear any odd noises last night?"

Glory's heart thumped. "Um, no. I don't think so."

"Papa thought it might have come from the courtyard. When he went out to look this morning, however, everything appeared normal." Mama shrugged. "It was probably just a cat."

After her mother left, Glory released a breath. Then she shook her head and smiled.

It was just like Wei to fix the drainpipe...and leave no trace that he'd done so.

TWENTY-FOUR

Glory and her maid arrived at the Hadleighs' on time. As Elsie departed below stairs for a cup of tea, Glory was greeted in the antechamber by Livy, the duke, and their daughter Esmerelda. All three were dressed to go out, the tot looking adorable in a bonnet and embroidered velvet jacket that matched Livy's. Seeing her friend with husband and child, Glory felt a pulse of longing she'd never felt before.

"Aunt Glo-wee!" Esme said, her brunette curls bouncing.

"Hello, dear." Glory crouched to give her a hug. "How is my favorite two-year-old?"

"Ouch," Esme announced, pointing at her mouth. "In here."

"The poor dear is getting the last of her teeth in," Livy said. "But Papa is our hero and taking her for ices to help the ouch."

"Papa hero," Esme agreed, holding her arms up to Hadleigh.

"Off we go, poppet," he said.

The duke scooped her up, swinging her in the air as she giggled. He paused to kiss Livy, murmuring, "Be careful, little queen," before striding off.

"I am shadowing Bryant today," Livy said, pulling on her gloves. "Which means you and Mr. Chen will have privacy. He is waiting in the library, and I've instructed the servants not to disturb you."

"Thank you," Glory said gratefully. "And good luck."

"You too, my dear." With a wink, Livy hurried off.

Glory went to the library.

The high-ceilinged room was bright with golden light, the shelves of books and plump velvet chairs adding to the cozy ambiance. Standing by one of the tall windows, Wei turned at her arrival, and her heart pitter-pattered beneath the bodice of her lilac carriage dress. The sunlight gilded his noble features; he was so handsome and virile she could scarcely believe that he desired her. That, last night, he had called her "mine."

In that moment, she didn't care about the differences that separated them. What she wouldn't give to belong to him. For him to belong to her.

They met each other halfway. Her chest tightened at Wei's grave expression. Instead of kissing her as she hoped he would do, he gave her a restrained bow. She curtsied awkwardly in return.

"Thank you for meeting me today."

His formality chilled her.

"I...it was no problem," she said falteringly. "We have much to discuss."

"Yes, we do. Shall we sit?"

They arranged themselves on a divan by the fire. As she fiddled with her skirts, willing herself to voice the questions burning in her head—*Do you still want me? Has something changed?*—he spoke first.

"I must beg your forgiveness for my behavior last night," he said calmly. "We ought to have had this discussion then instead of...of doing what we did."

His apology irked her. Suddenly, she was tired of the back and forth. Pippa was right: not knowing what he wanted might be worse than the truth.

"I *liked* what we did," she said. "I thought...I thought you liked it too."

She'd meant to sound bold, but the quaver in her voice betrayed her. Feeling her eyes heat, she looked down at her lap, willing herself not to cry.

Wei tipped her chin up. "I did like it. Too much, little tigress."

The passionate flare in his eyes relieved her. Told her he was being truthful.

"But I should not have made love to you again without telling you about my past. About things that will change how you feel about me...about us."

"My feelings for you could never change," she said with conviction.

"We shall see." A wistful look visited his gaze before he took a breath. "I told you that I must avenge my kin, but I did not tell you the full story. You see, their murder was not a random act but a calculated one."

As she absorbed the shocking fact, he added another.

"They were killed because of me."

Her heart hammered at his revelation. At the fathomless agony in his eyes.

"What happened?" she asked softly.

"I was eighteen and a selfish scoundrel." Self-loathing dripped from his tone. "I'd started attracting attention from the females in my village, and it went to my head. I thought that I could have any woman I wanted. When the most beautiful lady showed interest, I went after her. Had an affair with her even though I knew it was wrong."

Since he'd called the relationship an "affair," she asked, "Was it wrong because you were not married?"

Even as the question left her, Glory realized the irony. She and Wei had shared physical pleasure without the sanctity of marriage. Yet nothing they'd done together had ever felt wrong; to the contrary, everything felt *right*.

Once again, Wei showed his uncanny ability to read her thoughts.

"What we have is different," he said emphatically. "My intentions toward you have always been honorable, even when they didn't seem that way. I tried to deny my feelings for you because I wanted to protect you and keep you safe. But now that we have acted on our attraction—twice—things have changed. I want to do right by you, and that includes telling you about my past. Afterward, if you still deem me worthy, if you still want a future together"—his eyes blazed with intensity—"then I will have an important question to ask of you."

Her heart soared.

"Yes," she blurted. "The answer is yes."

His mouth suddenly twitched. "Why is your impatience so damned adorable, sweeting?"

He leaned in and gave her the kiss she'd yearned for. Their lips clung softly, sweetly before he broke away.

"Now, don't distract me," he said with mock sternness.

"All right, O Mighty *Shifu*."

She regretted her attempt at levity when he drew his brows together, frowning.

"I lied." He expelled a breath. "I have *not* been honorable where you are concerned."

It was her turn to frown. "What do you mean?"

"Wanting to teach you how to protect yourself wasn't my only motivation in becoming your *shifu*." His gaze was troubled. "I took on that role specifically to put up a barrier between us. In my culture, it is forbidden for a *shifu* to have a relationship with his student. Yet here we are."

His explanation relieved her.

"Surely there are exceptions to the rule," she argued. "Here in England, tutors and students fall in love and elope. As do footmen and ladies, dukes and scullery maids. In fact, my mama was working as a barmaid when she first met my papa. Such relationships may be seen as taboo, but that doesn't mean they are wrong for the people involved."

"The relationship is wrong if it violates universal principles," he said stubbornly.

She tilted her head. "How can love be wrong?"

"It can be wrong if it hurts other people. If it is selfish and uncaring of who gets injured."

She'd never seen him look so grim. A chill snaked up her spine.

"Are you talking about us," she said slowly, "or about the past? About what happened with the lady in your village?"

His jaw taut, he said, "Her name was Chun, and she was married."

Of all the secrets Glory thought Wei might reveal, an adulterous affair was not one of them.

"You had relations with a married woman?" she said incredulously.

"Chun was seven years older than me. When she was fifteen, her parents arranged for her to marry a man named Li. Li was in his fifties, a powerful merchant who was also the village governor. He abused her; when they did not produce children, he publicly laid the blame at her door. Chun hated her husband and was miserable in their marriage. After she and I had a chance meeting at the market, she sent me a note, and we met up. Became lovers."

"Were you in love with her?" Glory asked hesitantly.

She wasn't sure she wanted to know. While she was falling in love with Wei, she didn't know if he returned her feelings. He had admitted his desire for her...but passion wasn't the same as love.

"I thought I was." Wei rested his elbows on his thighs and stared into the hearth. "I was eighteen, the son of a soldier. While my father was a loyal member of the Imperial Army and fought bravely to eradicate opium, my family was not wealthy or distinguished. When I met Chun, she seemed so sophisticated...so different from me. She dressed beautifully, lived in a palatial home, and entertained the governor's powerful friends. I could not believe that such a refined creature would want to be with someone like me.

"But during the year of our affair, I knew what we were doing was wrong. The dishonor that our actions would bring upon not only us, but our families, was unthinkable. Several times, we almost got caught, and I tried to end the affair. But Chun started crying, saying that I was the only good thing in her life, and I...I couldn't do it. I was too weak to break things off. Even though nothing about our relationship felt right. I knew in my bones that the universe would one day punish us for our trespasses, and I was right."

Trepidation prickled Glory's nape. "What happened?"

"One night, I came home after a tryst with Chun. That is when I came upon the intruder I have since been hunting. After I fought him off, I found the bodies of my family and our servant, Old Wong." Wei's gaze was glassy. "The bastard slit their throats, and he took...took..."

Wei dropped his head into his hands, digging his fingers into his scalp. She'd never seen him this way, this *tormented*. It was as if all his barriers had come crashing down at once, and she now saw the enormity of all he'd been holding back.

She wrapped her arms as far as they would go around him, pressing her body to his. Offering what comfort she could. Feeling his shudders as if they were her own, she didn't pressure him to talk, knowing he would continue when he was ready.

Eventually, he said in a hollow voice, "Ling Ling had pretty hair. Thick and shiny black. She wasn't vain about her appearance, but her pigtails were the one thing she took pride in. And the bastard...he took them. Like a goddamned souvenir. It wasn't enough that he cut a ten-year-old girl's throat and left her lying in a pool of blood, he sheared off her hair as well."

Glory's insides churned. She felt physically ill.

"When I think of him having a part of my sister, I want to..."

Wei's clenched jaw and balled hands conveyed exactly what he planned to do to the murderous bastard. And Glory did not blame him. More than ever, she wanted to help Wei get justice for his family.

"I'm so sorry." Her voice was choked with emotion. "The blackguard will get his comeuppance. I know he will. When you first told me about this, you mentioned that he was after something in your family's home. Do you know what it was?"

Wei raised storm-ridden eyes to hers. "Me."

Self-revulsion poured like acid through Wei's veins as he confessed his sins to the woman whose opinion mattered most to him.

"The Englishman was sent by Governor Li to kill me," he said tightly. "Because of my affair with his wife."

Glory paled. "How...how did you find out?"

"By order of the Emperor, the English and other foreigners who wished to trade with China were only permitted to reside in certain housing called the factories. I went to the English factory to hunt the bastard down. The traders and their guards would not let me past the gates. Back then, I did not know *kung fu* and could not fight my way through.

"I demanded justice for my family and swore that I would return with Governor Li's army behind me. When the Englishmen's priest translated my words into English, the traders laughed in my face. The priest enlightened me on their reply. *'Governor Li is our ally and friend, scum. He will not take the side of a peasant over a trading relationship with the greatest empire on Earth. Especially a peasant dumb enough to stick his prick where it doesn't belong.'* And that was when I understood. When I knew that my punishment had come at last."

That moment of clarity had struck Wei like a red-hot brand to the chest, and he felt the sickening burn even now.

"It was Li who sent that assassin. He had my parents and sister killed." Wei stared down at his fists with futile rage. "Because of me."

"Oh, Wei," Glory whispered.

"He must have found out about my affair with Chun. He was within his rights to demand satisfaction," Wei gritted out. "But from *me*. If anyone deserved to die, it was me—not my sister, parents, or Old Wong. They did nothing wrong. The fault was all bloody *mine*."

He felt that hated burn behind his eyes. Yet the years had taken all the tears he had to shed. He felt Glory's gentle touch against his biceps, and it took him a moment to gather the courage to meet her gaze. To see what judgment those innocent-yet-wise eyes would hold.

"It was wrong to have an affair with a married woman," she said steadily.

"Believe me, I know. I was a selfish, worthless bastard—"

"I am not finished. While what you did was wrong, you were only eighteen. You were young, inexperienced, and you made a mistake...like we all do. I mean, look at how I trusted that drainpipe last night."

He shot her a dark look. "Do not remind me. Seeing you in peril took years off my life."

"My point is that while your actions did not show the best judgment, they in no way justified Governor Li's behavior. What he did was vile, cruel, and devious. He could have called you out, dealt with you man-to-man. Instead, he chose to vent his anger and injured pride on innocent people. You made a mistake; he committed a crime."

Wei let Glory's assessment percolate through him. She was not the sort of woman who would honey-coat the truth. And that truth felt like a balm, reaching deep inside him, soothing the wound that had never healed.

"Did you confront Governor Li?" Glory asked. "Confirm what he'd done?"

"I tried to, but I could never get near him," Wei said starkly. "Everywhere he went, he had an entourage of guards. But I did manage to see Chun one last time at the market. We only had a few minutes, and I wanted to know if she'd ever seen her husband with an Englishman with a tattoo on his arm. She said that about two weeks prior to my family's murder, Li had had visitors from the British factory. A group of traders who'd delivered a billiards table to him as a gift. She recalled the man with the tattoo specifically because he was one of the workers who'd carried in the table; he'd had his shirtsleeves rolled up, and the marking of vines and flowers caught her attention. She described him as being in his late twenties, with brown hair and ice-blue eyes."

Glory's forehead pleated. "If Chun's husband knew about her adultery, was she safe?"

It was so like Glory to be worried about Chun. Her compassion for others was one of the many traits that made her special and rare.

"I asked her the same thing. Even asked her to leave with me that day," Wei said tightly. "I felt responsible for her—felt I had to protect her however I could. But she refused to go with me. She didn't want to leave the life she had. As much as she hated her husband, she found the idea of being with a penniless nobody even less tolerable. I tried to change her mind, but she would not budge. Said she would be fine, that she could manage Li."

"I am glad you gave her a choice, even if she refused."

"It wasn't much of a choice," he said darkly. "Living a life of luxury under the thumb of a rich, murderous bastard or being on a flit with a poor nobody with only vengeance on his mind."

"You are not a nobody." Glory looked so deeply into his eyes that he wondered if she could see his very essence. "And I would go on a flit with you any day."

Her words made his throat tighten with wonder. Yet he couldn't let himself be distracted when he had more to tell.

"Let's hope it never comes to that." He inhaled deeply. "After what Chun said, I knew without a doubt that Li was behind the murders of my kin. There was as much blood on his hands as those of the villain who'd held the knife to their throats. And I swore on my family's graves that I would not rest until both men paid for their crimes."

"Did you, um, get your revenge against Li?"

Her brows knitting, Glory posed the question as if she wasn't certain she wanted to know the answer. Wei didn't blame her. At the same time, he was not going to lie.

"Li was the chief authority of the village. He decided how and if justice was served, which meant that I would get no help through official channels. I decided that an eye for an eye was my only recourse," he stated.

"You killed Li?" she whispered.

"I spent the first year trying to do so," he replied. "A hotheaded fool, I didn't consider that I had neither the skill nor the resources to carry out my plan. Unsurprisingly, I failed. On my last attempt, I narrowly escaped getting killed by his guards. I ended up a fugitive and had to flee the village and live under an assumed identity. I survived by finding work in the ports, living amongst the ruffians and pirates. I hated myself for my failure, was angry all the time. I drank, gambled, and whored. I got into brawls, most of which I did not win."

He slid a look at Glory, seeing the surprise she couldn't hide. Shame churned his gut at the man he'd once been. And maybe still was. The years of training with his *shifu* had changed some things, but how different was he at his core? Wasn't he still a failure, still making selfish choices...which included starting an affair with his lovely, innocent pupil who deserved so much better than him?

"That doesn't sound like you at all," she said staunchly.

"That was me." He dragged a hand through his hair. "Eventually, I got into debt with a dockside moneylender, and when I could not pay, he had his brutes beat me nearly to death. In that moment, I didn't care; I wanted to die." He released a slow breath, needing to stay in the present, to not get swept up in the tide of despair. "But Shifu Lam came to my aid. He, a frail-looking old man, took on a gang of ruffians and sent them running like curs with their tails between their legs. I couldn't believe it, begged him to teach me how to fight like him. And he said I would first have to prove myself worthy of being a student of *kung fu*."

"What did you have to do?"

"It was more what I had to *not* do. I had to give up my vices for a year—no drinking, no gambling, no women. No unprovoked fighting."

"Was it difficult?"

"At first. Slowly, it began to feel good, like I was applying a salve to a wound rather than tearing it open again and again." A pang hit Wei's chest as he recalled the start of his journey to recovery. "My *shifu* helped me to see that I was only hurting myself with my anger. That giving in to it was taking me farther and farther away from my goal of avenging my kin. He taught me different ways of managing my emotions."

"Like what you teach your students?" she asked softly.

He nodded. "At first, I was impatient. Even resistant. Why did I need to learn to sit and contemplate when I had enemies to kill? Why did I need to spend hours reading books and studying philosophy when what I wanted to do was learn martial arts?"

"I understand *completely*."

She spoke with such feeling that his lips quirked.

"Over time, I came to realize that my *shifu* was right. I wasn't ready. The studying cleared my mind—helped me to see my mistakes and how much I had to learn. Only when I reached that state of acceptance and humility was I ready to become a student of *kung fu*. For seven years, I trained day and night, practicing everything my *shifu* taught me."

"Your diligence certainly paid off," she said.

Her unabashed admiration made his face warm. As a *shifu*, he was used to getting respect from his students. Yet Glory had a way of making him feel good, not only about his skills and ability to teach others. But about...himself.

But will she feel that way when I tell her the rest?

He forced himself to go on.

"The day came when I was ready to confront Li. In the middle of the night, I infiltrated his compound and found him in his bed. He was asleep, a look of peace on his face, as if he hadn't a care in the world. As if the lives of my parents and sister didn't weigh on his soul—as if they didn't matter."

Fury sizzled through Wei's veins as he recalled looking down at the obese prick, snoring in his cocoon of silk.

"Li awakened with the edge of my blade against his neck. I told him why he was going to die, and finally, for the first time, I saw fear in his eyes," Wei said with dark satisfaction. "He tried to call for his guards, but I was faster. I left him the way he'd left my family, and I didn't look back."

Twenty-Five

There were no signs of remorse on Wei's noble features; if anything, his gaze glittered with defiance. He was not sorry he killed Governor Li and wasn't about to pretend that he was.

Glory swallowed. In her eyes, he was an honorable man, yet his streak of ruthlessness gave her pause. She couldn't argue that he'd had reason to take Li's life. The man had ordered the cold-blooded murder of Wei's entire family. Moreover, his position of privilege allowed him to get away with it...leaving Wei with a single path to vengeance.

Sometimes justice was complicated; other times it was simple. Black and white.

An eye for an eye.

"How did it make you feel?" she asked quietly. "Getting your revenge on Li?"

"If I had to do it over again, I would do the same," Wei stated.

"And the English assassin? The one you came to London to find?"

"When the time comes, I will do to him what he did to my family."

She bit her lip. "Isn't there another way to get your revenge? The laws are different here. After you find him, you could have him sent to prison—"

"You think your English law will be sympathetic to my situation?" Scorn dripped from Wei's words. "Your country has no qualms about wreaking havoc on entire nations. Do you think Britannia will care about the murder of four measly Chinese when she has poisoned millions? Do you honestly think that if I capture this bastard and hand him over to the authorities that he will get the punishment he deserves?"

She chewed on her lip, hating that he had a point. While she was an optimist, she knew that life was not fair. Justice, in particular, was not applied equally to all...which was why she'd become an Angel in the first place. To try to balance the scales where she could.

"I don't know what to think," she admitted.

She hadn't gone through his experience. Hadn't known the grief of losing those she loved most or the guilt of feeling like she was to blame for their deaths. She hadn't had to live each day knowing that the men behind their murders would not be held accountable.

"About me?"

Although Wei's tone was gruff, she saw the vulnerability in his expression. And that made up her mind. From the start, she had wanted to know what lay behind his wall of reserve. She'd wanted to know who he was...and now she did. He wasn't perfect. He'd made mistakes, ones he'd paid for dearly. His emotions were strong and sometimes not under his control.

At the same time, he had used his pain to help others deal with their struggles. For surely his own experiences with tragedy had shaped him into the formidable *shifu* and healer he was today. Even if she couldn't agree with his version of justice, neither could she say that what he'd done was wrong. In the end, what mattered most was that he had trusted her with his pain and darkest secrets.

"Yes," she said with hushed recognition. "My feelings have changed."

"I understand." His voice was as gritty as sandpaper. "I don't blame you."

"Before, I thought I was falling in love with you." The intensity of her feelings added a tremor to her voice. "Now I know that I *am* in love with you."

"You...you love me?" He stared at her.

"I wasn't sure because I have never been in love before," she said candidly. "I didn't know if what I felt was infatuation because you've always seemed so, well, perfect to me. Larger than life, if you know what I mean."

"I don't." Her mighty *shifu* drew his brows together, looking endearingly confused. "Explain."

"Well, you are so composed and unflappable. A veritable fount of knowledge. And you're good at everything."

"I am not good at—"

"You're good at everything that matters to me," she amended. "You are a warrior and a healer. You run a clinic that serves the greater good. You are a man of honor and integrity; you protect those who can't protect themselves."

He seemed to digest what she was saying. "You still believe this after all I have told you?"

"I believe it even more. Because now I know you aren't perfect."

"There's an understatement."

"But I like that you have flaws because it makes you more, well, like *me*," she said earnestly. "You have made mistakes, and sometimes your emotions have gotten the better of you. This makes you human. I don't see you as an idealized *shifu* any longer, but a man who has overcome tragedy and pain to be a better person. And that is how I know I love you, Wei. Because I see you for who you truly are, and you still take my breath away."

"Glory." He framed her face with his hands. Hands that were

powerful, capable of giving and taking life, and that were shaking with the force of his emotions. "I never knew what love was until I met you. But you've turned everything I thought I knew on its head."

"I have a way of making things topsy-turvy," she said breathlessly.

"Before I left for London, my *shifu* told me that I would only find what I was looking for by not trying. I did not understand what he meant until now. All I have been focused on is getting my final vengeance; the last thing I thought I needed or wanted was to fall in love. But I love you, Glory, and want to spend the rest of my life with you. Even if you deserve better."

"There is no one better for me than you."

"And you do not care that I am not an English lord?" he asked roughly. "Your life with me won't have the luxuries to which you are accustomed. Society will frown upon your choice to be with someone like me and—"

"And I won't care. Because I love you, Wei, and you love me. That is all that matters."

"What about your family?"

She swallowed, for this was the one sticking point.

"My parents might not agree with my decision at first," she admitted. "But they love me, and I am certain that, with time, they will get used to the idea. By the by, they have agreed to let our lessons continue...and Mama even said I could invite you to my birthday ball. If you, um, want to come."

"I want to."

Wei's intensity stole her breath.

"I want to be there for all your special occasions, Glory," he said. "From here on in. I want to love, cherish, and protect you. Will you do me the honor of becoming my wife?"

She gave him the answer bursting in her heart. "Yes, Wei. *Yes.*"

His eyes flared, and when he kissed her, passion ignited between them. For once, they had privacy, and their love didn't need to take place in shadows. Yet as Wei lowered her onto the divan, Glory realized that she wanted something different.

When she pushed at his shoulders, he looked surprised but helped her to sit up.

"You are right." He cleared his throat. "Now is not the time—"

"It's not that. I just want to, um, try something." She blushed. "Something I've been curious about."

He cocked his head. "What is that?"

She mustered her courage and brushed her fingertips over the bulge in his trousers.

"Will you teach me how to...to pleasure you?"

Glory's shy yet eager smile beguiled Wei.

Her offer wasn't one he'd expected. With Chun, he'd done all the pleasuring. With prostitutes, they'd done whatever he'd paid for. But he'd never been with anyone like Glory. A virginal lady whose wanton generosity made him want to burn an offering to the gods for his good fortune.

"You want to frig me?" he said thickly.

He saw her breath quicken at the naughty word.

"If you don't mind," she said, biting her lip.

No, I don't bloody mind.

He burned to feel her touch—the touch of his future bride. A woman who'd given him the gift of her love and acceptance. Whose sweetness and loyalty were almost too good to be true and everything he'd longed for. Everything he'd given up hope of having...until Glory.

Their passion deserved more than shadows: a thing of such beauty deserved to flourish in sunlight.

It felt like the most natural thing in the world to rise and shed his coat. He reached for his waistband, and Glory watched him with inquisitive eyes. When he unfastened his trousers, his rearing erection fell out, and she wetted her lips. Stifling a groan, he shoved down his pants, sat beside her, and took her hand.

"Ready for your lesson?" he said.

She nodded, trembling when he folded her hand around his shaft. Hell, he shivered too. Not just because it'd been a long time since he felt a woman's touch. It was because that woman was Glory—his little tigress whose sensual curiosity drove him wild.

"You're so big," she breathed.

His prick swelled even further, testing the limits of her grip. Her fingers looked so delicate against the veined length, the manicured tips just managing to meet around his throbbing girth.

"Touch me like this," he instructed.

With his hand over hers, he taught her the motion and pressure he liked, and she demonstrated her usual aptitude for learning...and testing his control. The years of honing his self-discipline allowed him to keep his pleasure in check. To prolong the bliss of his beloved's touch and revel in the knowledge that he was the only man to give her this lesson.

Soon she did not need his guidance, and he let go, pleasure blazing up his spine as she pumped his rod on her own, adding a squeeze at the tip that made him grunt and squirt a drop of seed.

She looked adorably pleased with her handiwork. "You get wet, too."

"And you are ready for a more advanced technique." He took her other hand, cupping it around his heavy balls, his breath hissing out at her exquisite touch. "That's it, love. Stroke my stones while you frig me."

Her lip caught beneath her teeth, she deftly learned how to make him lose his mind.

"Am I doing this correctly?" she asked.

Her gaze, brimming with a sweet eagerness to please, undid him.

"Bloody hell, *yes*," he grated out.

In the next heartbeat, he exploded. The pent-up need of years raged through him and out of him. Glory gasped as his hot seed blasted her fingers, creamy arcs escaping into the air. Even as he shuddered with bliss, he felt a feverish arousal watching her: her big, curious eyes and needy squirming as he unloaded in her lady-like hands.

Unable to resist, he hauled her face-down over his lap. Her gasp was muffled by the cushions as he shoved up her voluminous skirts. He ran a possessive hand over her linen-covered bottom, finding the slit in her drawers. Satisfaction welled inside him: her cunny was drenched.

"Did you like touching my cock, sweeting?" he murmured.

"Yes," she said bashfully.

"That is good, because I waited thirteen years to feel a woman's touch again." He felt her tremor of surprise. "And you were worth every minute of the wait."

Reaching under, he rubbed her pearl with firm strokes until she moaned. With his other hand, he breached her lush entrance. Her pussy clutched his thrusting fingers, so wet and tight that he turned rock-hard once more. He pressed inside her, groaning when she pushed against him, needy for more. He added another finger, ramming deep, again and again until she gushed around him, mingling his name with words of love.

In that moment, he believed that anything was possible.

"There is much we need to plan," Wei said. "How and when I should approach your papa to ask for your hand."

Cuddled against him, her body still thrumming from their lovemaking, Glory felt a prickle of anxiety. She drew a breath and sat up to face him.

"I want you to speak to Papa," she said hesitantly.

Wei narrowed his eyes. "But?"

"I think we should wait. Give ourselves time, to make sure we are certain—"

"I am certain," he said flatly. "Are you?"

"About us? Yes," she said with emphasis. "But there are other factors to consider. You know about Papa's bill. While I don't care if our marriage causes scandal, I don't wish to compromise his efforts to ban opium smuggling."

Wei's scrutiny was piercing. "This is just about the bill? Because if you are unsure of your feelings, I would understand. I would not pressure you—"

"You aren't pressuring me, I promise."

She caressed his jaw, marveling that this magnificent man loved her. That he'd waited thirteen years before being with a woman again...and he'd chosen to be with *her*.

"I would be honored to be your wife," she said softly. "But I don't want my happiness to be at the cost of my family's. You understand, don't you?"

Pain flashed in his eyes. "More than you know."

It took her a moment to realize what she'd done.

Horrified, she blurted, "I'm so sorry. I didn't mean to dredge up—"

"I am not made of glass, little tigress. You only spoke the truth." He took her hand and squeezed it. "What are you proposing?"

Reassured, she said, "I think we should keep our engagement secret until Papa introduces his bill. He said it will only be a month from now. During that time, we'll make sure you and my family get better acquainted. Once that happens, I know my parents will adore you as I do and support our marriage."

This way, I will not hurt Papa's campaign with a scandal. I won't distract or disappoint him. At the same time, I will prevent Wei from facing any potential rejection by my family. This is the best solution to make sure no one gets hurt.

Wei shook his head. "I wish I shared your optimism."

"Mama already expressed a desire to get to know you. Once you and Papa get a chance to talk—and my birthday ball will provide the perfect opportunity—you will get on like a house on fire," she said confidently.

After a pause, Wei said, "If you think the best strategy is to wait, then I'll wait."

"Thank you, darling." Flushed with success, she decided to push her luck. "I have another plan, too. Concerning Wulfric Scott."

Wei's gaze hardened. "I am going after him, Glory. After everything I've told you, you must understand why."

"I do understand, and I am not trying to stop you," she promised. "Trust me, the Angels want him too. To achieve our mutual goals, however, we must be patient and methodical."

The corners of his eyes crinkled. "*You* are advising me to be patient?"

"Perhaps I am learning from our lessons."

She beamed at him; he snorted.

"At any rate," she said, "getting your answers from Scott won't be easy. At the fight, you had him at your mercy, and he still would not talk. Even if you managed to get past his gang and corner him again, who is to say he will tell you what he knows about your enemy?"

"I will make him talk," Wei said.

"Torture is not your style," she chided. "Wouldn't it be preferable to have a better kind of leverage? One that would be, um, less messy?"

He frowned. "What kind of leverage are you referring to?"

"We obtain concrete proof of the Fancy's crimes. Say, for instance, their dognapping scheme," she said. "In exchange for not forwarding the matter to the police, we demand that Scott give you the information you seek and release all the dogs, with the promise to never again engage in the vile business. In that scenario, everyone wins."

"Your plan is to blackmail the Fancy?"

Wei did not sound as impressed as she'd hoped.

"We shall frame it as a trade," Glory replied brightly. "The Angels are taking turns shadowing Bryant and Scott. One of them is bound to slip up soon and lead us to the dogs. Then we'll have all the proof we need. I'm surveilling Bryant tomorrow; if you wish, you could accompany me."

During the ensuing silence, she held her breath.

Can we begin as I hope we will go on, as true partners in love and life? Will Wei see that we are stronger together than apart?

He expelled a breath. "I cannot believe I am allowing you to talk me into this."

Twenty-Six

The next day, Mr. Devlin drove Glory and Wei as they surveilled Bryant. Glory parted the curtains of the carriage and peered out. The hackney in front of them had stopped, depositing their blond and bearded suspect on the corner of a commercial thoroughfare in Chelsea.

"What business do you suppose Bryant has here?" Wei gazed at the street, which was lined by an assortment of middle-class shops.

"Hopefully, he has more in mind than shopping. Livy tailed him yesterday, and the most interesting thing he did was go for a shave."

Bryant crossed the street and entered a large corner establishment with a yellow awning. Seeing the name of the shop, Glory felt her heart pound faster.

Eady's Pet Emporium.

"Zounds," she said. "Are you thinking what I am thinking?"

"If you're thinking that a pet shop would be an ideal place to store stolen dogs, then yes." Wei frowned. "It is a diabolically clever scheme."

"Talk about hiding in plain sight." Excitement buzzed through

Glory; all her instincts told her that Sir Barkley was in that large brick building. "I must go in."

"Wait, little tigress," he said tersely. "I am not certain it's safe. Let me go."

"You are far too recognizable. Bryant is bound to remember you after you pounded his leader into a fare-thee-well. But he won't know me."

Today, she was disguised as a genteel spinster. A silver-threaded wig, face paint, and spectacles assisted in aging her, and she'd chosen a dove-grey walking dress that marked her as respectable.

"I don't want you in there alone," Wei insisted.

"I can handle myself." She touched his arm. "Besides, I will not be in the shop alone. While I keep them occupied in the front, you can go in the back and look for Sir Barkley."

With Wei's hard kiss tingling on her lips, Glory opened the door to Eady's Pet Emporium. A bell tinkled as she entered, setting off a cacophony of sounds. Birds, cats, dogs, and other more exotic species moved excitedly in their cages, which filled three spacious aisles. On the right side of the shop was a large wooden counter, over which Bryant was having a quiet but intense conversation with a fellow wearing a leather apron over his sizeable midsection.

The men barely spared her a glance before returning to their discussion. Glory had chosen her present persona for a reason. Middle-aged spinsters were the most invisible members of society, which had its advantages.

Reminding herself to be patient, Glory meandered about the shop like a patron would, pretending to examine the merchandise. At the aisle closest to the counter, she stopped to stroke the head of a baby brown ferret, eavesdropping all the while.

"...I cannot take any more inventory," the shop owner said.

"It's a legitimate business that I'm running, and I can't put it at risk."

Inventory? Does he mean the stolen dogs? Glory strained to hear more.

"You owe me, Eady." Bryant's voice had an edge of menace. "This is your way o' paying off your gambling debts."

"Well, I am done."

"You ain't done until I say you are," Bryant snarled. "You know what the Wolf'll do if 'e finds out you've been running a game behind 'is back?"

Scott doesn't know about the dognappings?

Glory tucked away the useful tidbit.

"But this scheme wasn't my idea," Eady sputtered. "*You* came to me."

"Who do you think the Wolf will believe? Me, his trusted lieutenant or you, a namby-pamby bugger who can't pay 'is debts? I 'ave the bloke's ear, and if you even think o' reneging on our deal, then I'll be telling 'im that you came to me wif this 'alf-baked plan."

"All right, all right. I'll do as you say." Eady made a sudden noise in his throat. "Good afternoon, ma'am. May I help you?"

Realizing that she'd been seen, Glory played her part.

"Good afternoon, sir." Adopting the manner of a retiring spinster, she stepped out of the aisle and came toward him. "I am shopping for a new companion and saw that you have quite a selection."

Eady sized her up, smirking as he judged her an easy target for his wares.

"I am sure I have whatever you need," he said.

Bryant dismissed her entirely, rapping his knuckles against the counter. "Eady, do we 'ave an understanding? I don't want to 'ave to drag my arse in 'ere again."

"Yes, yes," Eady said impatiently. "I'll expect the next, ahem, shipment as usual."

Bryant stalked past Glory without sparing her a look.

Just as well.

"Now, madam." Eady wore an oily smile. "Let me guess. You are in the market for a cat?"

Wei should be searching the backroom by now. Buy him time.

"How did you know?" Glory said diffidently.

"Feline companionship can be so rewarding to ladies such as yourself," Eady said. "May I suggest one of my newest arrivals, a lovely Siamese?"

"I was thinking of a less exotic breed." Glory made her tone timid. "A tabby, perhaps?"

"That would suit you. If you'll step this way, I will show you a pair of tabby kittens. They are siblings, and you would enjoy owning the pair."

Glory scrunched her forehead, pretending to think. "I was not planning to purchase two cats, sir. After all, I have ten of them already."

"Of course you do," Eady said with a condescending smile. "One can never have too many cats, can one?"

"I suppose you are right." Glory peered at him through her spectacles, as if he'd given her a bright idea. "The only thing better than ten cats would be a dozen."

"Precisely, ma'am..."

Eady trailed off as barks sounded faintly. He shifted his gaze to a door at the back of the shop.

"Do you carry accessories, sir?" Glory said hastily. "Several of my cats are in need of new collars and beds."

"Right this way, ma'am." Eady returned his attention to her, his eyes gleaming like the newly minted coins he was likely counting in his head. "I have everything you need and more."

Glory hurried out of the shop. Turning the corner, she walked down two blocks, keeping an eye out for Mr. Devlin's circling hackney. When she saw it, she waved.

As Mr. Devlin handed her into the carriage, he said in a low voice, "By Jove, we've done it."

Glory saw the triumph in his eyes before she boarded the vehicle. Inside, a white-and-brindle bull terrier was sitting between Wei's legs.

"You found him," she exclaimed as the carriage lurched into motion. "Hello, Sir Barkley! It is very nice to meet you at last. Mrs. Mumford-Mills will be so happy to see you."

The dog wagged his tail as she petted him between his pricked ears. Giving him a quick once-over, she found that he had a few scratches, and his short coat was crusted with dirt. His ribs also stuck out more than they should, but he seemed otherwise fine.

"There were at least two dozen dogs in the backroom," Wei said, his jaw taut. "The bastards crammed all of them in a single cage. I wanted to take more with me, but I didn't want to expose our plan. And we don't know who those dogs belong to."

"We will get those dogs back to their homes," Glory said determinedly. "Whilst in the shop, I learned some useful information that gave me an idea. A plan that will allow us to grow two plants from one seed. We can help the dogs and get the answers you need from Scott."

TWENTY-SEVEN

"How am I supposed to do a final fitting of your gown without you, Lady Glory? I am a dressmaker, not a miracle worker."

Two days later, Mrs. Quinton—Mrs. Q to intimates—folded her arms as she regarded Glory, Livy, and Fiona in a private dressing room of her celebrated atelier. The African modiste was much in demand, her list of clients ripped from the pages of Debrett's. It was rumored that the waiting time to secure an appointment at her Bond Street shop was over a year long. Given her friendship with Charlie, Mrs. Q made an exception for the Angels. Not only did she design their everyday ensembles, but she also created some special items for them.

In the secret workshop below her atelier, she designed frocks and accessories for the Angels that were both fashionable and functional. From umbrellas with retractable blades to dresses with detachable skirts, Mrs. Q made sure the ladies were properly outfitted for their missions. Her current project, however, was an ivory ballgown for Glory's birthday celebration, which was draped on a dressmaker's dummy.

"You have worked miracles before, Mrs. Q," Glory cajoled.

She was standing on a dais facing a looking glass. Instead of trying on her birthday ensemble, however, she was hurriedly getting into a male disguise.

"Hawksmoor certainly thought so." Winking, Fi helped Glory don a waistcoat. "He was most appreciative of the unmentionables you recently made for me."

Livy rolled her eyes as she adhered a mustache above Glory's lip. "Perhaps that is a bit too much information, Fi?"

"Hello, pot," Fi retorted. "As I recall, you boasted that Mrs. Q's stockings helped you smooth things over with Hadleigh."

A smile tucked into Livy's cheeks. "When all else fails, hosiery paves the path for marital happiness."

"I wouldn't ask, Mrs. Q, but I am in a bind," Glory pleaded. "My mama plans to return for me in three hours, and during that time I must complete a mission in Whitechapel."

Yesterday had led to several developments.

First, the Angels had the satisfaction of closing the Mumford-Mills case. Through their viewing holes into Charlie's study, Glory and her friends watched the touching reunion between the spinster and her beloved bull terrier. Having forgotten her own handkerchief, Glory had to borrow one from Fiona. Afterward, the Angels shared a celebratory toast with their mentor.

"Well done, Angels." Approval shone in Charlie's grey gaze. "Due to your efforts, Mrs. Mumford-Mills has been reunited with her faithful companion. I will also be sending a note to my contact at the Metropolitan Police about the stolen dogs being stashed at Eady's Pet Emporium. With any luck, the police will seize the pets and reunite them with the rightful owners."

"Before you do that." Glory cleared her throat. "I have a request."

"Oh?"

Having gained Wei's permission, Glory told her group about his quest to gain justice for his family and the role Scott might play.

Her mouth tight, Charlie said, "Such injustice cannot be tolerated. As Mr. Chen has been a friend to us, we will assist him however we can."

"That is very kind," Glory replied. "Being a private fellow, however, Wei does not accept help easily. I tried to convince him to let the society help, but he refused."

"*Wei*, is it?" Charlie's gaze was keen.

"Yes," Glory said steadily, despite her warm cheeks. "It is."

Charlie sighed. "Sometimes I wonder if I am running an investigative society or a matchmaking service."

"Why can't it be both?" Fi quipped.

Charlie cast her gaze heavenward as the Angels pealed with laughter.

"Wei only agreed to let me share his past because it affects the closing of our case," Glory said when the merriment subsided. "Charlie, could you delay alerting the police about Eady's? Only a few days, I promise. Wei has contacted Scott, requesting an audience. We are scheduled to meet with him tomorrow."

"You are going to see Scott without reinforcements?" Charlie frowned.

"Hadleigh and I can accompany you," Livy offered. "After everything Mr. Chen has done for us, we would like to repay his kindness. Ask him if that would be all right."

Wei had been open to accepting Hadleigh's help. At present, he and the duke were waiting for Glory and Livy in a carriage in the lane behind the dress shop.

Sighing, Mrs. Q said, "I suppose I can figure something out."

"Thank you ever so much!" Glory said gratefully.

"But decisions remain to be made." A divot formed between the dressmaker's brows. "The trimmings, for instance, and final adjustments to the cut, not to mention the accessories—"

"No need to worry," Fi piped up. "Since Livy will be accompanying Glory, I can stay to manage the fashion choices. Glory trusts me, doesn't she?"

"More than I trust myself," Glory said honestly. "Thank you, Fi."

"What are bosom friends for?" Fi placed a hat on top of Glory's dark wig, adjusting it to a rakish angle. "*Voilà*. You are ready."

Livy checked her pocket watch. "We had better not keep the men waiting. They are liable to follow their preferred instinct and go ahead without us."

Her duke was every bit as protective as Wei.

"Good luck on your mission, my dears." Although Mrs. Q shook her head, her lips had a slight curve as she turned to Fiona. "Now you and I have our own assignment: to create an exceptional birthday ensemble for Lady Glory."

Fi gave a saucy salute. "You can count on me."

At the Fancy's flash house, the guards performed a search for weapons.

"I'll take your blades and pistols," one of the brutes said.

"I did not bring any," Wei replied.

He didn't need weapons to inflict damage. Nonetheless, he suffered through the search, grinding his teeth when the guard repeated the process with Glory. She was posing as a dark-haired lad today and while the guard's touch was quick and impersonal, Wei did not like any man putting his hands on her. For any reason.

Once the group was pronounced free of threats, the Hadleighs and Yao were made to wait in the public area. Another guard led Wei and Glory deeper into the Wolf's den.

"Stay close," Wei said quietly. "Let me do the talking."

Knowing Glory's reckless streak, he did not find her jaunty nod all that reassuring. A part of him regretted allowing her to accompany him here. Yesterday, when he'd given her a lesson—her lightness *kung fu* was improving literally by leaps and bounds—he had told her about his appointment with Scott.

She had immediately insisted upon going. While he'd balked due to the danger, she had argued that since she had come up with the ploy to barter information, she deserved to see it through. When that hadn't convinced him, she had resorted to a sweeter kind of persuasion.

Even though the door to the music room had been open and her mother or servants could walk by at any moment, she'd kissed him. Their passion had been incendiary. Before he knew it, he had her backed up against a wall, his tongue planted firmly in her mouth. She'd wriggled against him as they feasted on each other, making him so randy that he'd had the urge to toss up her skirts and make her his then and there.

He hadn't, of course. When he made love to her for the first time, it was going to be special. Not furtive and rushed. He had other reasons to wait, too. While he did not like keeping their relationship a secret, he understood why she'd asked him to delay speaking with her father. He liked how loyal she was to the people she loved, how determined she was to do the right thing. Thus, he supported her decision, even though a part of him resented that their love had to be relegated to shadows.

Until then, Wei would not take his beloved's virginity. Even if their relationship could not yet be made public, he was determined to court her. To show her the respect a lady deserved.

Scott was waiting for them in a private chamber. He was the picture of menacing indolence, sprawled on a weathered, throne-like chair and surrounded by a coterie of armed brutes. The familiar little white dog was lying on the gang leader's lap, getting his belly rubbed. The juxtaposition between Scott's gentle treatment of his pet and the cold stare he leveled upon his guests was jarring.

Scott's throat was bare, his silvery-brown mane brushing his shoulders. He'd also rolled up his sleeves, showing his tattoo in its full glory. Wei knew it was a baiting tactic, yet his aggression simmered nonetheless.

Upon my family's honor, I will get my answers today.

"Welcome...or should I say, welcome *back*?" Scott's smile was more a baring of teeth. "I knew I recognized you. A member of the Limehouse Lads, you said?"

"It was a necessary ruse," Wei said curtly.

"You bloody lied to me." Scott petted his dog, his tone frigid. "Consider yourself lucky that your tongue remains in your head. I know how much you enjoy sticking it into the wench beside you."

Wei's muscles bunched, at the insult to Glory and the fact that Scott had recognized her. As he curled his hands, calculating how many moves it would require for him to take down the hovering half-dozen guards, Glory cleared her throat.

Stepping forward, she said brightly, "Good morning, sir."

What in blazes is she doing? I told her not to draw attention to herself.

Before he could stop her, Glory went on, "Please accept my apologies for any past misunderstandings. Believe me when I say we had a reason for the subterfuge, which I promise to explain. First, however, I would like to thank you for granting us an audience today and to assure you that we come in goodwill. In truth, we wish to negotiate a trade...one that will be beneficial to both parties involved."

Scott stared at her as if she were a creature he'd never seen before. Wei knew the feeling.

"You wish to bargain with me?" The gang leader's voice was tinged with disbelief and scorn. "What could you have that would possibly interest me?"

"Information."

"About?"

"Your, um, group." Glory cast a nervous look at the surrounding guards. "And their loyalty to you, their leader."

Devil take it. Wei closed his hand around Glory's arm, pushing her behind him as the cutthroats made threatening noises and raised their weapons.

"Stand down." Although Scott's wave was casual, his tone brooked no refusal. "No one touches a hair on this wench's head unless I say so. Am I clear?"

Muttering their assent, the brutes stepped back and sheathed their steel.

"As for you." Scott aimed his gaze at Glory, who was peering around Wei's shoulder. "You will clarify your last statement, or I will let my guards have their way with you. In whatever way they choose."

"Leave her out of it," Wei warned. "This business is between you and me. I want to know about the other man who shares that tattoo with you. In exchange, I will provide you with information concerning a problem in your gang. Your ship has sprung a leak; if you want to keep it afloat, you will listen to what I have to say."

Wei knew his plan—or Glory's, rather—hit home when Scott's eyes thinned. Despite his outward arrogance, the cove wasn't a fool. He likely suspected there was trouble afoot in his domain. He just didn't know if he could trust Wei and Glory.

"We'll go first," Glory piped up. "As a show of good faith. But perhaps you would like to have this discussion in private?"

She gazed pointedly at the guards.

By the gods, is she trying to get us killed?

Scott's smile was humorless. "I trust my men more than I trust your Chinese friend here and his lethal fists."

As Wei had surmised, the man was not stupid.

"You have my word that I will not use force of any kind," Wei said. "Unless it is to defend against attack."

Scott cocked his head, raking his fingers idly through Beauregard's fur.

"You are dismissed." He waved at the guards. "Close the door behind you."

"But, Wolf," a beefy ruffian protested. "The bastard could be playing a trick—"

"I said *leave*."

Grumbling, the guards shuffled out, aiming threatening stares at Wei and Glory.

When the door closed, Scott arched a brow. "Well?"

Wei looked at Glory, who gave a nod of encouragement.

"A member of your gang has been running a dognapping scheme," Wei said. "He is using your name and the reputation of your gang to carry it out. I assume you are unaware of this."

Scott sat up straighter. "Dognapping? What the devil do you mean?"

"He steals pets from unsuspecting owners," Glory burst out indignantly. "A friend of ours was out shopping, and a pair of scoundrels grabbed her dog, a bull terrier by the name of Sir Barkley. Then another fellow named Farwell, who said he was acting as a middleman, began to extort her. He came by regularly to collect her money, claiming the payments were ransom for her dog. But our friend began to fear that she might never see her pet again and sought our help."

"Why you?" Scott asked bluntly.

He regarded Glory with skepticism, and even worse, *interest*. Stiffening, Wei had to force himself not to interfere. To let Glory carry out the plan, for he could not deny she was doing it well.

Scott quirked a brow. "Do you belong to some lady's society for the protection of animals?"

"Something like that." Glory's gaze shone with sincerity. "As a pet owner myself, Mr. Scott, I know that the bond between animal and human is sacred. As strong, and I daresay sometimes stronger, than bonds between people. Thus, I could not stand by whilst a lady and her beloved companion were ripped apart in the name of greed."

"Wolf."

Glory tipped her head. "I beg your pardon?"

"You may call me Wolf," Scott said silkily. "As my friends do. And what should I call you, little dove?"

Wei could stand it no longer.

"We are not here to make friends," Wei clipped out. "This is business."

"But pleasure makes business much more palatable," Scott drawled.

He set his dog on the ground, and the animal headed for Glory like a furry bullet. Beauregard bounced on his hind legs, and crouching, Glory petted him, giggling when he bowled her over, licking her face. Scott watched on with a speculative expression that coiled Wei's insides.

Scott unfolded himself from his chair, strode to a cabinet, and poured himself a drink. When he held up the bottle of amber liquid, Wei shook his head. And with added emphasis when Scott pointed the bottle at Glory, who was busy playing with Beauregard as if they weren't in the middle of a perilous negotiation.

Scott took a sip of his drink. "You have proof, I presume, that one of my men is behind the theft of these dogs?"

"Yes," Wei said. "We followed him to a pet shop. The owner of the shop is paying off his debts to your man by holding the dogs. We rescued Sir Barkley from a cage crammed with dozens of other animals and have since reunited him with his owner. If you question the shopkeeper, he will tell you everything."

"I plan to." Scott's tone suggested the questioning would not be pleasant. "And now you will tell me who is the supposed mastermind behind this vile scheme."

Wei went with his gut instinct. "Bryant."

Surprise flashed across Scott's face, followed by the shadow of wrath.

"And he stashes the dogs at Eady's Pet Emporium in Chelsea," Glory added.

"I see." Scott tossed back the rest of his glass. "If I discover that you are lying—"

"We aren't." Giving the dog one last pet, Glory rose and dusted herself off. "Do you recall the charm on Beauregard's collar?"

"The one that went missing..." Scott's eyebrows elevated. "Or was stolen."

"Is it stealing to take back something that was stolen?" Glory asked ingeniously. "You see, Wolf, Sir Barkley's owner commissioned that charm for him. When I showed it to her, she verified that it was indeed the item he is wearing in this miniature."

Removing the small portrait of Sir Barkley from an inner pocket, Glory held it out to Scott.

The gang leader took it, staring at it for long moments.

"Bryant is going to pay for this," he said tightly. "The bugger had the bollocks to give me that charm as a *gift* for Beauregard. He must have been laughing behind my bloody back."

"I am sorry your friend betrayed you," Glory said quietly.

Her empathy seemed to take Scott aback.

"Not as sorry as Bryant is going to be," he vowed. "While the Fancy has engaged in its share of infamy, I made it clear when I took over that there were rules. Women, children, and animals were never to be harmed. Every single venture required my stamp of approval." His eyes flashed with an emotion Wei knew well. "Bryant broke both those rules, and by God, he will answer for it."

As if sensing his owner's ill-temper, Beauregard scampered over. Scott scooped him up, holding the dog against his chest as he stared into the distance. Perhaps contemplating Bryant's fate...but that was not Wei's concern.

"We have upheld our end of the bargain," he said.

After a moment, Scott expelled a breath. "The man with the tattoo like mine. What do you want with him?"

"That is my business." Years of training went into Wei's composure. "What I will say is that your friend has done grievous harm, and you cannot protect him from the consequences."

"He is no friend of mine."

Intrigued by the disgust in Scott's voice, Wei asked, "Then why are you protecting him?"

"I am not. Protecting him, that is." A muscle stood out along Scott's jaw. "The man you're looking for is named Leonard Kray."

Leonard Kray. Wei's breathing turned shallow, triumph and hatred swirling as he learned his enemy's name at long last.

He felt a small hand slip into his. Glory looked at him with wide, concerned eyes. He squeezed her fingers, reassuring her that he was all right.

"Kray is a twisted, murderous bastard. He deserves to sow whatever he reaped," Scott said.

"Then tell me where he is," Wei demanded.

"I don't know. Haven't seen the bugger in years. And before you ask me how I knew him, let me echo your earlier sentiment: that is my business. If you push me on this, I will end this discussion here and now."

Bloody hell. Of course, Wei did not expect things to be easy. He reminded himself that, thanks to Glory, he had the name of his family's killer. It was the most progress he'd made since arriving in London.

He calmed his tone. "If you could offer any additional information concerning Leonard Kray, I would be appreciative."

"Kray is the most devious and cold-blooded bastard of my acquaintance. And, in my line of work, I've met my share of bastards." Scott's gaze had that faraway look again. "Kray, however, was in a class of his own. A manipulator with no conscience. He lied so often and well that it was difficult to disentangle the falsehoods from the facts. In truth, I cannot guarantee the veracity of anything I am about to share."

"Tell me what you know, and I will judge for myself."

"Kray claimed that he was well-born, a younger son of a younger son. He had some falling out with his family; when he got deep into his cups, he would speak of them with rage. He was resentful of his grandfather, who refused to send him on a Grand

Tour and disowned him when he was caught for a crime which he did not elaborate upon. All I know is that he blamed some woman for 'seducing him' and landing him in Newgate.

"When Kray was released, he traveled the world on his own to spite his grandfather, funding his adventures, no doubt, through nefarious activities. He had a taste for pain and suffering, specifically inflicting it on others. He bragged about his visits to exotic places." Scott glanced at Wei. "Including China."

Hands curling, Wei bit out, "Go on."

"When Kray returned to England, he quickly spent whatever fortune he'd amassed abroad. Again, he turned to his murderous skills to make a living. I last saw him over six years ago and do not know where he is now."

"How do I find the blackguard?" Wei refused to accept a dead end.

"I know someone who might know where Kray is," Scott said. "If he is, indeed, alive."

He had better be alive. So that I can end his miserable existence myself.

"Who is this person?" Wei said tersely. "How do I contact him?"

"You don't. Not if you want answers. This person is particular about who she associates with, and she will not see you, let alone speak to you, without an introduction."

She. A woman can tell me where Kray is?

"Will you make an introduction?" Wei asked.

A beat of silence.

"I believe I will." Scott's expression held a peculiar mix of emotions that Wei couldn't decipher. "This will require time, but I shall do my best to sway her. Await my instructions."

Twenty-Eight

Three days later, Wei had not heard from Scott. He counseled himself to be patient. After fifteen years of chasing down the killer, what did another few days matter? The important thing was that he was finally making progress. He busied himself with the activities at the clinic, treating patients and teaching martial arts.

What made the time drag was Glory's absence. She'd sent him a letter, apologizing that a slew of social obligations prevented her from seeing him. Now that her parents were back, she had to attend various functions with them, including a boating regalia on the Thames yesterday. She was also working hard to plan a luncheon in honor of her papa's campaign.

The last thing Wei wished was to be the cause of friction between Glory and her parents. He liked that she was a dutiful daughter and did not want her to apologize for fulfilling her role. At the same time, he had to fight his demons. The ones that whispered that he was good for clandestine fucking and nothing else.

Rationally, he knew Glory didn't see him that way. She'd said she loved him—and shown him too. She'd stood by him in his quest and pleasured him so sweetly; she was giving, loyal, and adorable...everything he wanted in a bride. Yet the longer they kept their relationship in the dark, the more he questioned if they could ever step out into the light.

Even after her father's bill was presented, Wei would remain a liability in His Grace's political and social life. The duke's daughter would be married to a foreigner who helped opium users in the East End. Even if Glory's parents allowed the marriage—and that was a big *if*—was it fair of Wei to ask her to leave her life of privilege behind? To bring the woman he loved so far down in the world? Was he worth everything that she would have to sacrifice?

When Wei meditated, the questions whirled like shed leaves. It required more and more effort to empty his mind. To stay with his breath and not allow his thoughts to run amok. During other times, he managed to maintain his outward composure...at least to those who didn't know him well.

"Missing your little lady, are you?" Yao sauntered into the courtyard, an apple in hand.

Wei, who'd been working his frustrations out on a sparring dummy, paused for breath.

"I am practicing what our *shifu* taught us," he said. "You might do the same."

"Don't need to. Unlike you, I'm not as jumpy as a cricket on a hot stone." Yao took a large, crunchy bite of the fruit. "Don't blame you, though," he said through his mouthful. "She's a rare find. Pretty, rich, and bold as brass. *Shifu* would like her."

"You think so?" Wei couldn't help but ask.

"I *know* so. If for no other reason than the fact that she's proved his philosophy right."

Wei pitted his brows. "How do you mean?"

"You know Master Lam's favorite teaching. *Do not do.*" Yao mimicked their *shifu*'s voice. "He was always lecturing that striving has the opposite effect. Telling us to have the patience to let things unfold, etcetera, etcetera. Take your revenge, for example. You were focused on that for years and yet made little progress."

"I still don't understand what this has to do with Glory."

"Well, you met her, and for the first time since I've known you, *shihing*, you thought about something other than revenge. Something even sweeter, eh?"

Wei felt his face heat.

Yao took another bite of apple, chewing noisily. "The funny thing is that when you got distracted by romance, you started making progress on your vengeance. After all, we had been chasing dead ends for months until Lady Glory came along. Then you became obsessed with protecting her, which ironically led to you going to that fight and seeing the tattoo on that Scott fellow. Not only that, but it was her dognapping case that led her to Bryant which, in turn, gave you the leverage to get the information you needed to find your family's killer. See what I mean?"

The hairs on Wei's skin stirred as he soaked in the wisdom of Yao's observations. While Wei had first resisted his attraction to Glory, believing that it was a distraction that would take him away from his purpose, the opposite was true. Meeting Glory and falling in love with her had set him on the correct path.

"*Shidai*." Wei shook his head in wonder. "When did you get so insightful?"

"It wasn't for nothing that I was known as the 'Smartest Man in Shandong.'" Yao tapped his temple. "Most of the time I just can't be bothered to tell people what I'm thinking. Too much effort when I'd rather take a nap."

After the enlightening conversation, Wei was even more eager to see Glory. Luckily, she was available on the third day, and Wei went to give her a lesson at home. Unable to bridle his impatience, he arrived early; she was waiting for him in the music room, a vision of innocent sensuality in a frock the color of bluebells. She rushed to him, and her dazzling smile made him want to sweep her into his arms and kiss her senseless.

Since the door was open and her chaperone could enter at any moment, he had to settle for a bow.

"I've missed you, my love." He spoke in Chinese.

"I've missed you dreadfully," she replied in kind. "No news?"

Knowing what she meant, he shook his head. "Not yet."

"Scott did say it would take time."

She took his hand, her mere touch making his blood run hotter. For thirteen years, he had practiced celibacy without difficulty. Yet every minute he spent apart from Glory made him feel like a lad discovering lust for the first time.

"We will get to the bottom of this. You must have patience and faith that everything will work out as it should," she said earnestly.

As he was about to tease her about her newfound appreciation for patience, footsteps thumped in the hallway. Glory dropped his hand, the two of them parting hastily. Her brothers burst into the room, their dark locks mussed from what appeared to be a hurried journey. They skidded to a stop in front of Wei.

"Good day, sir." Theodore sounded out of breath. "We heard you arrive."

Wei nodded. "Good day to you, Masters Horatio and Theodore."

"Earlier, Glory was showing off the *kung fu* you taught her," Horatio said without preamble.

"I was not showing off. I was practicing," Glory retorted.

Her brother ignored her. "I want to learn how to leap over the pianoforte as well. Won't you teach me, Master Chen? I am free right now."

"Me too, sir!" Theo raised his hand, bouncing up and down.

Wei quirked a brow at Glory, who regarded her brothers with fond exasperation.

"Perhaps Mr. Chen can give you a *few* tips," she said. "But mind you don't take up my entire lesson."

"Hooray!" the lads shouted.

As Wei instructed the boys on the fundamental position of horse stance, he found himself enjoying their lively company. They took after their sister in their exuberance and curiosity...and impatience apparently ran in the bloodline.

"How much longer do I have to hold this pose?" Theo groaned.

"Longer than the thirty seconds you've held it thus far," Glory said.

"But it feels like *forever*. My legs hurt."

"Try focusing on a spot in the distance," she advised. "It helps the time pass more quickly."

She winked at Wei over the scamp's head. Warmth thrummed in Wei's chest. It had been a long time since he'd felt like a...a part of something. While he had found a family of sorts with Shifu Lam and Yao, he realized now that he'd been so wrapped up in his vengeance that he hadn't appreciated his time with them as much as he should have.

Yet Glory had a way of making him forget the darker side of life. She made him remember what it felt like to be happy and carefree. To look toward the future with hope...

"Am I doing horse stance correctly?" Horatio said, gritting his teeth.

"Set your shoulders back. Like this."

As Wei placed a hand on the lad's shoulder, intending to adjust his position, Glory reached out at the same time. Their hands touched, setting off a spark of electric awareness. Her breathless laugh revealed too much and made him hard as a rock...

"I thought I heard a ruckus in here." The Duchess of Ranelagh and Somerville swept in, looking regal in a striped navy dress. "Oh, hello, Mr. Chen. I did not realize you had arrived."

"I was early, Your Grace." Wei bowed. "I hope that is not an inconvenience."

"Not for me. It seems, however, that the boys have been pestering you when they are supposed to be working on their lessons." The duchess gave her sons a reproachful look. "Does your tutor know where you are?"

"We, um, told Mr. Welton that we had to use the necessary," Theodore admitted.

"Which we did," Horatio said virtuously. "We just stopped here on our way back to the schoolroom."

Her Grace rolled her eyes. "With arguments like that, I predict a shining career in politics for both of you. Now run along, and don't keep Mr. Welton waiting."

"Yes, Mama," the boys chorused before filing out.

"Now, Mr. Chen," the duchess said pleasantly. "Glory says you will be attending her ball."

"Yes, Your Grace. Thank you. I will be most pleased to attend."

Although Wei was not certain how he would fit in with the high-kick crowd, he looked forward to celebrating his beloved's birthday with her. In fact, he had a gift to mark the occasion... which he would have to give her in private to avoid suspicion. Nonetheless, he took it as a positive sign that Glory's mother had invited him—a tutor and therefore a mere cut above a servant—to a social event. Perhaps, with time, her family could accept him after all.

"Splendid," the duchess replied. "In that case, I was hoping you might lend a hand with something."

"I would be happy to assist if I can," Wei said.

"Since you have done a marvelous job of teaching Glory to curb her impetuosity, perhaps you could help her apply that principle to dancing. You see, my daughter is a gifted dancer, but she has a marked tendency to lead."

"*Mama.*" Glory glowered at her parent. "Must you embarrass me in front of my..." She caught herself in time. "My *shifu*?"

"Who better than your *shifu* to teach you to dance?" The duchess's rebuttal proved that she had contributed to her offspring's ability to argue. "Dancing is a form of movement, not unlike martial arts."

"I beg your pardon, Your Grace." Wei's face heated with

embarrassment. "I am afraid that I am not a qualified teacher for Lady Glory. Unfortunately, I...I don't know how to dance."

"Oh. I did not realize..." The duchess was obviously flustered.

Glory gawked at him. "You don't know how to dance?"

"Not in the English fashion." Feeling more self-conscious by the moment, Wei tried to explain without coming across as an unrefined idiot. "Given the demands of the clinic, I did not have time to learn. To be frank, there was also no reason. I do not attend many social gatherings and..."

He realized that he was digging a bigger hole. His lack of wealth and status were already huge obstacles to gaining the approval of Glory's family; he did not need to emphasize his lack of social graces as well. He was the impoverished soldier's son all over again, not knowing his place. Upsetting the order of things and asking for trouble. Aiming for a lady who wasn't just out of reach but out of his sphere entirely.

"It appears the tables have been turned."

Glory's voice brought him back. She was smiling, and her sweet dimples calmed his inner tempest.

"How so?" he asked, bemused.

"Today, I will get to teach *you* something."

TWENTY-NINE

After Elsie finished fastening Glory's ballgown, Glory saw the maid's eyes widen.

"What is it?" Glory asked. "Does something look wrong?"

"Not at all, my lady." Elsie busied herself gathering things. "Why don't you show the other ladies? I will collect your accessories."

The maid darted from behind the dressing screen, and Glory followed. Fi, Livy, and Pippa were lounging in her bedchamber, keeping her company while she got ready for the ball. They'd also thrown her a surprise celebration which included champagne, cakes from Gunter's, and other thoughtful gifts: a book about China from Livy, a garnet-studded comb from Fi, and a miniature of FF II that Pippa had painted herself.

Charlie, who'd left town again, had also sent a present. It was an exquisite filigree compass with an emerald marking north. The inscription read, "May you always follow your heart."

Glory went over to the full-length looking glass, turning to look at all angles. "Um, Fiona?"

Fi paused in her perusal of the iced cakes. "Yes, dear?"

"Where is the rest of my dress?"

"What do you mean?" Fi asked innocently. "It is all there."

The vee at the front of the ivory organza gown was more daring than usual, but it was the plunging dip on the other side that made Glory blink.

"What about the back?" she asked. "It appears to be missing."

Rolling her eyes, Fi selected a lemon cream cake with a pair of silver tongs. "Mrs. Q and I agreed that your frock needed a little something to make it unforgettable. Trust me, this silhouette is the latest rage in Paris. Ladies, do tell Glory how delightful she looks."

"You look a treat, dear," Pippa said absentmindedly.

Reclining on the chaise, she didn't seem to be paying attention since she was enjoying a foot rub from Livy.

She made a sound of pleasure. "Goodness, that feels divine. My feet have been killing me."

"I remember what it was like at this stage," Livy said.

"I cannot wait for this little one to make his or her appearance." Grimacing, Pippa patted her extended belly.

Concerned, Glory went over. "Are you certain you are well enough to be here?"

"I shan't be staying for the dancing." Pippa reached out to give Glory's hand a squeeze. "But I did not want to miss wishing you many happy returns, dearest. By the by...where is the rest of your dress?"

"I knew it was too scanty!" Glory exclaimed.

Pippa chuckled. "I am only teasing. You look stunning, dear. Mr. Chen won't be able to keep his eyes off you."

"Not just his eyes," Fi quipped.

Chuckling, Livy said, "Are you and Mr. Chen still waiting to speak to your parents?"

"Yes, even though I wish we didn't have to." Glory sighed. "But I cannot risk the damage a scandal would do to Papa's bill. Especially not now, when Papa is under such scrutiny."

"If your marriage to Mr. Chen affects His Grace's campaign,

the fault lies with close-minded gossips, not you," Livy said firmly. "Your papa would not blame you for it."

"He probably wouldn't."

But can I live with myself if I am the cause of Papa's failure? If I jeopardize his attempt to right a horrendous injustice by creating a scandal or distracting him?

"How do you think your parents will take the news when you tell them?" Fi asked.

"Mama will be supportive, I think." Glory perched on a chair next to her. "She has never put a fine point on things like money and rank. Papa might be a different story. He loves me, but he tends to be overprotective."

"Fathers can surprise you," Pippa replied. "I wasn't certain mine would approve of Cull, yet he and my husband have become best cronies. If we have a boy, Cull wants to name him after Papa. Mama says Papa can't stop talking about it and has already commissioned silver stamped with our 'son's' initials."

"Papa and Mr. Chen do have a lot in common," Glory mused. "When it comes to their character and interests...not to mention their shared Chinese heritage. I am hoping that tonight will give them a chance to discover their similarities."

If she and Wei announced their intent to wed now, without giving time for Papa and Wei to find common ground, the results were likely to be disastrous. The last thing she wanted was friction between Wei and her family: she didn't want her papa to reject Wei's suit or for Wei to experience that rejection. Thus, as hard as it was, waiting a few more weeks before revealing their love seemed like the best compromise.

"Shall we toast to that?" Livy suggested. "Glory's future happiness?"

"To Glory's future," the others said.

After they clinked glasses, Glory added, "We should also toast the successful closing of our case."

The newspapers this morning had reported that the police had broken up a dognapping ring. They had seized stolen pets from Eady's Pet Emporium and were reuniting them with their owners. Eady and Farwell were in custody, and the authorities were searching for Bryant, who'd gone missing.

"Here, here," the Angels chorused.

When Glory's parents came in soon after, her friends left to give them privacy.

"How charming you look, Glory," Mama said warmly. "Rhys, darling, our little girl is all grown up."

"Quite." Papa frowned. "But is your ballgown missing something? A cape, perhaps?"

"You do not like my gown?" Glory asked fretfully.

"Don't pay your father any mind." Mama gave him a chiding look. "He offered me a cloak this evening."

Since Mama looked ravishing in her ruffled cabernet gown, Glory felt reassured.

"Just trying to prevent a duel," Papa drawled. "Since I will be fighting off all the chaps who'll be sniffing after the two most beautiful ladies in London."

Mama laughed. "Since when have you had to fight a duel over me?"

"I would fight a thousand duels for you, Maggie mine."

When Papa gallantly kissed Mama's hand, she blushed like a schoolgirl.

"And this is for you, poppet." Papa withdrew a flat velvet box from his pocket. "From Mama and me."

"Happy birthday, dearest," Mama said. "We hope you like it."

Opening the box, Glory lifted out the beautiful gold locket. It was heart-shaped, a sparkling diamond set at the center. What made the necklace even more special was the smaller identical charm nestled next to it in satin.

"Is that for FF II?" Glory exclaimed. "It will look brilliant on his collar!"

"Why did we bother getting a necklace for our daughter?"

Papa asked Mama wryly. "When all she notices is the jewelry for the ferret?"

"I adore both pieces." Glory hugged her parents each in turn.

"Shall I help you put it on?" Papa asked.

Taking the jewelry box from her, he twirled a finger, and she obediently turned around. The necklace felt cool and smooth, the delicate chain comfortable to wear as Papa deftly fastened the clasp.

"How does it look?" she asked.

"You will be the belle of the ball," Mama declared.

"I hope I make a good impression," Glory said sincerely. "I know Papa invited some special guests this evening. I am looking forward to meeting Mr. Rothwell."

"As it happens, Rothwell will be bringing a guest." Papa cleared his throat. "Matthew Winslow, his nephew and private secretary, will be accompanying him this eve. I think you will like Winslow, poppet. He is a progressive thinker with a head for business; he has put together several successful investment schemes, and gentlemen are vying for shares. He's a widower but not too old—in his forties. Quite popular with the ladies, I'm told."

Glory frowned. She wanted to tell her father that it did not matter how charming or progressive Matthew Winslow was because her heart already belonged to Wei. But how would Papa react?

"Glory's *shifu* is coming tonight," Mama said.

"Chen?" Papa lowered his brows. "You invited him, Maggie mine?"

"Yes. Not only is he a respected master of his craft, but he is also a friend of the Hadleighs," Mama replied. "More importantly, Glory likes him."

Papa turned his gaze upon Glory. "Is that true, poppet?"

"I do, um, enjoy Master Chen's company." Glory prayed her blush wouldn't give her away. "If you spent time with him, I think you would too. You know about Mr. Chen's work, but did you know that his father also fought opium as a respected soldier in the Daoguang Emperor's Imperial Army?"

"How interesting." Papa's expression was inscrutable. "Perhaps I shall make an effort to converse with Mr. Chen this eve."

Glory could barely contain her joy. "That would be lovely."

"As long as you promise a dance to Winslow," Papa said.

It was a neat move, but Glory didn't care. She would do a jig with the devil himself if it meant Papa would give Wei a chance.

"I shall reserve Mr. Winslow a place on my dance card," she said.

"Isn't Glory in exceptionally fine looks this eve?" the Duchess of Hadleigh asked.

"She is always in fine looks," Wei said.

He was standing with the duchess and her husband, watching his beloved whirl across the dance floor. In his eyes, Glory was pretty no matter what her outer trappings were. Tonight, however, her rare beauty was showcased with an extravagance befitting a duke's daughter.

Her embroidered ivory frock was a work of art. The fitted bodice bared her lovely shoulders—and, in Wei's opinion, far too much in general. He felt a bite of possessiveness when he saw her current partner, a fair-haired gentleman, place his hand on the exposed skin between her shoulder blades as he deftly spun her into a turn.

Her fluffy skirts had an overlay of golden netting that was embroidered with peonies in shades of pink and peach surrounded by spring-green leaves. As she spun, the tiers unfurled like sparkling petals. Her partner said something, and the smile she gave him outshone the crystal chandeliers overhead. The fellow responded by subtly trailing his fingers across her back, and Wei experienced an urge to punch the cove in the face.

"Try to look like you are enjoying yourself," Hadleigh murmured. "Or, at the very least, like you are not planning to beat Winslow to a fare-thee-well."

Startled by his friend's acumen, Wei realized that his hands were balled. He relaxed them and took a deep breath. He still wasn't used to Glory's effect on his self-control.

"Thank you," he said in a low voice. "I do not know what came over me."

"I do," Hadleigh said wryly. "Punching Matthew Winslow, however, isn't going to accomplish anything."

It might make me feel better.

Wei knew the duke was right, of course. At this lavish event attended by the crème de la crème of English society, he was already a fish out of water. His goal of gaining the acceptance of Glory's family was not going to be helped if he acted like a barbarian.

Nonetheless, he had to ask. "What do you know about Winslow?"

"He's the nephew of philanthropist Emmett Rothwell. Son of a dead sister, I believe. Winslow acts as Rothwell's private secretary and manages some of his business interests. Winslow's a widower." Hadleigh turned to his lady. "Anything to add, little queen?"

"Only the most important fact." Her Grace gave Wei a knowing smile. "Glory has no interest in Winslow whatsoever. Her affections are entirely engaged elsewhere."

Beneath his cravat, Wei's neck burned with embarrassment. He wasn't used to feeling unsure of himself...like a lovesick mooncalf. He suddenly flashed to the last time he'd felt this way, and an icy droplet rolled down his spine.

From afar, he'd watched Chun during the Mid-Autumn Festival celebration her husband hosted for the entire village. Sitting next to the governor, distributing moon cakes to the peasants with a benevolent smile, she, too, had been garbed in the finest robes. She, too, had been the object of admiration. She, too, had been beyond Wei's reach. Only when the guests were gone and under the cover of shadows had she cavorted with Wei.

The poor soldier's son who was good for only one thing.

Who was a dirty secret and nothing more.

"I have it on good authority that what Glory would truly like for her birthday," the duchess said, her eyes sparkling, "is a dance with you."

Wei nodded gruffly, grateful for the reminder. Glory wasn't like Chun. For her, love wasn't a game, and when she pledged her affections, she did so with that enchanting, wholehearted sweetness that was part of her personality. She had promised to marry him, said she wanted a future together. From her, those words meant something—everything.

The gift he'd brought her bumped softly in his inner pocket. He couldn't wait to give it to her, and, if she was willing, maybe they could set a date for him to bring his suit to her father. Even if that date was weeks ahead, he could work with it. He could wait, as long as he knew that she was as committed as he was.

"Pay attention, old boy," Hadleigh said. "Here comes your lady's pater."

Wei straightened his shoulders as the Duke of Ranelagh and Somerville approached, accompanied by Emmett Rothwell. He made the introductions, although none were necessary. Rothwell was presently the darling of London, the papers effusive in their praise of his charitable character. He was shorter than His Grace, wider in the middle, and a couple of decades older. With thick silver hair and distinctively hawkish features, he radiated an aura of prosperity and power.

"How are you enjoying the ball, Chen?" Glory's father asked.

"It is a celebration worthy of the occasion, Your Grace."

"Prettily said," the duke drawled.

"His Grace tells me that you treat opium users here in

London." Rothwell addressed Wei in the manner of one used to commanding attention. "How taxing it must be to minister to those poor misguided wretches. I admire your tenacity in tackling such a difficult task."

Wei was aware of Hadleigh's tense posture. The duchess put a hand on her husband's arm, narrowing her eyes at Rothwell. Obviously, Rothwell did not know that Hadleigh had once been a "poor misguided wretch." While Rothwell probably didn't mean to let his condescension show, Wei knew that his friend felt it.

"The true tenacity is not mine, sir," Wei said. "But rather that of the men who fight for their recovery. In truth, I find the work more inspiring than taxing, for it reveals the resilience of the human spirit. It is a privilege to witness men find their way once again and be stronger for it."

In the awkward silence that followed, Rothwell's face reddened. The Duke of Ranelagh and Somerville said nothing, but his enigmatic expression was unlikely to be a good sign. Frustration welled in Wei; he wanted to kick himself. What had he been thinking lecturing the bloody philanthropist who was the cornerstone to Glory's father's success?

Am I trying to sabotage my chances of winning over my beloved's family?

"Well said, Master Chen." The Duchess of Hadleigh spoke up with determined brightness. "I find your informed viewpoint most elucidating. Accounts such as yours would certainly be useful in a campaign to educate the public...don't you agree, Mr. Rothwell?"

"Of course, Your Grace." Rothwell adjusted his lapels, his tone clipped. "If I may ask, Mr. Chen, how did your interest in combating opium come about?"

"My father was a soldier in China. On the Emperor's orders, he fought to suppress the smuggling of opium." Wei shrugged. "I suppose I took up the mantle from him, in a manner of speaking."

"A family vocation, one might say." Sir Rothwell's eyes

gleamed with interest. His irises were nearly black, blending with his pupils. "Where in China was your father stationed?"

"In a coastal village along the Pearl River Delta. Not far from Canton." Wei angled his head. "Have you been to China, sir?"

"I have not had the pleasure, no. But you ought to speak to my nephew, Matthew Winslow. He did a stint at the British factory in Canton. Ah, speak of the devil."

The memory of the British compound, of his powerlessness in the face of those smirking traders, rose like a spectre, causing Wei's insides to lurch. He turned and saw Winslow heading toward the group with Glory on his arm. He was saying something to her, but her eyes were on Wei. When she smiled, Wei found his equilibrium again.

"Winslow, you and my daughter cut quite the path on the dance floor," the Duke of Ranelagh and Somerville said.

"The credit goes to Lady Glory," Winslow said. "Her light-footedness made up for my clumsy partnering."

The man's gallantry was almost as annoying as his good looks. With Rothwell and Winslow standing together, the family resemblance between them was clear. Winslow had the same hawkish features, but they were tempered into handsomeness.

"You are a fine partner, sir," Glory averred. "I enjoyed our dance."

Even though Wei knew that Glory was being polite and responding to Winslow's self-deprecation, he couldn't quell a pang of jealousy. Which, in turn, made him feel stupid. Moreover, she had told him about her difficulties in social situations, and he ought to be happy that she was enjoying herself for once.

And he was. He wanted her to enjoy her success. To know how beautiful and desirable she was. What bothered him wasn't that other males were attracted to her: it was that he could not publicly stake his claim.

"Mr. Winslow, have you met my *shifu*, Master Chen?" Glory asked.

Winslow gave Wei a friendly nod. "Lady Glory was telling me that she is learning martial arts. That is a unique accomplishment for a young lady."

"And a useful one." Wei inclined his head curtly. "A lady can never be too careful."

"Isn't that what we gentlemen are for?" Winslow raised his brows, saying with a chuckle, "Careful, Chen, or you will render us obsolete one day."

I wouldn't mind rendering you obsolete right now.

Glory's brow pleated. "Just because a lady can take care of herself doesn't mean that a gentleman will have no uses."

"And here is such a use now," Hadleigh said smoothly. He turned to his wife. "I do believe they are playing your favorite waltz, my love. Will you do me the honor?"

"You know you're my favorite partner." The duchess placed a hand on his arm, adding, "And I believe this is Glory's favorite song as well."

Wei saw Winslow open his mouth, but he beat the other to it.

"Lady Glory," he said. "May I have this dance?"

She showed him those irresistible dimples, flooding his chest and his groin with desire. With longing greater than he had ever felt before.

"I thought you would never ask," she said.

THIRTY

Although Wei was a novice to dancing, he was the best partner Glory had ever had.

They started slowly, in time with the music. She shivered at his closeness and proprietary touch, the way his callused fingers rested gently on the exposed skin of her back. Unlike her other partners, Wei didn't try to engage her in pointless chitchat. They stared into each other's eyes, moving with a natural synchronicity that communicated far better than words. Glory felt the grace and joy of their pairing, and it was everything.

As the tempo of the music sped up, so did their steps. Wei spun her, then changed direction with a swiftness that made a laugh escape her like a bird from a cage. He was confidence and control personified; she didn't have to wait for him, urge him along, or modulate her pace to his. She could simply be herself and *dance*.

Joy and desire thrummed as Wei spun her again, holding her close, a hairsbreadth separating them from scandal. In that instant, she burned with memories: the scorching claim of his lips, the hard friction of his body against hers, the way he'd touched her deep inside. The heat in his eyes told her he was remembering and burning too. As they completed the turn, he adjusted their bodies to the proper distance, leaving her breathless and tingling.

The rest of the dancers, the ball, even the world fell away. There was only Wei, and how alive she felt when she was with him. How right. As Glory floated in her beloved's arms, she knew with certainty that they were born to do this. To be partners in the dance of life for as long as they both drew breath.

She gazed dreamily into Wei's eyes as the music began to slow.

"I wish this dance didn't have to end," she whispered.

"There will be other dances."

His heated promise sizzled through her.

"I brought you a birthday gift, but I think it must wait until we have privacy."

Anticipation fluttered in her chest. "Meet me in the conservatory in half an hour."

"Are you certain?" he said in a low voice. "I don't want to risk your reputation. And how will you manage to get away from your parents?"

Looking around the ballroom, she searched out the Angels' beaming faces. She lifted her hand from Wei's shoulder to give them a little wave.

Smiling, she said, "That is what friends are for."

As an anniversary gift, Papa had added the conservatory to the house several years ago so that Mama could cultivate flowers year-round. Glory had instantly adored the addition, which was a marvel of modern construction with its soaring glass walls and ceiling. Potted citrus scented the air, its lush foliage concealing cozy nooks. During the day, the room was bright and cheery, but tonight, illuminated by candles and moonlight, it had a sultry, romantic ambiance.

The perfect place for a lovers' rendezvous.

My first tryst...well, planned *tryst anyway.* Delight bubbled through Glory. On her twenty-first birthday, she was finally grown up and meeting with a lover.

She gave a start when hands covered her eyes from behind.

Her pulse racing, she said, "When are you going to teach *me* how to do that?"

"To do what, little tigress?" Wei dropped his hands and turned her to face him.

Even in the dimness, she could see the smile in his eyes.

"To move like a shadow."

"You are already nimble on your feet. As evidenced by your flawless dancing."

She gave him a mischievous smile. "As your *shifu* of dance, I must compliment you on being a quick study. I was not surprised, however. I knew you would be my favorite partner."

He raised her hand, brushing his lips across the back. The caress quickened her blood, her nipples tightening beneath her bodice.

His gaze was penetrating. "Only in dancing?"

She breathed, "In everything."

The next instant, she was in his arms, their mouths melded in a fiery kiss. She tasted his need and let him taste hers. The dancing and days apart fueled their passion, turning their embrace frantic. They stumbled into one of the secluded nooks, mouths fused, starved for each other. He backed her into a wall, the glass cool against her bare shoulders.

"How did you manage to get away unnoticed?" he murmured.

"The Angels are distracting my parents." Winding her arms around his neck, she peppered his jaw with kisses, inhaling his clean musk. Relishing the luxury of being close to him. "It seems like ages since we have been together like this."

"I know. I've missed you like the devil."

He took her mouth again. This kiss was long, thorough, drugging. The pressure of his lips and firm plunges of his tongue spun her senses. Her knees wobbled, but he leaned into her, a bulging wall of muscle trapping her against the glass, and the kiss burst into flame. Heat washed over her skin, her nipples chafing against her bodice, her pussy damp and fluttering. She gripped his shoulders, squirming and wanting him with every fiber of her being.

Suddenly, he broke the kiss, whispering, "Footsteps."

She froze, hearing the smack of soles against the tiled floor of the conservatory. Voices followed, and she couldn't hear what they were saying over her banging heart.

If we're discovered, the scandal will ruin everything. Papa's bill and my family's reputation. It will all be my fault.

Only when the footsteps retreated did she breathe again.

"That was too close," she said shakily.

"I know." Wei's gaze was unreadable. "We cannot continue sneaking around like this."

His words elicited a different kind of panic.

"What do you mean?" she blurted. "Are you tired of waiting for me? Am I not worth the trouble—"

"You are worth everything." Wei's steadfast reply calmed her racing pulse. "You are a rare jewel, Glory, and men could not keep their eyes off you tonight...Winslow especially." A pause. "I wanted to tear him limb from limb for touching you during the dance."

The growl that entered Wei's voice, as well as his admission, surprised her.

She furrowed her brow. "You were jealous?"

The emotion seemed so at odds with her self-controlled *shifu*.

"You are mine, Glory." His fierce expression told her he meant it. "Yet in the eyes of the world, I have no claim on you. I am tired of the secrecy that turns our love into something sordid. I want to walk through life with you, side by side, our heads held high."

"I want that too," she said tremulously.

He reached into his pocket, taking out a silk pouch and handing it to her. With trembling fingers, she removed the object inside. Her breath clogged as she beheld the delicate jade bracelet. In the moonlight, it seemed to glow from the inside, a halo of swirling translucence.

"This is for me?" she whispered. "It is so beautiful."

"The bracelet belonged to my mama, her favorite piece of jewelry. It was given to her by her mother-in-law on her wedding day, and she intended to give it to my future wife."

Glory's breath lodged in her throat.

"I want you to have it. To take it as a symbol of our engagement. A token of my promise to you and yours to me." Wei's eyes were intent, lines of concentration pulled between his brows. "I know we agreed to keep our relationship a secret until after your father's campaign, but I want us to set a date when I can speak to him. I need to know how much longer I must wait."

"We can pick a date, of course," she said in a rush. "And I...I'm sorry you've had to wait for my sake. I never meant to imply that our love was sordid—"

"You didn't." He shook his head.

"But I know I am asking a lot—"

"Glory, my reaction has to do with me, not you." He raked a hand through his hair. "It has to do with Chun...with how I felt during the affair."

Glory stilled, listening.

"Our relationship consisted of sneaking around. I would see her in public, but I could never lay claim to her. We could only be together in the shadows, never in the light, and it made me feel like...like a dirty secret."

"Oh, Wei. I'm so sorry." Glory's eyes welled at the realization that she'd unintentionally aggravated an old wound. "You do know that I am *proud* to be yours? And I want the world to know it. If it weren't for my papa's bill—"

He placed a finger on her lips. "I understand. Truly, I do. Your loyalty to those you love is one of your finest qualities." His mouth crooked ruefully. "I am just impatient to publicly claim your affections."

She came to a decision. "How about four weeks from today? That should give Papa sufficient time to launch his bill...and even if he hasn't, we will go forward. I know that seems like forever, but—"

"Four weeks it is."

Wei's gaze was bright...with relief, she realized, and remorse panged.

"I will count the days, my love," he said.

He took the bracelet from her, and they both watched as he slid it onto her wrist. A symbol of their commitment and love.

He kissed her tenderly on the forehead. "I cannot wait for the day when you can wear my mother's bracelet in public."

"I shall do it with pride," she promised. "I saw you chatting with Papa tonight. How did it go?"

Wei's expression turned somber. "Not that well, I'm afraid. It was my fault for offending Rothwell. His attitude toward opium users was patronizing, and I could not remain silent."

"Especially not with Hadleigh there," she said with under-standing.

Wei gave a gruff nod, and his loyalty to his friends made her love him even more.

"We can think of the next four weeks as an opportunity then," she said. "We'll arrange for you to spend time with my family. Once Papa gets to know you, he will give his approval for our marriage."

"Are you certain?" Wei's question was stark. "I am a foreigner and neither titled nor rich. I cannot give you the things that someone like Winslow—"

"You are the only one I want," she said. "And you are not a foreigner to me, Wei: you are home."

His smile was raw and real, warming his eyes. "All right, little tigress. I should go before anyone catches us. But before I do, I will leave you with a lesson for this eve."

"What sort of lesson?" she asked.

Bending his head, he kissed her throat, and she shivered as his lips coasted upward. When he suckled her earlobe, she moaned, her nerve endings pulsing.

His breath caressed her ear. "Are your pretty nipples tingling beneath your dress?"

She gave a bashful nod.

"And your pussy...is it wet?"

She bit her lip, nodding again.

"Tonight, when you are alone in your bed, I want you to pretend that I am there with you. That your hands are mine, moving over your body. That I am the one touching your breasts, pinching those lovely stiff buds. That I am the one petting your cunny. Rubbing your pearl until you come apart with bliss."

Zounds. She might have come a little then and there. She found this wicked side of Wei utterly irresistible, probably because it was such a contrast to his reserve. Only she knew this part of him, her future husband.

"While I am completing this naughty assignment, what will *you* be doing?" she dared to ask.

His smile was lazy and made her heart pitter-patter. He snagged her hand, bringing it to the front of his trousers. His aroused length pulsed beneath her palm.

"The same as you," he said huskily. "I'll be touching myself, imagining your hands on me. Your sweet touch milking my cock, pleasing me until I can't help but spend."

Stirred beyond bearing, she clenched her thighs together against a moist rush. Her hand closed spasmodically on his steel-hard ridge. He growled before lifting her hand away and placing a kiss on her palm.

"I must go, my sweet." His gaze consumed her. "Don't forget your lesson tonight."

"I won't," she breathed. "I love you, Wei."

"And you have my heart. Forever."

They shared another lingering kiss before he vanished into the shadows.

Thirty-One

Glory surfaced from the depths of a delightful dream, prodded awake by a wet nose. She blinked up at FF II's bright eyes and twitching whiskers.

"What time is it?" she asked, yawning.

FF II made chiding sounds.

She glanced at the clock on a nearby table. "Nine o'clock is not *that* late. Considering I went to bed well after three..."

She trailed off, memories of what she'd done under the covers assailing her with shameful delight. She looked at her wrist and smiled dreamily at the sight of Wei's bracelet. Not wanting to arouse suspicion, she'd removed it before returning to the ball. But she'd slipped it on again before going to bed and engaging in a very naughty lesson...

Her body thrumming, Glory turned onto her side. FF II wandered off in search of more interesting company. For once, she wasn't in the mood for adventure. She wanted to stay in bed and bask in her fantasies. *Did Wei do what I did last night...is he doing it now?* Images of him lying in his bed, all his rippling muscles on display sent a quiver through her thighs.

With the exception of the time he'd let her frig him in the

Hadleighs' library, Wei had always focused on her. She wasn't complaining—far from it—but she wanted to explore him too. To learn how to pleasure him. Languorously, she imagined running her hands over his sinewy shoulders, the hard-paved blocks of his chest. Her nipples budded as she recalled the attention he'd lavished upon them. She wondered if he would enjoy having her touch him there...kiss him there.

As the fantasy took hold, she saw herself kissing his flat brown nipples. Kissing her way down his chest and stacked abdomen... and even lower. Licking a path down the slope of muscle that ran from his hip bone to his cock.

Heat flashed over her insides, her palm tingling with the imprint of his arousal. The memory of holding that big, meaty rod caused a liquid trickle at her core. She'd loved undoing him, watching his reserve melt in the heat of passion. Furtively, she raised the hem of her nightgown, slipping her hand between her legs.

It felt wicked and strange to be touching herself, but she lost herself in the fantasy of stroking Wei's cock. In her mind's eye, she went even further, kneeling before him, pumping his thick shaft whilst he watched with his calm *shifu*'s eyes. Eyes that held her with such assurance. That told her she could be as curious and brazen as she wanted. That she could try anything, be anything, and still be safe with him. She saw herself leaning forward and licking the glistening dome of his cock...

Pleasure crested, a quick release pulsing through her. She rolled onto her back, heart thudding, and gazed at the shell-pink canopy of her bed. While she probably ought to be shocked by her behavior, she felt more...in awe. In the past, she'd wondered if there was something wrong with her, why she didn't have the same curiosity about romance that she had for other things. Now she knew what the answer was.

She had been waiting for Wei. Everything he'd shown her—including the naughty things—felt natural and right. He had unlocked her inner wantonness, and she could not bring herself to be embarrassed about it. She wanted to spend the rest of her life having passionate adventures with him. Thinking of his vulnerability, of what he'd shared about feeling like a "dirty secret," she felt a stab of guilt.

During the next four weeks, I must make sure my family is welcoming toward Wei. I will ask Mama to invite him to supper after he gives me my lesson today. And I will encourage Papa to get to know Wei...for surely when he does, he will respect Wei and accept him as the man I wish to marry.

Full of hope, she bounded out of bed and rang for Elsie to help her get dressed.

"Papa, may I have a word?" Glory peered into her father's study.

"Of course, poppet. Come in." Papa rose from his mahogany desk. "I did not realize you were up. The ball ran into the wee hours this morning."

"You know I've always been an early bird," she said cheerfully. "Back in Dorset, I used to wake up before dawn to comb the cliffs for fossils before school."

"That was then." Papa's forehead furrowed. "Now your only responsibility is to enjoy yourself, my dear. You ought to sleep in as long as you like."

"I couldn't stay in bed and do nothing..."

Flustered, she remembered that she hadn't exactly been idle in bed this morning. To hide her blush, she went to the tea tray and poured herself a cup.

"Is everything all right, Glory?"

"Yes, Papa."

The cup rattled slightly in its saucer as she turned to face him, searching for an inconspicuous way to start a conversation about

Wei. The problem was that her papa was no fool. People often underestimated him, not realizing that behind his dashing good looks was a mind like a steel trap.

"Is Mama still abed?" she asked.

Papa nodded. "She stayed up late after the ball."

The hint of satisfaction in his voice made Glory want to cover her ears. Heavens, for years she'd been oblivious to sexual signals and now she was noticing them everywhere. Whilst her parents had always been affectionate with each other, she hadn't thought too deeply about what went on in their private lives...and she wanted to keep it that way.

Papa led the way to the seating area, waving her to the divan whilst he folded his long frame into the studded wingchair.

"I have been meaning to speak with you," he said.

Uh oh. His serious expression did not bode well.

She took a fortifying sip of tea. "What about?"

"How are you enjoying your Season?"

"You and Mama have given me everything a debutante could ask for," she said sincerely.

"It is our pleasure to do so." Papa drummed his fingers on the arm of his chair, his signet ring glinting. "But you haven't answered my question, poppet. Do you find the life of a debutante to your liking?"

I like being part of the Angels. I like solving cases and helping others. And I adore being with Wei and want to spend the rest of my life with him.

Yet she realized that none of these things had anything to do with being a debutante. Quite the opposite. All were activities that she had to sweep under the rug.

"What is not to like?" she countered.

"Where shall I start?"

At Papa's wry rejoinder, she had to chuckle, some of her tension ebbing. Even before she knew Papa was her father, they had always had a special connection...an ability to understand each other and a shared way of viewing the world. Perhaps he could understand her desire to marry Wei. Perhaps she ought to throw caution to the wind and tell him about her feelings for her *shifu* and ask for his blessing.

She tested the waters. "Perhaps I find myself not entirely suited to convention."

"You come by that naturally." Papa stroked his trimmed beard, obviously choosing his words with care. "I haven't been a paragon myself, particularly not in my younger days, and I can understand that Society's rules can seem arbitrary and stifling. Being my daughter—the daughter of a peer—is a double-edged sword: whilst you have certain privileges, you are also subject to added scrutiny."

"I know, Papa." She canted her head. "What is this about?"

"Of late, I have noticed some changes in you."

She stilled. *Does he know about Wei?*

"You seem uninterested in balls and the usual diversions," Papa went on. "While Mama and I were away, Hypatia said you spent an inordinate amount of time with that society of yours. And you started taking lessons with this Chen fellow."

Glory forced herself to stay calm and breathe.

"Master Chen is an expert in his field who has taught—"

"I don't give a damn what he is. Glory, you are a duke's daughter, and he runs a clinic treating opium users. It is not proper for you to be in his company." Papa paused. "At the ball last night, there was talk when you danced with him."

"What sort of talk?" But she already knew.

"The kind that can ruin a reputation if it continues," Papa said flatly. "I think I understand what this is about, poppet."

Her heart thumped. "Do you?"

"You are intelligent, curious, and independent. It is only natural that you should chafe against the restrictions of Society, some of which are stupid," he acknowledged. "Trust me, I understand the desire to defy mindless convention."

Is that what Papa thinks? That I am feeling defiant? Rebellious?

"In my youth, I rebelled against the polite world. I made mistakes that nearly cost me everything...that shame me even now. Through that, I learned that my defiance was not hurting anyone but me. I discovered this the hard way, and I don't want you to repeat my mistakes."

Seeing the concerned lines etched on her father's face, knowing that this could not be easy for him to discuss, she felt a surge of love.

She set down her tea and leaned forward. "I promise you I am not trying to deliberately flout convention, Papa."

It just sort of happens when I follow my heart.

"Then you are wiser than me, poppet." He studied her. "It took me years to realize that defiance wouldn't bring me happiness. That took meeting your mama again. Her love and steadfast influence helped me to become the man I am today. One who understands how to channel my inner fire toward a more productive end."

"You and Mama are a perfect match," Glory said sincerely.

"What do you think about Matthew Winslow?"

The abrupt question caught her off guard.

"Um...he is nice, I suppose."

"He is a decent chap with bright prospects. Last night, he had to fend off gentlemen wanting to buy shares in his and Rothwell's latest venture. And he's not bad-looking, eh?"

"I guess not," she mumbled.

"Mama thinks he's too old for you, and she may be right," Papa amended. "But it wouldn't hurt for you to spend time with him and see what you think. He asked me if he could take you for a ride in the park this afternoon."

"But I have a lesson with Mr. Chen—"

"I have taken the liberty of canceling it for you."

She bolted upright in her chair. "*Papa—*"

"I told you about the gossip last night and do not wish for

rumors to circulate about you." Her father looked uncommonly stern. "For now, your lessons with Chen are on hold."

Now the fire of rebellion did blaze in her heart.

"For how long?" she asked with trembling outrage.

"Until such time that I can be certain that he poses no harm to you or your reputation."

I love Wei. I want to marry him. Not having him in my life is what would hurt me.

Yet if she told her father now, he clearly would not understand, and she risked causing more friction between him and Wei. He was pushing her toward Mr. Winslow, for heaven's sake. Frustration knotted her insides.

"Mr. Chen would never hurt me," she protested. "He is a good, honorable man—"

"If that is true, he will understand why he must stay away for the time being." Papa's face softened. "I am trying to protect your reputation, poppet."

"Mine or yours?"

Seeing the startled hurt that flashed in his eyes, she instantly regretted her words.

"I...I am sorry, Papa." Shame shortened her breath. "I didn't mean it."

"You would be within your rights if you did." His sigh was heavy. "My campaigning has taken its toll on you and the family. If the work were not so important, if it did not have such an impact on innocent lives—"

"Please, you needn't explain." She felt worse than ever. "I am so proud of your fight against the opium trade and support your endeavors wholeheartedly."

"You are a good girl, Glory. A far better daughter than I deserve," he said quietly. "You've never complained, but I know that the circumstances of your birth haven't made things easy for you in Society. And I am to blame."

Glory chewed on her lip, hating that Papa felt guilty after all these years. "You didn't know that you'd fathered me. And you did something about it as soon as you did."

"Adopting you at age nine is not the same as giving you my name when you entered this world. I will never forgive myself for how my reckless behavior affected you and your mama."

The remorse in his eyes constricted Glory's throat.

"But I swore to myself that I would make up for it. That I would do everything in my power to guarantee your happiness." Papa's expression hardened with resolve. "That is why I must insist that you stop seeing Chen."

But I love Wei. And he loves me. How can I make you understand?

All along, she'd been confident that Papa would come to respect Wei and see their commonalities. Now she was forced to confront the chilling possibility that he might not. That he might not support her decision to marry Wei.

"You are one of my life's greatest blessings," Papa said, his tone gentling. "And I hope I can be the same to you. Trust me to have your best interests at heart."

Her bottom lip quivered. "I do trust you, Papa."

But she didn't know how to convince him that her happiness lay with Wei. She didn't want to choose between following her heart and her father's wishes. Either way, someone she loved would get hurt.

I need to think. To regroup and plan.

"If there is nothing else." She rose. "I should freshen up before Mr. Winslow's visit."

"Of course, poppet."

She exited, aware of her father's troubled gaze following her.

Thirty-Two

"I am sorry I brought you into this," Wei said gruffly. "I should be doing this on my own."

"No, I want to be here." Sitting beside him in the dark carriage, Glory squeezed his hand. "And you need me. Scott said specifically that Mrs. Swann wants to see us together. That she would not share anything about Leonard Kray unless we met her terms."

In the two days since Glory's ball, a lot had happened.

After their interlude in the conservatory, Wei had been full of foolish hope. Glory had committed to a timeframe, agreeing that he could seek her father's permission in four weeks. He would win over the Duke of Ranelagh and Somerville, do everything in his power to prove that he was worthy of Glory.

That night, Wei had spent over and over again, imagining Glory was with him. Dreaming of being inside her, a part of her. Even coming half a dozen times didn't sate his desire; he'd awakened with a cockstand, her taste and scent teasing his senses. Lying in bed, his body and heart hungry, he had wondered if he could steal a kiss from her during their lesson that day.

Then reality had reared its ugly head.

Yao had been the bearer of bad news, bringing Wei a note sealed with the Duke of Ranelagh and Somerville's stamp. The message had been brief and to the point, thanking Wei for his services and stating that they were no longer required. To add insult to injury, the duke had enclosed a generous bank note.

Another note had arrived soon thereafter, this one from Glory. She had asked Wei to wait for her. To give her time to persuade her father. Before Wei could pen his reply, yet another message had appeared.

This one had been from Wulfric Scott. The gang leader's contact, a woman by the name of Susanna Swann, had agreed to see Wei on two conditions. He was to bring his female companion and convene at Mrs. Swann's shop at midnight tomorrow. If Wei failed to meet these requirements, Mrs. Swann would not speak to him.

Foreboding had filled Wei. He did not know who this Mrs. Swann was or what she would want. Desperate to discuss the situation with Glory, he'd gone to her home, planning to scale her balcony if need be. But he didn't have to...because she'd been returning from a drive in a sporty barouche with that bastard Winslow.

Luckily, she'd spotted Wei's carriage. After Winslow left, she'd met Wei in the back lane, and they'd managed a quick and furtive conversation. Glory had insisted on accompanying him to Mrs. Swann's, saying that she would tell her parents she was staying with the Hawksmoors and Wei should pick her up there.

When Wei had arrived this evening, Glory and Lady Fiona Hawksmoor had been waiting for him.

"Be careful tonight," Lady Hawksmoor had said. *"Hawk and I met Mrs. Swann during a case. While I do not think she is malevolent at heart, her manner can be cagey and unsettling. I do not doubt that she will test you...and you must decide how far you will go to get your answers."*

Thinking of what lay ahead now, Wei clenched his jaw. Had he been selfish to involve Glory in his quest? What kind of nefarious demands would Mrs. Swann make?

"Everything will be fine," Glory said.

She was developing a disconcerting ability to read his thoughts.

"We do not know that," Wei said grimly. "We have no idea what Mrs. Swann will want in exchange for information."

"Actually, I have some idea."

At Glory's hesitant words, Wei raised his brows.

"Fiona didn't want me to go in unprepared," she explained. "And while I haven't met Mrs. Swann personally, I know some facts about her based on a prior case."

"What do you know about this woman?"

"She is, well, there is no polite way to say it…"

Her dithering heightened his unease. His little tigress was never one to mince words.

"Then just say it."

"She bills herself a purveyor of sexual fulfillment," Glory said in a rush. "She isn't a bawd, exactly, since she does not employ prostitutes. But her 'shop' is a club of sorts which gives her patrons —couples, mostly—a place to, um, explore their desires."

As the revelation percolated through his brain, apprehension morphed into disbelief, then anger. At himself for involving Glory in this sordid mess. For being so focused on his vengeance that he'd compromised her safety.

"Bloody hell," he bit out. "We are turning this carriage around *now*."

"*No.*" Glory grabbed his arm, her chin rising to a determined angle. "For fifteen years, you have been hunting your family's killer. Now you have the opportunity to find out where he is, and I can help you. I love you, Wei, and I will not let you down. Trust me."

Wei felt something twist in his chest, and it took him a moment to recognize it: the agony of longing. After everything he'd done, the unpardonable mistakes he'd made, he had never expected *yuan fen* to give him this. A woman like Glory. Who gave him her love and loyalty. Who offered everything of herself, asking only for his trust in return.

And he did trust her...in all respects.

Earlier, she'd told him that her papa had arranged her outing with Winslow, and Wei believed her. Knew she wasn't playing him false, that she was committed to him and gaining her father's blessing for their marriage. Just as he knew that she was a capable partner, one he was lucky to have by his side on the present undertaking.

"Glory." His voice hoarse, he cupped her face. "What did I do to deserve you?"

Her mouth crooked in an impish grin. "You mean that as a compliment, I assume?"

"Minx." Shaking his head, he traced her bottom lip with his thumb. "How can you be so perfect?"

"I'm really not," she said, adorable as always. "But perhaps what I am is perfect *for you*."

"That you undoubtedly are."

Unable to resist, he claimed her with a kiss that left them both wanting more. But the carriage was slowing, rolling to a stop. He looked out the curtain and saw an unremarkable two-story brick building with a beige awning. It looked closed for the night... except for the ominous red glow coming from behind the shuttered windows.

"We're here." He fought an inner battle. "Are you certain you want to do this?"

"Yes," she said resolutely.

"Then you must promise me something."

She canted her head.

"You will tell me at once if anything makes you uncomfortable," he said firmly. "If Mrs. Swann's conditions are unacceptable, I will find another way to get the information I need. I will not have you coerced into anything or hurt because of me. Is that understood?"

"Yes," she said.

"You mean too much to me." He trailed his knuckles along her jaw. "If anything happened to you, I could not bear it."

"You know I can take care of myself. And together we can do anything."

He exhaled, hoping he didn't regret his decision. "Once we are inside, you will follow my lead."

With a saucy wink, she said, "Don't I always, O Mighty *Shifu*?"

He was doomed.

Given the Angels' previous case involving Mrs. Swann and what Fi had described, Glory was not going into the evening's mission blind. Even if she were, it would not matter. She would take on any danger with Wei.

They were greeted by a female servant, who took them through the front of the shop. The place was like any other fashionable atelier, with glass-fronted cabinets displaying accessories ranging from vinaigrettes to stockings. Behind the locked door at the back of the shop, however, was another story. Glory felt Wei's tension as the servant unlocked the door, leading them down a carpeted corridor and into a sitting room.

Their hostess was waiting for them. Seated in a black damask chair by the fire, Susanna Swann was a diminutive woman with blue-black ringlets and feline features, her violet gown contrasting with the paleness of her golden skin. Although Fi had said Mrs. Swann looked to be in her mid-twenties, the sharpness of the woman's blue gaze made her seem older. As if there was little left in the world that could surprise her.

"Good evening, Mr. Chen," Mrs. Swann drawled. "Bring your little friend over and have a seat."

Wei took Glory's hand, and together they sat on the divan facing the proprietress.

"Now, my dove, I don't believe we have been introduced."

Beneath Mrs. Swann's stare, Glory felt like a butterfly pinned for inspection. While she could obviously offer an alias, Fi had warned her that the proprietress insisted upon honesty and was a bloodhound when it came to scenting lies. At the same time, Mrs. Swann prided herself on discretion and kept her patrons' secrets.

"This has nothing to do with her." Wei cut in, his expression hard as granite. "This is between you and me, Mrs. Swann. I am looking for a man named Leonard Kray, and Scott said you know where he is."

Glory recognized the flicker in the proprietress's gaze. *Pain.* Her heart squeezed with intuitive empathy. According to Scott, Kray was a cold-hearted bastard who had an appetite for pain. Had Kray hurt Mrs. Swann...or someone she loved?

Mrs. Swann fiddled with the lace on the high collar of her dress.

"I do not run a charity, Mr. Chen," she said in cool tones. "My assistance comes with a price."

"Name it."

"We shall begin with your lover's name."

Wei rose, pulling Glory with him toward the door. "Our time here is done."

"Wait." Glory dug in her heels, turning to the proprietress. "I believe you are acquainted with my friend Fiona. She said that I could speak to you in confidence."

"I can neither confirm nor deny an acquaintance with your friend," Mrs. Swann replied. "However, it is my policy to safeguard the secrets of all those who visit my establishment. What I demand in return is honesty."

"Let's go," Wei growled.

Glory darted a glance at him, then blurted, "My name is Glory Cavendish."

Wei swore; Mrs. Swann smiled.

"Pleased to meet you, Miss Cavendish." She rose in an oddly soundless manner given the fullness of her skirts. Gliding over to a cabinet of spirits, she said, "May I offer you refreshment?"

Glory knew when an olive branch was being extended. "Yes, please."

She tried to tug Wei back toward the divan, but he was immovable.

Mrs. Swann came over, and Glory took the glass of blood-red port with murmured thanks. When Wei shook his head in refusal, the proprietress shrugged and took a sip from the glass herself. She returned to her wingchair, not seeming to care that her guests remained standing.

Glory politely tasted the drink, finding it fruity and sweet.

"Will you tell us where Mr. Kray is?" she asked.

"Not until we have arrived at a price for this information."

Wei folded his arms over his chest. "What do you want?"

Mrs. Swann sipped her beverage as she studied them.

"An equal exchange," she said after a moment. "You are asking me to share a secret from my past. In return, I wish to be privy to your deepest secrets."

Glory swallowed. "What...what do you mean?"

The proprietress flicked her gaze between Glory and Wei. "The two of you will pleasure each other while I watch."

"Out of the bloody question." Wei's chest surged with outrage. "We will not be pawns in your perverse games. Glory, we're leaving."

"Leave, and you will never find out what happened to Kray." Mrs. Swann's eerie singsong statement was threaded with steel. "I guarantee it."

Glory's breath lodged, for she knew the woman was speaking the truth. Wei was so close to achieving his mission; all they had to do was gain Mrs. Swann's cooperation. Although the proposition was outrageous and ought to have been abhorrent, Glory felt a strange tingle inside.

A thrill of wanton curiosity.

"Let's go," Wei insisted.

He held out his hand to Glory and looked surprised when she didn't take it.

Instead, Glory directed her gaze at Mrs. Swann. "Why?"

The proprietress quirked a dark eyebrow. "What do you mean, dove?"

"Why would you wish to...to observe such a private moment?"

Mrs. Swann's mouth curled at the corners. "Why does your lover wish to find Kray?"

"To get the justice he is owed," Glory replied.

"Then my reason is the same. I want to get back what was taken from me." Mrs. Swann propped her elbow on the chair, leaning her head into her hand. "You have my promise of discretion, of course. I will be viewing from another room; you won't even know I am there. You may pleasure each other in whatever fashion you wish as long as you do so honestly. There is to be no playacting, no faking, nothing but authentic desire. Trust me, if you hold anything back—from me or each other—I will know, and you will forfeit our bargain."

"This is ridiculous," Wei snapped. "We don't need to bargain with her."

But we do. Glory knew it was only a matter of time before Wei arrived at the same conclusion. *And what she wants is within our ability to give. If we wish to.*

She knew with certainty what she wanted: Wei. Always Wei.

Did she really care if Susanna Swann knew it?

"Mrs. Swann, will you give us a moment?" she asked.

The proprietress rose. "Ring when you have come to a decision."

As soon as the door closed, Wei bit out, "We are getting out of here. The very idea of what that woman is asking—"

"It is the only way to get to Kray. Unless you have another suggestion?"

Wei raked a hand through his hair. "I am not subjecting you to—"

"No, you're not. I am choosing to do it. Willingly."

When Wei stared at her, Glory felt her cheeks heat, but she didn't look away.

"I love you, and I like...like being with you," she said haltingly. "There is no shame in that, is there?"

His eyes simmered with emotion. "Of course not, sweeting. That isn't the point. What happens between us is a private matter, and the bloody woman has no right to be a part of it."

"But she wouldn't be. She'll be in another room. She said we won't even notice her watching."

"You cannot seriously be considering this."

"Fi intimated that Mrs. Swann asked something similar of her and Hawksmoor," Glory admitted. "She said that it wasn't a bad experience, and in fact, their relationship may have benefited from it. And Mrs. Swann kept her word."

Wei drew his brows together. "As the Hawksmoors are married, their situation is different."

"In our hearts, are we any less committed?"

"No, but in the eyes of society, we most certainly are." His gaze turned penetrating. "What is this really about?"

Feeling very exposed, Glory looked at her shoes. "You told me that you hated being treated like a dirty secret. By Chun, I mean. It occurs to me that I have been doing the same—not intentionally, of course. And you have been so patient, agreeing to wait—"

"Glory." Wei tucked a finger under her chin, lifting her gaze to his. "I understand. And you don't have to worry because I will wait for you—weeks or years. Even a lifetime, if that is what it takes. Because you are everything I want, and I will not settle for less. I will have my freckled, ferret-loving little tigress or no one at all."

His devotion stole her breath and filled her heart to bursting.

A tear leaked down her cheek. "You...you truly would wait that long for me?"

He thumbed the droplet away, his gaze so fierce and tender. "How could you doubt it?"

"Then let us not waste tonight," she whispered. "I've missed you. For this one evening, let us celebrate our love, and the rest of the world can go hang itself."

He swallowed, and she could see him fighting his desire for her. Fighting his own needs because he wanted to protect her. Because he loved her.

He looked deep into her eyes. "Are you certain you want this?"

"I want you." She let everything she felt for this extraordinary man shine in her gaze, her smile. "Make love to me, please?"

Thirty-Three

Glory's dimples had always been Wei's undoing.

He blamed them for the fact that he was heading down a perfumed corridor with her, toward a room that Mrs. Swann had claimed would be the ideal setting for them to explore their fantasies... as if the bloody woman knew anything about Wei's desires. He and Glory reached the room at the end, the flower upon the door matching the one stamped on the key in his hand.

"This is it," he said. "There is still time to change your mind—"

Glory squeezed his hand. "I want this. I want you."

Bloody hell. Despite his misgivings, his cock stiffened in anticipation.

He slid the key into the lock, and a silky click later, they were inside. Disbelief thumped in his chest as he beheld the room.

How did that blasted Swann woman know?

Red lanterns bathed the chamber in a seductive glow. The latticed screens and carved rosewood furnishings, combined with the sultry spice of incense, brought him back to his debauched youth. The nights he'd sought oblivion through lustful vices. A beaded curtain swayed gently to some invisible current, the movement making the carpeted floor seem to rock beneath his feet.

Silk peonies bloomed in a porcelain vase. There was a round table, set with a decanter of rice wine and two small cups. Beyond that, visible through the beaded curtain, was a large bed set upon a dais.

"What is this place supposed to be?" Glory said in a hushed voice.

"A flower boat." At her inquiring look, he clarified, "The Pearl River Delta is infamous for its floating brothels. The flower boats, as they are known, pride themselves on offering every vice under the sun. On satisfying any desire, no matter how depraved."

"Oh." She peered at him. "Have you, um, frequented a flower boat?"

He nodded gruffly. "After my family was killed and before I met Shifu Lam, I visited a number of disreputable places."

Although his chest burned with shame, he didn't want to lie to her about the past. About anything.

She tilted her head. "And did you, um, satisfy your desires?"

"Whatever relief I found was temporary." His gut twisted at the sordid memories, that feeling of dirtiness and despair. "Afterward, I felt worse. Angrier at myself for being a selfish bastard."

With every whore he'd fucked, he'd hated himself more. For his lustful weakness which had allowed Chun to lead him by the cock. For being the cause of his family's slaughter.

"You are not selfish." Glory touched his jaw. "You made a mistake in your youth, and you have spent every moment since trying to atone for it. You have helped and protected so many people...including me. I wish you could see yourself as I do: honorable and kind, a gentleman in every sense of the word."

He held her hand against his jaw. Feeling her delicate strength twined with his, redemption seemed not only possible but imminent. As if happiness was close...close enough to touch.

"How can you be mine?" he said with rough wonder.

"I've been yours since the first time you kissed me." Her smile lit up the room, his bloody world. "Tonight, I wish to prove it."

"You don't have to prove anything."

"Prove isn't quite the right word," she acknowledged. "But I want you to know that I am committed to our future. That my heart is pledged to you."

She pulled back the lacy cuff of her sleeve, and his throat cinched at the sight of the gleaming jade circling her wrist. Proof of his claim. The fact that she'd worn it swelled his chest...and his prick. Already he was hard for her, hungry for her in a way he knew he always would be.

He pulled her close. "I love you, little tigress."

"Then be with me," she said simply.

He needed no further encouragement. He took her mouth, possessiveness pounding in his blood. He tasted her sweetness mingled with port, an intoxicating flavor. The feminine hunger of her response made him wild. Lifting her into his arms, he carried her through the swaying curtain, the smooth bamboo beads sliding over their heated skin.

He stepped onto the dais, setting his precious girl on her feet. The "bed" was a mattress set upon a platform...designed, no doubt, to give Mrs. Swann an unobstructed view. Tensing, Wei scanned the room, looking for peepholes.

The brush of Glory's fingertips returned his gaze to her.

"It is just you and me." Her lashes framed her wide, earnest eyes. "Nothing else matters."

The truth reverberated through him, and his entire being quaked with desire.

"You are everything to me," he said in a low voice.

Then he kissed her again, on her forehead, nose, lips. When he dragged his lips to her ear, she gave a delightful sigh. He nibbled on the tender lobe, sucking it as he freed her from her layers. One by one, the garments dropped to the ground until she was left in a thin shift.

"Arms up," he said huskily.

Her eagerness made his lips twitch. He pulled the chemise over her head, his lungs straining at the beauty he revealed. He palmed her breast, teasing the rosy tip between finger and thumb. She sank her teeth into her bottom lip as he pinched her nipple into a tight, velvety point.

"You are so beautiful," he said raggedly.

Blushing from head to toe, she said, "I, um, want to see you too."

He complied with her request, stripping off his own clothes even as he feasted his eyes on her. It struck him that this was the first time they were seeing each other fully naked in the light. Beyond the shadows, their desire blazed to new heights. He knew then that Glory was right: nothing about their love could ever be shameful.

In some ways, he was as much a novice as she was in this moment. While he'd been with plenty of women, he'd only fucked in the dark. Making love in the light was something different entirely.

Glory watched him undress with unabashed curiosity, and when her innocent eyes widened at the sight of his jutting erection, desire forked through his belly. Her fingers alighted on his chest, soft and tentative against his madly thumping heart.

"You are splendid."

The awe in her voice, the reverence and care in her touch, undid him. No one had ever made him feel this wanted. This worthy of desire.

He tumbled her onto the bed, smothering her gasp with his mouth. He ran his palm down the length of her, her skin a river of silk from her throat to her pussy. Between her sleek thighs, she was warm and wet, drenching his hand as he fingered her. One of these days, he was going to teach her the pleasures of delaying satisfaction, but right now he was as impatient as she was.

He'd had a lifetime of restraint, of waiting and biding his time.

Tonight, he was going to revel in the excesses of love.

He plunged his tongue deep into Glory's mouth, plundering her sweetness while he rubbed the bold little bud between her legs. The twin sensations made his little tigress squirm, her hips bucking as he swirled his fingers. The juicy sounds of her quim hit him straight in the cock, wetting the crest with pre-seed. He knew she was close and wanted to take her over the edge.

Releasing her mouth, he bent his head over her berry-ripe nipple and suckled hard.

Her thighs clamped his hand like a vise, and she spent, panting his name.

He took his hand from her pussy. In the light, his fingers glistened with her desire. She watched with pleasure-darkened eyes as he painted her nipples with her own dew, then drew a path back down to her lush, quivering petals.

"You look almost too pretty to eat," he rasped. "Almost."

"Oh, heavens. Oh, my goodness. *Wei.*"

Glory clutched Wei's hair as another climax broke inside her. She arched her spine, and he growled, burying his tongue deeper inside her spasming passage, teasing out every shiver of bliss until she lay trembling and boneless.

He crawled up her body, kissing her deeply. The taste of her own pleasure made her nerves flutter anew.

"I love it when you come in my mouth," he murmured.

"That's good," she said breathlessly. "Since you made me do it so many times."

His eyes crinkled at the corners. "Are you complaining, my sweet?"

"Of course not."

But I'd like to do the same to you.

The thought flashed in her head, but she didn't say it.

He read her mind anyway. "But?"

She hesitated, a lifetime of modesty making it difficult to admit what she wanted. She recalled her naughty fantasy, and heat flashed over her skin. What were the rules in lovemaking? Was it like dancing where a lady was supposed to follow a gentleman's lead? True, Wei hadn't seemed to mind the time she'd asked to touch his cock—actually, he'd seemed to enjoy it—but asking if she could kiss him there was brazen, even for her.

Wei looked down at her with brows drawn. "You can tell me anything, Glory. If I did anything that you did not enjoy or made you uncomfortable—"

"It's not that," she said hastily. "I enjoyed everything you did. But I...I..."

Mrs. Swann's voice was the devil whispering on her shoulder. *If you hold anything back—from me or each other—I will know.*

"Tell me," Wei said.

"I want to kiss you," she blurted.

With a baffled smile, he leaned toward her. "That's easy enough—"

"Not on the mouth. Well, there *too*, but what I mean is that I'd like to kiss you, um, elsewhere. The way you've kissed me. I don't know if ladies are supposed to want to do that, but I'm curious," she confessed. "I...I want to try it. If you don't mind."

At Wei's stunned look, she stopped babbling and squirmed. Had her curiosity finally shocked him?

He abruptly rose, and her breath jabbed her throat like a fishbone. *Did I go too far?* He stood at the side of the bed, the muscular grooves and ridges of his form limned by the red light, his eyes dark and unreadable. She blinked when he crooked a finger at her.

"Come here, little tigress." His voice had a primal edge that matched the way he fisted his cock, holding the meaty shaft as if it were bait. "Come take your first taste of me."

The mingled heat of embarrassment and arousal were almost too much to bear. Yet she'd asked for this, and he was giving it to her. It was too late to turn back...and she didn't want to. Certainty flooded her: Wei was the one man who truly valued her, curiosity and all. Who treated her oddities like they were treasures. With him, she was safe to be who she was.

Giddy with newfound confidence, she crawled playfully toward him like the pet name he'd given her. Amusement flashed in his gaze even as he pumped his cock in a lazy motion that made her pussy flutter. When she reached the side of the bed, she knelt and looked up at him.

"Ask for what you want, love," he said.

At his command, her tummy quivered.

"May I kiss you...there?" She darted a glance at his member.

"You can do better." He chided her the way he'd done during their lessons, his stern tone causing heat to bloom at her core. "I want to hear the naughty words you were using in your head."

Botheration, he knows me too well.

She drew a breath. "May I kiss your cock?"

"There's my good pupil."

His approval made her tingle from head to toe. With his free hand, he threaded his fingers in her hair, bringing her mouth close to his cock. The head was wide and rosy, shiny with his essence. Shivering, she leaned forward and placed a kiss on the tip.

She ran her tongue over her lips, his salty male flavor making her hungry for more. But she didn't know what to do.

Looking up into her beloved's watchful eyes, she whispered, "Teach me."

"Take my cock," he said huskily.

She circled her fingers around him, quivering at his virile abundance.

"Now lick the tip again."

Bending forward, she swept her tongue over the broad dome, gauging Wei's reaction. His chest surged as she lapped at him, his fingers tightening in her hair. Remembering what he'd done to her, she tried quick flicks back and forth, a steady motion that had driven her wild. He grunted, and she tasted a burst of salt. Emboldened, she mouthed his entire head and gently sucked. He rewarded her with another burst of him upon her tongue.

He dug his fingers into her scalp, the pressure exciting in its demand.

"Take me deeper," he growled.

Holding her head in place, he pushed his cock inside her mouth, and his mastery thrilled her. Instinctively, she opened wider, wanting to take more of him, moaning as he slid in deeper. Watching his gaze grow heavy-lidded, his torso rippling as he enjoyed her mouth, filled her with a sense of feminine power.

"You suck my cock so well, sweeting."

Wei's praise, uttered in a gravelly voice, spurred her to do even better. By relaxing her jaw, she discovered that she could take even more of him. He seemed to know her limits, just how far to thrust, and she surrendered dreamily to his care and experience.

"Is this what you thought about during the lesson I assigned you?"

His words pierced her floaty bubble. When she didn't answer, he pulled out and gave her a stern look. She didn't know how she could feel shy given what they were doing, but she did.

"Yes," she whispered.

When he traced her lips with his glossy tip, her pussy clenched on a fresh wave of dew.

"Did you touch yourself doing it?" he inquired.

She managed a nod.

"Show me."

Heavens. I can't do that...can I?

Yet her hand had a life of its own, creeping bashfully between her splayed thighs. She was so swollen and wet that she whimpered at the contact with her own fingers.

"Such a good student," Wei rasped. "Now rub your hot little pussy while you pleasure me with your mouth."

His eyes holding hers, he drove between her lips, his movements less gentle and more demanding. Mindless with need, she touched herself whilst he filled her mouth, deeper, harder, the taste of him delighting her senses. Arousal, need, and love sizzled in their locked gazes, making her feel safe to experiment. To swirl her tongue around his plunging head. To suck him deep. To grip his hard, flexing buttocks and urge him on.

Perhaps she got a bit carried away, for he surged powerfully, his cock butting depths that made her choke around him. Groaning, he pulled out. His eyes darker than coals, he fisted his shaft, jerking with mesmerizing roughness. Then he took aim at her breasts, and with a hoarse shout, sprayed her with his pleasure. His hot, primal marking triggered her own climax. He tumbled her onto the bed, kissing her as he stroked her pussy and extended the waves of bliss.

Afterward, they lay entwined, exchanging tender kisses as their heartbeats steadied.

Wei traced her mouth with a callused fingertip. "I didn't hurt you, did I?"

"Of course not. It was lovely." She nipped at his finger.

His eyes gleamed down at her. "Is your curiosity satisfied then, little tigress?"

She thought about it. "Mostly."

"Mostly?" He lifted his brows. "What else have you fantasized about?"

She bit her lip, wondering if she could possibly say it aloud.

"You can tell me anything," he prompted.

"You know how you enjoyed having me, um, come when you were kissing me intimately? Well, does it work the same way—"

The rest of her question was smothered by Wei's hungry kiss.

THIRTY-FOUR

Two days later, Wei sat across from Susanna Swann in her carriage, heading north out of London. When he and Glory had left the shop, Mrs. Swann had said she would be in touch, and he'd heard nothing from her until she showed up out of the blue at the clinic this morning.

"If you wish to find Kray, come with me," she'd said.

Wei's immediate thought had been of Glory. He knew she was helping her parents host a luncheon today. She had worked hard planning the event—been on pins and needles about making it a success. Not wishing to distract her from her familial duty, Wei had dashed off a note explaining where he'd gone but instructed Yao not to deliver it until after the luncheon.

Yao had wanted to accompany Wei.

Eyeing Mrs. Swann, he'd said in their native language, *"I don't trust this woman. She looks like trouble."*

"Mr. Chen comes alone." Mrs. Swann had replied as if she'd understood Chinese, but Wei suspected she was just good at reading people. *"He has nothing to fear from Kray."*

As the carriage bumped along the muddy country road, Wei brooded over what she'd meant. *Why is Kray not a threat? Is he incapacitated in some way?* At any rate, if anyone had cause to be afraid, it was Kray. Wei curled his hands as he contemplated taking his vengeance. He'd wanted this for so long, yet as he was about to achieve his goal, he felt a strange lack of anticipation. Instead, he was plagued by uncertainty.

Years ago, he'd served justice to Governor Li without blinking an eye. He hadn't cared about the consequences. If Li's crooked officials had caught him, he'd have been put to death, but it would have been worth it because revenge had been the only thing that mattered. Yet now things were different...because of Glory.

Because of her, Wei had love and hope and happiness to look forward to.

Images flitted through his head of what their married life might be like. By day, they would practice *kung fu* and run the clinic together. By night, they would make love, and he would indulge her every carnal curiosity...especially the one she'd expressed at Mrs. Swann's. If she wished to continue with her Society of Angels work—and he did not doubt that she would— he would support her in that too.

And if fortune smiled upon them, he saw their clinic overrun with children. Imps who would inherit Glory's beauty and goodness and spirit. Who would smile at him with her dimples and pester him with countless questions and make him so very glad to be alive.

At the same time, he felt guilty for hesitating to end Kray for the sake of this dream. If he put his love for Glory first, he was letting down his family again. Failing to honor his vow to them.

"Thinking about your lovely dove, Mr. Chen?" Mrs. Swann drawled. "After your performance two nights ago, one would think you'd had your fill. But I cannot blame you. It is rare to find a lady with Miss Cavendish's freshness and sensual nature."

The anger that smoldered in Wei's chest was a welcome distraction from his inner turmoil. Although he could never regret making love to Glory, he resented having their privacy violated by the smirking bitch across from him.

"You will leave her out of this," he said tersely. "How much longer until we get to Kray?"

"All in good time."

Propping her chin on her hand, Mrs. Swann regarded him with a piercing gaze. Today, she'd forgone the face paint and wore a modest grey dress. With her black ringlets tucked under a lace-trimmed cap, she looked surprisingly respectable.

Which proves that looks can deceive.

"From your impressively extended pleasuring of our little Miss Cavendish," she said, "I would have taken you for a more patient fellow."

"She is not *our* Miss Cavendish." The bloody woman wasn't fit to utter Glory's name. "She's mine, and you will stop bandying her name about."

"My, my. Protective, aren't we? One cannot blame you for staking your claim." Mrs. Swann's ringlets swung with mock sympathy. "A duke's daughter, and such a pretty one at that, must be in high demand. I cannot imagine that the Duke of Ranelagh and Somerville will find you a suitable son-in-law."

Wei's blood chilled at the woman's knowledge. *Is she issuing a subtle threat? To expose my relationship with Glory?*

"We had a bargain," he said through gritted teeth. "You promised discretion."

Mrs. Swann waved a hand. "Your secrets are safe with me, sir. You and Miss Cavendish gave a delightful and genuine performance, which is why I am taking you to Leonard Kray."

While Wei didn't trust her, he was relieved that she made no attempt at extortion.

"What is your relationship to Kray?" he asked.

"I promised to help you find him." Mrs. Swann's gaze was hard. "Not to discuss my past."

"Then why do you say that Kray is not a threat now? Fifteen

years ago, the bastard murdered my family, and I fought him—I know how lethal he can be. Does he know that I am coming for him?" Wei narrowed his gaze. "Am I walking into a trap? Are you his partner in some nefarious plan?"

Emotion flared in Mrs. Swann's gaze.

Rage.

Wei recognized it well.

An instant later, she snuffed it out.

"Kray is no friend of mine," she said coolly. "As for the rest, you will have your answers soon enough."

"It's been a while since you visited your uncle, Miss Smith." The male attendant dressed in a white uniform, who'd introduced himself as Bremerton, glanced at Wei. "And you've brought a friend, I see."

"Mr. Wong, here, knew my uncle in the past," Mrs. Swann said smoothly. "He wanted to pay his respects."

"That's good of you, sir. Mr. Smith doesn't get many visitors, and I'm sure your presence will lift his spirits."

Wei returned Bremerton's friendly smile with a neutral nod. Inside, he was reeling—had been since he'd arrived at the gated asylum located in a barren field outside of Camden Town.

What in blazes is going on?

As the attendant led him and Mrs. Swann down a corridor that smelled of urine and old shoes, bloodcurdling screams erupted from one of the locked chambers along the way.

"How is Uncle Walter faring today?" Mrs. Swann asked.

"Same as always, I'm afraid. Poor bloke." Bremerton took out a ring of keys, pausing in front of a scarred wooden door. "Madness affects folks in different ways, and in your uncle's case, it's made him angry. Angry and confused. The physician believes Mr. Smith is subject to disturbing delusions...but of course it's difficult to know since your uncle has such difficulty speaking."

"Poor Uncle Walter. I hope my presence today won't upset him the way it has in the past."

Was it Wei's imagination, or was there a trace of malice in Mrs. Swann's smile?

If there was, the amiable Bremerton missed it. "I hope you don't take it personally, miss. Your uncle isn't in his right mind and doesn't realize how fortunate he is to have you looking after him. Because you gave advance notice of your visit, I was able to make some preparations. For your safety and that of Mr. Smith, of course."

"How kind of you," Mrs. Swann murmured.

Nodding, Bremerton took a breath as if to brace himself and slid a key into the lock. "Let's see the patient then, shall we?"

His chest tight with anticipation, Wei followed the others in.

The chamber was dark and resembled a cell with a tiny, barred window framing a bleak patch of sky. There was a small cot with a single pillow. In a corner, a man sat in a chair with a high back and wheels. From his profile, he looked disheveled and frail.

"Hello, Mr. Smith," Bremerton said with exaggerated cheer. "Your visitors have come like I said they would."

The man turned his head slowly in their direction.

At the sight of the pale eyes that had stalked his nightmares, Wei's heart raged with stunned recognition.

It's him. The bastard who slaughtered my family.

Only, Kray had changed.

When Bremerton turned Kray's chair in their direction, the blackguard's condition struck Wei fully. His chest surging, he took in Kray's vacant stare and skeletal features. The slack mouth, drool dribbling down the sunken chin. Kray's clothing draped his emaciated figure, bones jutting against the stained linen. His limbs were spindly...as if he hadn't used them for some time.

"Alas, my poor uncle had an accident," Mrs. Swann

murmured. "He cannot move from the neck down, and even speaking is difficult. Perhaps it is for the best that he lacks conversation, for his mind also suffered much damage."

At the sound of her voice, Kray's gaze suddenly sharpened. It was as if a mask slipped off, and Wei saw a glimpse of the cruel killer. Instinctively, he took a step forward, ready to take down the bastard. With his bare hands and a great deal of pleasure.

Kray's face was mottled with emotion, yet all he could do was sputter, *"You...you...you."*

"Do you recognize me, Uncle dear?"

Mrs. Swann glided over, and Wei could have sworn he saw fear in Kray's eyes.

"Bi...bi," Kray managed.

"I am happy to see you too." She glanced at the table next to his chair, which held a tray of shaving implements and a folded newspaper. She picked up a razor. "Having a shave, were you? Let me help you with that."

With her free hand, she gripped his jaw, turning it this way and that whilst he wriggled his head like a worm on a hook. She brought the blade a hairsbreadth from his throat.

"It looks like someone missed a spot," she crooned. "Shall I fix it for you?"

Kray shrank away from her.

"I'm afraid I didn't manage a clean shave today," Bremerton cut in, his tone apologetic. "Your uncle isn't cooperative with grooming. It helps if I have one of the other attendants read to him whilst I wield the razor."

He gestured to the newspaper, and Wei noticed the blazing headline: *Ransom and Rothwell, Rising Stars in the Fight Against Opium.* It made him think of Glory, how pleased she would be for her papa. Wei realized how lucky *he* was to have won her love and loyalty as well...gifts he'd done nothing to deserve.

The doing is in the not doing.

Something clicked in Wei, unlocking the door to awareness.

The simplicity of the insight made his breath catch even as it grounded him. Filled him with conviction for what he had to do.

"But even reading the newspaper didn't calm Mr. Smith today," Bremerton went on. "Made him worse, in fact. I had to give him a sedating elixir."

"Perhaps he was anxious for my visit," Mrs. Swann said. "If it is not too much trouble, I would like to review my uncle's care. Perhaps we could speak in private whilst Mr. Wong keeps my uncle company?"

"Of course, miss," Bremerton said. "Shall we talk in the front office?"

As the pair headed out, Mrs. Swann turned and looked at Wei.

Her gaze glittering, she said, "Enjoy your visit, Mr. Wong."

Alone with Kray, Wei strode over, looking down at the pathetic figure. He grasped Kray's right sleeve and tore it off. The familiar black vines crept over Kray's bony arm, the blooms withered upon his skin.

Balling his hands, Wei said, "Do you remember me?"

Kray's eyes widened, lucidity glimmering in the pale depths.

"I can see that you do," Wei said. "Which means you must know why I am here."

He reached for Kray's bobbing throat and felt the fragility of his enemy's existence.

"You slaughtered my family. Why did you do it? For money? Because that bastard Governor Li paid you coin and turned a blind eye to your opium smuggling?"

When Kray didn't answer, Wei tightened his grip on the other's throat.

"Did you even know their names? My father was Chen Qiang, my mother Chen Jumei. And my sister Chen Meiling was only ten years old when you cut her throat."

Kray gurgled, his eyes bulging.

"I swore to them that I would find you and make you suffer for what you did." Red misted Wei's vision as he squeezed harder. "It would be so easy to smother you with your own pillow and say you had a fit and choked to death. No one would know. No one would care."

Wei saw the moment Kray gave up the fight. Felt the bastard going limp, his head lolling in acceptance of his fate. Maybe even welcoming it.

And Wei let go.

Kray gasped at the sudden rush of air.

"But I am not going to do it," Wei said with cold finality. "Because you deserve to live out this miserable existence you have earned. *Yuan fen* has done my job better than I ever could. My revenge will be leaving you here." Gripping the arms of the chair, he leaned down and stared his demon in the eyes. "Right where you are."

He turned and walked to the door.

The screech stopped him. The inhuman sound raised the hairs on his nape and was followed by thumping. Pivoting, Wei saw Kray banging his head against the back of his chair as he emitted awful sounds.

Although Kray could only move his head, he managed to move his chair with his thumping, knocking it against the table. The shaving implements rattled; the newspaper flapped to the ground. The noises were so loud that Bremerton and Mrs. Swann burst into the chamber.

"What is going on?" Mrs. Swann asked sharply.

"Your uncle is having a fit of lunacy, I'm afraid," Bremerton said. "As I mentioned, the same thing happened earlier."

The attendant hurried to Kray's side.

"There, there, Walter. Calm yourself now, or we'll have to use restraints. You wouldn't like that, would you now? Why don't I read something to take your mind off whatever's bothering you, eh?" Bremerton picked up the newspaper. "Well, here's an interesting article on the Duke of Ranelagh and Somerville and Emmett Rothwell—"

Kray's shrieks filled the room. This time, the sounds had the shape of words.

"*Kill her...kill her...*" Spittle flew from Kray's lips, his eyes wild. "*Kill her...*"

"I think we'd best take our leave," Mrs. Swann said with a brittle smile. "I am afraid my visit brought out the worst in my poor uncle. Are you ready to go, Mr. Wong?"

Watching Kray bang his head, thrashing his withered, frozen body, Wei told the truth.

"More than ready," he said.

Thirty-Five

"Sweeting, you shouldn't have come here."

Wei's actions belied his words, for he strode toward Glory as she dashed toward him. They met in the middle of his study, his arms enfolding her in a fierce embrace. She held him just as tightly as their mouths fused with tender passion. Even when the kiss ended, they stayed as they were, breathing each other in.

"I had to see you," she said tremulously. "When I got your note about going after Kray, I was mad with worry. Are you all right? What happened—"

"I will tell you everything. After you answer my question, impatient one."

When she saw the smile in his eyes, relief percolated through her. She hadn't known what state she would find him in after he confronted his enemy at long last. Yet whatever events had occurred, Wei seemed none the worse for the wear. He was calm and composed, every bit the commanding *shifu* in his elegant dark-blue tunic and trousers.

She tilted her head. "Ask away."

He sized her up, taking in her outfit, which was considerably less elegant than his. She'd thrown on a shirt and pair of trousers, jamming her hair beneath a battered cap.

"How did you manage to slip out?" he asked.

"It wasn't difficult." She shrugged. "After the luncheon, I told my parents I was feeling peaked. They went to bed early themselves. Once everyone was abed, I made my exit."

Wei aimed a stern look at her. "You didn't climb down the drainpipe again?"

"Oh no. I used the tried-and-true method of tying bedsheets together."

"Well," he said after a pause. "That is a relief."

"Enough about me. I want to hear how things went with Kray."

"I shall tell you. Over tea."

They sat side by side at the round table, and over cups of a fragrant chrysanthemum brew, Wei shared the events of his day. The appearance of Mrs. Swann, the asylum, the meeting with Leonard Kray. As Glory listened to Wei's description of Kray, his conflict over how to mete revenge, and his final choice, her eyes welled. Not with sadness but pride. At his wisdom, strength, and honor.

What a man I've fallen in love with.

"You did the absolute right thing, darling." She placed her hand atop his on the table. "Kray got his just deserts. There was no need for you to stain your conscience."

"After what he did to my family, I don't know that killing him would stain my conscience," Wei said matter-of-factly. "I wish, though, that the bastard could speak. That I could hear him confess that he'd murdered my parents and sister and why he'd done it."

"I am sorry you did not get all your answers," she said softly. "The proper closure you and your kin deserve."

"I may get it yet. Mrs. Swann said that she had some of Kray's things. She plans to sort through them and deliver any pertinent items."

"That is helpful of her. She is a woman of her word, and I admire that."

Wei shot her a dark look. "Steer clear of her, Glory. She's dangerous. I wouldn't be surprised if she was somehow responsible for Kray's present state."

"*Amicus meus, inimicus inimici mei,*" Glory said. "The enemy of my enemy is my friend."

"With friends like Susanna Swann, who needs enemies?" Wei's expression grew somber. "Regardless of how Kray ended up in that asylum, seeing him that way made me realize something."

"What, darling?"

"There is justice in the world," Wei said. "Fate meted out his punishment far better than I could."

"I am glad you came to that conclusion," she said softly.

He rubbed his thumb over her knuckles. "I came to another one as well."

"Oh?"

"I don't want revenge to be my sole purpose any longer." His gaze was clear and passionate. "I want to live for love. For you."

Joy spilled like a bowl of sugar, sweetness spilling into every nook and cranny of her being. His certainty triggered her own decision. Made her aware that life was short and love too precious to waste even a moment.

"Then come speak to my father," she said.

Wei stared at her. "What about his campaign? The bill he plans to propose is important—"

"We won't go public with our engagement quite yet, but I don't want to hide our relationship from my family any longer," she said with resolve. "My papa may resist, but we will convince him that you are the only husband for me. That I will have my wise, strong, and noble *shifu* or no one."

"My love." Wei cupped her face with such reverence that her eyes stung. "You have made me the happiest of men."

His kiss was passionate and possessive. She opened to him, eager for the feel of him inside her. He growled, and the kiss caught fire. He pulled her onto his lap, her cap falling off and hair tumbling free over her shoulders. He threaded his fingers in her tresses, holding her head steady as he raided her mouth. With equal fervor, she kissed him back, wanting more. Everything.

He tore his lips from hers, breathing raggedly. "Bloody hell, you drive me wild, little tigress. But we ought to stop and get you home before your absence is discovered."

The brewing need in his eyes gave her courage to voice her desires.

She fiddled with his collar. "I want to stay the night. Here, with you."

His pupils flared, but he firmed his jaw. "Soon we'll be able to spend every night together, love. After I speak to your papa—"

"I don't want to wait to be with you. We are committed to each other, and that is what counts." Despite his arguments, she felt the hard bulge of his agreement beneath her. "In my heart, I am yours, Wei, and you are mine. What other legitimacy does our love need?"

He caught her chin, looking into her eyes, and her breath held.

"Do you know how people are married in my village?"

At his unexpected question, she shook her head.

"It is an intricate process. Marriage is seen as a union between two families, not just two people. Matchmakers are used to pair bride and groom, making sure they are compatible."

Curious, Glory had to interrupt. "How do they do that?"

"By consulting birth dates, astrological charts, and other means."

"Do you think we would be compatible?" she mused.

"To be honest? Not really."

She frowned at him. "Why not?"

"You were born in the Year of the Tiger. As was I." He lifted his brows. "Two tigers make for a rather intense relationship."

"Intense isn't bad," she argued.

"According to Chinese astrologers, you would be better off with another sign."

"Which one?"

"A pig." His eyes gleamed with laughter.

She cuffed him on the shoulder. "Very amusing. Tell me more about a Chinese wedding."

"Well, there are many rituals. Betrothal gifts, a procession from the bride's home to the groom's, ceremonies, and banquets. As for the wedding clothes, the bride and groom both wear red for luck."

Fascinated, Glory said, "I would love to wear a red wedding dress."

"Red would suit you, little tigress." Wei's smile was tender. "Now, despite all the rigamarole that goes into a Chinese wedding, there is a specific ritual that unites the bride and groom, and it is quite simple."

"What is it?"

"Three *kowtows*," he said. "One to heaven and earth, paying respect to the deities and our ancestors. One to our parents. And one to each other." He paused, his eyes searching hers. "Will you *kowtow* with me, Glory? Bind yourself to me in the eyes of heaven and earth?"

She gave him the answer thumping in her heart. "Yes."

Triumph blazed in his eyes. He set her on her feet, taking her hand and leading her to his ancestral altar, where she'd burned an offering to Ling Ling on her birthday. The spirit tablets bearing his family's names were polished and gleaming, the perfume of burning incense rich in the air.

Together, they knelt.

"*Baba, Mama, Mei Mei*," Wei said in a gravelly voice. "Earlier today, I informed you of the fate of your murderer, and I hope the justice he is serving brings you peace. Now I have brighter news. I want you to meet Glory Cavendish, who is to be my wife. I pledge to love and protect her and any children we are blessed to have for as long as I shall live. We humbly ask for your blessing."

The gravity of the moment cinched Glory's throat. As Wei turned to her, she saw their future in his brilliant gaze. A lifetime of *kung fu* and adventures. Pursuing their passions by day and making passionate love at night. Raising a family together.

He is everything I could ever want.

"Are you ready?" he asked.

She nodded.

"First bow is to heaven and earth," he said.

She followed his motion, bending her forehead toward the ground.

"The second to my parents."

They *kowtowed* to the altar.

"And the last to each other."

When she lifted her head the final time, Wei was staring at her with a mix of love, wonder, and hunger that made her tremble. In the next instant, he swept her onto her feet and into his arms. She barely managed to loop her arms around his neck before he crushed his mouth to hers.

As Wei set his woman next to his bed, he felt a surge of pride and awe.

Glory is mine. She has bound herself to me. Nothing can come between us.

Love burgeoned his chest and his cock. Making love to Glory was always an exhilarating experience, but tonight there was an added freedom. A headiness in knowing that they'd made their vows, and there was no need to hold back. He could claim his sweet girl fully, once and for all.

He kissed the silky curve of her neck, inhaling her scent. "I've wanted this for so long."

"Me too." She gave a delightful shiver as he tongued the rim of her ear. "Since the first time you kissed me at the Fancy's flash house."

"I wanted you even before that." He kissed her nose and cheeks, trying to catch every freckle. "Even though I tried to resist. Even though I told myself it was selfish and wrong to want you for my own."

She drew back. "You don't think that now, do you?"

"No." He tucked a strand of her rich hair behind her ear, smiling into her eyes of sunlit jade. "Now I know I was meant to love you for all our days."

"That's just as well," she said, dimpling. "Because I am going to love you just as long."

She was so adorable that he had to kiss her again. Soon, they were panting, straining to get closer, and he wanted no more barriers between them. He undressed her, unwrapping her like the precious gift of fate that she was. In his eyes, there was no finer woman than Glory. Her lithe perfection made him harder than a rock.

Blushing beautifully, she whispered, "I want to see you too."

He stripped, his eyes on her face. Loving the cute yet carnal way his little tigress looked at him. When he shed his trousers, her eyes locked on his rampant erection, and he groaned when she moistened her lips.

He tumbled her onto the bed, and the feel of skin on skin was sublime. She was soft and supple beneath him, her nipples stiff buds poking into the wall of his chest. His mouth watered to taste her everywhere, and he did. From her sweet little tits to her dainty toes and luscious cunny. He ate her until she arched against his mouth, rewarding him with her nectar.

Still ravenous, he turned her over to explore more of her graceful terrain. He nibbled down the silken rung of her spine.

Tasted the pretty dip above her bottom. Spreading her enticing cheeks, he tongued her from behind until she squealed another climax into his pillow.

Flipping her over once more, he kissed her. Feeding her the taste of her own pleasure sent a blaze up his spine. When she wrapped a hand around his throbbing prick, he groaned against her lips.

"I want you," she whispered. "I want to know what it feels like to belong to you fully."

"And you will." He sat up, guiding her head toward his lap. "Suck me first, love. Make me wet so that I can fit into your snug little slit."

Whimpering, she dove for his cock, taking him with enchanting enthusiasm. As usual, she was a quick study, improving leaps and bounds since their previous lesson. His fingers gripped her hair as she pleasured him, her tongue a teasing flicker, her lips an exquisite seal as he guided her up and down his length. Suddenly, she plunged down of her own accord, the squeeze of her throat drawing his stones up taut.

Grunting, he pulled out. "By the deities, you're getting too good at that."

Her grin was playful. "You taught me well, *Shifu*."

He shouldn't have been aroused by that, but he was. Everything about his naughty pupil made him wild with lust. He rolled atop her, driving his turgid shaft against her dewy folds, grazing her little nub with his hardness until she began to shake once more.

Only then did he notch his head to her opening. As he pushed into the tight clasp of her body, it felt like his first time. Not because he'd been celibate for years, but because he'd never truly made love before. Never wanted a woman with his body, heart, and soul.

He stared into Glory's eyes. Into his future. His everything.

"You're mine," he rasped.

"Forever."

Her sweet vow expanded his chest with pride and a primal need to claim.

With a guttural sound of exultation, he thrust home.

Glory gasped as Wei entered her. His manhood felt like a hot bar of steel driving into her core. Even though she wanted him, she wasn't prepared for the bite of pain and deep stretch that pushed the breath from her lungs. Just as she feared that he might not fit, he stilled, his forehead creasing.

"Are you all right, love?" he said.

She managed a nod. "Is it always this, um, tight?"

"I wouldn't know." His eyes roved over her, so hot and possessive that her heart fluttered giddily despite her discomfort. "I've never been anyone's first lover before."

"Oh." She liked that—liked that this was a first for him too.

"I'm told some pain can be normal at first." He rubbed his thumb over her bottom lip. "Breathe, love. I won't move until you ask me to."

She hadn't even realized that she was holding her breath. She exhaled, then inhaled deeply. As she repeated the cycle, the pain began to ebb, replaced by a feeling of fullness.

"Better?" he asked.

Nodding, she said hesitantly, "I'm ready, I think. If you want, you can try moving now."

His eyes had a wicked twinkle. "We'll know you're ready when you ask me nicely."

Before she could ask what he meant, he bent his head, closing his lips over her nipple. His tongue sent licks of fire over her skin. When he drew on her sensitive tip, her pussy clenched, the sensation tender yet strangely exciting. He moved his attention to her other breast, suckling until she began to squirm, the fullness at her center morphing into unbearable need.

"Please, Wei," she gasped. "Do something. Please."

As he continued lazily tonguing her nipples, he moved his hand between them, his thumb circling another peak where she throbbed. The combined sensations built and built until she was desperate for relief. Instinctively, she shifted her hips and felt his cock go deeper. But there was no pain now, only a pulsating desire for more.

"Now you're ready." Satisfaction gleamed in his gaze. "Move with me, sweeting."

He thrust slowly, and his movements felt good, then better than good. They felt as essential as the way he looked at her, as if she were the most precious thing he'd ever seen. She ran her hands over his shoulders, biceps, and chest, reveling in his rippling power. In the fact that this splendid man was hers.

"You feel so bloody good," Wei grated out. "Can you take more?"

"I want everything you have to give."

He gave her what she asked for, the vigorous drives of his cock pushing a gasp from her lips. There was only pleasure, building and building with the rhythmic slaps of his skin against hers. Suddenly, he shifted his angle, hitting some high, exquisite place inside. She cried his name as her release rushed over her, bliss blasting through every cell of her being.

"You're so damn beautiful," Wei said fiercely. "And you're mine."

He surged inside her. Again and again and again, stimulating that spot until the waves of pleasure began anew. Suddenly, he pulled out, and even as her pussy clenched on emptiness, her breath caught at the virile display. His fist flashed up and down his huge, glistening shaft, his biceps bulging, the muscles of his chest standing out in stark relief. Then he threw his head back on a shout, and she gasped as milky streams shot from his cock and rained hotly upon her belly.

Lowering himself onto his forearms, he blanketed her body with his. His solid weight and the scent of his satisfaction added to her own fulfillment. She floated in the warmth of his proprietary gaze.

"Is your curiosity satisfied, little one?" he asked huskily.

She thought about it. "For the time being. But I still have questions."

"About?"

"Positions, amongst other things. I think I will be requiring additional lessons."

His eyes bright with laughter, he said, "I shall be happy to oblige, my love."

And he did, all through the night.

Thirty-Six

Wei surfaced from a deep sleep. Without opening his eyes, he sensed the emptiness beside him. But he smiled because he could smell Glory's orchid scent, lingering like the sweetest aftermath.

Last night hadn't been a dream.

He and his little tigress had committed themselves before heaven and earth. They'd declared their love with words and their bodies. She belonged to him now as surely as he belonged to her; there was only one more barrier to cross. Wei didn't fool himself that the Duke of Ranelagh and Somerville would readily accept his suit, but he was determined to prove his worth to her family.

When he'd dropped Glory off at home in the wee hours of the morning, they had agreed that Glory would tell her papa to expect him this afternoon. This gave Wei a few hours to work on his proposal. While he was neither wealthy nor titled, he had sufficient means to give Glory a life of comfort and security. She'd even expressed excitement at the prospect of living at the clinic. Nonetheless, he knew that she was giving up a lot for him, and he would dedicate himself to her happiness, protect her, ensure that she wanted for nothing that was within his power to give.

Hopefully, that would be enough to satisfy her papa.

Wei sat up, stretching before he rose naked from the bed. At the sight of the small stain on the sheets, he felt a twinge of guilt... and a proprietary jolt in his cock. Bloody hell, he couldn't wait to have his little tigress in his life and his bed permanently.

Getting dressed, he went in search of breakfast and ran into Yao in the courtyard.

"Didn't think you would be up this early." Yao waggled his brows. "Not after your little pupil's visit last night."

"Show some respect," Wei said shortly. "She is going to be my wife."

"About time you admitted it." Yao grinned. "When will you be bringing home my future *shimu*? God knows this place could use a female's touch."

"I have an appointment with her father this afternoon."

Yao grimaced. "Good luck with that, *shihing*."

Wei would need it.

"By the by, a package just arrived for you. From the Swann woman. I put it in your study."

Wei's nape prickled. Mrs. Swann's delivery had come sooner than expected.

"Thank you," he said. "Have breakfast sent to my study, will you?"

Parting ways with his *shidai*, he headed to his study. A box was waiting for him on his desk, and he paused, dread creeping over him. Whatever he discovered in there was bound to be painful—a veritable Pandora's box of the past. Yet there might be answers in there, the closure that Kray had been in no condition to give.

Wei owed it to his family to see this through to the end. To honor their deaths with the truth. And to give himself peace by laying the matter fully at rest.

Inhaling, he opened the lid.

His gut recoiled, his eyes blurring as he saw what lay inside. With shaking hands, he lifted out his sister's hair, wetness sliding down his cheeks as he held the dull and lifeless skeins. At that moment, his grief and rage merged again, and he wished he'd torn out Kray's throat.

He drew a hitched breath. Gently, he set down his sister's hair and forced himself to remove the other item from the box. The leather-bound journal was tattered, his chest constricting when he saw the title scrawled on the first page: *The Adventures of Leonard Kray 1835-1836.*

The time of his family's murders.

Wei made himself read on. Kray was meticulous and depraved, detailing his exploits with bloodless precision and pride. In the story he told, he was a self-made hero. To him, robbing, assaulting, and even killing were valuable skills he'd honed over time. His words showed no remorse or moral conscience, an early entry summing up his view of the world.

I never wanted to be a sailor, but the bleeding Peelers left me no choice but to get out of London with all due expedience. Bastards somehow tied me to the old mort in Clerkenwell. How I don't know for I left her with a cleverly broken neck at the foot of the stairs...an accident, by all appearances. My recent stint in Boarding School— the whore responsible for my stay is lucky I didn't cut her throat for her stupid bleating—makes my current flit all the more necessary.

P.S. The mort's idiot nephew didn't pay me nearly enough for the job, and now that he has his greedy paws on her inheritance, I'll be reminding him that he owes me for my silence.

Kray's entries simmered with resentment and spite. With the belief that life had cheated him, and he deserved better. Therefore, he felt entitled to take what he wanted.

Grandpapa, that cheeseparing bastard, didn't want to send me on a Tour, and I hope he's turning in his grave as I make my own way around the world, doing the Kray name proud. In India, I parted ways with my last ship due to a misunderstanding. The captain wanted to discipline me for the alleged coercion of a native—as if a man ought to be punished for picking fruit off a tree he owns. India is a jewel in the English crown, ours to do with as we please. The nabobs' estates are teeming with their half-Indian bastards, but as always, wealth makes the rules while men like me suffer unfair consequences.

Battening down his rage, Wei forced himself to read about the path of destruction Kray carved all the way to China. Kray had his usual litany of complaints about the Middle Kingdom: from the food to the culture and people, everything was inferior to England. Having yet again parted ways with his ship, Kray had found work as a guard for one of the British opium traders in Canton. A man named Erasmus Trimble who'd earned a rare modicum of respect from Kray.

Now Trimble, he's a man of action. He wasn't born with a silver spoon in his mouth, and he's made something of himself. An intelligent fellow, he values all I have to offer. He won't let the rules of ordinary men get in the way of ambition and greatness.

More glowing accounts of Trimble's "greatness"—which amounted to bribes and violence in the service of opium smuggling—followed, until Wei arrived at an entry dated three days after his family's deaths. His blood turned to ice as he read the words.

There was a fly in Trimble's ointment, and I got rid of it for him. That's what the stupid soldier gets for getting in the way of progress —for interfering in the British right to free trade. By disposing of the interfering captain and his family, I've not only restored the healthy flow of opium, but now Governor Li owes Trimble a favor.

Apparently, the soldier's son is fucking the fat governor's wife...a pretty piece I wouldn't mind sampling myself.

Too bad the son got away. But Trimble says not to go after the peasant—Li is satisfied that the bastard who cuckolded him is suffering a fate worse than death, having his kin massacred before his eyes. I took a souvenir to prove I'd done the others, and that was enough for Trimble. He's giving me my purse today for completing the job, and I'm headed out on the next ship out of this godforsaken place. Back to London I'll go, where I can start life anew as a gentleman of means...

Bile rose in Wei's throat even as a terrible numbness spread and spread. All this time, there'd been another villain hiding in the shadows. Erasmus Trimble had wanted Wei's father out of the way because the captain was incorruptible and dedicated to stamping out opium. Trimble had given Kray the assassination orders and parlayed the murders into an advantageous relationship with Li.

Where can I find Erasmus Trimble?

Feverishly, Wei tore through the pages, looking for a description, a clue, anything. But soon after Kray committed the murders, he collected his earnings and left—with no more mention of Trimble. Gritting his teeth, Wei read every despicable word until there was nothing left to read.

Just another dead end.

With a roar, Wei hurled the useless journal. It crashed into a wall, exploding in a flurry of paper. Pages rained through the study as he cursed himself for failing once again. For letting his family down. For selfishly focusing on his happiness when their murderer was still out there, carefree and unpunished.

When the red mist cleared, Wei dragged his hands through his hair, his chest surging as he took in the mess he'd made. The journal's pages had separated from the cover and scattered bloody everywhere. His *shifu* would chastise him for his lack of control and rightly so. He should know better than to give in to temper, which accomplished nothing. What he needed to do was think... and to talk to Glory.

The thought of his little tigress anchored him. She would listen, support him, and help him work on finding Trimble. With her in his corner, he was no longer alone.

Expelling a breath, he went to gather the pieces of the diary, pausing when he picked up the cover. The binding on the back cover had unraveled, a corner poking out from beneath the leather. Frowning, he brought the cover over to his desk and used a letter opener to cut through the rest of the binding. He tipped the cover to the side, and something slid out.

A daguerreotype.

The image was of two men standing together in front of a building, which Wei recognized as the British factory in Canton. Kray was on the left. And on the right...recognition slammed into Wei.

Bloody hell, it can't be him...

Turning the daguerreotype over, he saw that Kray had identified his companion.

British Factory, Canton, with Erasmus Trimble. 1836.

But Trimble went by another name now. Wei flashed to Kray shrieking when the attendant had picked up the newspaper, and suddenly he knew what the blackguard had been trying to communicate.

Killer, killer, killer.

Wei left his study in a sprint.

Thirty-Seven

That afternoon, Glory wished the guests would leave. After talking business with Papa, Mr. Rothwell and Mr. Winslow had stayed for tea in the drawing room, and she hoped they did not plan on lingering. Wei was due to arrive in two hours, and she wanted him to have privacy when he spoke to Papa.

Given that her father had forbidden her from seeing Wei, she'd thought it wise to keep mum about her lover's impending visit. Instead, she'd asked if Papa would be free to help her with something at four o'clock. She'd told him it was a surprise, and, looking faintly puzzled, he had agreed. In her head, she planned what she might say when Wei came...perhaps a little speech that appealed to the unconventional way her own parents had found love.

"May I compliment you again on yesterday's luncheon, Lady Glory?"

Sharing a settee with her, Matthew Winslow gave her a charming smile. He was dapper in a Prussian blue frock coat, embroidered yellow waistcoat, and biscuit-colored trousers. From his pomaded hair to his brass buttons, he was polished to a shine... one that Glory found a bit overbright. She preferred Wei's understated elegance.

"I cannot take credit, sir," Glory demurred. "My mama did most of the work."

"Nonsense, my dear," Mama said from an adjacent sofa. "You planned the menu and selected the entertainment. The Chinese illusionist was a hit with the guests."

"I will never understand how the chap links and unlinks *solid* rings," Papa muttered from beside Mama. "Even though I footed his bill, he wouldn't tell me his secret. All he would say is that one sees what one wishes to see...whatever the devil that means."

"I think it is more apt to say that the guests saw whatever the illusionist wanted them to see, Your Grace." Mr. Rothwell took a sip of tea and smirked. "A useful trick, that. We should take a page out of his book for our campaign."

"I think His Grace's speech accomplished that nicely," Mr. Winslow said.

"I agree." Glory beamed at her papa. "You spoke eloquently about the impact of opium on the Chinese people. About the human cost of the trade."

"There was not a dry eye in the ballroom." Mama squeezed Papa's hand. "Well done, darling."

Papa turned a bit ruddy. "I only hope it was enough to gain the guests' support."

"Between your savvy and my resources, this is a battle we will not lose. I hope you will not forget your friends, Your Grace, when you soar into the political stratosphere," Mr. Rothwell said indulgently. "The papers are hinting at a position for you in the Prime Minister's cabinet, and I have several ventures in the works that could use your leadership."

"I am not interested in politics," Papa said. "Only in putting an end to a heinous injustice."

"Never say never, Your Grace—"

Mr. Winslow was cut off by the arrival of Greaves.

"Pardon, Your Graces. Mr. Chen is here," the butler said.

Why is Wei so early? Looking at the guests, Glory felt a thrum of panic.

"What the devil is he doing here?" Papa clipped out.

"I told him you were occupied at present," Greaves said. "But he is being rather insistent."

Seeing the gathering storm on her father's face, Glory cut in hastily.

"I invited Mr. Chen," she blurted. "Please bring him in."

Lines bracketed her father's mouth as he shot her a foreboding look. Because they had company, however, he could not say more. Hearing Wei's approaching footsteps, Glory got to her feet. She tried to keep her manner casual; it wasn't easy because her impulse was to run to him and greet him with a kiss.

She needed to do this right, however. To gain her parents' consent for their marriage, she and Wei had to put their best foot forward.

And that includes not betraying that we consummated our love last night.

Her intimate muscles quivered in memory, the slight ache making her feel a bit strange. Making love with Wei had been everything she'd dreamed of and more, and she didn't regret it, not for a second. This morning, however, she'd felt a sudden vulnerability, an awareness that, in following her heart, she had crossed a threshold of no return.

For she had committed the ultimate sin for a well-bred lady: she'd given her virginity to a man outside of marriage. She was a woman of experience now. It was exciting...and a teensy bit scary.

Anticipation welled as the door opened. Wei came in, cutting a handsome figure...although she was surprised that he'd chosen to wear his native attire rather than the English fashions he usually favored in public. His eyes met hers, and her smile faltered.

Something is wrong. Why does Wei look so...so agitated?

To the outsider, he might seem his usual calm self, but she

knew him far too well. His eyes were the black of a starless night. The kind of dark that drained all brightness from a room.

"Mr. Chen," she said haltingly. "You...you're early."

But he wasn't looking at her. His gaze had locked on Mr. Rothwell, and her heart stuttered at the bloodthirsty rage that contorted his features.

"*You*," he said in a savage tone. "You are going to pay for what you did to my family."

Mr. Rothwell blinked, looking uncertain. Papa and Mr. Winslow both rose.

"What is the meaning of this, Chen?" Papa said shortly.

"That blackguard." Wei jabbed a finger at Rothwell; his voice trembled with unleashed fury. "He murdered my parents and my sister. And he is going to pay."

Wei moved, lightning fast. So fast that Rothwell didn't have a chance to react. In a heartbeat, Wei had him pinned to the wall, a hand on his throat.

Shaking off her paralysis, Glory dashed over.

"What is going on?" Hearing Rothwell's desperate gasps, she tugged at Wei's arm, but it was futile, his grip like steel.

"Stop, darling," she said desperately. "You're going to hurt him."

"I'm going to *kill* him," Wei snarled.

Rothwell made a choking sound, his eyes bulging. Then Papa, Winslow, and Greaves were there. The three of them barely managed to wrestle Wei away from Rothwell.

Rothwell sagged against the wall, wheezing.

"Calm your bloody self, Chen," Papa bit out. "Before I summon the police."

Wei struggled against their hold. "My family is dead because of Rothwell. He deserves to die."

"How is Mr. Rothwell involved?" Glory asked, stunned.

"I don't know what the scoundrel's talking about," Rothwell

said hoarsely. "He's mad—or maybe he's an opium eater. Around the stuff enough, isn't he?"

Wei let out a bellow of rage.

"Uncle, get to the carriage." Winslow was panting, his brow sheened with exertion. "We cannot hold him back much longer."

Rothwell staggered out the door.

Growling, Wei wrestled with his captors, including Glory's father.

"Papa, don't hurt Wei," she pleaded.

"You're worried about *him*?" Papa shot her an incredulous look as he tried to twist Wei's right arm behind his back. "He's lost his bloody mind—"

At that moment, Wei shook off Winslow, swatting him aside like an annoying fly. Glory gasped as he struck out wildly with his free hand. He hit Papa in the chest, the latter stumbling backward.

"Rhys, darling!" Mama dashed toward him.

Glory moved to stand between her parents and Wei.

"Stop it!" she cried. "What are you doing?"

Wei's gaze swirled with blind fury. "Rothwell is behind my family's murders. He paid Kray and was in cahoots with Li. Back then, he was an opium trader and went by the name Erasmus Trimble."

"The man's a liar." Dusting himself off, Mr. Winslow glared at Wei. "My uncle has never even been to China. I have visited the bloody British factory and never heard of anyone named Trimble."

"Glory, get away from that madman," Papa growled.

"Wei is not mad." Her mind spinning, she tried to explain. "He's been hunting down his family's killer for years. We found a cutthroat named Kray who committed the crime, but now it sounds like he was paid—"

"Devil take it, what has the bastard involved you in?"

Papa made a grab for her, but Glory found herself pulled in the opposite direction.

Wei's arm circled her waist, holding her tight to his side.

"They won't listen, Glory." He circled his gaze around the room as if all its occupants were his enemies. "Their kind never do. Leave with me now."

"My father will listen," she said desperately. "You just have to explain."

"There is no bloody time for explanations," Wei snarled. "I will bring Rothwell down, no matter how long it takes. No matter the cost. And you swore to heaven and earth to be with me no matter the path before us."

"Release my daughter this instant," Papa thundered.

Seeing that Papa meant to lunge for her, she twisted free of Wei's grip. Backed away, swinging her gaze wildly between their hostile faces. She was torn, helpless to stop the violence brewing between the two men she loved most, her worst nightmare coming true.

Through hitched breaths, she said, "If you would just listen—"

"Last night you gave yourself to me." Wei's stare sliced into her soul as he held out a hand. "Now prove that you're mine."

"You *touched* my daughter, you blackguard?" Hellfire blazed in Papa's gaze. "By Jove, I am going to tear you limb from limb!"

He launched himself at Wei.

"Don't do this," Glory cried. "Stop!"

Mama was shouting for them to stop as well, but neither man listened, grappling and landing blows. Their aggression had a mind of its own, making them oblivious to anything but the desire to do bodily harm. Frantic, Glory tried to wade in—and stepped into the path of her father's oncoming attack. Greaves yanked her back in the nick of time, Papa's fist whooshing by.

"Stand back, my lady," the butler shouted. "You'll only get hurt."

He shouted for the footmen to come help, and a pair came running in...followed by Theo and Horatio. Seeing her brothers' stricken expressions, Glory ran to intercept them before they could try to enter the fray.

"Why is Master Chen fighting with Papa?" Horatio asked in a trembling voice.

"Stop hurting my papa!" Theo yelled, struggling against Glory's hold.

At that instant, Wei sent Papa arcing backward through the air. Papa slammed into the spirits cabinet, his head smacking against the wood. Decanters rained around him in a symphony of glass.

"*Rhys.*" Mama pushed past Glory to kneel by him, her face ashen. "Greaves, send for Dr. Abernathy. Quickly!"

Glory stood paralyzed as her brothers raced to Papa. Her heart seized at her father's closed eyes, the blood trickling from his lip. She lifted horrified eyes to Wei, who stood unmoving, his torn fists clenched at his sides.

This is my fault, she thought numbly. *I thought by keeping my relationship a secret, I was protecting Papa and Wei. Instead, I hurt them both.*

"Glory, I..."

Wei gave her an agonized look, then staggered over to Papa. He crouched, fumbling with Papa's sleeve, placing his fingers on Papa's wrist.

"His pulse is steady," Wei said hoarsely. "He should be fine—"

"Get away from my papa!" Theo shouted.

He shoved Wei with all his might, and Wei stumbled back.

At that moment, Papa coughed. Glory crossed over to him, her breath held.

Please be all right, Papa. Please.

He opened his eyes. Looked blearily at Mama.

"What...what the bloody hell happened, Maggie mine?" he sputtered.

"You were acting foolishly, Rhys," Mama scolded. "Don't ever do that again."

Then she burst into tears.

As Papa stroked Mama's hair, Glory knelt beside him.

"I'm sorry, Papa," she choked out. "Wei didn't mean to hurt you. He and I were going to tell you today—"

"You lied to me."

She swallowed, fearing her Papa's anger far less than the hurt in his eyes. He looked betrayed...and he had every right to.

"You gave me your word to stay away from Chen," he said ominously.

Through suffocating guilt, she pleaded, "I love him, Papa, and he loves me. If you would just listen to us..."

She turned around, looking for Wei. Needing his help to manage this disaster.

But he was gone.

Thirty-Eight

D r. Abernathy arrived within an hour. After a thorough examination, he pronounced that Papa had suffered a mild concussion but should be right as rain after some rest. Relief bloomed in Glory. She watched her mama sitting by her father's bedside, tenderly brushing a lock of hair from his forehead whilst he slept, and guilt twisted around her heart, the thorns digging in deep.

This is my fault. I should have told Papa the truth from the start. How will he ever give his blessing to me and Wei now?

Her fear of disappointing him had led to a calamity worse than she could have imagined. She didn't know what to do with regards to her father...or with Wei.

Recalling his rage, she shivered. She didn't know if Wei had gone after Rothwell. She tried to reassure herself that he was a skilled fighter who could take care of himself, and despite his wrath, he wasn't foolish.

I want to help you, my love, she thought in despair, *but I don't know how. I don't know if you even want my help any longer. If you want* me.

She slipped out of her papa's room and was greeted by Greaves in the corridor.

"I am sorry to disturb you, my lady," the butler began.

She gave him a wan smile. "I ought to be the one apologizing, Greaves, for the disturbance *I* caused. I hope you didn't suffer any injuries?"

"Thank you for your concern, my lady, but it is unnecessary." The old retainer's eyes were kind. "I wanted to inform you that Matthew Winslow is still in the drawing room and wishes to speak with you. Shall I tell him you are indisposed?"

Glory exhaled. "I'll take care of it."

Mr. Winslow rose the moment she entered, his face creased with concern.

"How is the duke?" he asked.

"Papa is fine," Glory said. "Thank you for staying."

"I am relieved to hear His Grace suffered no damage." He paused. "But there is another reason I am here."

She tilted her head. "Oh?"

"It concerns Chen's slander of my uncle," he said.

The truth is not slander.

"Such nonsense cannot be credited, of course," he went on. "I am familiar with my uncle's history inside and out, and I can, and will, vouch for the fact that he has never stepped foot in Canton. It will be my word, the word of an English gentleman, over the lies of a foreigner. A crazed and violent one at that."

Anger surged in Glory, but her instincts told her to keep it in check. To find out what Winslow was after.

"What is it that you want, sir?" she asked.

She saw him calculate his next move.

His expression turned charming. "You are a young and sheltered miss, Lady Glory, and to be forgiven for not understanding the ways of the world. For being misled in matters of the heart. It is not your fault that you were taken in by the Chinaman's lies."

She bit her tongue. Hard.

"But your innocent error in judgment could have devastating consequences...not only to your reputation but that of your papa. You see, His Grace's future is tied to my uncle's. Any scandal that reaches Rothwell will taint your papa as well. It will destroy His Grace's chances of stopping the opium trade and his political ambitions."

The threat was even more chilling due to the pleasant way it was uttered.

"There is a way to sweep this mess under the carpet, however," Mr. Winslow said. "A way to protect your good name and that of your family. A way to codify my uncle's support for your papa's campaign and fulfill all His Grace's aspirations." He took her hand. "You would like that, wouldn't you?"

"What, exactly, are you proposing?"

To her astonishment, he went down on one knee.

"Will you do me the honor of becoming my wife?"

After Mr. Winslow departed, Glory went to her papa's room. He'd awakened, and Mama was helping him take a sip of water.

"Papa. Mama." Glory took a breath for courage. "We need to talk."

THIRTY-NINE

Rothwell's estate was a fortress set atop a grassy knoll in Hamstead Heath. It was surrounded by a towering iron gate and guarded by a battalion of armed men. From the shadows of the surrounding trees, Wei searched for points of entry, chinks in the armor of Rothwell's lair.

He found none. No way to get in. No weaknesses to exploit.

He'd seen no sign of Rothwell, didn't even know if the bastard was inside. Wealth shielded Rothwell the same way it had Governor Li. It had taken years of planning and preparation to penetrate Li's defenses, and Wei's current challenge was even greater.

For Rothwell was rich as Croesus and the toast of London. He had important men in his pocket. With a wave of his hand, he could have Wei arrested, thrown in gaol...or worse. Who would believe Wei's version of events that Rothwell had been a villainous opium trader who'd ordered the murder of an innocent family? Who would even care that four Chinese had been slaughtered?

Years ago, Wei had been caught unprepared when his enemy attacked; he wouldn't make that same mistake. Before coming here, he'd gone to his clinic. Told Yao about the potential attack, instructing his *shidai* to get the patients and pupils to a safe place and shutter the clinic until further notice.

Surveilling Rothwell's stronghold now, Wei's vision blurred with rage—and with sudden grief. It wasn't over closing the clinic, even though he'd worked hard to build it and regretted leaving those under his care in the lurch. The aching emptiness was because of Glory...because he had destroyed any chance of a future with her.

At long last, he'd found true love. Glory had given her loyalty, her faith, even her sweet body...and he'd repaid her by beating her father. By acting like a goddamned ruffian and showing the world what a failure he was.

It was as if the years of training and hard work had been stripped away. Without the mantle of *shifu*, who was he? Nothing, that's what. Nothing but a worthless brute, a selfish scoundrel who'd caused the deaths of his family and taken a lady's virginity.

Wei's despair felt suffocating. *How can Glory's family accept me now?*

How could *she* forgive him? He had ruined everything, and he had no idea how to fix things. If things could even *be* fixed. Even the prospect of destroying Rothwell failed to console him. Failed to bring him any sense of peace.

"When you can relinquish that which drives you, then you will find your way," his *shifu* had once told him.

Wei was finally beginning to understand what the other meant.

For so long, he had been obsessed with the idea of avenging his family. But what if killing Rothwell meant giving up Glory? Wei could not expect her to go on the flit with him, spend the rest of her life dodging the authorities because he'd killed a man, no matter how justifiable his reasons. Earlier, it hadn't been fair of him to ask her to leave her home, the family she loved, in order to prove her loyalty.

With pounding remorse, he recognized that he'd reacted out of fear born of his past. Chun had loved the excitement of bedding a rough-and-ready fellow, but she hadn't loved *him*...and he had secretly feared Glory would come to the same conclusion. That he was good for fun and adventure, for carnal pleasure, but he wasn't good enough for *her*. Wasn't fit to be her husband, the father of her children, the man she would give her heart to forever and always.

Yet had Glory ever given him reason to doubt her? She had never deceived him, never let him down. On the contrary, she'd been loyal and true. Hell, if it hadn't been for her, he would never have picked up the trail that had led him to Rothwell. *She* had negotiated the trade with Scott and Mrs. Swann. She had listened to him and supported him and given him her love.

The greatest gift he'd ever been given. What he'd been searching for his whole life.

Glory...she's my true path.

The recognition was simple and stunning, the way the truth often is.

His mind suddenly clear, Wei knew what he had to do. He didn't know if his plan to win Glory back stood any chance of success, but he would try. And he didn't care if it took months, a year, forever...because love was worth it.

His little tigress was worth everything.

Wei took a wooded path away from the estate, heading back to the main road. He would have to walk to the village to find a hackney. The lamps of an oncoming carriage appeared, and he quickly took cover behind some trees.

The carriage pulled to a stop in front of his hiding place, and he released a breath when he recognized the occupant looking out the window.

"Thought you could use a ride," Hadleigh said.

"Good timing." Wei guessed that his friend must have been by the clinic. "Did Yao send you?"

The door swung open, and Wei saw that Hadleigh wasn't alone.

The duchess smiled at him. "Actually, it was Glory."

As Greaves announced the visitors the next morning, Glory took a breath and prepared to play the most difficult role of her life. The thought of Wei bolstered her. She wouldn't let her beloved down.

"Ready, poppet?" Papa murmured.

She straightened her shoulders. "Yes, Papa."

"Whatever happens," he said, "I want you to know that I am proud of you, Glory. I could not ask for a better daughter."

Her throat swelled, but she didn't have time to answer for Rothwell and Winslow entered. They'd brought a retinue of guards, all six of them armed to the teeth. Uncle and nephew swept a gaze around the room, their lips curling as they saw no threat in the tranquil drawing room.

Glory curtsied as Papa welcomed them.

"Thank you for coming," Papa said. "May I first apologize for the events of yesterday?"

"No need to bring up the unfortunate incident, Your Grace. I am relieved that you suffered no damage from that barbaric fellow," Rothwell said magnanimously. "Winslow assures me that we are united in our desire to ensure that the malicious lies are never repeated—the same way we are united in our efforts to stop the opium trade. Indeed, my hope is that we are soon to be connected in another way as well."

He came over to Glory, and she tried not to cringe as he kissed her hand.

"I hope you have given my nephew's offer the consideration it deserves, my dear," he said.

"I am honored by Mr. Winslow's offer." Glory widened her eyes like a naïve debutante. "Papa says I am most fortunate to receive it on the heels of my, um, indiscretion."

"His Grace is quite right. It is all water under the bridge, however." Rothwell wagged his finger at her as if she were a puppy in need of training. "As long as you do not make such a silly mistake again, young lady."

From the corner of her eye, Glory saw her papa stiffen, and she willed him to follow the plan. To see this through, for all their sakes.

"I see the error of my ways, sir," she said penitently. "And I am ever so grateful that Mr. Winslow has given me a chance to redeem myself. But there is something I must tell you, even though I am afraid you will be angry."

"As we are soon to be family, my dear, you can tell me anything."

"Last evening, Mr. Chen made an attempt to contact me," she said in a rush. "I would not see him, of course. But he...he sent this."

She picked up the leather-bound journal from a nearby console.

"It is the diary of a man named Leonard Kray. And it...it makes horrid accusations, Mr. Rothwell." She looked at him, her lip trembling. "There's even a daguerreotype of you and Mr. Kray, and the inscription labels you as Erasmus Trimble."

"Give me that diary," Rothwell snapped.

He made a grab for it, but Glory artfully stepped out of reach and went to pace in front of the fire like a ninny with an attack of nerves.

"If any of this gets out, we shall all be ruined," she cried. "You, me, and Papa!"

Winslow intercepted her path, snatching the diary out of her hands. He tossed it into the flames.

"There, my dear." His charming expression was every bit as sinister as his uncle's as the pages crackled and blackened, turning into ash. "The problem is solved."

"But there is still Mr. Chen." She peered fretfully up at him. "He knows everything."

"We will take care of Chen," Rothwell said calmly. "He will not bother you—or any of us—again."

"What exactly are you suggesting?" Papa asked.

"The specifics are unimportant. All you need to do is back my version of events, Your Grace."

"You mean I will have to lie. I read the journal, Rothwell." Papa's voice had a betraying tremor of anger. "I know what happened in Canton."

"A mere peccadillo, Your Grace. We all have skeletons in our closets—you, yourself, had quite the wild reputation in your younger days." Rothwell's smile was knowing. "Great men, however, do not allow inconveniences to get in the way of larger ambitions."

"By inconveniences, you are referring to the fact that you ordered the murder of the Chen family and their servant," Papa said in a foreboding tone.

"And by ambitions, I am referring to your campaign to stop the opium trade. You need my financial backing and influence." Rothwell dropped any pretense of humility, clearly believing that he held the upper hand. "Come now, our fortunes are tied together. If my history gets out, your reputation will suffer the consequences. Who would back the campaign of a duke who partnered with an opium trader accused of murder? What will happen to your career in politics then, Your Grace?"

Papa stood very straight and said, "I don't give a damn."

Glory had never been prouder of her father.

"You heard Mr. Rothwell's confession," she said loudly.

Rothwell and his nephew looked confused as the door to the adjoining room opened. Wei strode in, his gaze fierce and fury restrained. The Angels, their husbands, and Yao came to stand behind him.

"You murdered my family, Erasmus Trimble." Wei's tone was cold and controlled. "And you will answer for your crimes."

"There is no proof of anything," Rothwell spat. "My nephew burned the damned journal."

"Actually." Glory cleared her throat. "He burned a fake copy."

"And we heard your confession," Hadleigh said. "All of us here will swear to it."

Rothwell looked furious, but then he sneered, "Those deaths took place years ago and on Chinese soil. English courts have no jurisdiction over what happened, and I cannot be found guilty of anything."

"Not in a court of law, perhaps," Wei said calmly. "But the real jury will be that of your peers, the society that you've fooled into thinking that you are a man of charity and success. My friends and I will see to it that your crimes are on the front page of every newspaper and gossip rag. Everything you've built as Rothwell—your reputation, projects, and schemes—will fail. Your name will be less than dirt. You are finished."

Glory saw the instant that Rothwell realized he'd been cornered. He looked stunned—as if he'd never found himself in the position of not getting his way. His face turned apoplectic.

"You cannot do that to me," he hissed. "I bloody own London, and you are nobody!"

Wei's stare did not waver. "I am the nobody who is bringing you down."

"Guards, kill this bastard," Rothwell yelled.

The guards glanced at one another, then at Papa and the other lords in the room. Not one of them moved. Apparently, they'd decided whatever Rothwell was paying them wasn't worth the trouble of public, cold-blooded murder.

Even Winslow backed away. "Father, it isn't worth it. We should go—"

Father? Glory raised her brows. The men were apparently closer kin than they'd let on.

"You spineless bastard," Rothwell snarled. "I always knew you would never amount to anything. I should have left you in the streets with your whore of a mother."

"It's over." Winslow's face hardened. "People are going to discover that you faked your death as Erasmus Trimble. That your wealth doesn't come from investments but opium smuggling. No one is going to buy shares in our schemes now. We need to cut our losses."

"A great man does not accept losses," Rothwell declared. "He dictates the terms. Always."

He punctuated his statement by yanking out a pistol—and turning it on Glory.

"Take away what's mine, and I'll take away what's yours." His eyes were feverish, wild. "You can watch another person you love die, Chen."

Glory's instincts kicked in—or her lightness *kung fu*, rather. Her breath snapped into a trained rhythm, and she was off. Everything around her seemed to slow—Rothwell's finger moving on the trigger, Papa's shout of warning—as she leapt through the air. Her shoes barely touched the ground as she sped past Rothwell, soaring gracefully over the settee and taking cover behind it.

Wei had moved as well. From behind her cover, she sighed with admiration: she still had much to learn from him. Her *shifu* possessed the stealth of shadows and the power of a tempest. He slammed into Rothwell, the force knocking the pistol from the bastard's hands. Rothwell swung at Wei; Wei dodged, then landed a strike to the other's chest. Rothwell staggered backward as Wei continued with a barrage of punches, the final one hurtling him into a wall.

Wei towered over his defeated foe, his knuckles cracking as he tightened his fists. Glory's breath jammed as he hauled the moaning, bloodied blackguard up by the throat.

"I could kill you," Wei said softly. "But I won't. Because revenge won't give me what I truly need. What I've already found."

He dropped Rothwell like a piece of rubbish and walked away.

As the Angels and their husbands surrounded Rothwell and his associates, Wei came toward Glory. She ran to him, meeting him halfway. He took her hands and clasped them tightly.

"Your plan worked, little tigress." His voice was husky.

"Did you doubt that it would?"

"I know better than to doubt you," he said tenderly. "Thank you for believing in me. For standing with me against all odds. But most of all, for showing me that what I needed wasn't vengeance but love. I don't deserve you, but I will do everything in my power to make you happy. And that includes earning your family's approval. Whatever it takes, I will do it...because you are my path. My everything."

Brimming with joy, she twisted her head to look at her papa. Willing him to understand.

He sighed, then shrugged as if to say, *It's up to you*. But his eyes were warm and full of pride, and she knew that whatever choice she made, she would have his support and love.

Her heart full, she turned back to Wei.

"I think you already have Papa's permission," she said.

Wei slid a wary glance at her father. "I should probably wait to kiss you."

"Probably." She wound her arms around his neck, bringing him close. "But you know how impatient I am."

He kissed her with a love that they no longer had to wait for.

FORTY

With a feeling of triumph, Wei carried his new bride into his bedchamber.

"Welcome to your new home, Mrs. Chen," he murmured.

Her arms around his neck, Glory dimpled at him. "I am glad to be here at last. Our engagement felt like it lasted *forever*."

He didn't disagree, because the last two months had felt interminable. It was his own fault, he supposed, for insisting that they stick to proprieties. But he hadn't wanted to give Glory's parents any reason to regret accepting his suit, nor had he wanted to compromise His Grace's political efforts. Thus, he and Glory had only seen each other during chaperoned visits and hadn't made their engagement public until after the duke had introduced his bill.

Unfortunately, the bill failed to gain support.

While disappointed, the duke had taken the result in stride.

"You can only lead a horse to water," His Grace had said philosophically. *"I shan't give up. The next time, however, I shall refuse the help of any backers who belong behind bars."*

He was referring to Rothwell, aka Erasmus Trimble, who was

presently a resident of Newgate. While Trimble had been correct that the English courts held no jurisdiction over the crimes he'd committed in China, the local authorities did have something to say about the attempted murder of a duke's daughter. Given the many witnesses, the case had been open and shut, and Trimble would spend the rest of his days where he belonged.

Yuan fen was a powerful thing.

Wei set Glory by his bed, cupping her face in his palms. Stroking his thumbs across her silky cheeks, he murmured, "Did I tell you what a beautiful bride you are?"

Standing at the altar, surrounded by the beaming Angels who'd served as her bridesmaids, Glory had stolen Wei's breath. He hadn't been able to believe that his little tigress, who'd been accompanied by a flower-bedecked FF II, was his at last.

"I am glad you like my wedding dress," Glory said earnestly. "I wanted Mrs. Q to make it in red in accordance with Chinese custom, but Mama said there is such a thing as too much scandal."

Wei had to hide a smile. His new mama-in-law had been gracious, welcoming him into the family, and he liked her very much. In fact, he was surprised by how well he was getting on with all of Glory's kin. Over the last several weeks, he and her papa had gotten better acquainted, discovering that they shared similar values and views of the world.

Like his daughter, His Grace was curious about his Chinese heritage, and he and Wei had spent hours discussing the nation's culture and politics over brandy and cigars. He had even asked Wei to assist in his next campaign to stop the opium trade. Wei respected his new father-in-law and was gratified that the feeling was mutual. Most of all, he was glad the duke trusted him to take care of Glory.

Gazing at his bride, Wei said, "You are a vision just as you are."

It was no lie: Glory looked like a princess in her frothy ivory gown trimmed with lace. His mother's bracelet circled her wrist.

"You look very handsome yourself, *Shifu*." The look she gave him made his heart thud as if he'd been practicing *kung fu* for hours. "And I cannot wait for a lesson on my wedding night."

Her sweet naughtiness undid him as always. He snatched her into his arms.

"I shall be happy to instruct you," he said.

He kissed her with the impetuousness that only she roused in him. She returned his passion eagerly, showing him that she'd missed their physical connection as much as he had. As their kiss raged out of control, he had the thought that perhaps he should douse the lights for his bride's sake.

He discarded the idea immediately. First of all, his wife was more curious than modest, and he was quite certain that she would complain if she didn't get to see everything. Second, he was done with shadows. He'd waited a lifetime for Glory, and their love deserved to be celebrated in the light.

He managed to get her wedding dress off...and his heart stuttered.

"By the deities," he said in a low voice.

"Since I couldn't wear red on the outside," Glory said mischievously, "I thought I'd wear it on the inside. For luck."

By "inside," she was referring to a cherry-red corset and garter belt. Combined with her demure white stockings and blushing cheeks, she was wanton innocence come to life. His cock swelled to new heights.

"I am a lucky man all right," he said reverently.

She giggled as he pounced, tumbling her onto the bed. But she wasn't laughing when he removed her corset and kissed every inch of her pretty breasts. She started panting as he nibbled his way down her belly. By the time he buried his mouth in her pussy, she was moaning with abandon. He ate her until she came, savoring her cream as it coated his tongue.

He crawled over her shivering body and kissed her, sharing the taste of her bliss. When he lifted his head, the sparkle in her jade-and-sunshine eyes told him she was far from done.

"Now I want to try something," she whispered. "Do you mind?"

"Be as curious as you want, my sweet," he said huskily.

He didn't think he could get any harder, but she proved him wrong. Unbuttoning his shirt, she kissed her way down his front, her tongue investigating every groove, every quivering sinew. By the time she tugged down his trousers, his cock stood upright, leaking seed.

Nestling between his thighs like a playful cat, she wrapped her delicate fingers around his shaft and licked the dripping tip. Then she took him, her kiss so deep and generous that he groaned, weaving his fingers in her hair. He tried not to lose his mind as she bobbed on him, but the sweet hums she made, the loving seal of her lips was too much.

"Bloody hell, love," he grunted. "I'm going to spend—"

He tried to move her head away, but she wouldn't budge, kept on sucking and sucking him. Pleasure boiled over, and he came with a harsh cry in his bride's wanton mouth.

When he caught his breath, he hauled her up and rolled atop her.

He was still hard, and the sight of her glossy lips made him harder.

"Is your curiosity assuaged, my love?" he asked.

"I liked it," she said, blushing.

By the gods. How did he get to be so lucky?

"What about this?"

He entered her slowly. Pleasure sizzled up his spine at the snug, tender clasp of his wife's body.

"This is lovely too," she breathed.

He began to move, sheathing himself in her damp heat. He thrust harder and deeper when he saw no discomfort on her expressive face. In fact, she bit her lip, arching to take more of him.

"Wrap your legs around my hips," he instructed.

She did, the feeling of being surrounded by her silken limbs pure bliss. He drove more forcefully, and she liked it, rocking her hips for him, chanting his name. His control unraveling, he pounded into his sweet bride, his match in every way. His stones slapped her pussy, and she dug her heels into his arse as her release pulsed around him, bathing him in liquid silk.

He couldn't resist teaching her something new. Flipping her onto her hands and knees, he pushed his cock into her from behind. The fit was exquisitely tight, but she was so wet that he went in easily. Her gasp of surprise turned into a moan as he slammed his hips against her sleek bottom. Gripping her hips, he watched her pretty pussy spread to take his veined girth, and it made him crazed with lust and love.

No woman had ever taken his body and his heart this completely. No woman had ever owned his soul. No woman was like his Glory.

Wei felt the warning sizzle at the base of his spine. Reaching one hand beneath her, he found her bold little nub, rubbing it as he shafted her. She purred, pushing back on his thrusts, arching her spine like a wildcat. He managed to hold back until she came. Her release milked him of everything, and his neck arched with bliss as he emptied himself inside her.

Afterward, he cuddled her close and looked into her eyes.

"I love you, Glory," he said. "My beautiful wife. May you be curious forever."

Her dimples lit his world.

"And I love you, my husband. Forever and ever."

EPILOGUE

"Wei," she panted. "I have to move..."

"Patience, sweet tigress," her husband murmured. "You are making such good progress at waiting."

"This is different." She trembled, feeling the proud length of him throbbing at her core. "It is too much."

When they'd awoken, Wei had been hard and ready...which she'd discovered during these first few weeks of marriage was a typical state for him. This morning, however, he'd decided to teach her a new variation. One that involved sitting on his lap with her back to his front, his cock buried deep in her pussy. The position was novel and arousing...except he wouldn't allow her to move.

She whimpered as his hands roved possessively over her front, his touch light and teasing.

"You can take it." His voice was low and wicked in her ear. "Let the pleasure come to you; there is no need to chase it. Just feel how hard I am inside your tight little quim."

She felt it all right; being impaled on his thick cock was making her wild with need. The harder she tried to resist squirming, the greater the need to do so. It didn't help when his lips coasted along her neck, his callused fingertips brushing over her taut nipples. Staying still heightened her awareness of all the sensations: the sinewy ridges of his thighs beneath her bottom, the hot pulsing of his prick filling her up.

Her climax burst upon her with no warning, a deep ecstatic quaking that started at her center and spread outward into her limbs. She heard Wei's hoarse groan of pleasure as he joined her, injecting her with his heat. Even then, he didn't stop, rubbing her pearl with masterful roughness until she came again around his still-hard cock.

Limp with bliss, she turned and wound her arms around his neck.

"That was new," she breathed.

His eyes were sated and warm. "Did you like it?"

"If that is the reward for waiting," she decided, "then I don't mind being patient."

He laughed. It was something he did more and more, and she loved the sound of it. Loved everything about their new life together.

With her dowry, she and Wei could have bought a house in a more fashionable area of London, and Wei had offered to do so if she wished. She chose instead to live at the clinic, which had felt like home from the moment he'd carried her over the threshold. She liked the hustle and bustle here; there was always something interesting to do and learn. She continued to practice *kung fu*, and Wei said she was one of his best pupils. In the evenings, they retreated to the privacy of their own building, where he gave her lessons of a more intimate nature.

"We had better get dressed." Kissing her on the temple, Wei set her on her feet. "Your parents are bringing your brothers by this morning."

Horatio and Theo worshipped their new brother-in-law and were relentless in their desire to learn martial arts. Glory was glad

—and unsurprised—that her family and Wei got along famously. Before everyone arrived, however, she had something to share.

"I have been meaning to ask," she said as casually as she could. "Did you have plans for the area behind this building?"

"Eventually I had planned on adding another wing." Wei pulled on his tunic. "Why do you ask?"

She went to him, helping him to button his collar. "I think you should consider doing that soon. Say, in the next nine months?"

He blinked. "Do you mean...are you...we're going to...?"

It was the first time she'd seen her husband flummoxed.

"Yes." She could barely contain her excitement. "We're going to have a baby."

"Glory, my love." Wei cupped her face, his face lit with joy. "I can't believe it happened so quickly."

"Given the frequency of certain activities," she pointed out, "is it really surprising?"

"I suppose not." Male satisfaction glinted in his eyes. "How do you feel, little tigress?"

"Absolutely fine, so there is no need to hover."

"But I like hovering." He pulled her close. "And I love you."

"I love you, too."

Their kiss left them both breathless.

"Before your family arrives, I want to burn incense at the altar," he said. "To share the good news and ask my ancestors to watch over our little one."

She nodded, loving his deep connection to his kin. She had been by his side when he made an offering of Ling Ling's hair, finally giving his sister the peace she deserved. Since then, he had seemed lighter, shadows lifting from his eyes. He shared happy memories about his past, and even though Glory had not met his sister or parents, she felt like she was beginning to know them. That she was becoming as much a part of his family as he was of hers, their legacies weaving seamlessly into the fabric of the life they were creating together.

Wei and Glory finished getting dressed. They were walking hand in hand through the courtyard, FF II bounding ahead of them, when they ran into Yao. He was accompanied by the Angels.

"Good morning, ladies." Glory regarded her friends with surprise. "I thought we were meeting to discuss the new case this afternoon. What are you doing here so early?"

"It's Charlie," Livy said urgently. "She is in trouble and needs our help."

Author's Note

Readers often ask where the ideas for my stories come from. It's not always easy for me to pinpoint the specific seed that germinated and blossomed into one of my books, but I can say that a thread of the plot for Glory and Wei's story was sparked by a conversation I had with my *baba*, who is a Chinese Canadian immigrant from Hong Kong, when I was eight years old. My father and I were walking around the Legislative Building in my hometown of Winnipeg, Canada and came upon a statue of Queen Victoria. To me, she looked grand, sitting there with her crown and scepter. I said something along those lines to my dad, who replied, "She was not a great monarch in everyone's history books."

"Why?" I asked.

My eight-year-old self didn't fully understand his explanation, which involved an example of the tragic and egregious consequences of British imperialism during Queen Victoria's reign. But I remember him mentioning something about the English smuggling drugs into China and forcing an unjust war, and it wasn't until I began the research for *Glory and the Master of Shadows* that

I remembered that conversation I had with my father all those years ago.

As a writer of historical fiction, I believe that history depends on point of view. How we view the past is influenced by our experiences, the information we are exposed to, and the prevailing zeitgeist of our time. Thus, to some, Victoria is a matriarch who reigned during the expansion of an empire known for its technological and social advancements. To others, she is a symbol of oppression who sat in power while policies of colonialism, dispossession, and violence were enacted on other nations and peoples[1]. To others still, she may be a combination of the above. For me, how we interpret the past—and perhaps learn from it—is what makes history so interesting.

The writing of this book involved substantial research. Of note, I am indebted to Stephen Platt's *Imperial Twilight: the Opium War and the End of China's Last Golden Age* for its compelling analysis of the two opium wars (1839-1842 and 1856-1860) between Britain[2] and China. Platt's work explores the fascinating personalities that influenced the course of this iconic clash between civilizations. It also examines how factors such as the British appetite for Chinese goods and use of "gunboat diplomacy" combined with the internal rebellions and corruption within China to result in a war that William Gladstone, the Prime Minister of the United Kingdom, described thus in a famous speech:

"I am not competent to judge how long this war may last, but this I can say, that a war more unjust in its origin, a war more calculated in its progress to cover this country with permanent disgrace, I do not know, and I have not read of."

In his diary, Gladstone further wrote, *"I am in dread of the judgments of God upon England for our national iniquity towards China."*

For those interested in learning more about the Opium War, the Asia Pacific Curriculum, an initiative of the Asian Pacific

Foundation of Canada (https://asiapacificcurriculum.ca/) offers some excellent resources.

I should also make a note about the Chinese words used in this story. For consistency, I tried to use the Hanyu Pinyin system. However, there were cases where the Westernized version of a Chinese word was more recognizable to the average Western reader than the Pinyin version: for example, "Confucius" (Westernized) versus "Kongfuzi" or "Kongzi" (Pinyin); "kung fu" (Westernized) versus "gong fu" (Pinyin). In such instances, I made an authorial decision to go with the Westernized version due to its greater familiarity to a Western-based readership. Any mistakes in translation are my own, for which I humbly apologize.

While the context of the opium conflicts informed Wei's background story, I was also inspired by the many Cantonese martial arts dramas I watched growing up. These powerful tales of loyalty, duty, revenge, and love have stayed with me...as have episodes of Charlie's Angels. I have always loved stories of intrepid women like Glory and her friends.

While I am mish-mashing cultural influences, I should also note that the dognapping idea came from a real-life incident: Victorian poet Elizabeth Barrett Browning had her spaniel Flush stolen from her...not once, but three times! Luckily, the story has a happy ending: Elizabeth managed to ransom Flush, who lived with her and her husband, the poet Robert Browning, into peaceful old age.

NOTES

AUTHOR'S NOTE

1. Interestingly, when I looked up that statue of Queen Victoria to see if it lived up to my childhood memory, I discovered that it had been destroyed during an anti-racism rally in 2021. The protest centered around the deaths of Indigenous children who were forced to attend Canada's residential schools from the 1870's to the 1990's.
2. It should be noted that while British traders were responsible for smuggling the majority of opium into China, traders from other countries, including the United States, were also profiting from the trade.

ALSO BY GRACE CALLAWAY

LADY CHARLOTTE'S SOCIETY OF ANGELS

Olivia and the Masked Duke (Book 1)

When Lady Olivia MacLeod volunteers for a genteel lady's charity called the Society of Angels, she discovers to her delight that it is a front for a female investigative agency. Working on a dangerous case throws her into the arms of a masked vigilante...who may or may not be her secret girlhood crush, the notorious Duke of Hadleigh. *Winner of the Daphne du Maurier Award & the Passionate Plume.*

Pippa and the Prince of Secrets (Book 2)

After the tragic ending of her marriage, Lady Pippa Longmere (nee Hunt) is determined to forge her own destiny as a member of Lady Charlotte's investigative society. A deadly case brings her into the path of Timothy Cullen, a lad from her past who has grown up to become the powerful and mysterious leader of the mudlarks. Cull's protective nature and secret devotion threaten her investigation...and the walls she has built around her heart. *Winner of the Maggie Award; Finalist for the Daphne du Maurier Award & Gold Leaf Award.*

Fiona and the Enigmatic Earl (Book 3)

When celebrated debutante Miss Fiona Garrity weds stoic widower Thomas Morgan, the Earl of Hawksmoor, the pair agree to a marriage of convenience. Both plan to use their marriage as a cover for their clandestine activities: she is a lady detective, and he is a spy for the Crown. Neither expect to find passionate love...or to unravel dark secrets that threaten not only their happiness, but their very lives. *OKWG Heart Award Finalist.*

Charlotte and the Seductive Spymaster (Book 5)

The only thing more dangerous than Lady Charlotte Fayne's present case is her past. Preorder for Jan 2024.

Mrs. Peabody and the Unexpected Duke (Holiday Novella)

When former lovers Hawker and Mrs. Peabody are paired on a spy mission over the holidays, the pair battle a deadly enemy...and a desire that neither can deny. In chronological order, this steamy, enemies to lovers Christmas novella falls between Book 3 (Fiona and the Enigmatic Earl) and Book 4 (Glory and the Master of Shadows).

GAME OF DUKES

The Duke Identity (Book 1)

Shattered by betrayal, ex-scholar Harry Kent finds new purpose as a policeman. Sent to infiltrate a family in London's criminal underworld, he lands a job guarding the family's clever and wicked daughter, Tessa Todd. Neither is prepared for their passionate attraction—or the rising peril that threatens their lives. *Winner of the Daphne du Maurier Award and Finalist for the National Excellence in Romance Fiction Award.*

Enter the Duke (Book 2)

A hunt for a legendary treasure reunites the Duke of Ranelagh and Somerville with Maggie Foley, a former barmaid and his ex-lover. Her shocking secret triggers a journey of redemption for the devil-may-care rake. Together they must fight for their future and that of their daughter...all while defending themselves against a dangerous foe. *Finalist for the NECRWA Readers' Choice Award, the Maggie Award for Excellence, and the Golden Quill.*

Regarding the Duke (Book 3)

Shy, sweet wallflower Gabriella Garrity has everything she's ever wanted: a husband she loves, beautiful children, and a home of her own. Then she discovers the secret that shatters all her illusions. Ruthless moneylender Adam Garrity has a life-long goal: revenge on the man who nearly destroyed him. He has his enemy within his grasp...until amnesia makes him see his life—and his wife—with new eyes. A hot and heart-melting journey to happily-ever-after! *Finalist for the National Excellence in Romance Fiction Award.*

The Duke Redemption (Book 4)

A gentleman in search of redemption finds a lady looking for a sin. Can one night of passion change their destinies forevermore? A steamy twist on Beauty and the Beast starring charming rogue Wickham Murray and the clever and spirited Lady Beatrice. *Winner of the Maggie Award and the Golden Leaf; Finalist for the Booksellers' Best Award.*

The Return of the Duke (Book 5)

Tinker's daughter Fancy Sheridan longs for a passionate fairy tale romance. Newly minted duke Severin Knight needs a cool-headed duchess. When Knight accidentally compromises Fancy, their marriage of convenience is anything but convenient. Will they find their happily ever after? *Winner of the Maggie Award & Finalist for the Passionate Plume.*

HEART OF ENQUIRY (THE KENTS)

The Widow Vanishes (Prequel novella)

Fate throws beautiful widow Annabel Foster into the arms of William McLeod, her enemy's most ruthless soldier. When an unexpected and explosive night of passion ensues, she must decide: should she run for her life—or stay for her heart?

The Duke Who Knew Too Much (Book 1)

When Miss Emma Kent witnesses a depraved encounter involving the wicked Duke of Strathaven, her honor compels her to do the right thing. But steamy desire challenges her quest for justice, and she and Strathaven must work together to unravel a dangerous mystery... before it's too late.

M is for Marquess (Book 2)

With her frail constitution improving, Miss Dorothea Kent yearns to live a full and passionate life. Desire blooms between her and Gabriel Ridgley, the Marquess of Tremont, an enigmatic widower with a disabled son. But the road to love proves treacherous as Gabriel's past as a spy emerges to threaten them both... and they must defeat a dangerous enemy lying in wait.

The Lady Who Came in from the Cold (Book 3)

Former spy Pandora Hudson gave up espionage for love. Twelve years later, her dark secret rises to threaten her blissful marriage to Marcus, Marquess of Blackwood, and she must face her most challenging mission yet: winning back the heart of the only man she's ever loved.

The Viscount Always Knocks Twice (Book 4)

Sparks fly when feisty hoyden Violet Kent and proper gentleman Richard Murray, Viscount Carlisle, meet at a house party. Yet their forbidden passion and blossoming romance are not the only adventures afoot. For a guest is soon discovered dead—and Violet and Richard must join forces to solve the mystery and protect their loved ones... before the murderer strikes again. *Finalist for the National Readers Choice Award and the Daphne du Maurier Award for Excellence in Mystery/Suspense.*

Never Say Never to an Earl (Book 5)

Despite their outer differences, shy wallflower Polly Kent and wild rake Sinjin Pelham, the Earl of Revelstoke, have secrets to hide—and both desperately fear exposing their true selves. Yet the attraction between them is too strong to deny, and they become entangled in a passionate adventure. Both will have to face their greatest fear in order to win the love of a lifetime... and to survive the machinations of the enemy who lies in wait.

The Gentleman Who Loved Me (Book 6)

What happens when fate throws a headstrong miss on a mission to find a titled husband together with a powerful and notorious club owner who is anything but a gentleman? Find out in this final passionate installment in the Kent family series, which stars Primrose Kent and Andrew Corbett in his long-awaited return. *Winner of the Passionate Plume Award and Finalist for the Maggie Award for Excellence.*

MAYHEM IN MAYFAIR

Her Husband's Harlot (Book 1)

How far will a wallflower go to win her husband's love? When her disguise as a courtesan backfires, Lady Helena finds herself entangled in a game of deception and desire with her husband Nicholas, the Marquess of Harteford ... and discovers that he has dark secrets of his own. *Finalist for the Golden Heart Award.*

Her Wanton Wager (Book 2)

To what lengths will a feisty miss go to save her family from ruin? Miss Persephone Fines takes on a wager of seduction with notorious gaming hell owner Gavin Hunt and discovers that love is the most dangerous risk of all.

Her Protector's Pleasure (Book 3)

Wealthy widow Lady Marianne Draven will stop at nothing to find her kidnapped daughter. Having suffered betrayal in the past, she trusts no man—and especially not Thames River Policeman Ambrose Kent, who has a few secrets of his own. Yet fiery passion ignites between the unlikely pair as they battle a shadowy foe. Can they work together to save Marianne's daughter? And will nights of pleasure turn into a love for all time?

Her Prodigal Passion (Book 4)

Sensible Miss Charity Sparkler has been in love with Paul Fines, her best friend's brother, for years. When he accidentally compromises her, they find themselves wed in haste. Can an ugly duckling recognize her own beauty and a reformed rake his own value? As secrets of the past lead to present dangers, will this marriage of convenience transform into one of love?

Acknowledgments

In writing the acknowledgements for this book—my 20th full-length novel!—I have so many people to thank.

First of all, my readers and book family: none of this would be possible without you. When I wrote my first book, Her Husband's Harlot, I had no idea where the journey would take me. Now, thirteen years later, I am still dreaming about my characters and writing their stories, and I couldn't do it without your support, so thank you, thank you! And special appreciation goes out to those of you who have reviewed, posted about, and recommended my books: I am so very grateful!

This book is dedicated to my parents and my sister; I am so lucky to be part of our family. *Baba*, the first storyteller in my life—every story you've told me has shaped the writer I've become. *Mama*, thank you for filling the house with books. *Mei Mei*, thank you for cheering on my characters.

Huge appreciation goes out to all the talented folks who helped me bring my vision to life: my developmental editor Peter Senftleben; copyeditors and proofreaders Faith Williams, Judy Rosen, and Alyssa Navarro; cover artist Erin Dameron-Hill. Special thanks to my friend and photographer Jenn Le Blanc for shooting the amazing cover image!

A shout out to the many writer friends who make this profession a joy. Barbara, Anne, and Veronica—thank you for the weekly brainstorming sessions and lunches. The Carlsbad crew...thanks for the fun and inspiration and plot tub :-)

To Brian, Brendan, and Bo: my reason for everything. I love you.

ABOUT THE AUTHOR

USA Today & International Bestselling Author Grace Callaway writes hot and heart-melting historical romance filled with mystery and adventure. Her debut novel was a Romance Writers of America® Golden Heart® Finalist and a #1 National Regency Bestseller, and her subsequent novels have topped national and international bestselling lists. She is the winner of the Daphne du Maurier Award for Excellence in Mystery and Suspense, the Maggie Award for Excellence in Historical Romance, the Golden Leaf, and the Passionate Plume Award. She holds a doctorate in clinical psychology from the University of Michigan and lives with her family in a valley close to the ocean. When she's not writing, she enjoys dancing, dining in hole-in-the-wall restaurants, and going on adapted adventures with her special son.

Keep up with Grace's latest news!

Newsletter: gracecallaway.com/newsletter

facebook.com/GraceCallawayBooks

bookbub.com/authors/grace-callaway

instagram.com/gracecallawaybooks

amazon.com/author/gracecallaway